BEFORE
THE
RAIN FALLS

ALSO BY CAMILLE DI MAIO

The Memory of Us

BEFORE THE RAIN FALLS

THE

RAIN FALLS

CAMILLE DI MAIO

LAKE UNION
PUBLISHING

Text copyright © 2017 by Camille Di Maio
All rights reserved.

No part of this book may be reproduced, or stored in a retrieval system, or transmitted in any form or by any means, electronic, mechanical, photocopying, recording, or otherwise, without express written permission of the publisher.

Published by Lake Union Publishing, Seattle

www.apub.com

Amazon, the Amazon logo, and Lake Union Publishing are trademarks of Amazon.com, Inc., or its affiliates.

ISBN-13: 9781503939974
ISBN-10: 1503939979

Cover design by Rachel Adam

Printed in the United States of America

A story about sisters would not be complete without dedicating this to my own sister, Catherine Remmert. She was the best Christmas morning present ever and continues to be a daily gift to me.

Others come to you later in life, and through the blessing of marriage, I am grateful to my sisters-in-law, Sarah Vogt Remmert and Julie McCall Di Maio, for their love, support, and friendship.

The drops of rain make a hole in the stone, not by violence, but by oft falling.

—Lucretius

PROLOGUE

Hidalgo County Courthouse, Texas—March 1943

Observers in the standing-room-only gallery fanned themselves with newspapers, fidgeting and grumbling as they waited for the decision. Sketch artists scratched away at their canvases, shading with their pencils, rubbing with their fingers until they'd created adequate representations of the scene.

Whirl click. Whirl click. A lopsided ceiling fan cut through the air, its four blades drooping from years of deep southern heat. *Tick tick tick tick.* The second hand of the defense attorney's wristwatch crawled around the numbers. One . . . two . . . three . . . four. Before it began a new minute, the wood-paneled door squeaked open, and the jurors filed out, collapsing into their seats on the platform. Twelve men, twenty-four unsympathetic eyes.

Della Lee Trujillo sat in the low-slung chair, its slats cutting into her back. Slow-spreading dampness gathered behind her knees, and the chafe of the shackles left her wrists raw. The death of her younger sister, Eula Lee, had dominated the headlines for weeks.

Beautiful Songbird of Puerto Pesar Murdered!

The tiny border town was devastated, for the second time, by the Lee family.

She knew Tomas was sitting in the first row behind her, his fingers chapped from gripping the railing as the arguments played out. He'd been there every day, every moment, abandoning what few crops and livestock were left on the homestead. She could feel his eyes boring into her now-stringy hair. They'd been married only four hours when it happened, their newly minted future ripped apart by an ivory-handled knife.

Tomas said he understood why she'd done what she did.

The door at the front of the courtroom groaned open. "All rise," the bailiff announced.

Della struggled to her feet, using her elbows to push herself off the arms of the chair. Her court-appointed attorney offered no assistance, much the way the whole trial had gone. In contrast, the prosecutor acted as if the murder presented a personal affront, so dogged was he in his determination to win.

Judge Fuego, filling every inch of his otherwise billowing black robes, wiped his forehead with a handkerchief and sank into his leather chair.

Whirl click. Whirl click. The fan kept pace with Della's heartbeat. She closed her eyes and remembered.

Wedding dress. Lace. Eula's long brown curls fell in a fan-shaped pattern. Red pooled on white, growing, spreading.

"Has the jury reached a verdict?" the judge asked.

The foreman stood, clearing his throat before speaking. "We have, Your Honor." He handed a slip of paper to the bailiff, who placed it on the desk. The judge opened it and nodded, handing it back.

The man continued. "We, the people of the jury, in the matter of the death of Eula Lee, find Della Lee Trujillo . . ."

Everyone leaned in.

"Guilty."

CHAPTER ONE

Puerto Pesar—Today

Della had trouble sleeping.

It was surreal being back in the place that had consumed her memories through seventy years in prison. The homestead had been almost mythological, as if it existed for a different woman altogether. She had the same arms, hands, feet, toes of the girl who long ago ran barefoot in the natural grasses. And yet they were not the same. They were wrinkled, spotted, fragile.

A new person carved from the same material.

Tomas had lived in the house for a few years until going off to war, but he'd had the foresight to take care of all the legal bits that Della never had the chance to consider. It had been rented out over the years to several long-term tenants, the rents covering the cost of a property manager. By the looks of things, the landlord had maintained the bare minimum, put the agreed-upon amount into savings for her each month, and kept the rest for himself. The roof was in disrepair, easy to see even with her aged eyesight. Paint cracked, wood rot plagued the porch.

There was also a little money left over in an aging bank account Tomas had set up, and she supposed after enough interest over enough years, she'd have some to live on for a while. But not enough for work to be done on the house.

It surprised her that even some of the furnishings were the same. New in their day—Mama wanted the best—but antique now.

The feather bed was too soft, and the dust on it made her sneeze. Her frail body, nearing the end of its ninth decade, had grown used to the thin mattress provided by the Texas Department of Corrections. It had been cheap, surely purchased from the lowest bidder, its sole purpose to fit the minimal requirements of humane treatment during incarceration. But Della never had trouble sleeping there, not once. Not when the whooping cough struck in 1949. Not when everyone was edgy about the Cuban Missile Crisis. Not even when the parole board told her that she was going to be a free woman. It wasn't until she returned today to her childhood home that phantoms and memories stirred her, making it impossible to rest.

Everywhere she looked was a reminder of a time when her skin was sun-kissed, when she could swim in the lake naked without catching a chill, when her heart clenched every time she watched Tomas work in the fields.

The Before Days, she called them, when she dared to think about them at all.

She looked around at the house, still solid, built with the kind of craftsmanship that few could have afforded at the time. A stone fireplace reached to the ceiling, with niches thoughtfully made to accommodate matches and firewood. Fossils and pebbles found on long-ago childhood walks with Eula and their mother were placed sporadically into the mortar, a notion Papa had had when his girls came home with their treasures. Thick beams lined the ceiling in a perpendicular pattern that created not only a support system but a subtle nod to the money it took to produce such things primarily for their aesthetic. Front and back porches offered shade in the brutal Texas heat and maximized the respite that could be found in even a gentle cross breeze.

Nearly everything was in its logical place, arranged by the property manager before her return. But the mattress lay forgotten, and she doubted that she had the strength to beat it until the dust left. She found the tobacco tins in the shed along with other things that would probably be considered junk to an unemotional eye. Like the red and green toy top, whose sides had rusted and whose tip was bent. But they weren't junk. The top had entertained Eula for hours and hours, as Della spun it for her without tiring. The tobacco tins were what they'd used for lunch boxes, and their proper place was in the kitchen cupboard. Hers had been mustard colored, and Eula's was red. Della had actually preferred the red one, but Eula had thrown a tantrum until her sister gave in. Papa shot holes in them for ventilation so the food wouldn't spoil, and Della packed them with dried jerky and bread and hog lard.

The crucifixes were all gone. They'd hung above every door, mostly little ones, almost unnoticeable but always present.

Some things were unfamiliar—left over, she supposed, by tenants. A museum of sorts, curated by one family after another. Strangers who must have made their own memories in this home. Were there births, deaths, marriages, joys, sorrows that were absorbed into these walls over the years? Did their ghosts mingle, along with those of Herman, Eva, Tomas, and Eula, all watching her, this old woman in an old house?

Unchanged was the lavatory, an addition Papa made to the house when Mama insisted. By today's standards it was surely outdated, but it had been quite the talk of the town at the time—the first one for years to come. Della was just happy that it was in working condition and afforded the kind of privacy that was nearly nonexistent in prison.

In the Before Days, Della and Eula would sprawl out on the floor with sugary Abba-Zabas in hand and flip through pages of Sears and Roebuck catalogs, imagining what it would be like to have bosoms that fit into the kinds of brassieres in the pictures. When they grew the bosoms later on, Eula's were much bigger. And although she complained that they were hot in the summer and hurt her back, she did not miss an opportunity to pull down her blouse a bit when she left the house, letting a little of the line between them show. Their mother would have been appalled if she hadn't run away with the painter, and Papa was oblivious to all the ways that his girls were growing into women.

The portraits were definitely not where they belonged. They had hung over the bed, side by side, the two girls immortalized by the painter at the seaside. Now there were two spots of floral wallpaper, patches of brightness surrounded by faded print on the rest of the wall. Della's painting was likely in the shed somewhere, and the other was said to hang in the church, in a little shrine made to the town's beloved girl. She'd heard some nonsense about it crying. Well, if it was, there was a lot to cry about.

In the morning, she planned to go to the church itself—Our Lady of Guadalupe. Her first foray into town. She'd found an old hat with a black veil, fashionable in its time and perfect for whatever anonymity she could retain. She did not yet know if her notorious celebrity of the forties was still of interest to anyone today, but it felt too soon to find out.

She looked forward to venturing out. To breathe in fresh air, to see the sky and the trees and the clouds and the birds. The yard at the penitentiary was vast but surrounded by tall brick walls and taller barbed wire that blocked the scene. Besides, one had to look out, not up, and be mindful of theft from fellow inmates and groping from the restless hands of the guards. Though that last part had not been an issue for her in the past few decades.

Funny how she could view her life in ten-year spans. The forties— when she learned to be a champion catcher of greased pigs. The fifties— when she discovered a love of reading. The sixties—when she sabotaged her chance at parole. And so on. How long they all were. And yet they seemed like yesterday. Time was a droll companion when looked upon with such distance.

Those were the After Days, the ones that comprised most of the years of her life. More than most people lived. The days in which her sister was no longer the belle of Puerto Pesar, drawing crowds from around the county to the little church on Sunday mornings. The days, instead, when Eula resided six feet below the parched soil in the churchyard.

Della didn't know what to call this new time. The Freedom Days, perhaps, but that didn't seem quite right. It wasn't enough that she could now walk around without bars to block the view. That was only one kind of freedom.

It was the freedom in telling your secrets before it was too late. Like the confessional of her youth, whispering things to Fr. Medina that she told no one else. About how she missed her mother. Her guilt over not being a good enough caregiver for her sister. Della had a story, and she was ready to tell it.

She would think of this time as the Truth Days. That was it.

The Truth Days.

And it would start by visiting Eula.

CHAPTER TWO

Puerto Pesar—Today

Mick Anders exited Highway 77 in a cheap red rental car, wondering if the narrow road really led to where the map said it did. He couldn't get a signal, just one measly bar on the phone, so GPS was out of the question. He was stuck with a flimsy map he'd bought at a gas station, the kind that required an engineering degree to refold. It was already starting to tear at the creases, dampened by the oppressive heat.

He looked up. There was nothing around him save for a weathered billboard advertising a Buc-ee's road stop a hundred seventy-five miles to the west. But he pressed on. Scant homes appeared on the endless horizon. Boards covering broken windows. Rusted bars covering the boards.

It reminded him of the place he'd grown up. Across the tracks from a moneyed East Coast prep school. Single mom living in a trailer, cleaning toilets in smoky bingo halls in exchange for tuition. Those long-ago playground voices had revisited his dreams lately. "Mr. Nobody," they'd taunted.

He ignored them. He'd worked his ass off trying to make something of himself. Politicians elbowed one another for his attention. Colleagues envied his bylines.

Until things went wrong.

Just a few miles farther, the GPS kicked in, and the houses improved somewhat. Builder-grade starters. But they were tidy, at least, even if they were plain. They lined the main road, heralded by a lone, dangling stoplight. To the right was his destination: La Palma Inn, the only lodging in Puerto Pesar. No rewards points to earn on a platinum card.

Mick stepped out, the sunburned remnants of grass shattering into fragments beneath his leather slip-on shoes. He shut the car door behind him. It echoed a sound of finality, the proverbial nail in the coffin, just as his editor's door had as it slammed behind him. Had that really been only three days ago?

"You need to lie low for a while, Mick," he'd said. "The owners are breathing down my neck to fire you, and I have to at least look like I'm a good company man. We're in enough hot water with circulation down and every two-bit blogger thinking they're the next William Randolph Hearst." He'd leaned in closer, enough that Mick felt the warmth of his cigar-saturated breath. "You're a good guy. I know you did what you thought was right. But this fiasco with the senator isn't the only reason you should go."

Mick had flinched at the truth in it and braced himself for what his editor might say next. Craig was known for his crackpot ideas as much as he was known for being right about them.

He leaned back and used his sausagelike index finger to slide a manila envelope across the desk. "Look. This was going to be a joke, a little laugh for your birthday. But after this week, well, I guess the joke's on me. I had an intern research the screwiest story possible, and she dug up a gem from a Podunk paper, a few months old. Who knows? Work your magic and turn it into the next Pulitzer winner. But more important, get out of town, go to Texas, and clear your head until this blows over."

This reeked of stupidity. But Mick didn't have any other choice. His editor had given him an ultimatum: two weeks of leave. Find a knockout story. Or you're finished.

Of course, there was no per diem, since it wasn't a real assignment, so Mick had decided to forgo the airline seat he would have preferred and hit the highway in a rental. Stephanie had taken the keys to the Lexus and kicked him out of their Copley Square condo. No doubt she was already on the prowl for the next man whose ambition rivaled her own.

He hadn't fought her over any of it. The condo was bought at the top of the market and had little equity. The Lexus had been hers to begin with, a present from her parents for her twenty-seventh birthday. Not even a milestone one like thirty. What would they buy her then? A dealership? Just like the kids he'd gone to school with. He never had an expensive car to park in the student lot. He and his mom took the city bus in—he with his Goodwill backpack, and she with her cleaning rags.

Well, at least he'd gotten a great education out of it. And made enough money to buy his mom a small house in Florida.

He'd proven himself once. He could do it again.

In and out. He was going to get the story he came for, spin straw into gold, and return to the newspaper as the prodigal son. He was young enough that he could still work his way up to the top of the masthead as he'd always planned. Until then, he had to buckle down and make something out of this far-fetched errand.

A little bell announced his arrival, waking the woman at the desk.

"Sheets get washed only between guests," she said as she handed him the keys. "But if you're here more than a week, we'll go ahead and change them out. And towels are on the bed."

He did not plan to be here any longer than he had to.

"And we're on drought restrictions," she continued. Her skin sagged with spotted folds that indicated a life of sun exposure and cigarettes. "Keep your showers to five minutes."

Mick found the room at the end of the parking lot. He forced the key into the tarnished brass lock, pushing and pulling until finally shoving open the door.

He was certain, now that he was captured by its unrelenting grasp, that humidity was a natural disaster worthy of the emergency aid and national outpouring that was bestowed upon more traditional afflictions like earthquakes and hurricanes. While it did not cause homes to crumble to their foundations, the same could not be said for visitors from Boston, who enjoyed moderate summers and blessedly cold winters. Never again would he curse the ice he scraped off the windshield as he hurried to cover a story.

Mick tossed his Tumi suitcase onto the bed. It landed next to a leftover newspaper, three days old, suggesting, disturbingly, that the room hadn't been cleaned since the last occupant.

He read the headline: One hundred eighty-two days and counting since the area had seen anything close to rain, and the temperature felt as if it were keeping pace with that number. The accompanying photo showed rosaries and holy cards strewn on the ground outside the church as people begged for salvation from this particular hell. But, like the once-green flora that surrounded it, the hopes were eventually abandoned, and the sacramentals lay forgotten.

It was just too hot to pray.

Mick searched for the air conditioner and found a note attached:

AC BROKEN. **R**EPAIRMAN DUE IN THE MORNING.
UNTIL THEN, PLEASE USE THE FAN. **M**ANAGEMENT.

He rolled his eyes and turned on the television. It flickered low-resolution images of a ballet recital broadcast over local cable lines.

He checked his watch. Eight fifteen now. Two hours past dinner-time, three if he were still on the East Coast. The ache in his stomach confirmed it. Surely there must be a bar nearby and a bartender to talk to. They always had the best information. And the sooner he got his story, the sooner he could leave.

He took a swig of room-temperature water and imagined that it was a beer, dripping with condensation that he could trace across his forehead.

Now or never. He couldn't procrastinate any longer.

Mick slid an envelope out from the bottom of his suitcase, creased under the weight of his clothes. It contained printouts of stories by lesser papers, mostly regional ones, and the sparse results of the intern's research. He ripped open the packet, leaving jagged lines along its edges.

It all boiled down to this: a portrait was found in a thrift store and was thought to be leaking tears. The image was that of a young girl about four years old—Eula Lee, whose father owned the fish cannery that had been the town's largest employer at the time. Her sister had murdered her years later. Della Lee had gone to prison and recently returned to the family house after seventy years of incarceration.

It seemed that all was dead and buried, so to speak, and the town had spent the last few decades more concerned with an endangered economy than the sororal antics that few were alive to have witnessed. But news of the crying saint had brought believers to the town for a short time. And for that time, Puerto Pesar enjoyed a regional notoriety it had not known in two generations.

12

Then, all too quickly, the heat, the drought, and skepticism sent the pilgrims right back to where they came from.

And sent Mick his Hail Mary pass.

Had one mistake, one reckless grasp at advancement, been worth banishment to a Hades that seemed so out of place in a civilized country? And could any kind of salvation be found in a convicted nonagenarian and the portrait of a long-dead girl named Eula?

CHAPTER THREE

Puerto Pesar—Today

Paloma Vega fidgeted in the house that was once again hers to call home, but she felt like a stranger. Ten years living away had produced a bona fide New Yorker who was already nostalgic for Thai food that could be delivered in the middle of the night and sirens that mellowed into an urban lullaby.

She liked noise. It calmed her, made her feel steady in a world that was moving swiftly around her. Growing up in Puerto Pesar had been so quiet that she could hear her own restless heart beating. Its rhythm ached for something more. That came to fruition when she graduated from high school and received a letter from her father in Connecticut.

He and his wife had just divorced. She'd never wanted him to contact his daughter, the product of a long-ago spring-break fling. But he'd always thought of Paloma and had set up a trust in her name years ago. And there was enough in it to pay for college, and maybe grad school.

Her only hesitation was leaving her sister, Mercedes, who was only six at the time. Paloma would miss their nighttime routine of reading before bed and all the time they spent together, but Abuela encouraged her to take this unbelievable opportunity. Nineteen and free, she left for a new future.

Now she was a few months shy of thirty. A whole different person whittled out of a decade. Four years at NYU and four more at Columbia for medical school. A two-year residency at Lenox Hill Hospital with a job offer from them for a permanent position. Her father was proud. But she wondered if, as a board member, he'd pulled any strings.

It was hard to know if you were truly good at something when the way had been paved for you.

"Where does Abuela keep the bleach? And the funnel?" she shouted.

Mercedes adjusted her earbuds and nodded her head to a beat that Paloma couldn't hear. She wanted to give her sister the benefit of the doubt. To believe that she just hadn't heard the question.

She tried again. Something more relatable.

"What are you listening to?"

But Mercedes shrugged and left the room.

Paloma sighed. There was no manual for Things to Talk About with a Sixteen-Year-Old. She'd actually looked online. In the last week, she'd tried to engage her in anything she could think of. Movies. School. Now music. She didn't ask about boys, though. She still wanted to think of Mercedes as the girl who rode a bicycle that had plastic streamers cascading from the handlebars. Not the one who'd just gotten her driver's license.

Who was this creature with the dark eyeliner and darker mood?

Paloma gave up and opened cabinets around the house, finding everything except the items she was looking for.

Abuela's own mother had been a product of the Depression, and she had learned to hoard items for reuse. The green movement didn't arrive in Puerto Pesar as a politically correct trend but as a matter of necessity, and thrift was no stranger to this house. Plastic bags and aluminum foil were meticulously rinsed and folded. The dish towels were threadbare, their once-colorful party images of Fiesta San Antonio frayed into near oblivion, a decade passing since they were new. The toaster looked like one of those replicas that could be found in upscale catalogs that advertised retro styling, but this one was an original, a wedding gift to Abuela. It had outlived her husband by twenty years and counting.

At last, Paloma found them on a shelf in the carport. She wiped her forehead with her arm and worried, not for the first time, whether she'd stayed away from Puerto Pesar for too long. Four visits in ten years. Not often enough to witness the intricacies of her sister growing up or her grandmother growing old.

Puerto Pesar. Family. There was something comforting about returning home, even if you'd always dreamed of leaving it.

But she'd done what any girl from a small border town would do when her upper-class father offered her a way out: escaped. She'd been too young to think twice. Too starry-eyed to feel guilty.

Until recently.

The administration at Lenox Hill Hospital agreed to hold her new position for a month so she could go home and help Mercedes take care of Abuela after her heart attack. Paloma caught a plane the next day, nonstop to Houston, then an impossibly long bus ride. With every mile, she willed the tires to spin faster. That was a week ago. Abuela was able to come home yesterday after recovering at a hospital in Harlingen and had already spent the day cooking enough *caldo de pollo* to feed an army.

Paloma knew better than to dissuade her. This was the woman who had raised her while her own mother flitted in and out of town. Who added homework to the school's load in the name of better education. Who supported her plan to move east and go to medical school.

It was simple: Abuela needed her, even if she denied it. So here she was. If an eternity were at her disposal, she could never repay her grandmother for all she'd done, raising Paloma and then Mercedes, while holding down three jobs to do it. But Paloma was quickly realizing the toll her absence had taken on her sister. How had she not seen it before? And what could she do about it with three more weeks here?

Paloma took a drink from the quart of water she'd set on the counter. Four of those a day. One gallon. Stave off the dehydration that came with the indomitable heat.

She returned to the task at hand. She'd promised to clean the drain line to the air conditioner after dinner. It, too, was a relic, and although Paloma had offered on four separate occasions to buy Abuela a new, energy-efficient unit, her grandmother insisted that the original worked as long as it was maintained. She stood over the piping, watching the bleach chug its way into the interior, and grimaced at its pungent scent. Catching the excess droplets with one of the kitchen towels—and eradicating what was left of the aged fiesta revelers in the process—Paloma gave them a final resting place in the trash bin.

"What is that you are throwing away?"

Paloma turned and saw Abuela standing there in her frayed bathrobe, arms folded.

"An old towel, Abuela. I'm ordering you some from Williams-Sonoma. You need new ones."

"You don't have to do that, *mija*. That one was just fine."

It wasn't worth arguing. It was easier to change the subject.

"How about some warm milk before you go to bed?"

"That sounds good. I'll start a pot."

"No. You're supposed to be resting. Let me do it." She pulled out some kitchen chairs and led her by the elbow. "Here you go. Sit on this one, and put your feet on that one. Remember, you have to elevate them. Doctor's orders."

The refrigerator door was covered in photos of Paloma and Mercedes through the years—pigtails, braces, graduations from kindergarten on up. But one was unfamiliar to her. It was a saint card, the kind that Abuela liked to hand out to trick-or-treaters along with the candy they wanted. She kept a vial of holy water in a reused perfume bottle in her purse along with a stockpile of Saint Michael cards to protect against evil.

But this one was different. Paloma pulled off the magnet that held it in place. It was a very young girl with long brown hair wearing a blue taffeta dress. A golden halo had been drawn above her head, and her name was printed at the bottom.

EULA LEE—SANTA BONITA

The back was blank.

Eula Lee. Paloma remembered the stories—legends, practically— of the murder. And she heard that Della Lee was just released from prison after all this time. She must be ancient. She'd have to ask Abuela about it.

But first, she wanted to talk about Mercedes. There had to be some way to connect with her sister. Maybe Abuela would have the answers. Paloma poured the milk into a kettle and turned up the heat. When it was ready, she poured it into two mugs. Flea market finds, if she remembered correctly. She joined Abuela at the table.

"She's going to lose her hearing with all those drums she listens to," her grandmother said as Paloma set the mug in front of her.

Paloma traced her finger along the vinyl tablecloth, the green leaves scattered in a patternless display, and a hole revealing its sinewy cotton batting. "She might, Abuela, but she didn't listen to me when I told her. I even showed her an article about it."

"I don't know where I went wrong, *mija*. I was too strict with my own daughter, and look how that turned out. So I lightened up with Mercedes. Didn't push too much. But it didn't make a difference. If she had two pennies to rub together, she'd be off on that road, just like her parents. Stubborn, that one."

Abuela looked out the window to the dusty street that led to the highway. The one where her daughter had driven off with her latest boyfriend, leaving behind the latest child. Where the semi that had hit them as they raced onto the on-ramp ensured that this departure was the last one.

Paloma wondered how Abuela managed to even get up in the morning with memories like that. What did life promise except more of the same? Hard work. Heartache. She'd have to think of some special things to do for her grandmother while she was in town. Maybe buy a new tablecloth. Or introduce her to flavored coffee.

"You know that she wants to go to California?" Abuela went on. "That she wants to change her name to Madison and to color her hair blonde? She doesn't even want to be Latina. That's why she won't go outside. Doesn't want to get any tanner than her God-given color allows."

"That's not true, Abuela. No one is going outside if they can help it. It's too hot. And she's a teenager. You know these ideas come and go, and I'll bet all her friends feel the same way. Remember I wanted to be a dancer and a flight attendant and a business owner before I wanted to be a doctor?"

The older woman shook a wrinkled finger. "You haven't been here, *mija*. You just watch—that girl is going to run off with the first boy who promises her a ticket out. Breaks my heart."

You haven't been here. The words pierced her, echoing exactly what she had been accusing herself of.

Paloma patted her grandmother's hand and laid it back on the table. The older woman's skin felt paper-thin. Abuela was getting old. Paloma leaned in, a habit she'd acquired this week as she'd realized that Abuela's hearing was not what it used to be. "But I'm here now. Maybe things will be different."

"Three weeks. It's going to go by too quickly. Much too quickly, my darling."

Paloma smiled at the old endearment. Abuela had always said that when she put Paloma to bed as a little girl, and it slipped in throughout her teenage years. She missed it. No one in New York talked like that.

They curled their fingers around each other's, the older set dotted with liver spots, each one earned as another year of worries came and went. The younger one was somewhat lighter, almost the identical shade of her father's, and smooth from meticulous applications of lotion she applied after the antiseptic soap that she used in the hospital.

Abuela continued. "But never mind about that. You grew wings and flew off, and I'm proud of you for it. Maybe you'll set an example for your sister. But what about the rest, *mija*? I worry about you. It's all well and good to have your career, but not if you don't have love. Do you ever slow down long enough to find a man in that city of yours?"

"Abuela." Paloma squeezed her hand and sighed at the refrain that her grandmother asked every time they were on the phone. Still, she hated to disappoint her. "There's no rush. I'm not even thirty yet."

"Next birthday, though. And then what? A few years to get settled into your new job, a few more to get married. What about babies? You girls wait so long now and then have problems getting pregnant."

She did want those things. But there was never enough time. Not if she wanted to establish her own practice someday. She needed this position at Lenox Hill to gain more experience and to add to her résumé.

"All right, Abuela. Work. Husband. Babies. I'll put them on the to-do list. But right this minute, I'm just happy to sit here with you and try not to melt in this heat."

Her grandmother pushed her chair back and cleared away the mugs before Paloma could stand up.

"I'm going to bed, *mija*. Don't forget to lock the doors and windows. And turn off the porch light, please."

"I will, Abuela. Sweet dreams." Paloma kissed her on the head and watched her until she made it into her bedroom. The roles were reversed. There was a time when Abuela would have been the one to send her off with a kiss and a prayer. It occurred to Paloma how full-circle life could be.

But how could she take care of her grandmother from New York? Paloma pursed her lips and did a quick mental calculation of her new salary, minus taxes, rent, and other expenses. There should be enough left over to have a nurse look in on her a few times a week.

And she still had to determine what help, if any, Mercedes provided to their grandmother. So far she'd seen little on her sister's part, but she'd brushed it aside with the excuse that Abuela had been in the hospital for the last week, and Paloma just hadn't been around before that to see how Mercedes might be helping out.

As if on cue, Mercedes came into the kitchen and grabbed a bottle of Big Red out of the refrigerator. Without a word, she headed toward the front door.

"Where are you going?" asked Paloma.

"Out." Mercedes put her hand on the doorknob and didn't look up.

"Out where?"

"You're not my mother."

"You're right. But I'm your sister. I should know where you're going to be. Especially at nine in the evening."

Mercedes muttered something and headed out, slamming the door behind her.

Paloma thought it sounded like "some sister." But she didn't want to believe it. That would hurt too much.

A quiet took over the house. Paloma looked around the living room, every corner reminding her of things she never thought about anymore. The table where she'd played Candy Land with Mercedes, always making sure that her little sister got the Queen Frostine card, advancing her toward the win. The recliner, where Mercedes would tell Paloma to lie down so she could examine her. It made Mercedes giggle to realize that she could hear their heartbeats through the Fisher-Price stethoscope.

Ironic that Paloma had become the doctor. Did it ever cross Mercedes's mind to pursue something like that?

Paloma realized that she had no idea what Mercedes wanted to be. Her hand rushed to her lips, holding back a gasp that had formed in her throat. Had she failed her sister with her absence? Had she really thought that the occasional Skype calls and less occasional visits were enough?

She hoped it wasn't too late. She hoped three weeks would be enough to reconnect with the girl who she'd let become a stranger.

CHAPTER FOUR

Road to Goree State Farm for Women—1943

Justice was swift, and the judge applauded the jury for being so decisive.

Della Lee Trujillo was sentenced to life in prison, with the possibility of parole in twenty years, and would live out those days at Goree State Farm in Huntsville.

Panic gripped her as the reality of what she'd done set in. Life in prison. She hadn't imagined it could have gone that way.

After an initial cheer erupted from the people who had packed into the building's largest courtroom, everyone trickled out, save for her husband of two weeks. Tomas stood and walked forward as she shuffled through the courtroom on the arm of the bailiff. He put his workman's hands on Della's thin arms and brushed her cheek with a light kiss. She felt warmed by his touch, the last they would have for a very long time.

"It wasn't supposed to be like this. You didn't have a chance."

She nodded, but words would have unleashed the tears that she desperately wanted to hold back. He needed to remember her as someone who was strong. Maybe he would worry less.

"I'll wait for you," he said.

"Don't," she answered, and turned before she lost all her resolve. She didn't look back.

"I love you," he said in a voice that filled the room.

She spent only one more night in the cell in Edinburg before being transported on the longest journey she had ever taken. This one was on the dime of the state of Texas.

Della hoped that the start of the four-hundred-mile trip might include a coastal route. It would be nice to see the water one last time. She had vague memories of visiting the Gulf of Mexico with her mother and her sister when they were all much younger. A weathered boardwalk that splintered her toes. Translucent crabs burrowing into little black tunnels in the sand. Children tossing multicolored beach balls. Sitting for a commissioned portrait and waiting while Eula did the same.

Eula had been fidgety, and Della could tell that their mother was agitated. But she didn't lash out like she usually did at home. Instead, she sat very close to the painter, touching his knee sometimes with her long, painted fingernails, all while glaring at Della in a way that she interpreted to mean that she had to keep her younger sister in line. Even at the ripe old age of six, Della knew that a girl of four was not much more than a baby and that it was difficult for her to keep still. She stroked Eula's hair and whispered to her that it would be over soon. Until Mother told her to get away because she was mussing Eula's curls.

It went on for days. The girls were ready for the beach right after breakfast, but Mother made them sit and sit and sit and sit in front of the painter until he declared that he was finished for the afternoon. Only then could they don their swimming clothes. Della

24

would hold Eula's hand in the surf to make sure that she wasn't swept into the turquoise-green water. She'd look back at her mother, who held the hand of the painter, crossed her legs, and giggled while fanning herself with a magazine. Della thought it odd, as it seemed like behavior that would make Papa sad, although she didn't know why and had never seen her parents act like that together. But the painter was so nice and patient with the girls. Perhaps their mother simply appreciated that.

Papa had not taken the trip with them. He was at home in Puerto Pesar, something about having to work. Something about having to provide. Della thought she knew what that word meant. It meant paying the grocer's bills and giving Mother pretty clothes and curtains and flowers. Papa was always giving her flowers.

Della missed Papa while they were away, and although the painter stayed over some nights at the rented house a block from the water, he did not have Papa's caramel candy scent, and he did not fly them up above his head while twirling them around the kitchen.

These recollections came to her as Della sat in the backseat of the black-and-white car with her hands cuffed in front of her and her ankles secured to the floor. Maybe it was better that they weren't driving by the coast. Because it was after that last trip that everything had become sad. Mama ran away with the painter, and Papa buried himself in the business. Della became a mother to Eula in their absence.

They'd taken Della's rosary when she was arrested. The one her mother had carried at her own wedding years ago. Something old. Maybe that had been a mistake. Maybe her mother's great sin had imprinted on it somehow and created a chain reaction of bad luck. Still, she had ten fingers—one for each Hail Mary in a decade. She tried to pass the time by praying. It had always calmed her in the past.

She paused at each Our Father.

Forgive us our trespasses.

But she couldn't finish. The heat and hunger masked an underlying unease about where she was, where she was going, and she kept losing her place.

She was denied more than a crack of the window for fresh air while the driver on the other side of the glass had his rolled down nearly all the way. His right hand was on the wheel, and next to him on the red vinyl seat was a revolver. She didn't know what kind, but it had a large barrel and faced the windshield. His left arm was propped on the open window, and his shirtsleeve flapped in the wind created by their speed. Back and forth. Back and forth. It reminded her of a kite. Her kite, the one that Papa, in a rare moment of lucidity, had bought for her fourteenth birthday. The last birthday before he left when he found a lead to her mother's whereabouts. Her kite was white, like the driver's shirtsleeve, but it also had a blue border that made it look like part of the sky.

The driver spoke only once, halfway there when he stopped for gas. He stood next to her window with his hands clasped in front of him, rocking on his heels while the pump sputtered into the car. "You's a lucky girl, ridin' in style today. If you'da been here last week, it woulda been Bud Russell and that bitch of a wife for company escortin' ya on the One-Way Wagon. No cushy seat for yous then. Just a hard bench in the back o' his there flatbed. But ol' Bud gone get sick this week. So you's a lucky girl. Mighty lucky."

He leaned in for that last part, filling the small opening of the window. The toxicity of his breath with the backdrop of gasoline fumes made her feel sick. But she held back a gag and turned her cheek. She closed her eyes tight, wishing she could escape this awful *luck*.

The plan had been to make it all the way to Huntsville by the end of the day, but when it started raining outside of Houston, he said that visibility was difficult, and they would have to wait it out. Della had never learned to drive and did not think the rain to be much more than a sprinkle, but she supposed she was not a good judge of what it was like to be behind the wheel.

The driver pulled into a motel. A sign on the outside featured dusty black letters that seemed to indicate availability. Both of the *C*s were missing, and it read **Va an y**. He put the gun in his pocket, the grip sticking out, and then draped a brown overcoat over his arms to cover it up.

A chill flittered up her arms.

He came around to her side, opened the door, and unlocked the shackles. He handed her a coat as well and told her to put it on because they might not let them stay if they knew she was a convict.

"You best keep quiet about that," he said in a hushed tone. And he patted his pocket.

The motel was L-shaped, with its stucco walls colored baby blue, and its long line of identical doors colored dark brown. Its trim might have once been white, but wood rot and peeling left it rather grayish. The driver knew which one was the office without a second guess, and a little bell on top of the door jingled as they arrived.

A radio blared in the background, as Perry Mason fought for his client in court. A girl accused of killing her sister. But this one sounded innocent. The clerk was facing the Emerson, a newer model of the one they had at home in Puerto Pesar, and he did not turn around when they entered. The driver put some money on the counter and picked up a key for room number twelve.

One room. She'd never been in a bedroom alone with a man. Not even her husband. She bristled at the thought.

The clerk raised his arm, causing his chair to let out an anemic squeak, and with a halfhearted wave said, "Have fun, Eddie."

What did that mean?

Three cars were parked between doors one through seven, but the rest of the lot was bare as they approached the one at the very end.

The room contained two beds—a relief, the only one of the day. It had pink paisley coverlets, a round table with two tweedy chairs on either side, a lamp between the beds, and one hanging by a heavy black chain above the table. A long bureau stood opposite the beds, and an Emerson radio identical to the one in the office sat upon it.

Occasionally Papa would take the family with him on business trips. She still remembered the Adolphus in Dallas with its painted ceilings and dazzling chandeliers that mesmerized Eula. They tried orange duck in the French restaurant nearby and a dessert called a Napoleon.

Della looked around the room and sighed. How far they'd fallen since those happy golden days.

The driver slung his overcoat across the chair and was irritated when Della said that she had to use the toilet. He patted his pocket once again. "Be quick about it," he told her. "And don't pull any funny business." He tuned the radio to a news program.

Della managed, despite the handcuffs, to pull down the drab prison jumpsuit, whose shoddy elastic waistband gave away the fact that it was old and used. She sat on the toilet with her head in her hands and used her foot to close the door.

"Open that back up," he yelled, startling her. The hinges squeaked as she opened it again, just enough to give her the illusion of privacy. It was horrifying enough to share a bedroom with this foul man. To be exposed in this way made her want to cry.

"Damn no-good machine," he said, hitting the radio as he tried to get a clearer signal.

She might have stayed there forever, but she didn't want to risk his ire. So she flushed and washed her hands with soap that made them smell like ammonia.

In the mirror, she saw someone she didn't recognize. Her brown hair was pulled back into a severe ponytail, with flyaways that had escaped during the many hours in the car. Her eyes were expressionless and wan, her cheeks pale, and her lips cracked. Eula had always been the prettier one, no doubt, but Della now sunk to a new low and was glad that Tomas was not here to see her like this.

She looked nothing like the bride she'd been just a few weeks ago.

She walked back into the bedroom. The lampshades threw a golden pall across the floor, and it reminded her of the color of vomit. The driver was sitting on the bed closest to the door, and he instructed her to sit on the other. He leaned over to reshackle her feet and lifted her legs onto the bed. He took her wrists, unlocked the handcuffs from one arm, and reattached them to the bedpost.

Her heart pounded in fear, and she tugged at the handcuffs, afraid of what he might do to her. But after pulling them to make sure they were tight, he nodded and walked to the door.

"No funny business," he said again. "I'm going to go get something to eat."

Relief. He was just securing his charge until he could return. As she calmed down, she thought ahead to what he might bring back. She hadn't eaten since yesterday—forgotten, she supposed, in the clamor as she was escorted to the car. Reporters shouted at her. *Why did you kill your sister?* Spectators gawked, and some even threw dirt and pebbles at her back.

Now she'd reached that point where she was so hungry that she didn't even feel it anymore. But all strength had left her.

He stopped when the door was halfway open and turned back. He walked to the Emerson, tuned it until he found some band music, and dialed it up to a high volume. She wondered if he were afraid she would scream, although it would do no good even if she did. She was not a victim held by a captor. She was a convicted murderer, being lawfully transported by an agent of the state.

Murderer. The word sounded so foreign to her, although she should be fluent in its meaning, as it had been bandied about endlessly ever since—ever since her wedding day.

The glow behind the curtains vanished, and darkness descended until it was impossible to know what time it was. Della lay there, immobile, and stared at the ceiling until finally falling asleep, despite the radio.

She woke to the sound of his return, startled at first, forgetting where she was for one glorious second. It was impossible to see, but she could hear as he fumbled with his keys and tossed something onto the other bed. She felt the driver stagger over to her, reeking of cheap alcohol. The black juice of chewing tobacco dripped down his chin onto her hand. Instinctively, she balled it into a fist, but he held her down by the wrist. He slapped her across the face and told her that she had been a bad girl and that she was going to get what was coming to her. He began to unbuckle his belt.

Della gasped at the realization of what was happening, but she stiffened with fear, paralyzed.

She tried to lift her arms to push him away but was too weak from hunger, and he had the strength of one who was emboldened by the bottle.

He lowered his face to her neck, and its scruffy texture scratched her and made her feel sick. Then he climbed on top of her, fumbling with her top, pulling down her pants.

"No," she tried to utter, but his weight crushed her voice.

She dug her heels into the mattress, bracing herself. She shut her eyes and turned her head, hoping to block out what was suddenly, horrifyingly inevitable.

"You're not like the other girls," he grunted. "Where's your fire? Don't you want to fight?" He shook her, grabbed her jaw, and squeezed it hard enough to leave a bruise.

She yelped, too quiet to be heard, especially over the radio.

It was not supposed to be like this. A cruel mockery of the wedding night she'd never had. Instead of Tomas, a brute. Instead of love, savagery.

Della might have cried, but she had no fight left in her, and her last hope was that he might kill her, reuniting her with her parents and sister. Bringing an end to a misery that had started years ago.

With painful strokes, he finished what he had started, mercifully brief. He rolled back onto his own bed and passed out. Della's heart raced, and her nails cut into her palms as she tried to grasp what had just happened.

A grim thought occurred to her. Her sentence carried more than the words spoken by the judge. In one quick moment, she'd now lost the last thing she had to call her own.

Della lay there, exposed, wet, silent. The music blared on.

CHAPTER FIVE

Puerto Pesar—Today

Paloma flipped through her closet for a cotton dress that was not too wrinkled after a week of sitting in a suitcase. The army-green one with spaghetti straps made the cut. She pulled her long brown hair into a sleek ponytail and checked the mirror. At the last minute, she added gold chandelier earrings and tiptoed to Abuela's room to check on her before heading out. The old woman was breathing deeply and clutching her rosary beads.

The night had reached the threshold where the heat abated into an almost bearable captor. Paloma jiggled her car keys but decided to walk and enjoy the air before it roared again the next day.

Not much had changed since she'd last visited, an unexpected comfort that made her feel as if she'd never left. Abuela's garden was still the pride of the neighborhood, even in its shriveled form. The Zamoras' house was now coral instead of teal, and the Rueles' home was abundantly protected by what must have been fifty statues of the Blessed

Virgin Mary in as many incarnations. She walked over chalk-drawn elephants, the faded doodlings of a child, remaining because there was no rain to wash them away. Just the thought of the drought made her feel thirsty.

It reminded her of when she'd taught Mercedes how to draw a hopscotch grid with the chalk she'd gotten for her third birthday. Her little legs had struggled to jump out and then together. Paloma and Abuela hid their grins so as not to hurt her feelings.

Two more blocks brought her to what was once called Travis Square but had been changed a few years ago to Cesar Chavez Plaza. It was lined with one-story cement-block buildings. Half were boarded up, and the faint lettering of past, failed businesses gave an almost ghostly feel to it. Telephone poles stood at every block, connecting sagging lines, and a lone palm tree looked as if it had gotten lost on its way to a more tropical destination.

Still as depressing as the day she'd left.

The fountain remained dry, but teens still sat around its perimeter, some smoking what was surely illegal, some groping one another in a drunken lack of inhibition. Nothing changed, she supposed, and why would it? This had been a popular hangout when she was in high school, and there was no more to do here on a Saturday night than there had been ten years ago. Even then, Paloma had looked at her classmates and wondered why they seemed so complacent about being in Puerto Pesar. Every minute that wasn't spent working the cash register at the thrift store had been spent studying. Whatever it took to get out someday.

She wondered if Mercedes were here, but it was too dark to tell.

The only lights came from opposite ends of the plaza. On the right was the church, Our Lady of Guadalupe, the requisite name, it seemed, for any Catholic church in South Texas. The windows were illuminated from within, their stained glass muted from the outside but brilliant on the inside, from what she could remember. A glow from the rectory told her that Father Reyna was awake, and she smiled. He had baptized Paloma when she was a baby, and her mother before her. Slipped peppermints to the children if they'd behaved in Mass. Paloma had always earned one.

She hadn't stepped inside a church since the last time she visited Puerto Pesar, except for Saint Joseph's in Greenwich Village when they did a "Messiah" concert before Easter one year. And not for any reason other than valuing her sleep on a Sunday morning. Abuela probably suspected but never reprimanded her.

Another light came from the left. Year-round Christmas bulbs scalloped around the roofline and cast Impressionist-like circles of blue, green, and red upon the sidewalk. The volume of recorded Tejano music rose and fell as patrons of Arturo's opened and closed the door. It wasn't crowded, though, not yet. She recalled that the place would really pick up around eleven or so, after bored husbands had finished their dinners and tucked their children into bed before leaving for the bar to meet their buddies.

She hadn't seen Arturo since she'd come home, and she couldn't let too much time pass without a visit. She'd fallen off her bike once when she was about ten, just outside of his restaurant. He'd brought out a first aid kit and cleaned up her knees and elbows, and given her a bowl of tapioca pudding while she waited for Abuela to pick her up. After that, he'd always waved to her as she passed by on her way home from school. And at least once a week she'd stop in for more tapioca.

She smiled at the memory. There were some nice things about being home.

People were scattered sparsely around the tables. Plates were cleared, their contents either consumed or packaged into foam boxes as leftovers. Only the far left side of the bar was crowded, with a rowdy bachelor party in progress, the group already drunk.

A man sat in the middle of the bar, alone save for the Shiner Bock that he was nursing. His skin was pale, and his hair was only a slight shade darker. He had a lost look about him.

Her strap fell off her shoulder, and she put it back in place as she slid onto the brown vinyl stool just in front of her. Crumbs had nestled permanently into the grooves where decorative buttons attempted to add style to the seat cushion.

"Paloma, my girl. You're back!"

Arturo was talking to her from behind the counter, and she smiled at the man who had become like an uncle to her. His shirt hung on his thin frame like a king-size duvet on a twin-size mattress. He still wore his sleeves rolled just past the elbows. All that was different was his hair, artificially black now while the gray traces in his mustache betrayed his real age. What had inspired Arturo to lapse into this particular vanity? He always struck her as a no-frills kind of guy.

"Yes, in the flesh. For a little while, at least."

He took her hands in his and kissed each one. "So good to see you. How's your grandmother? We don't see her except for Sundays after Mass."

"She's recovering from her heart attack. I'm trying to get her to rest up, but you know how she is. Mercedes is a handful, though. I wish I could figure out a way to help them both out."

His eyebrows wrinkled. "*Sí, sí*. I can certainly understand. But don't be too hard on your sister. She's a good kid underneath. And as I recall, you weren't no picnic either when you were her age. A bit lead-footed. Is that what they call it? I could hear that engine as you sped out of town. Lord knows where you were going."

"Nowhere, Arturo. Just for a drive. And I didn't even know you knew that."

It felt good to have someone know you so well. It took a long time to develop that kind of familiarity with someone in the city.

"Aw, Paloma. These thick glasses give me a superpower. I see everything. Did you know that?"

"Well, then, will you use your superpower to keep an eye on Mercedes when I go back to New York? Call me if there's anything I need to step in for?"

"I wouldn't need to call you if you decide to stay."

"Nice try. But I have a new job waiting for me."

He nodded as he wiped the counter with a dishrag. It was an impossible task, given the cloudy white haze that had overtaken the heavily lacquered surface. Hard Texas water. She had forgotten about that.

"Your grandmother told me as much. Big hospital there, right? She's so proud of you. You should see her smile when she says your name. But if she can live without you, I suppose I can, too. What will you have? It's on the house. A homecoming present. Some tapioca like old times?"

Oh, Arturo knew how to aim straight for her heart. But she'd actually had something else in mind.

"Would you consider me ungrateful if I just have a Dr Pepper?"

"Are you trying to look out for poor Arturo? Yeah, it's been slow, but I can afford much better than that! How about a nice plate of enchiladas *verde* and a margarita? Corrina's been getting fancy with the flavors. We have mango now, and even prickly pear cactus."

"Impressive! I'll tell you what. Let's take a rain check on the alcohol and stick with the Dr Pepper. Crushed ice, if you have it. But I'll take you up on the enchiladas. I never could resist them, and that's one thing that no one else gets right, not even in New York."

"Yeah, you don't be needing to go to no big city wannabe *cocina* when I can make you all the good food you need. You're too skinny. A few servings of my Corrina's tomatillo sauce and we'll have you looking healthy in no time."

"You sound just like Abuela. And you have no room to talk. What do you weigh now, forty pounds?"

"Forty-one," he joked. "But if you're not nice to me, I'm going to throw in the batch of sopapillas that just came out of the oven. Guaranteed to add two pounds!"

He waved his finger in the air and disappeared into the kitchen before she could object. She admitted to herself that the honey-drenched puffs sounded perfect. She hadn't had them since she left and hoped he still sprinkled powdered sugar on top.

She picked up the menu. They were laminated now, giving a sense of permanence to the changes that Arturo's wife had made. He wasn't kidding about the margarita selections. It was a veritable cornucopia of possibilities. She traced her finger down the page and then pushed it back across the counter.

The man with the sandy-colored hair followed the menu with his eyes and then looked back at his own place. The side of his hand rested next to a manila envelope, and Paloma wondered again if he were a recent local or a visitor. But not for long. Arturo handed him a plate, holding it on both sides with a towel and warning that it was hot. The man placed his arms on the counter on either side of it and stared at the food as if it were a crossword puzzle. At last, he took a knife and fork and started digging into it.

Definitely not local. Anyone who lived within thirty miles knew that whole *lengua*—beef tongue—was Arturo's specialty. And that it was best with chili sauce on it. He'd come in second place at the state fair years ago for his chili sauce.

"You might want to try this." She slid the bowl a little closer to him.

He looked up, and she warmed at the feeling of his glassy blue eyes on hers. They took a second longer than necessary to look away.

～

Mick turned to see the woman with slender shoulders and the slightest circles under her eyes. There was a glow behind her hair from the unseasonable flicker of the Christmas lights. Still, she had a younger Demi Moore kind of look, and a previous version of himself might elect to take her statement as an invitation that he was likely to consider. But New Mick had been screwed over recently, and he was damned if he was going to go through that again, no matter how pretty the girl.

He tried the dish the way she suggested, surprised at how much he liked it.

Arturo walked up and pointed to the small bowl on the plate, which was now empty. "That's more like it. We'll get you up to speed soon enough, *gringo*." He slapped the larger man on the shoulder.

"I won't be here long, but thanks anyway."

The bartender looked at him and then at the woman, smiling before walking back into the kitchen.

He saw the woman staring at him.

"What?" he said.

"I'm curious. Why did you order the *lengua*? It's not the kind of thing that people usually think of when getting Mexican food."

"Hey, when in Rome, and I heard it was a specialty here. Even without the chili, it's not the worst thing I've ever tried."

"No?"

"Ever eaten *balut* in Vietnam?"

"Can't say that I have."

"It's embryonic duck, still inside the egg—beak, feathers, and all. You add a little salt and suck it out." He mimicked the action, drawing it out a little longer than necessary.

She flinched, almost imperceptibly, and he couldn't help but feel a little bit of a kick at getting a reaction from this beautiful woman.

"Thanks for that. If I had an appetite before, I'm not sure I do now."

He held back a smirk.

She continued. "It's too bad you're not here in the fall for Arturo's *chapulines*."

He shook his head. "Nope, that's a new one, too. Lay it on me. What are *chapulines*?"

"They're *grasshoppers* with garlic and chili." She said the word as if she were trying to one-up him. It intrigued him. "Arturo adds lime juice to his."

"And why does he serve them only in the fall?"

"Because you can't get the right kind of grasshoppers here, but that's when his mother visits from Oaxaca and brings them."

"Well, thanks for the heads up, but I'm going to be out of here as soon as I can. Sorry to miss *that* delicacy." He dug into the *lengua* again.

"What a pity that we don't have anything here that can give you bragging rights. Maybe you'd be happier with your fetal duck."

She lifted her chin and turned toward the kitchen. In Mick's experience with women, this could either mean that she was being coy or that he had bombed in a situation he hadn't even crafted. Or wanted. Attractive woman or not, if he were going to get this story over with, he needed to keep his head on straight. She didn't entirely look as if she belonged here, but maybe she could help.

He swiveled to his right on the stool, hearing the faint metallic squeak above the music.

"Hey, I—" But she never looked his way.

"Arturo," she said. "I'll take those enchiladas to go. And save the sopapillas for the gentleman here. It's not Saigon, but I'm sure if he'll condescend to eating them, he might find something not to like." She waited until the bar owner came out with a Styrofoam box and slid off the chair without another word, exiting into the night.

Mick Anders, named Journalist of the Year by the New England Newspaper & Press Association just last year, sabotaging his first attempt at conversation with a local. Clearly his smoothness with women had turned to sandpaper with lack of practice. He raised a finger to gesture for another beer.

"Don't feel bad, man. You wouldn't be the first one to fail with her." Arturo popped the top off another Shiner Bock and handed it to him, leaning in to speak conspiratorially. The mist rose out of it in willowy ribbons, and the ice flecks fell, making puddles on the bar.

"What do you mean?"

"Paloma Vega. Didn't date much in high school and ran off to the East Coast right after that to live with her dad. She's a pretty girl, isn't she?"

"Mmmm." Mick glanced at the door she had just walked through, recalling how her hips moved as she hurried off.

"So, what you doin' all the way in Puerto Pesar, man? Ain't exactly on the way to anything. It's no tropical paradise." He pointed to the wall. Mick saw the weathered posters that hung on either side of the counter. Palm trees and oceans, the pride of Mexico, reminders of what might have been. They laughed at him, creases and stains and all.

He took a swig of his beer as the bartender continued.

"Let me guess. Wife left you, your rich uncle died and left the money to a bimbo girlfriend who took your dog."

"Well, no, but close enough."

"Hey, you know what happens when you play a country music record backward?"

Mick had heard this one before, and he didn't find it funny the first time. But he had nothing better to do than to humor the man, and as the town bartender, he could be a useful source of information later.

"You get your wife back, you get your dog back, and you win the lottery!" Arturo laughed and slapped the counter. Mick smiled to be polite, the maximum effort he could put forth without a few more beers in him.

"Actually, I'm here to see the portrait. And maybe interview Della Lee, since she just got out of prison."

But his attempt at a lead-in was interrupted.

"Sopapillas up!" A husky female voice came from the kitchen. Arturo held up his hand and disappeared through the slatted swinging doors.

Mick looked around. The bar wasn't any busier than when he'd come in. The drunks at the end of the counter were now shrouded by a haze of cigarette smoke and engrossed in a game of who could make the bigger pile of peanut shells before it toppled. Arturo returned with a plate of puffy pastry, drizzled in powdered sugar and honey.

"Compliments of Miss Paloma Vega, for our visitor."

Mick remembered her tart remark as she had left, but he couldn't deny that the dessert smelled like beehives and heaven. He grabbed a fork from a nearby table setting. The hot, flaky pillow collapsed on his tongue as he took a bite. The cooler honey settled into every corner of his mouth, and he closed his eyes at this contradictory treat. Much, much better than *balut*.

When he opened them up again, Arturo was standing there, hands on his hips.

"Hey, man," the bartender said. "Did you say something about the portrait?"

"Yes. The one that's supposedly crying."

"Yeah. The one in the church. *Santa Bonita*, they call it. I seen it happen, just once. It sure did bring in the pilgrims to little old Puerto Pesar for a few weeks. Me and Corrina finally had the money to get married, what with all the business that came to town."

Mick pulled out his notebook and clicked his pen. "So religious pilgrims came to the bar? I wouldn't have thought."

"Oh, no. Not the bar. But Corrina—she's a smart woman, that one. She had this idea to make T-shirts. And when they sold out, she printed more and added mugs to the line. Five dollars each, or two for ten dollars."

Mick cocked an eyebrow at him as he continued.

"I know, I know. Same thing. But Corrina, she thought that wording it that way would appeal to different buyers. Alls I know is that she made a tidy bundle, and we got married. She'd been yapping about it for enough years. Guess it was time."

"What a romantic."

Arturo waved his hand in the air to shrug it off. "Don't pay me no mind. I know I'm a damn lucky man to have a woman like Corrina. Don't know what she sees in old Arturo here, but who am I to argue?"

"And the portrait? Do the visitors still come?"

"Oh, no. Not since we got the heat, at least. That was months ago. And it didn't seem to cry no more after a time. But there was a frenzy while it was. People sayin' that they was cured of cancer or getting all epileptic when they was prayin'. I don't know nothin' about that stuff. But Corrina even sold bottles for them to take water from the holy font. Well, until Father Reyna found out. He didn't like her doin' business like that on church property. But they made up. She still goes to Mass on Sundays. Even makes donations to the poor box. Fifty cents for every margarita sold."

Mick's pen remained hovering over his legal pad, and he silently cursed his editor. Yeah, this was a joke all right. But he wasn't going to leave this town without a story. And he wasn't going to get a story without some better leads. He pulled out a twenty to cover everything plus a sizable tip and stood up. "It was good to meet you, Arturo. I'm going to turn in now."

He stopped a few steps before reaching the door.

"Thank you for the sopapillas."

~

Paloma liked this time of night better than any other. In New York, ten o'clock was when she could finally get some dinner after a long shift at the hospital, barring an emergency. It seemed like the city was just coming alive at that time of night.

In Puerto Pesar, ten o'clock was the time that the humidity relinquished its death grip and a still coolness nudged it away until the morning. Normally, the euphoria would be tempered by the preponderance of mosquitos, but it seemed this year they had been equally smothered by the heat. They departed for places unknown and were certainly not missed. It was just as well. Paloma disliked the residue left by drugstore repellants as equally as she resisted the stench of the oregano-based concoction that Abuela swore by. Still, either was a better alternative to itchy welts and West Nile virus.

The cicadas, however, chirped with that constant mating hum that sounded like a rattlesnake on a roller coaster. Molted skins littered the ground, their shape a hollow shroud of their round little bodies. She used to take Mercedes for walks, and they'd laugh at the crunchy sounds the shells made as they stepped on them.

That was what first got her interested in anatomy as a teenager. Paloma would pick up the skins, so perfectly detailed, and found a book in the Harlingen library that illustrated all its different parts. She was fascinated by the males who would sound their tymbals, creating the drumlike beat, while females would flick their wings in response. Amazing how bodies worked. And romance.

Her high school didn't have the budget for specimens, so dissection happened via textbook pictures. Just another reason she jumped at the chance to move east when her father called. New York had everything Puerto Pesar lacked, times a million. When she first entered the formaldehyde-scented biology rooms at NYU, she felt as if she were a student for the first time. Her premed path was sealed.

Paloma sat on a bench outside the church and opened the box with the enchiladas. Rooting around in the plastic bag, she realized that Arturo hadn't added a plastic fork. She stood up to go back in, but the man from the bar was just exiting, and she didn't want to run into him.

Those blue eyes when he'd looked at her. Even as they sniped at each other, there was something about him. Maybe they had something in common in visiting a place that rarely saw visitors. A kinship of sojourners.

But she had no interest in continuing a conversation. In and out. Back to New York. The fewer complications the better.

Paloma breathed in the air. Hot but clean, free of the smog that sometimes hovered, cloudlike, over the city. A piece of her was happy to be home, although even a week back had opened up her eyes to deficiencies that she hadn't noticed as a kid.

For example, she found it appalling that Abuela had had to go all the way to Harlingen when she had her heart attack. What if she'd died along the way? The town doctor had retired years ago and moved to Colorado for better weather, and there was no clinic in town for even minor medical needs. So residents of Puerto Pesar had to either drive up to the valley or down to Mexico, where they could get cheap prescriptions. Paloma begged Abuela not to choose that route, dangerous by all accounts, and sent her money to buy her medicines in the United States.

A truck rumbled from a street behind her, and she turned to see a bright-red Chevy with tires as high as mountains speeding toward the square. A girl in a lightweight tube top hung out the passenger window, her hair blowing over her face, a beer bottle in her hand. Several people held on to the side of the truck bed. They hollered like werewolves as the vehicle careened around the fountain several times. It kicked exhaust into the air, and Paloma had to cover her nose and mouth to avoid breathing it in. They nearly hit a dog that was crossing the street. She caught a glimpse of the driver, with his left arm hanging out the window. It was adorned with tattoos, sleevelike, and from where she was sitting, she could make out a globe and a skull. But the others were too small to see the details.

It was like being in high school all over again. Paloma watching her classmates from the thrift store window, rooted in the responsibilities she'd fashioned for herself but envying the freedom of those joyrides. Her freedom would be hard-won, and a better kind.

The truck changed direction, and the girl's hair fell to her back. Paloma saw her face.

Mercedes. And they were accelerating out of the square at a dangerous speed.

She shouted out to her sister, waved her arms, but she was either ignored or unseen, as they drove off faster than Paloma could run. She dialed her sister's phone, but there was no answer.

Maybe this was typical. Maybe a decade had emboldened the teens to be even more reckless than when she'd lived here. But Paloma felt a knot in her stomach, telling her that something wasn't quite right.

CHAPTER SIX

Goree State Farm for Women—1943

Della passed the night at the motel in sleepless silence, hurting and curled into a ball, trying to think of anything that would distract her from what had just happened. It was hard to remember the good stuff.

Papa reading an article that sent him chasing across the world to find their mother, nearly a decade after she'd left. News of his plane crashing into the Atlantic. Della selling off land to pay debts. Eula singing her first solo in the choir. Well, that memory was good, at least. The voice of an angel. The star of the county.

She had been so proud of her sister. Proud but afraid.

The driver stirred and called her to her feet as he thrust a half-eaten bag of peanuts into her shackled hands and said it was time to go. She shuddered at the sound of his voice, his very nearness, and dreaded the thought of being confined in a car with him for several more hours.

Most people would have called it justice—the fact that the driver stepped out of the motel room in the morning and straight into a pile of dog excrement. The kind that looked as if the dog, nowhere to be seen, had a stomach bug. The kind that would have to be hosed off the sidewalk.

That was the cherry on top of the justice, one would suppose, and the driver swore and used some *Jesus Christs* liberally while he scraped his shoe and pants leg across the tire of a car that had been parked next to his sometime in the night.

Della grimaced at his sacrilege. It was right there in the second commandment. *Thou shalt not take the name of the Lord in vain.*

The fifth had haunted her for the past few weeks. *Thou shalt not kill.*

Fr. Medina preached on the commandments regularly in the hell-fire-and-brimstone way that Della grew up with.

It did not occur to Della to use the driver's diversion as a means to escape. Not merely because her feet were still shackled, but because she had not yet recovered from the blow of the verdict. She did not think about her husband or what he might be doing at this very moment. She did not think about the future that lay ahead of her. Nor did she even think about last night. The violation. The humiliation.

The only escape to be had was to think of something else, to push out her fears of the driver and replace them with things that she could hold on to. Like the red and green top of her youth. Spinning here and there, landing on whichever memory it pleased.

Eula. It always came back to Eula. How she had trouble sewing when she was little because the thimble would slip off her thumb. How they tried to teach themselves to play the fiddle that Papa abandoned long ago. Or the time they saw eight horses pulling a whole house down the road.

When Eula was five and she cut off a chunk of her hair, and Della found her crying in the closet and managed to shape it into a bob that made the girl smile. The time that Eula tried to root out bees from a tree by setting fire to some old rags, and Della had to treat her stings with kerosene oil. Della and Eula. Essentially momma and daughter. Only two years apart.

Della recalled the time when they pretended that the sheets on the laundry line were a snowy forest in Switzerland, and the girls hid behind them, and the flapping in the wind concealed the sound of their breathing as they listened to Mama tell Papa that she was leaving because he smelled like a factory and refused to sell the cannery to the man from Dallas who offered a fortune. Mama gripped that ivory carving knife—a gift from that man from Dallas, sent along with the legal papers that Papa wouldn't sign. She threw it at him along with the hinged wooden box lined with red velvet that it came in.

Della tried to avoid thinking about the time that Eula started to change. When she began parading about in a thin nightgown whenever Tomas came over to visit. When she stopped helping out with chores. When she'd come home long after dark with no explanation and breath like whiskey. Or, only weeks ago, when that knife sat in her sister's belly, and Eula's crimson blood spread across Della's gauzy white gown. The one that she had spent weeks creating from old curtain sheers.

The ordeal was over. What was done was done. Della had accepted the consequences.

They drove on for half the day. With each mile, fear rose in her chest, nerves waking her from her cocoon. She should be a new bride, packing a lunch for Tomas as he set out for the day. Sharing his bed, beginning the large family they wanted. But instead, the expanse of nothingness as she looked out the window created a sort of vertigo. She felt small, alone, sinking into a pit that was swallowing her into itself.

At last, they turned in to the area known as the Goree State Farm for Women. It was surrounded by a tall chain-link fence and topped with triple rows of barbed wire. To the left of the car, as far as anyone could see, were fields of cotton, tended by fifty-something Negro women and overseen by two white ones. They alternated between wiping their brows and hoisting hoes over their shoulders before bringing them crashing down into the land. In the middle of the field was a man-made ditch, long and narrow, filled with water, with siphon tubes running perpendicular across it to hydrate the crops.

To the right were orchards—peaches and apples and pecans, she would learn later—and a bunch of white women were climbing on ladders and sorting the fruit into baskets. They, too, wiped their brows, but not as often, as the shade from the trees offered some protection from the temperature that would reach its peak later in the afternoon.

All moved in a slow, sun-drenched symphony of efficiency, and Della wondered if she would be taking her place among them. After Papa left, she'd worked much of the land on their homestead. But never during the peak heat of the day, and always with the chance to go inside for a glass of lemonade.

Ahead lay a rectangular fortress of reddish brick, two stories with countless barred windows that gave her a claustrophobic feeling just looking at it. If Della had thought about what the Goree Unit would look like, she might have imagined something towering, something imposing. But it was no more than an unadorned rectangle. Two towers housing men with binoculars stood at either corner. The driver stepped on the gas pedal, and they arrived at the front in less than a minute.

She shuddered at the thought of spending the rest of her life here. The labor. The isolation. The walls. It was one thing to understand that everything you'd ever known or hoped for was gone. But to see it in all its bleak reality was jarring.

A man in a dark uniform came forward, and the driver turned off the ignition.

"You're late," the man said without a trace of surprise or irritation.

"Yeah, well, we ran into some rain in Houston."

The man stood still, eyeing the driver and never looking at the passenger in the back. Della felt invisible, and she'd only been here a matter of minutes. "Let's not let it happen again, Eddie." He handed him a white envelope, which Eddie the driver opened immediately. He counted its contents and nodded.

The man opened the door next to Della. "Come on, you." Della caught a whiff of the dog shit, and yet it was not easy to differentiate from the outside, surrounded as they were by fertilized farmland. Her nose tickled her, and she brought her two handcuffed arms to her face and rubbed it with her sleeve. Her ponytail had all but loosened itself out of existence, and she could feel the hair tie hanging off her longest strands.

The man bent down and unlocked the shackles. She flexed her legs one at a time before ducking out of the car and into the sunshine. He slammed the door behind her, and the driver sped off, spewing dust onto both of them. It occurred to her that this had been Tomas's last glimpse of her—driving off in that car, finality hitting in the way it did for her now. She felt relief that she had seen the last of the monster behind the wheel, but a pit grew in her stomach at the feeling that it was her last tangible connection to her husband.

"Welcome home," the man said with sarcasm. His polished brass tag read Roy Hildebrand.

The guard gripped her elbow, another sign that her life was no longer her own and she had to go where she was led. He walked her past a reception area through a pair of heavy double doors to an office. A middle-aged woman sat behind a desk, and a thin chain around her neck pinched her skin. She laid a nearly new cigarette in the ashtray in front of her and adjusted the glasses on her face. Her thin lips barely moved as she spoke and never cracked a smile.

"Miss, uh . . ." she said as she flipped through the file in front of her. "Mrs. Trujillo."

The name brought tears to her eyes. She wanted more than anything for it to be true, for her to be the wife of the man she loved. But one terrible moment had taken away that possibility forever.

"Miss Lee," Della corrected. She did not want to add the Trujillo to her file, for when she thought of Tomas, she hoped that he would forget her soon and give the name to someone else. It would be better for him that way.

"Suit yourself," the woman said. "I don't care what they call you. But for our records, you're Mrs. Trujillo."

The woman turned to a girl to her right, who was dusting the bookshelves. The girl could not have been any older than Della, probably younger, and her white prison uniform lay limp across her bony frame. "Yes, ma'am?" she said.

"Go fetch Gertie and tell her that The Murderess has arrived. And bring out the camera."

She was no longer Mrs. Trujillo. She was "The Murderess." How low things had sunk, exposing deeper and deeper levels of humiliation.

When the camera was placed on its tripod, Della was instructed to stand against the black wall on the opposite side of the room and hold a chalkboard sign, where her name and a seven-digit number had been hastily written upon it. The accordion-like lens extended, and the camera flashed, startling her already stinging eyes. She shut them as she was told to turn to the right so they could capture her profile.

The woman called her over to the desk. "Sit down," she said. "And hands out."

Della placed her hands just above the desk, watching them shake. The woman pulled out a black ink pad and a sheet of paper with ten boxes on it.

D-E-L-L-A L-E-E T-R-U-J-I-L-L-O, she printed in heavy-handed pencil. "That's it," she said. "Now, place those fingers one at a time in the ink and then roll each one slowly into one of the boxes." Della did as she was told, a response that was too quickly becoming instinctual. With each new print, she felt the weight of the criminal moniker that was now hers, and yet wholly unfamiliar to someone who prided herself on being a good girl.

When all ten were complete, the woman waved the paper in the air to dry it. She peered at it and held it up to her face. "Hmm," she said.

"What is it?"

"Oh, nothing. Just that a friend of mine reads palms, and seeing as the kind of work I do, she showed me how to read fingerprints. It's become a little hobby of mine. Helps me size up the new arrivals."

Della didn't ask what hers meant, nor did she dare to believe in superstitions like that. Fr. Medina wouldn't approve, as horoscopes and astrology and the like were forbidden—damning—sins akin to the original one, where Adam and Eve presumed equality with God. That part of her was not lost, at least. The part that believed that beyond this new, miserable life, there was another one waiting. One where she was reunited with her family and where she was not known as The Murderess but as Della. She needed to cling to this hope with every ounce of strength she had. It was the only antidote to the despair that was already taking over.

"Look here," the woman said as she laid out the paper in front of Della. "The different fingers mean different things, and the kinds of swirls they have indicate character traits. Yours, for example. Not a loop in the bunch. That would mean someone is lighthearted. Easygoing. Not you, though. See here."

She pointed to the middle finger. "This one is your moral finger. You have an arch. That means you're pragmatic. Responsible." She leaned in closer. "Yep. You're a tough one. Mostly arches and whorls. Whorls tend to be intense. Uncompromising."

Della didn't like to think of herself that way. It sounded so strident. And yet she couldn't deny the descriptions, either. Was it circumstances that made her that way? The need to have mothered Eula at such a young age? Would things have been different if their mother hadn't left? Or were these traits written on her hands from birth, preordaining her very identity?

Someone knocked on the door, and the woman quickly slipped the paper into the file. "Gertie," she said. "We've got her booked, and she's all yours."

Della could hear Gertie before she saw her, with the click-clack of her shoes tapping against the saltillo tile floor. Her shoes were boxy, with hard soles, and the socks around her ankles were frayed. Her dress looked homemade because the hem was longer on one side, and the buttons didn't match up correctly to the holes. Her face had the fundamentals to be rather pretty, with the kind of symmetry that her attire lacked, and her braided blonde hair looked two days overdue for a wash.

"Miss Lee," she said firmly but kindly, in a voice that had a hint of musical quality. "Come this way with me. I'm going to get you settled in."

They walked to another set of double doors, and Gertie removed a key from an oversize ring that she had attached to her wrist. The *thump* echoed in the hallway and sent a shudder through Della's body, followed by the *snap* of the key as it bolted the lock. Nothing up until this moment, not the drive, the night in the hotel, the fingerprinting, reflected the tone of finality quite like this did. She was barricaded behind those awful, heavy doors.

Gertie began a soliloquy that carried all the lightness of a docent in a museum tour and belied the gravity of where they really were. It reminded her of the time Papa took her to Houston to hear a talk about dinosaur bones before seeing the exhibit.

"This is the Goree State Farm for Women. We call it the 'Goree Unit.' We're just four miles south of Huntsville, where the men are. I'm sure you've heard of Huntsville—John Wesley Hardin, the Old West gunslinger. Satanta, the Kiowa war chief."

Della didn't recognize the names that seemed to make Gertie so enthusiastic. But it made her feel, distressingly, as if she were now one in a long line of notorious criminals.

"Goree was opened in 1911, just a year after the legislature abolished the convict lease system. Until that time, prisoners were leased out to private companies for labor. In fact, it was prisoners who built much of the state's railroad system, and it was prisoners who quarried the limestone and granite that make up the Capitol building in Austin. They even built much of the furniture there."

Gertie seemed to speak about them with the pride a mother might have for her child, and Della hoped that there might, at least, be small kindnesses in this place.

She continued. "But not to worry. That's all done with, and now the work we do here is for the sustainment of Goree itself. Plantation-style."

To demonstrate, they stopped by a window. "You see there, those are the fields. We grow our own cotton and our own fruits and vegetables. Beyond that and over some—but you can't see it from here—is the dairy barn and the henhouse. On the other side of this building—you probably noticed it as you drove in—are the orchards, the cannery, and beyond that is the cemetery. The Negro women make up more than sixty percent of our population, and they work in the fields. The white women who are on good behavior work inside with clerical work, laundry, sewing, etc. The ones who are on discipline are out in the orchard. And, if not enough are on discipline, then they're chosen by lottery." She stopped and smiled. "Well, not the kind of lottery that anyone would want to win!"

On cue, the frantic staccato of sewing machines came from down the hall, and as they walked by, Della saw through the tiny window a bevy of women in starchy white overalls hovering over their worktables.

Her eyes opened wide, which was the first trace of sentiment she allowed herself. Her mother had been an excellent seamstress, embellishing their garments and their home to make everything more beautiful. Gertie noticed. "You like sewing, do you? Maybe that's where we'll put you. Here at Goree, we make all the clothes and bedding for the whole state penal system. See over there"—she pointed toward the back corner—"those are the beginners. They're making pillowcases."

Then she pinched at the top of her own dress. "This here is a gift from a graduate of that corner. You can see she was just starting to get the hang of buttonholes."

Della noticed a progression of expressions on the girls' faces as they did their work. The new ones were easy to spot. They seemed to struggle with learning the machines. Others were adept enough at the tasks in front of them, even turning their heads a time or two to talk to others around them. But she shuddered at the third group. They were proficient in their work but appeared thoroughly bored. No, not bored. Expressionless. Their skin was a pasty white, and they seemed as if they'd been there a long time, all personality drained until they seemed part of the machines.

Were they lifers like herself? Would she be sitting there someday looking so thoroughly vacant? Maybe there was a safety in that, though. It was better than pain. Already she was feeling an ache return to her as she took in her surroundings and the reality of her actions set in.

This was her new forever. Perhaps those women had it right: numbness was a virtue to strive for. Her survival might depend on it.

They continued through the rest of the main building, where rooms were set aside to teach other skills to the women. "All our girls are in for felony charges. Some of them are truly a bad sort, getting in with gangsters and laundering more than the laundry. Some of them were just mamas who fell on hard times and went to forging checks and stealing and the like. Poor things."

Panic rose in Della's throat at the thought of being trapped with such criminals, forgetting for a moment that she, herself, was a convicted murderer. It felt like being buried alive. Surrounded by darkness, she wanted to push her way out and scream, *You've got it all wrong! I don't belong here!* And yet Justice had wielded its mighty sentence as she took her place among the notorious rolls of lawbreakers at Goree.

She stopped in front of one room that was filled with bottles and looked like a laboratory of sorts. "This here's the salon for the girls who want to be beauticians when they get out of here. Now, I know that you're a lifer, but if you're good, you might get paroled, and if you're not, well, it doesn't hurt to learn another skill anyway. Might keep you out of the heat."

That, at least, seemed like a small blessing.

They left the main building after Gertie told her about the cafeteria and the infirmary and the nursery. The latter being for women who had their babies in prison, a thought that seemed too appalling to dwell on. They entered the yard, where two buildings stood on either side.

Gertie pointed to the left. "That's the Negro dormitory, and the other's for the white girls. We've got about a hundred and fifty inmates altogether. Used to be cells about five or six years ago. But the public started to complain. The Texas penal system didn't have the best reputation, so this is one of their nods to more humane treatment. Especially for the women." The dormitories were lined with small windows, each barred with iron.

"But before we go there, we have to hit the showers." She walked ahead and looked over her shoulder. "And I apologize in advance."

Della tensed up. *Apologize for what?* she thought. But she obeyed.

Gertie led Della to a room that smelled both gamey and stale. In the middle was a drain and, on the side, a concrete bench. The door echoed as it slammed into its locked position.

"Just take off your clothes and put them there."

Della began to shiver, not only because she was cold but because she felt like a chicken at the slaughter, unaware of what was happening until she sensed danger and flapped her wings trying to escape. Her blood pulsed in protest of whatever was going to happen next. But she had no choice. She slowly rolled the jumpsuit off her body and covered herself with it as she walked to the bench.

"And now, stand over the drain."

Gertie looked to the side as she handed Della a bucket of water and a slab of lye soap. "Go ahead and wash."

Della dipped the soap into the freezing water, and goose bumps sprouted across her limbs as she lathered herself. Gertie picked up the jumpsuit and checked its pockets before folding and replacing it. By then Della had rinsed herself and covered herself with her hands in a futile attempt at modesty. Gertie returned, averting her eyes when possible. She pulled a comb out of her pocket and had Della lean over so she could check her head for lice. Bit by bit, she parted the long brown hair until she pronounced Della to be clean.

"Well, that's good news for you. The delousing soap is a stinker, and we have to use it more times than not. Stand straight now, and open your mouth."

Della had thought last night that it was not possible to feel any more broken than she had been in that motel. But she was mistaken, as Gertie lifted her tongue, spreading her arms and legs; wiggled her fingers and toes; and subjected every crevice to inspection, for health and for contraband. Della closed her eyes, trying to imagine being someplace else, but the intrusion was so intense. As if she were an animal being prepped for the slaughter, not a human being who stood terrified at every mortifying indignity.

Yesterday morning, no one had ever seen her undressed, not even her husband, and now, two days in a row, her body was no longer her own. It was the possession of the state of Texas and those who worked for it, to do with it what they would.

Gertie, at least, was perfunctory in her actions, and Della figured that this was probably not her favorite part of the job. This sentiment was reflected in her eyes when she at last turned to a nearby cabinet and pulled out a towel and a stained white frock. She handed it to her charge.

"Now there, I'm sorry that had to be done, but it's the rules. The doctor usually does the inspection, but he's out delivering a baby in town. So, between him or me, I'd like to think that you got the better deal."

Della just nodded, feeling as if her voice would be a mere caricature of the empty shell she was becoming. She stepped her legs into the jumper, followed by the arms, obeying orders.

"Right. Now that's done, and I can tell them that you're as fit as a fiddle and there wasn't a razor or drug to be found on you."

They continued until they came upon the dormitory once again. Gertie pulled out her keys as they entered through one door and knocked so that a guard could open a second one.

"A bed just became available here, so we're putting you next to a woman who's been at Goree for five years. She's got three left. In here for horse thieving with her husband. Says it was to feed their babies after he couldn't find work, but she didn't get a sympathetic jury." She leaned in slyly. "Nor did she really have babies at home."

They stopped at a bed made of white iron, identical to every other one. Mattresses showed the outlines of springs pushed against the worn ticking, emaciated from years of use. Thin cotton coverlets were folded at the feet. One was bare, waiting for its newest occupant. Above the others hung pencil drawings of animals and seascapes and world landmarks. Della recognized the Eiffel Tower. The Taj Mahal. Niagara Falls. And others were decorated with quilts and embroidered pillowcases brought, presumably, by loved ones to add a cheery touch.

"This will be yours. You're next to Hazel. She's got a thick old Mississippi accent, but you'll get used to it. But before you settle in, I'll finish showing you around."

The hall was bright inside, with an endless single row of rounded fluorescent lights, the kind that took a minute to adjust to and gave you a headache after prolonged exposure. Down the long hall, a female guard paced with a baton that she tapped against her hand, and Della wondered what infraction might merit a beating with a stick like that. Most of the beds were empty, and Gertie explained that the inmates worked ten-hour days. That, at least, was something familiar to a girl who was raised on land.

Through unseen corridors, Gertie told her that there were special wings: those for girls who came in with venereal diseases and those who came in pregnant. Della couldn't have imagined there was anything that could make a prison sentence worse, but apparently there was.

Near the end, the barred doors to a large, old cell were open, and Della heard the refrain of a song that seemed to be about lost love. It was beautiful, haunting, even. She thought at first that a radio was on, but the song stopped suddenly and voices rose in disagreement over how to proceed.

Della looked quizzically at Gertie, who placed a finger over her lips. She leaned toward Della's ear. "That's the Goree Girls practicing for their show tomorrow night."

Again, Della was confused, and Gertie continued. "You've never heard of 'Thirty Minutes Behind the Walls' on WBAP? Well then, you are in for a treat. The Goree Girls are one of the biggest names in country music, honey, made up of female inmates. And that voice you hear in there belongs to the one who started it all—Reable Childs. Now there's a woman who knows something about how to make a life in a place like this. And how to win back her freedom."

Music. Freedom. The words rushed through her, awakening a small part of her that was slowly dying.

CHAPTER SEVEN

Puerto Pesar—Today

It was 7:50, and the sun was already as strong as if it were midday. The driver Della had hired for getting around town was due to arrive in an hour or so. The girl was sixteen, newly licensed, and happy to make a few dollars helping out an old lady when she needed it. Mercedes Vega. She said she was saving for something but never said what. Probably shoes. Or clothes. That's what Eula would have done.

Della stretched her arms and stood up as quickly as her body would allow.

If there was one thing she liked about the heat, it was that her arthritis didn't hurt so much. In Goree, and later, when the women all moved to Mountain View, the nights could get cold, and her bones would stiffen. She supposed it was a malady that afflicted many people her age, but decades in prison could not have helped. She couldn't deny that the medical care had been reasonable, though, and she had been a favorite of the nursing staff ever since her brown hair turned gray and then white. They'd nicknamed her "Old Lady Lee" and "Granny D," and she was no longer spoken of as "The Murderess." There were not many senior citizens behind the walls of the Texas State Penal System.

In fact, the news that she was going to be released was met with disappointment all around. Even Della herself hadn't been entirely happy about it, though she had chosen to finally behave before a parole hearing. The walls had been her home for nearly all her life, good or bad. At the end, the younger inmates had looked to her as sort of a grandmother figure.

She smiled as she lifted a housecoat over her head, one made with a zipper by young inmates who were practicing that skill. She tugged at it halfway through, where a bit of fabric was stuck. She remembered when Gertie first took her through the sewing room on her first day at Goree.

Dear Gertie. She had written letters to Della up until the day she passed away in her sleep, an old woman herself. Prison had been difficult, despite what the politicians wanted you to believe. But there were good memories. Good people.

Puerto Pesar, on the other hand, held nothing but memories of two lives snuffed before their time. Eula was buried just outside the church, never to sing again. And the Della of the Before Days might as well be there next to her.

Mercedes arrived right at nine o'clock in a cream-colored Oldsmobile that she said belonged to her grandmother. A little heavy-handed with the eye makeup, but Della remembered Eula experimenting with cosmetics at the same age. This girl could be so much prettier without it, but she'd learn that in time. She was punctual, at least, and Della appreciated that. Time ran with precision in prison, something that provided a modicum of predictability in a place where one could rely on so little. Nine meant nine, not 9:05. She would ask the girl to drive her to the corner of town, but after that, she wanted to walk.

"Drive slowly, please," Della told her. "And you can drop me off at the market."

Mercedes gripped the wheel, hands firmly on the two and ten, as Della had read but never practiced. She had read everything in the prison library, from the classics to the mysteries to the magazines to the auto manuals. Whatever was donated.

"Here you go, Miss Lee," said the girl as she eased next to the curb. "But it's closed on Sundays. You need something? I can bring you something from home before I pick you up later."

How sweet. A helpful child. She was a tad younger than Eula had been when she died. And with a better disposition.

"I'll manage," Della answered. "Just drop me across from the church, then."

The lawn in front of the church was packed, people filing out of an earlier Mass and others into a later one. The board outside was new. Black with removable white letters. Sunday Mass at eight and at nine thirty. Just like when she was growing up. She and Tomas had attended the early one. Eula sang later.

Mercedes pulled over and helped Della out of the car.

Della walked the long way around the crowd, not ready to see or be seen by the congregants. They were likely the great-grandchildren of the people she'd once known, and that brought up nothing but thoughts of how hateful they'd all been in that courtroom.

She walked through the cemetery gate, painted over a thousand times, she supposed, with black gloss. Weeds popped up through the many cracks in the pavement, and graves were overgrown and unkempt.

Except for Eula's.

She remembered exactly where it was but was surprised to see the wreaths and bouquets at various stages of freshness and decay that lay across it. Della had considered bringing some herself, but the market's Sunday hours had made that decision easy. Just as well. On the one hand, she loved her sister. Of course she did. On the other hand, Eula was the reason that she had been shut away, the reason that she had lost her chance at happiness with Tomas.

Tomas. He was here, too. At the thought of it, her face flushed with tears. One by one she hobbled past the graves, trembling as she stepped over the stones. She recognized a name here and there, disbelieving, despite the math, that everyone she ever knew in Puerto Pesar was gone.

And there it was. It was hard to find at first. One of those flat ones that lay on the ground. Humble, just like him.

Her knees couldn't hold her any longer, and she knelt down, using her cane for support. She kissed her fingers and then traced them along each letter.

Tomas Trujillo

Beloved Brother and Friend

Just like Teresa to have left off the *husband* part. Maybe four hours didn't count for much in his sister's eyes, but there'd been all the years before that, at least, to merit a mention of his role, the one that Della knew had for a short time been his favorite.

She brushed off the dirt from each of the corners and stood up one creaky inch at a time. She would return with flowers soon. It was the least he deserved.

A gathering hall was adjacent to the chapel, an addition after her time but still weathered with age. A sign pointed the way to *Santa Bonita*.

Della entered the candlelit room and avoided glancing up. Seventy years since she'd seen it. It could wait a minute longer. She needed to breathe.

For an offering of a dollar, she could light one and pray for the intercession of the would-be saint. Leaving the coffer empty, Della picked up a long wooden stick and placed its tip in a nearby flame. Her hand shook as she tried to connect match to wick, but at last they collided, and the smoke from her prayer was released. The fire sprang to life before mellowing into a subtle and comforting flicker. She snuffed the end of it in the bowl of sand and took her seat.

She looked up. And shivered. It was as if no time had passed.

There was Eula, beautiful Eula, immortalized in her innocent childhood. Her heart softened for this little girl who didn't know what pain lay ahead.

It was just as she remembered it, save for the delicate white streaks that fell from the eyes, barely perceptible. They did indeed look like tears.

Once inseparable, the sisters were apart now, life from death, canvas from canvas. One relegated to eternity, one left to languish in this hellish South Texas heat. The house had become Tomas's after her incarceration, by merit of their four-hour-long marriage, and only he might have known how the portraits got to be where they were. But he had been dead now for such a very long time.

Della folded her arms and studied it, adjusting her glasses. The dress that Papa had bought for Della, which she had treasured and managed to wear for two Christmases. By the second holiday it was too short, and she couldn't fasten the top two buttons in the back. But she loved that dress, and imagined that she was a princess. She didn't mind, though, when she outgrew it completely and handed it down to Eula. By that time, Papa had bought her another one, the blue one that she wore for the sitting. It had been similar, with its taffeta fabric and lace trim, but this one had puffier sleeves, a fact that was not lost on Eula, even at so young an age. Papa promised her a new one the next time he went to Houston for business. But by then Mama had left, and he forgot about all sorts of promises.

Papa had inherited the cannery from his own father, who had the crazy idea to bring iced fish and oysters inland from the coast where the labor would be cheaper to process them and the land for the factory cost less to buy. The journey took just over an hour, and the fish were still fresh, so the consumer saw no difference in taste and appreciated the savings that were passed along to them. In fact, Lee and Son's Fine Fish created a proprietary pickling blend that the bigger companies could never copy. They even wrangled a lucrative contract with the military to put their fish into army rations. So time after time, they were offered dazzling incentives to sell, and Mama would look at the zeros, and her fingers would tingle with anticipatory pleasure. But Papa had the tenacity of his father, who'd died earlier of a stroke. And he had a loyalty to the poor people of Puerto Pesar, who would surely lose their livelihood in exchange for his one chance at wealth.

After he left and took his acumen with him, the cannery declined in the face of his absence and the lack of modernization. It was sold to the highest bidder for far fewer zeros than it once would have, with promises that the people would keep their jobs. But the ink was still soaking into the paper when the recipe was turned over to the buyer and the outdated plant was rendered unnecessary.

The town never recovered, living up once again to its name. Puerto Pesar. The Port of Regret.

Regret. A word she knew intimately. Only three people knew the truth about what happened that day, and two of them resided in this cemetery.

"Stop, stop, stop." Abuela brushed Paloma's hands away as she dressed for church. "I'm not an invalid yet, and I can do it myself." She contorted her arms and stretched her neck, and managed to zip the green cotton smock all the way to the top. Paloma remembered her hand embroidering the colorful flowers that were splayed across the front. Abuela had tried to teach Mercedes and her, but it didn't hold the interest of either.

"I'm just trying to help. No need to be a ninny." Paloma kissed the top of her head, in the oval-shaped spot where the hair had thinned and her brown scalp was exposed.

Abuela reached for her veil, the long kind that covered all her hair and not the little round doilies that had become fashionable in the years right after the Second Vatican Council. She pinned it to her braid, spun it into a tightly coiled bun at the back of her head, and took one final look in the mirror.

"I know you are. I'm sorry. I guess I just don't want to believe that I need the help. But if you really want to do something, you can knock on your sister's door and remind her that Mass starts in half an hour."

"I thought I heard her leave with the car this morning. I meant to ask you about that."

Abuela put her hand on her cheek. "Oh, that's the thing about getting older. You forget so much. Yes. She is earning some spending money helping out an old woman. Della Lee."

"The murderer? Abuela—do you think that's wise?"

Their eyes met in the mirror. "*Mija*, she's ninety years old. I can't imagine that Mercedes would be in any danger. Besides, I'm sure the woman has had more than enough time to atone for what she did and make her peace with the Good Lord."

Paloma sighed. She didn't share Abuela's faith in people. But she had to admit it was unlikely that Della Lee could do anything to harm Mercedes. Or would want to. Still, the thought was chilling.

"Well, speaking of questionable company, Abuela . . . I saw her in a guy's truck last night. She was hanging out the window with a beer in her hand. Is that as bad as it gets, or should I be worried?"

"Oh, she's just like your mother was. Don't think I haven't tried to lay down the law, but I'm an old woman. It's not as if I can physically hold her back." She patted Paloma's hands. "That's just one more reason why I'm glad you're here. I've been worried, too, and I'm counting on you to help me figure out what to do."

Paloma sympathized with her grandmother. Their mother's fate was exactly what she wanted to spare Mercedes from. The generations before them didn't have a lot of options, but today women could become anything they wanted to be. She was living proof. There was a right path to leaving Puerto Pesar, and she wanted to help Mercedes find it.

Abuela continued. "It's the best I can do to give her a roof over her head and food on the table."

This tired woman was not the grandmother Paloma had grown up with. The one who was a taskmaster about behavior, education. This one was older, aged by one more decade in this town and one more teenager to raise. And poor health on top of it. But there wasn't much Paloma could do from the other side of the country.

"Do you think she might meet us for Mass?"

Abuela placed her hand on Paloma's shoulder. "Probably not. But I still ask every Sunday. At least when I meet the Lord on my judgment day, He won't be able to say that I gave up. The rest, well . . ." She waved her hand in the air to dismiss the thought, and then brought it down into a sign of the cross. "Let's just say that I pray enough rosaries to make up for it just in case."

Paloma leaned in to share the mirror space. She had put her own hair in a bun to keep it off her neck in this hot weather. But standing side by side with the older woman, she saw more of a resemblance than she wanted to, and she quickly let it down. It fell into gentle waves, layered recently by the stylist a friend had recommended. She liked how it looked on her, and she was inspired to add a little mascara and lip gloss to finish off the effect.

"What do you call that color?" Abuela asked.

Paloma checked the label at the bottom. "Nude Bliss."

"Holy Mother of God." Abuela crossed herself. "That's no kind of name for a lipstick."

"It's not a lipstick, just a gloss. To moisturize."

"In my day, it was popular for girls to wear *red* lipstick. Some were bright like poppies, and some were dark like blood."

"Is that how you got Abuelo? Smacking your red lips at him?" Paloma made puckering noises into the air.

"Heavens, no. Your grandfather didn't care for red lipstick at all. He'd say, 'No woman of mine is goin' to go 'round lookin' all hussied up.' And I'd say, 'Manuel—*guarda silencio y bésame.*'"

Paloma laughed. "'Be quiet and kiss me,' right?"

"Good for you. Not too rusty on your Spanish."

"And would he? Kiss you?"

"*Claro!* Of course!" She grinned at the memory. "And you could use a little color, since he's not here to make a fuss over it. I'll get some for you next time I'm at the market."

Paloma knew that it was pointless to disagree. Abuela was determined to see her meet a man, get married, and have babies, and if the perfect shade of lipstick would help make that happen, then there would be no stopping her. Whatever it took to make an old lady happy.

She returned to her room and slipped another sundress over her head, this time a pale-blue one. She worried that Abuela would scold her about the spaghetti straps and the indecency of bare arms in church, but she figured it should be good enough that she was even going.

"Abuela," she said as she peeked out her doorway. "How do you plan to get to church, since Mercedes has the car?"

"I walk, *mija.* Every Sunday I walk. It's good for me."

Paloma couldn't disagree with that. The doctor in her approved. It would be good for both of them.

Mick went for a run just after the sun came up, and he felt the adrenaline entering his body as the sweat left it.

He showered for a long time, dismissing the sign on the bathroom counter that requested the conservation of water. It felt too damn good. He grimaced at the cheap gardenia-scented soap that came with the room and resolved to find a more masculine brand in town. But it was all he had for now. He lathered it in his hands and rubbed it on his wet skin while the water washed it away on its highest setting. He turned his face to the spray and slid his hands down his stubbly cheeks. Stephanie had refused to kiss him if he hadn't shaved in the last few hours, and he had gotten in the habit of doing it twice a day if necessary.

The water started to run cold, although he had been in there for only ten minutes. He reached for the undersize towel and dried off, wrapping it around his waist when he was finished. He looked in the mirror. It was full-length, unlike the one in his bathroom in Boston, and he gave himself the once-over. He added to his new list of resolutions: *lose ten pounds by my thirty-sixth birthday*. His arm muscles were still impressive, well defined, the product of daily visits to the gym. But that habit had waned, and he knew they could disappear if he didn't take it up again. His stomach hadn't fared so well. It was probably better than most, but it had lost its tautness as he indulged in pasta and beer whenever the vegan princess wasn't home.

That was one thing he didn't miss. Stephanie had been stick-thin, a size double zero, he thought they called it. She claimed to be healthy but bordered on emaciated. Give him some hips any day. But she wouldn't hear of it. If it had more than ten calories and didn't come certified organic, gluten- and GMO-free, and from the farmers' market, it was banned from their home. What she could do with that skinny little body . . . well, let's just say that there were compensations. They'd been a good match in that regard.

And not just in the bedroom. He had to be fair. He'd been attracted to her ambition. No one was more driven than Stephanie Kaye. She wanted to be at the top of her game, just like him. She had plans to start a fitness empire. A television show. Bicoastal gyms. What a turn-on. But their growing commitment to their careers eclipsed their commitment to each other.

The first time he realized it was just a few months ago when they had a rare evening where both were home. She agreed to rent a movie with Mick but offered no opinions on what to get. She spent the whole time on her laptop. She was always on that thing, screen time replacing face time, and if it wasn't that, it was her phone, texting. Constantly texting.

What he'd loved about her he began to loathe.

She always had time for someone else. Her trainer. Her accountant. Her nutritionist. Her chi adviser.

What the hell was a chi adviser?

Mick got the leftovers, and while that might be the pot calling the kettle black, he realized that there couldn't be an actual relationship in such a void. That thought and a cold shower were enough to put a damper on those kinds of memories. He placed the razor back in his toiletries bag and decided to live for himself today.

He chose linen shorts from the closet and set out to pay a visit to the portrait of little Eula Lee, the *Santa Bonita*.

As he got close, he remembered the side effect of being a newsman. Sunday was Wednesday was Friday was Monday. There was a story every day, and every day was like the other. There was no Lord's day, there was no church, so he forgot that today was a day of worship and that the town would be as crowded as it ever would be.

The sign on the outside of Our Lady of Guadalupe posted Mass times for the next several hours, so if he wanted to see the portrait, he'd either have to join the congregation or wait several hours. And he didn't even know if it would be locked after that.

The churchgoers mingled near the steps. Tables stood on either side of the courtyard, with coffee on one and doughnuts on the other. A group came out of the eight o'clock service and greeted one another, picking up their modest breakfast. The ones arriving bypassed the food but still hugged everyone they met before walking inside.

Quaint. Real small-town America stuff, the doughnuts and coffee. These people probably didn't think in terms of Beltway and Bulls and Bears. Their big headline was water rationing. The basics.

Awful, yet simple.

A doughnut didn't sound half-bad right now, come to think of it, but Mick thought of his goal to shed a bit of weight. And he didn't know if you had to show some kind of membership card to get the goodies. There was no way he wanted to walk through that throng, so he found a bench across the street and planned to wait until it thinned out. He sat down and laid his arm over the side, taking in the surroundings. The sun was not yet halfway up in the sky, and with the lack of clouds to obstruct it, it was still bright. He slipped his Oakleys over his eyes.

On his left he saw Arturo, recognizing him even under his hat. Next to him was a large woman who wore a brightly colored dress with the kind of horizontal stripes that stretched until they were a washed-out version of themselves. They said hello to some friends in front of the doughnut table, and he recognized the throaty laugh from the kitchen last night. Corrina, the queen of the sopapillas.

"Hey, *gringo*," called Arturo. He stepped forward and put his hand on Mick's shoulder. "Good to see your face again, my friend. You joining us for church?"

"Just walking by."

"Word to the wise, my friend. Don't get a doughnut after Mass. The icing melts, and what's a donut without icing? Bread. Come over to my place instead. Sopapillas on me."

"That's nice of you, Arturo. I might take you up on that."

"You do that. Hey, man, I got to catch up or I'm gonna catch hell from Corrina." He laughed and slapped Mick on the shoulder once more. "That woman keeps old Arturo on the straight and narrow!"

He waved to Mick as he walked off, and Mick returned it before sliding his hands into his pockets.

Not even twenty-four hours here, and he'd already run into someone from yesterday. Small-town America. In the city, walking down the street was anonymous. He liked that. But this wasn't so bad.

71

He saw another person from the bar—Paloma Vega. She wore a light-blue dress this time, flowing but unable to hide the kind of body that would catch any man's attention. Slender but not gaunt. Her skin had the look of a natural tan that some women would pay a lot of money for. She reached for a cup of coffee until the woman beside her pushed her hand away and pointed to the church. She set it down, nodding, and followed her inside.

Mick waited until the area had cleared. Then he walked up the stairs and opened the arched wooden door.

He'd read that Our Lady of Guadalupe had been a mission church nearly two hundred years ago, and it did look like those he'd seen in his California travels. The plaster walls were white, surprisingly clean, and culminated in a wide, gold-painted dome above the altar. The perimeter of the dome was lined with red and yellow tiles. The icons at the rear were primitive but appealing in their generous use of color. Mick didn't know the names of the saints portrayed, nor did he see one that seemed as if it could be *Santa Bonita*.

Churches were not familiar territory for Mick. His mom worked three jobs and got paid a dollar an hour extra for working Sundays. He would have liked to wander around the side chapels, most of them illuminated with black iron stands full of flickering tea lights. But he followed some latecomers into a rear pew and sat down. Within seconds, the congregation was standing at full attention while an off-pitch cantor sang a hymn.

He'd heard of that. Catholic calisthenics. The ups and downs.

The priest walked up the center aisle supported by a tree limb that was fashioned into a cane. In front of him, an altar boy led with a brass crucifix attached to a pole. The people genuflected or bowed, as their age dictated, and Mick observed that their reverence was not limited to the cross but extended to the priest. He seemed unaware of it, though. If a Boston politician was fortunate enough to receive such adulation, he would have been glad-handing it the whole way, slapping the backs of the would-be donors and patting the cheeks of the babies. Senator Worth was a master at such showmanship, making it appear so genuine that even the harshest critic of his voting record couldn't help but smile when his name was mentioned. "Charismatic," they called him.

Mick had been among the admirers of both the politics and the person until what happened at Harbor House. Underage girls, trying to better their lives. Taken in by that charming man who promised them all sorts of things that he never delivered on. Mick had had weeks of research and interviews on file and was close to breaking the story.

And then a picture came across his desk. The smoking gun—the senator in bed with one of the girls, half-naked, snorting cocaine. He ran with it, having been tipped off that a blogger in DC was about to break the story.

The story was real. But the photo was a fake. When that came out, it discredited everything he'd done. His paper paid a huge settlement, and Senator Worth, victimized, rose in the polls.

Mick shut it out. It hurt to think about it, and doing so was contradictory to his purpose here. What was done was done.

Hymn 223 in the Praise Book was announced, and Mick decided to go along with it. He flipped through the pages until he came to "The Body of Christ Is the Food of My Soul." Strange language, if you asked him, and the melody sounded like a throwback to the seventies. The priest started talking through the last refrain, and over a subpar sound system, all that Mick could make out was something about a procession. Then the congregation stood and filed out silently through a side door, singing "*Pan de Vida.*" *Pan. Vida.* Bread. Life. Remnants of high school Spanish.

How strange. They'd just arrived; now they were filing out. Regardless, this would give him his chance to be alone and find the painting. Mick lingered in the back and saw that someone else had stayed behind, too.

Paloma.

She sat on the left side of the church in a pew near the front and raised her hands over her head, gathering her long hair into a crude ponytail. She picked up a Praise Book and fanned the back of her neck. Mick felt a charge throughout his body and supposed that, irreligious though he was, he should not be having these kinds of thoughts in a church. Still, there were things a man couldn't help when faced with a beautiful woman.

She slid down to her knee, crouching over and resting her head on her arms. He'd grown up with a single mom. He knew what a woman in distress looked like. But how to approach her, especially when he'd made such a poor impression last night?

He debated whether to make his presence known and find a reason to talk to her. To apologize. But before he could decide, she leaped up from the pew and screamed.

Mick's nerves prickled all at once, and he raced over to her without even feeling the floor beneath his feet.

She was brushing her hands down her legs and looked startled when she saw him approaching.

"Are you OK? What happened?" His heartbeat slowed as he realized that she wasn't hurt.

She pointed to the floor, where a six-inch lizard was racing away. Its black and tan stripes became a blur as it ran, probably as frightened as she was.

"Did it bite you?"

"No." Her cheeks looked pink, and he thought he might have embarrassed her by rushing over. "I don't usually freak out about those sorts of things. But I was just kneeling there and felt it crawl up my leg."

The creature was gone now, as far as he could see. He almost wished it had been a spider. Slower moving, something he could catch and kill. Knight in shining armor stuff.

"Well, at least we know your lungs work."

That was a stupid thing to say.

But she laughed. Thank goodness.

"Yeah, well, my lungs, my reflexes. Check and check."

Mick cupped his hands over his mouth. "This has been a test of the fight-or-flight system."

"Exactly. I just waited for the church to be empty so as not to startle everyone."

"Very considerate of you."

"I try."

Banter. This was good.

"Anyway, thanks for coming to my rescue," she said, sitting down. Mick joined her but kept a couple of feet between them, as he didn't want to make her uncomfortable. Her voice was beautiful. Light. Laughter was good on her. She wore it better than the sarcasm of last night. Maybe they'd both just been in a snarky mood. The heat could do that to a person.

Mick folded his hands in his lap and nodded. "You bet," he said. He paused and looked around the church—at the arches on the sides, the old lanterns that had been repurposed with electrical wiring—trying to think of what to say next. The ends of the pews were finished with carved scrolls, and the tiniest crevices harbored colonies of dust specks. A spider the size of a thumbtack trekked across a brown leather kneeler. It stopped at the end, turning back a few steps before continuing on its path and clinging to the wooden bottom until it made its way to the floor. What was it with critters here?

It took a lull like this to notice the intricacies woven into a scene. Mick rarely slowed down enough to see them, and he found it strangely rewarding.

He caught Paloma's eye and said the first thing that came to mind. "Those sopapillas were fantastic, and I have you to thank for leaving them behind."

Her smile. A smile that made him feel warm inside. Like there was goodness in the world, and it was right in front of him. Refreshing for a journalist who too often made money off reporting the negative. Maybe it was just the glimmer from the candles that surrounded them, but regardless, he felt the nearness of peace for the first time in months.

"I'm glad they met with your approval," she said. "You're a tough critic, you know."

"I'm an ass. That's what I am." He stopped. "Wait—can I say 'ass' in church?"

The smile spread, and Mick felt like a juggler who was trying to keep all the balls in the air before they came crashing down.

"Well, seeing as I'm going sleeveless and talking during Mass, perhaps I'm not the best authority."

"What Mass? Didn't everyone leave?"

"No, they're just outside for the Corpus Christi procession."

"Oh. I thought it seemed like a short service. Corpus Christi as in the city?"

"No, like the Latin. It means 'Body of Christ.' Today is the feast."

"OK. I understand. Sort of."

Paloma's shoulders began to relax, and her eyes searched his face. She said, "Why are you here, anyway?"

He laughed. "Do I really seem that out of place in a church?"

She grinned and nodded. "I'm sorry, but you do."

"You have the perceptive skills of a reporter, then." He held her gaze. "I'm here to find out more about this *Santa Bonita*. I thought it would be here in the church, but I don't see it."

"*Santa Bonita?*"

"Yes—the portrait that is supposed to cry."

A look of recognition flickered in her eyes. "Oh, yes. I know what you mean. Abuela has a holy card of the little saint on the refrigerator. I haven't seen the original yet, but I don't think it's here in the sanctuary—maybe in the gathering hall?"

"Why would it be there? There're so many other icons in here."

"Well, Abuela says she's not a *real* saint, or should I say not one sanctioned by the Church. So it can't hang in here. But she said that there's a little shrine in the hall, and once in a while people still come to see it."

"Do you believe that it cries?"

"I haven't really given it much thought. You know, I grew up with Abuela believing all sorts of apparitions. Like the tabloids that would show the image of Jesus in a pancake or a potato chip. Beeswax candles in case the end of the world came. You would have thought it was the Second Coming in our very house."

"Still, people said that there were miracles . . ."

She looked at him sternly. "I'm a doctor. I don't believe in miracles. I don't believe in what can't be proven, what I can't see under a microscope. What I can't test."

"Well, I don't, either."

"Then why are you here?"

"Would you believe me if I said it's a destination vacation?"

"Yeah, right."

"Let's just say that it started as a little joke on the part of my editor, one that morphed into a favor. Gave me a reason to get out of town for a bit. I guess it's a little penance—that's a church word, right?"

He didn't like being vague, but he hadn't thought ahead about the questions he might have to answer. But of course they would be asked. What was a political journalist from Boston doing in a border town researching an outdated religious story?

It sounded just as ridiculous as it was.

She opened her mouth to respond but must have heard the ambling musical notes of the procession returning. This time they were coming in through the main door, and their sound rose and expanded throughout the cavernous church. She leaned in conspiratorially. She smelled like peaches, his favorite. In another time and place, he would have kissed her.

"Look. There's no air-conditioning in here, and this place is going to be even more of an inferno as soon as everyone returns. If you want, I'll take you over to the hall, and we can find your portrait."

"Sounds like a plan." He would have loved, then, to take her hand and lead her out the door, but again he had to remind himself that he was here on a mission. In and out, his current mantra. The beautiful Miss Vega could not become a distraction.

Paloma stepped outside the pew and genuflected on her right knee, crossing herself at the same time and kissing her fingers. Mick followed her lead in this confusing choreography and stood up when she did. They tiptoed out the side door just before the people started entering.

The path to the gathering hall was made of packed earth, with weeds sprouting up on either side. It was a terrible irony that weeds could survive so heartily in this drought while everything else struggled. Seemed to be a metaphor for his life right now. Bad wins; good tries hard but ultimately loses.

The path was adjacent to the cemetery, where some of the tombstones dated back to the early 1800s, even before the church was complete.

Mick stopped. "Huh," he said.

Paloma looked at him. "What is it?"

"In Boston we have cemeteries right in the middle of downtown. Lots of famous people are buried there. Paul Revere. Sam Adams. In fact, there's a bar across the street from one that serves Sam Adams beer. I always thought that was funny. Anyway, I enjoy the history that can be found there. So it got me thinking about the history of this place. Why is it called 'Puerto Pesar' if it's not near the water? What's the story with that?"

She rested her hand on the iron fence that separated the living from the dead. "You're right. It doesn't immediately seem to make sense. In English it means 'the port of regret.' But not 'port' like the kind on the gulf. This is a border town. See that hill over there?" She pointed south.

"Just on the other side of that is Mexico. This was once a major cross-ing point between the two places. It used to be called La Jolla, I think. Like the one in California. But Santa Anna's men renamed it to Puerto Pesar after their defeat at the Battle of San Jacinto. They had to cross through here to get back home, leaving behind thousands of soldiers on the soil of *Tejas*."

"Oh. I get it."

"And it's apt today, too. There is a deportation station not far from here, and it's the last stop before Immigration Services brings people back over the border after they've been caught."

"I see—so it's a sad place to leave?" He looked around and didn't quite see the appeal.

"Well, I suppose it is, depending on your reasons. Not for me, though, and not for my sister, apparently. Mercedes is crawling the walls wanting to go out west. Not that I can blame her. I wanted out, too, when I was her age. There isn't much of a future here."

"And you—why did you come back from New York?"

Her head snapped around as she looked at him, and her ponytail followed a second later, landing on her shoulder. "How did you know I live in New York?"

He saw her tense up.

"While I don't usually reveal my sources, I can neither confirm nor deny that sopapillas may have played a role in that particular conversation."

"Oh." She relaxed. "Dear Arturo. He's a little yenta, I tell you. Got to watch out for him. No better than my grandmother." She walked a few more steps. "I'm just here for a few weeks. My grandmother had a heart attack, and I negotiated a window of time before I start my new job. It's just as well. I haven't been back in a couple of years, and I can see that Abuela needs me. And my sister . . . it's like she went from cute kid to moody teen overnight, and I didn't notice. I feel a little guilty about that. A lot guilty. Not that I think a few weeks can fix anything. But I'm going to try."

She put her hands on her hips and smiled. "Well, that was a lot to unload on someone I've just met."

"What do you mean, 'just met'? We had dinner together last night, as you might recall. Well, yours went out the door in a Styrofoam box with you, but still. I think it counts."

"Way to cover for my rambling."

"How is she doing?" Mick asked.

She rubbed her temples. "My grandmother or my sister?"

"Both."

"Could be better."

Here he was, wallowing in his own self-pity, aching for the comforts that he was used to. Counting down to his escape. How entitled he'd become, keeping at arm's length his disadvantaged past and anything that reminded him of it. Assuaging those thoughts with the checks he wrote to his mom but not really calling very often. He even kept an envelope of dollars in his sun visor to give to the homeless people holding signs at street corners, and he patted himself on the back for not questioning whether or not they'd use that George Washington on alcohol or drugs. He'd kept himself busy with cocktail parties and people who vied for his attention, and he forgot that there were people in the world who really struggled.

Where had his initial fire gone? The one that made him want to tell the story of people like his mom? To shine a light on their plight?

Journalists and politicians were exactly alike. Most got into the business for altruistic reasons. Voices of the voiceless. But the lure of power, money, pride, all the major vices, was enticing. The truly good-hearted got eaten up and spit out. The ones who learned how to play the game made it.

Mick had decided to play. Shame on him.

Talking to Paloma reminded him of those early days—back when he wanted to be the Champion of the Downtrodden. Here was someone who had a palpable dilemma on her hands: Work a good job in New York or take care of two people who could use her help? And not the kind of help that would get better by throwing money at it.

"Penny for your thoughts?" she asked.

He hadn't realized that he'd let his mental soliloquy go on so long. "You'd be paying too much."

"Are you always so hard on yourself?"

"Probably not often enough."

She waved her hand. "Let's go see this portrait."

Mick opened the door and stepped back to let Paloma enter. A gentle wave of cooler air washed over them, and he closed his eyes for a moment to enjoy the bliss that came from even such meager relief as that.

The gathering hall was no more than a modular steel building, the kind you could buy on the Internet and have shipped to you unassembled. Air-conditioning it would cost a small fortune, evidenced by the hand-drawn fund-raising thermometer on a yellowed poster board that ironically showed red-marked mercury lingering about a quarter of the way up.

There were two doors on either end of the building. The closest one was open, leading to a classroom that was plastered with posters like SUNDAY Is SONDAY. They started walking toward the other one.

Mick asked, "So, if the painting is so important, why don't they hire security for it?"

"I don't think it's *actually* important, as in highly valuable. Just sentimental, I guess. Abuela told me that when the pilgrims were coming, some of the men in town volunteered to man the door round the clock. But now visitors are rare, and no one thinks of it anymore."

She stopped and turned to him. "Why *are* you here, anyway? That wasn't much of an answer earlier. And you don't strike me as the kind of person who follows apparitions and signs."

He stuck his hands in his pockets. He supposed it was as good a time as any to tell her.

"It's a long story, so here it is in a nutshell. Someone sent me a photograph of a popular senator doing some, uh, questionable things at a halfway house he supports. My research told me that the story was true, although the photograph itself turned out to be a fake. But in my enthusiasm, I ran with it. I barely escaped getting sacked, and the paper had to settle with him out of court. So I'm on suspension. My editor read a clip somewhere about *Santa Bonita* and thought the change of scenery would do me some good. I'm supposed to write an article and buy some time until I come back. Unofficially, of course." He left out the Stephanie part.

"Why would an East Coast newspaper be interested in *Santa Bonita*? No one even comes from McAllen anymore."

"Ah, you haven't met my editor, then. It's not the screwiest idea he's ever come up with. He gets a hunch and won't let it go until it either crashes and burns or makes him a hero."

Paloma narrowed her eyes. "I'm not so sure this one will be a success."

"I'm *certain* that it won't. But he was right that I needed to take a break for a while. I worked too hard and got cocky about the small stuff. As much as I liked the senator's politics, he was really hurting people. The best hope I have is that he's at least on guard not to do it again."

"So you're a hero, then."

Well, that was a stretch of the highest proportions.

"Don't polish my halo just yet. I can't deny that there was a certain attraction to having a story that would undoubtedly make national headlines. One person's career-breaking story is another's career-making one. This just happened in the reverse of what I expected."

"So this scandal really put you that low on the ladder at your newspaper?"

"Lower than the lowest rung. I am the termite that is burrowing into the heel of the ladder, trying to make it up to the top again."

"Again? So you were at the top before?"

"It's a tall ladder. It's a long fall." He put his hand on her back lightly, to move her forward. A shot like electricity ran through his arm, and he pulled back. "Let's keep going."

She opened the door that said **La Capilla de Santa Bonita**. Time to see what all the hubbub was about.

CHAPTER EIGHT

Goree State Farm for Women—1943

Introductions at Goree went like this:

"What is your name?"

"Where are you from?"

"What are you here for?"

"How long are you in?"

"Did you do it?"

For the first question, Della kept the Trujillo silent. "Puerto Pesar," which no one had ever heard of, was her answer for the second. Then: "Killing my sister."

"Life."

"Yes."

Her answer for the last one raised eyebrows, because most inmates were quick to proclaim their innocence. After Della had been there some time, she learned that those who did so were usually guilty, and the ones who admitted it said they had done it out of self-defense or impoverishment. There were even those who, as hard times descended at the end of the war, had come here intentionally. They were known as "Three Hots and a Cot" or "cotters." Commit a felony, and you were practically guaranteed three square meals and a roof over your head compliments of the taxpayers in the state of Texas.

Two weeks in, Della returned from a shift in the chicken coop, her least favorite task so far. Feathers and down dotted her jumpsuit. She flopped onto her bed, arms and legs splayed out. There was a time when such filth would have sent her running for a water bucket, but the heat was brutal today, and she was just too wiped out.

"Hey. You're lyin' on your letters. And there's a bunch of them." The words were spoken to her by Hazel McKay, the woman whose bed sat next to Della's. From Lubbock, via McComb, Mississippi. Here for horse thieving. Three years left. Of course, she didn't do it.

"You hear me? You're on your letters."

Della closed her eyes and breathed deeply before fumbling around for them. There they were. Under her back. She pulled them out.

"Must be nice, that I-don't-care attitude. Most girls would die to have even one."

Della did care. She cared so much that it ripped her up inside.

"Thank you," she whispered. She flipped through them. There were seven. All bearing Tomas's tight, scratchy handwriting.

She rubbed her palm across her nose. She would not cry.

The letters were open in a clean cut, read in advance by Matron Heath to ward off escape plans and conspiracies, collected until she could get to them.

Della traced her finger along the top of one. With her fingernail, she pulled down the edge. It was tempting. Tempting. Just pull a little farther and she could slip out the first letter.

She pinched it shut, and her heart beat until it felt as if it would break through her chest.

"What are you waitin' for?" Hazel sat up, and the bedsprings squealed in protest. "'Cause if you're hopin' for a private moment, surprise. There aren't any."

Della slid them under her mattress. "I'll look at them later."

Hazel shrugged. "Suit yourself."

And then came the tears. They started in Della's cheeks, gathering and tingling, moving up until she could feel her nose run. Then up to her eyes, where she couldn't have stopped them if she'd tried.

She couldn't try anymore. It was exhausting.

Hazel's face softened. "Darlin', don't cry. I didn't mean anything by it."

Della shook her head. "It's not you."

"Do you want to talk about it?"

"No." She hung her head. "I can't."

Hazel sat down next to her, sighed, and patted Della's lap. "Let's try this. You like music?"

Mama had bought a piano when the girls were little. She played beautifully, taught them all the names of the great composers. Eula, newly three, picked up simple tunes as if she'd played them all throughout her short life, one finger at a time. Her hands weren't even big enough to make a whole chord. But she could play discernable songs. Della, on the other hand, never moved past scales. She got pretty good at scales.

"Yes. I like music."

"You know about the Goree Girls?"

"I've heard them practicing."

"I might have joined myself, if it were not for havin' a voice that makes cats cry." Hazel laughed. "But I've been able to head over to the Walls Unit a few times on account of helping carry instruments. You should see the crowds. Eight, nine hundred people every time. Seven *million* listenin' to 'em on the airwaves. 'Course, there're other acts—the opera man from Huntsville and the one who tells the jokes. But believe me, those people are a-comin' for the Goree Girls, no doubt."

Hundreds of people to hear a band of female inmates sing. Amazing.

She said the idea for "Thirty Minutes Behind the Walls" came from the shared need of WBAP in Fort Worth to fill a dead slot at ten thirty in the evening on Wednesday nights and from the Texas state prisons to have a good public relations opportunity in the wake of recent gunfights and attempted escapes in the system.

A natural marriage.

At first it was all men. A mariachi band, a jazz group, gospel singers. In their former lives they had been murderers, thieves, and extortionists. But on Wednesday nights, across the country, they became symbols of rehabilitation and hope, and the show attracted unexpectedly high numbers of listeners.

The girls got in on the game a little later, when Mrs. Reable Childs, convicted for conspiring to kill her husband, Marlie, with a .22-caliber rifle, decided that she wanted an earlier parole than her twenty-five-year sentence was going to allow. She got wind that the governor of Texas, "Pappy" O'Daniel, who had campaigned by traveling the state with his band, the Hillbilly Boys, might take a liking to a girl group. And the power to parole rested with him. She planned to sing her way out of prison.

Reable had studied music and possessed a nearly perfect voice. She got along well enough playing the steel guitar and the banjo. The group was rounded out by seven other women—Mozelle and Ruby Mae as lead singers; Lillie and Burma on bass fiddle; and Georgia, Ruby Dell, and Bonnie on guitar. Like the men, they were here for assault, heroin possession, burglary, murder.

The Goree Girls received gifts, fan letters, and marriage proposals from as far away as the Arctic Circle. Besides playing in the Wall Unit once a week, they were sometimes hired to play at private events and carnivals and got to enjoy a brief freedom that other inmates only dreamed about—like motorboating and Ferris wheels. Rumors floated that their activities were not limited to daytime endeavors, and they were happy to earn extra spending money on the side by demonstrating other talents between the sheets—cutting, of course, a piece of their earnings to the guards who procured the arrangements. Whether it was true or merely a vicious tale spun by envious prison mates, Della never did know.

For their performances, they wore dark pants, light-colored shirts, and dark matching cowboy hats. They were managed by the matron, whose husband "the Captain" oversaw the inmates working the farm. They played with radiant smiles, all-American girls, save for their backgrounds. Models of contrition. Stars of salvation. Primed for parole.

One by one, the girls were indeed released from their sentences, first by Pappy and then by his successor, Coke Stevenson. By the time Della arrived, only Reable remained of the original group, and other inmates filled the positions. The band continued.

The highlight of their year was playing the prison rodeo in Huntsville in October, but this time around it was canceled due to the war. So they rehearsed as usual for the weekly radio nights instead.

"Just think of it, darlin'," Hazel said. "It'd be a great way to get your mind off whatever it is that's botherin' you."

Della caught her breath. The very idea of it sounded as if it could be the hope that she needed to survive.

~

The next Tuesday night, Hazel shook Della from a brief nap, much needed after a day in the orchards.

"On your feet, darlin'. It's time."

She pulled her up by the sleeve and led her down the hall, where Della could hear the sound of guitars being tuned.

"Reable Childs!" she shouted. "I've got a new one for you."

A woman with dark-brown bobbed hair turned around, setting her fiddle on the nearest chair. "I told you, Hazel. No more room in the Goree Girls for now."

"I ain't deaf, woman; I heard you. But sooner or later you'll lose another one. Think of her as an apprentice. She can be learnin' the guitar and working on her voice and be ready to step right in when you're short someone."

"You can't play, then?" Reable looked harshly at Della.

She realized that she needed to make a case for herself. This could be a welcome pastime, and the idea of being around music sounded appealing. "No, ma'am, but I'll try to be a quick learner."

"Ma'am! You hear that, Hazel McKay? She called me ma'am. The girl has some respect in her bones. Take a bet on how long it will take to get that beaten out of her here at Goree."

Della flinched.

"Quit your yappin', Reable; you know I'm right."

Reable looked Della over from head to toe. "Well, at the very least, she'll be a pretty one on the bandstand. All right, girl. It might be months before you play live, but if you want to carry some instruments and learn some chords in the meantime, we'll give you a go, so long as the matron signs off."

A wave of relief washed over Della. She'd wanted this more than she let herself believe. A distraction from the backbreaking work and the worry about Tomas. Something that would feel normal.

She desperately wanted to feel normal.

∽

Tomas continued to send letters. Three times a week trickled to two, then one, interspersed with a guard telling her one Saturday a month that he was there for a visit.

"Baby girl, why don't you go out to see that boy?" Hazel asked her one weekend.

Della spoke muffled words to the pillow she'd buried herself into. "It's for his own good."

He hadn't sent word of the annulment. She knew that such a thing would take months—years—having to go all the way to the Vatican and back to the diocese, but they had grounds: no consummation. Should be clear-cut, if he would only get it started. Then he would be free to find another girl. The idea hurt more than she wanted to think about. But she loved him too much to make him sacrifice his happiness for her.

She continued to pile his letters under her mattress. Reading even a word might have broken her resolve.

He knew she was stubborn. It was one of the things he was most proud of in her. It was necessary, especially when raising a girl like Eula, who became more headstrong as the years went by.

It was with this trait that she first ingratiated herself into the Goree Girls. Matron Heath approved her joining, since one of the guitar players was scheduled for release in less than a year. As long as Della got her regular work done, she could practice with the band in the hopes that she'd be ready to take her place this time next year.

Della pushed through her exhaustion. At the end of the day, it was so tempting to curl up on her bed and not wake until the morning. It surprised her that she could feel this tired; she'd grown up working the land. Maybe it was something about the prison environment. Something in the food. Still, the lure of rehearsing with the band was just strong enough to keep her going.

The first time Della held the guitar, a wave of relief washed over her, as if she were breathing for the first time since arriving at Goree. The resonant echo of a C, a G, an E, strummed as individual notes and then together as chords, created a flutter of excitement in her as she imagined the possibilities of what could be played with enough practice.

It was amazing to think about the future again, even if it was a future behind these walls.

Della practiced at every available opportunity, impressing the band members, bloodying her fingers until they hardened and grew the calluses that made her feel like a real guitarist, albeit a beginner. She added F and A and B, interweaving them to create new chords. Soon Reable would teach her the minor notes, expanding the possibilities of what could be played.

Not that Della thought herself to be any more than average. She just worked really hard at it. Music was Eula's domain. Her sister had been the kind of artist who heard songs in her head, sang them without knowing it, tapped her fingers to inaudible tunes even at the dinner table.

Della rehearsed because it made her feel, for those hours, that she was not a prisoner. Eula rehearsed because it was a part of her soul.

It was at a Christmas midnight Mass when life took a turn, the first Mass they attended after their father died. Eula was fifteen, on the cusp of blooming into a woman and already standing straighter when she saw a man looking at her. Della, two years older, began to feel what little influence she had on her sister slipping from her hands. Eula was taller, more beautiful, more driven, and it wouldn't be long before she realized it. Della knew that, before she sang one note in public, Eula had the potential to really become somebody, whereas Della was quite content with the idea of falling in love with the ranch hand and spending her life on the homestead.

That evening, as people gathered early for the best seats in the small church, whispers that the vocalist at Our Lady of Guadalupe had fallen ill made their way to the sisters. Della watched Eula's fingers move almost imperceptibly, as if playing a piano. Inching to the right on a high note. Sliding to the left for a low one.

"Go," she whispered. "I know you want to. I hear you sing at home all the time, and it's beautiful. Maybe it's time to share the gift you have."

How she wished she could take back those words.

Eula had hesitated, glancing at Della as if she needed one more word of approval. Della squeezed her hand and nodded. Eula approached the choir director to say that she could step in. She never looked back at her sister.

Della remembered the night as if it were yesterday. It was the beginning of everything that was to come. And the end of all that had been. Eula made her debut.

The only lights were the flickering candles. The congregation stood as the procession began. The altar boy processed out of the sacristy first, carrying the large brass crucifix that began every Mass. He was followed by Fr. Medina, who carried a life-size baby Jesus, carved and painted by a long-forgotten parishioner, nameless to history. As all eyes watched, a single note broke through the silence.

"O . . ." The long sound was held with unwavering perfection before embarking on the song that would forever move souls. ". . . Holy night. The stars are brightly shining."

Eyes shifted to the choir loft where Eula stood, sheet music in hand, held steadily.

"It is the night of our dear Savior's birth."

Even Fr. Medina had stopped and turned to watch what was unfolding.

She finished the first verse and then the second, and if everyone else's hearts were like Della's, they were starting to beat quickly in anticipation of the crescendo of the familiar song.

And it was perfection. It was as if an angel inhabited the body of the girl.

"Fall . . . on your knees."

Della's heart swelled with pride as she looked around. People were bringing their hands to their eyes, wiping away tears. Or clutching their chests, rapt in the sound coming from up above.

Baby Jesus lay forgotten in Fr. Medina's arms.

Then the second refrain. Della held her breath.

Please let her hit that note, she thought. The one that, sung as a congregation, sounded like a bunch of bellowing cats, everyone straining as they hit pitches that fell short.

And then she did it.

"O night divine."

And it was indeed. *Divine* was about the only word that summed up the evening as Eula soared through the score.

"Silent Night." "Joy to the World." And at the end, "Angels We Have Heard on High," in which the magnificent "Gloria in Excelsis Deo," with the impossible notes that defied breathing, were mastered effortlessly by Eula.

After the final blessing, Eula came downstairs, and the hordes of people who would usually have gathered around the now-complete nativity set swarmed instead around the girl as baby Jesus lay abandoned.

Della watched her sister from a pew, standing on a kneeler to see her over the crowd. Her first thought was to rescue her. The people were grabbing at her as if she were some kind of living relic, and she thought she'd pull her out of there with the excuse that they needed to get home.

She could see only the top of Eula's head, but one by one the people left, and she could see her sister's face. She expected to find her frightened and frantically searching for the harbor of Della's arms.

But that was not the case. It was as if she were electrified, powered by an internal light, glowing and radiant.

"Straight from heaven," Della heard people say as they walked toward the door. But that was not what came to her mind. She looked at her sister until their eyes met.

There was something about Eula that seemed to recognize the effect she'd just had on everyone. A kind of vainglory shone in her eyes, the same look Della remembered seeing on her mother's face on that last day at the beach with the painter. An unspoken triumph.

Della realized the name for what she'd been feeling. What had been brewing for the past several years.

Della was frightened.

CHAPTER NINE

Puerto Pesar—Today

Paloma watched Mick as they walked down the rest of the hall. He looked like he belonged in a Tommy Bahama catalog, with lightweight shorts and leather sandals. He wore a loose-fitting shirt in light-green cotton, which suited his equally light coloring. His sunglasses were perched on his head, a feature that she had always found attractive. Much better than tying them to a cord or sticking them in the back of his shirt.

He seemed to be a study of contrasts. Sarcastic yet sweet. Arrogant yet gentle. Self-absorbed yet considerate. It was an odd thing to make such observations in so short a time, but Paloma moved in a fast-paced world where judgments had to be made in an instant. New York— watch the light, cross the street, hail the taxi. Emergency room—stop the blood, set the bone, start the IV.

One week in Puerto Pesar had put the brakes on that kind of pace. Abuela was her only patient, and there was only so much tidying up one could do. And living with Mercedes was like living with a mannequin that had earbuds. All attempts to engage her in conversation ended with a shrug despite Paloma's continued research online.

Talk with *your teen. Not* to *him or her.*

Don't ask yes *or* no *questions. Engage him or her in discussion.*

Psychobabble. None of it worked on Mercedes. And none of Paloma's friends had kids, let alone teens.

Maybe what she recognized in Mick was a reflection of herself. A walking contradiction. Fast. Slow. Busy. Bored. Maybe that was why she understood him so quickly.

"Here we are," he said. *"La Capilla de Santa Bonita."*

He pronounced the *L*s correctly—*Cap-e-yah.* She liked that he knew that.

"Ready or not, here we come, Eula Lee." He opened the door and let Paloma walk in first.

The room was dim, lit only by the same iron stands with candles that illuminated the church. Six chairs and kneelers were arranged in two rows. And on the wall opposite the door hung the painting.

The canvas measured about eighteen by twenty-four inches and was outlined with a wooden frame, ornately carved, and dotted with flecks of gold leaf. But, beautiful as that was, it didn't compare to the image inside it.

A child was portrayed, a girl about four years old, but with an expression that seemed much more mature. Her mouth was rosy, upturned at the ends just enough to indicate a smile. Her cheeks were flushed, as if she'd come in from a game of tag, and her large brown eyes were mirrorlike in their glassiness. The eyes were remarkable, in fact, almost glistening. The hair, too, was magnificent. It was nearly black, with curls down to her waist, gathered in a burgundy satin ribbon over the shoulder. The bow matched her dress, finished in ivory trim along the neckline. Obviously expensive.

She sat with poise and none of the restlessness you might expect in someone so young. Resolute, if that wasn't too mature a word to attribute to a small child.

Mick and Paloma stood transfixed, neither one breathing while they studied it. Finally she spoke.

"Look at the folds in the dress. As if, when you touched them, you would feel their texture."

"And the lace," he added. "I've never seen such detail." He waved his hand over it, keeping a breath of space between himself and the canvas.

"Amazing," she agreed.

"Did you see a signature anywhere?"

Paloma strained to read the markings that were smaller than her fingernail. "T. B.," she said at last. "Abuela told me they don't know who painted it. I wonder what it stands for."

"I have no idea. But here's the million-dollar question: Does it look like it's crying to you?"

She focused more intently on the eyes. They were mesmerizing, no doubt. There was a glossiness to them that in the right light might be construed as tears. But she was convinced that it was the mastery of the artist that made them appear so. She stood to the left and then to the right, but the perspective stayed the same, no matter where you were. All that looked out of place were two white streaks that looked as if they had dripped from her eyes. But could that be attributed to tears?

She shook her head.

"I agree," said Mick. "But it certainly is unlike anything I've ever seen."

"So you're not a believer?"

He looked one more time, then told her the streaks didn't seem as if they'd done the kind of damage that salt could. Wouldn't tears be salty?

"So, if you don't think it's crying, you don't have much of a story. What are you going to bring back to your editor?" she asked.

"Beats the hell out of me."

"That's two foul words spoken on hallowed ground in thirty minutes. Are you trying for a record?"

"I'll pass. Let's go before I'm beyond salvation."

Paloma nodded and headed toward the door.

"I'm sorry," she said, feeling oddly disappointed herself.

"For what?"

"It looks like you've wasted your time coming here."

Mick again noticed how the candles caught the highlights of her hair. He might be struggling to come away with something he could write about, but for the first time, he found himself thinking of someone other than Stephanie.

"Miss Vega—" He suddenly realized that they had never actually introduced themselves, and that it was Arturo who had told him her name. But he had already told her that he knew about New York. "May I take you to breakfast?"

She hesitated, and he forced himself to steady his breath while he waited for her answer. Never had he wanted a woman to say yes as much as he did now, and never to a question as simple as this one.

At last she spoke. "I have another idea. I'll take you to the best place to eat in town."

Relief flooded him. "You lead the way." He swept his arm out to open the door for her. "Is it close, or will I need to get my car?"

"Everything is close in Puerto Pesar. We can walk."

She didn't offer up anything else. He followed her out, past the church, where the singing indicated that Mass was still going on. He looked at the strewn holy cards and prayer intentions that littered the ground near the stairs.

"When you were growing up here, did you always have such terrible droughts?"

Paloma stopped walking and looked up at the sky. The few clouds that graced it were bright white, save for some that hinted at gray far off to the east.

"Every few years there would be one, and we were on water rations more often than not. But not like this. This is epic."

She pulled up her ponytail and fanned herself with her hand. Mick usually liked it when women wore their hair down, but Paloma was stunning no matter what she did with it. He traced the curve of her neck with his eyes, thinking about what it would be like to kiss her right there at the base of it, at that little indentation.

He found himself growing impatient with the small talk. Weather. Ha. He could talk about the weather with anyone. He wanted to know this woman. To know what she saw herself doing in ten years. To know what book had had a profound influence on her. To know her thoughts on political issues.

It was a surprise to him. He and Stephanie had thrived on a dual spirit of ambition. But they were never the sort to do the Sunday crossword together and talk about the headlines. An image of spending that kind of morning with Paloma crossed his mind, and just as quickly, he shut it out.

It was premature to be entertaining that kind of thought. Probably just the stuff of rebounds, anyway. Safer to stick to weather.

"I'm not one of those stop-and-smell-the-roses people, but I have to say, this drought makes me grateful that I don't have to think about these kinds of things in Boston."

"Nor New York. Although in the cities, we have other things to worry about. Traffic. Subway strikes. Eight dollars for a box of cereal."

"Yeah. That one's a killer. Are you wishing you were there now?"

"No, although I know I'll look forward to going back in a few weeks. It's good to get out of the city once in a while. Even to come to Puerto Pesar. I think it's more a part of me than I realized."

Not for Mick. The smallness, yes. He liked the slower pace here. But the run-down feel of it, no. It reminded him too much of the trailer park he'd grown up in.

They continued toward the dried fountain, where they saw an old woman crossing the street toward an Oldsmobile.

Paloma grabbed him by the arm. "Mick. Do you know who that is?"

He peered out, shading his eyes from the sun. "No. Should I?"

"That's Abuela's car. She told me that Mercedes borrowed it this morning to pick up Della Lee. That has to be her."

He felt the familiar tingle in his fingers that itched to hold a pen. The sensation that always told him there was something brewing. "Can you imagine returning after seven decades in prison?"

"Can you believe that she was capable of murder? Look at her. I know it was eons ago, but it's hard to imagine."

A million questions raced through his mind. "I think there may be a story here after all."

CHAPTER TEN

Goree State Farm for Women—1943

Della felt worse with each passing day.

Fatigue was compounded by nausea, which was triggered by the slightest scent, all-consuming. She managed to swallow the urge to vomit until she was in a place where she could do so unnoticed. Maybe the prison food didn't agree with her. Maybe she was dying. The thought actually gave her hope. She didn't mind the idea of ending her sentence so prematurely. So she did not visit the infirmary.

It grew worse one particularly fitful night, where the smell of the freshly laid manure in the fields consumed the part of the dormitory she shared with Hazel. Della felt the familiar knot in her stomach that rolled its way up until she held it back in her throat, where she choked as she tried to keep it from exiting. But this time it was too strong for her, and in seemingly one move, she sat up and grabbed the empty, worn enamel basin between the beds. Violent waves came over her, and as much as she tried to stifle the sound, Hazel woke up and immediately sprang to her side. Without question, she held back Della's long hair with one hand and stroked her back with the other.

"There, there," she said. "Let it out. That's a girl."

When Della's heaving finally came up empty, Hazel took the now-brimming basin and in two strides placed it in the corner of the room. She picked up the steel water pitcher, warmed from the heat of the night, and brought it to her side. She lifted it to Della's lips, and Della obeyed by taking a drink and swishing it around her mouth to clean out the bile that poisoned her taste. When she looked around to see where to spit, Hazel went to retrieve another basin, but an empty wave overtook her again, and the water spilled onto her clothes.

Unfazed, Hazel lifted the corner of Della's shirt and wiped her mouth until she took in a deep breath and nodded in indication that it was over. Sweat dripped down her forehead until she felt as if she were melting.

Della looked up at her companion, seeing her as if for the first time. Lately they'd worked in different areas of the prison during the day and were too exhausted at night to do anything but capture every moment of sleep until they were woken to do it all over again at dawn. She saw Hazel only at rehearsal on Tuesday nights.

Hazel was older than Della, by perhaps as much as two decades, but it was unclear as to whether her wrinkles and smile lines came from natural aging or the burden of incarceration. She seemed at least as old as Della's mother would have been, but she lacked the grace and charm that Eva Lynn Lee had possessed. The contrasts didn't stop there—Eva had been tall and lean, with silken brown hair that she pampered into perfection and eyes that were commonly called brown but were more like the color of the dark melted chocolate they used to receive in their cups at Christmastime. Hazel, on the other hand, had ornery hair that was pulled into a low ponytail and a gently plump body rounded into a pillowy shape. When she pulled Della toward her, Della sank in and found the kind of peace that she used to feel when Eula would crawl into her bed during a roaring Texas thunderstorm to look for protection. But since the roles were reversed—Hazel was Della and Della was Eula—she reveled in the comfort for a minute before lifting her head and apologizing.

"Whatever for, darlin'?" Hazel asked as she loosely braided Della's hair to keep it out of the way.

"I don't know what came over me. Usually I can control it."

"You mean this isn't the first time?" Hazel held Della's gaze with a look of concern.

Della felt guilty, and she didn't know why; she lowered her head and shook it.

"How long has this been going on?"

She whispered, "Since about a month after I got here."

Hazel hesitated before responding. "And that's all that's unusual?"

Della sighed and shook her head. "Cocaine Maggie ran into me the other day in the laundry"—she wrapped her arms protectively around her breasts—"and it hurt more than it should have."

Hazel snorted. "Well, that old bulldagger didn't do that by accident."

Della knew her confusion showed on her face.

"You really are some kind of innocent, aren't you? A bulldagger. A woman who likes women. You know, doin' things with women that are usually done with men."

Della's eyes squinted and then widened as she began to understand.

"Cocaine Maggie's always finding a way to touch someone. That's why they took her out of the dormitory and put her in a cell. She's usually harmless enough, but did she hurt you?"

Della shook her head again. "No, at least, she didn't mean to." She tightened her arms around herself. "But they are so sore." She took a deep breath and whispered, "And they're bigger than they used to be."

"And your rags? Have you been needing your sanitary belts every month?"

The younger girl stared at the wall, and she squeezed her eyes shut. *Oh, please do not let it be true. It cannot be true. Not like this.*

Nothing was how it was supposed to be.

Hazel took both her hands in her own and patted them. "You understand, don't you?"

Della nodded.

"Are you married?" Hazel asked.

Della didn't respond either way. She didn't know how to. Yes, she had said vows, worn the dress. The dress that was buried in some evidence vault in Harlingen. But no, she had never lain with Tomas. The only man she had ever been with had forced his way in. How did you tell that to another person, when the deed was unspeakable?

She curled up on her bed, wrapping herself around the child inside her that had been uninvited.

Hazel didn't speak again but unbuttoned Della's shirt and slid it off her arms, replacing it with her own larger one. She brushed the strands of hair that had already loosened, tucking them behind Della's ear. She reached for her prison-issued brassiere, dark gray and ill-fitted. She put it on Della and returned to her bed. She hummed a lullaby so softly that Della could barely hear it.

She was frightened. And yet amazed. A baby. What was that going to mean?

～

The driver had taken something of Della's that could never be returned and never given to Tomas. Now he had also stolen the very chance of her husband being the father to her child. It was a theft of a most devastating nature and felt, even in light of a life sentence, like the biggest injustice she could imagine.

She'd tried to put Tomas out of her mind as much as she could, but it proved especially impossible as the daily reminder of what had happened that night grew inside her. It also became impossible not to draw comparisons between the two. The monster and the man.

Tomas was a man who gave everything he had, and when the Lee girls had lost their father, he stepped in to look after them.

She remembered the first time she met him. She was nearly fourteen. Only five short years ago, but it made up a quarter of her lifetime.

Papa had mentioned that he'd hired a boy to help mend the places where the fence was coming down.

Della first noticed the boy at a distance about a hundred yards from the house. She had just soothed Eula into sleep after her sister had worked herself into a frenzy over the hemline that Della had taken out in a dress that had come by the mail. Della's hands were raw from the sewing, scratched from the gardening, and she went for a walk to find some of the aloe vera that grew wild on the edge of the property.

She gathered some sunflowers as she walked, thinking that they would look nice on the kitchen table.

"Stop right there!" She heard his voice, though it was still too far to make out the features of his face. The boy sat on the fence, hunched over, and Della looked around her to see if there was a rattlesnake or tarantula or some other danger that was not uncommon out here.

"Aha," she heard him say after a minute. He hopped down and walked over to her. He was not tall, maybe just six inches taller than her, a couple of years older. His face was brown, either by birthright or sun exposure or both, and his eyes were kind. He had a sack of tools slung over his left shoulder and a shotgun over his right, but in his hands he held a notebook. A pencil hung out of his mouth.

"You're one of the Miss Lees?" he asked.

"Yes, I'm Della."

He took the pencil out of his mouth, and she could see the indentations left by his teeth.

"Sorry if I startled you. I was looking for a break from fixing the fence and thought I'd draw a picture of your house to say thank you to your pops for giving me this job. But then I saw you coming this way and thought, *Wouldn't it be nice if I put his daughter in it for him?* So there you were, picking flowers, looking pretty, and I just had to add you to it. You want to see it? Tell me if he'll like it?"

Della didn't hear anything after *pretty*, a word usually reserved for Eula, who even at twelve was already showing herself to take after their mother. But she liked it coming from his lips and liked the smile with which he said it.

Tomas didn't wait for an answer, and he flipped to a page in the notebook, where she saw a crude drawing of a landscape with their house in the background and a female figure.

There was no doubt that it was her. And yet she'd never seen herself this way.

"It's not done, mind you," he said slowly. "I'll work on the details later, but it's enough to get it started."

"Nice. It's nice." She nodded. "I've always wanted to be able to do that."

"Have you now?" He smiled as he looked down at her. The sun shone from behind him, and she tried to convince herself that it was only its intense rays making her feel light-headed. "Well," he continued, "I don't exactly know what I'm doing, but I'd be happy to teach you what I can."

She didn't know what to make of the flutter in her heart, but she let the edges of her lips curl up rather than speak the nervous words in her mind.

He put out his hand. "Well, good to meet you, Miss Della. I'm Tomas Trujillo. I think I forgot to tell you that. I'm mighty glad your pops gave me this job. Mine worked at the cannery until he died a few months ago of a heart attack. I'm too young to work there, but Mr. Lee said he was going to take care of me and my sister. So here I am, mending your fences, and he said that he'll have more work for me if I do this one well."

"I'm sure he'll see to that." Her mouth felt dry as she spoke, and she struggled to get even those words out as his hand lingered on hers.

"Yeah, he's a good man, that Mr. Lee." He let go and put the pencil behind his ear. "Well, I'm off to finish up for today. I hope I see you again, Miss Della."

"And you." The boy turned around and sauntered back to where he'd started. Della watched until she couldn't see him any longer and then turned toward home. She forgot about the aloe vera, for her burning cheeks and beating heart were now of a more immediate preoccupation than her aching hands.

But the fairy tales that Della had imagined for them ever since that day were over now.

And what would Tomas do when he found out?

CHAPTER ELEVEN

Puerto Pesar—Today

Paloma led Mick through the square and down an alley, where a line of about thirty people wrapped around the block.

"Must be a good restaurant," he said.

"It is. Norma's is an institution here. Abuela took us here every Sunday after Mass. And I've been back every time I've visited."

She winced as she said that, a reminder that it hadn't been often enough. She'd spent a few Thanksgivings with Abuela and Mercedes on school breaks, but summers and Christmases were with her dad and his wife. She'd justified it by saying that she was making up for lost time with him. But she just didn't feel the draw to come to Puerto Pesar, and Abuela declined Paloma's offers to fly them out. She never gave a reason, so Paloma imagined what they might have been. Fear of flying. Discomfort at seeing the man who knocked up her daughter. Pride.

A boy of about ten approached them. "Umbrella?" he asked, holding out a flimsy red one.

"Thank you," said Paloma, taking it. She opened it with a little struggle and raised it over their heads.

"That's optimistic."

"It's not for the rain. It's for the sun. Norma hands them out at the front, and as you get your food, you bring yours to the back for the last person. Sometimes they have misters, too."

Mick looked up at the eaves, presumably searching for piping.

"This isn't Boston, Mick. Not actual misters. Kids who come by with spray bottles to cool you down. Norma's grandchildren sometimes come out and do it, and she slips them a few dollars."

"Well, I've seen everything now."

They turned the corner, and Mick's eyes widened when he saw the silver bullet trailer.

"Oh, a food truck. We have those in Boston."

"Yeah, but Norma was doing it before it was trendy. And I'll bet you've never had food like hers."

The line moved quickly, and they were at the front before long.

Paloma shouted over the giant fan that sat by the stove. "Three *carne guisadas*, two on corn tortillas and one on flour." She knew Abuela loved them, and they had always been Mercedes's favorite. She hoped that was still the case.

"Sounds good. I'll take two of the same. On flour, please."

Mick took out his wallet before Paloma did and insisted that he pay for them.

"But I also ordered for Abuela and my sister."

"Well, that nine dollars might break the bank, but I can probably sell some blood to make up for it."

"Aren't you the comedian?"

Paloma was glad that she was getting a chance to know the Mick of today instead of the one at Arturo's last night. Then again, she hadn't been in the best of moods, either. She was having a difficult time wearing all the different hats that she had right now: granddaughter, caregiver, older sister, employee. Add to that the fact that she was still reconciling how she fit in here. In some ways, she fit right back in like the proverbial glove. And in other ways, she felt like a New Yorker through and through. She and Mick had that in common—two East Coasters here for a brief time.

She enjoyed being with him. Their little jaunt to see *Santa Bonita* and even getting the breakfast tacos was a respite where she could just be Paloma with no other qualifiers. It had been a long time since she'd made the effort to just hang out with someone.

"So, what's the master plan?" Mick asked. "Are we going to find a park bench or something?"

"Actually, I thought we'd bring them back to Abuela's. She should be coming home from Mass any minute, and you can ask her about Della Lee. Not that she knew her, but I'm sure the stories were told for decades, and she might be able to point you in the right direction."

"She won't mind a stranger coming over on a Sunday morning?"

"Abuela almost doesn't know what to do with herself if she's not taking someone in or bringing people a meal. And besides, I'm kind of intrigued myself. Could be interesting."

She was right. When Abuela walked in through the front door, Paloma expected a reprimand for leaving Mass without telling her, but instead Abuela lit up when she saw Mick with Paloma, and her eyes didn't leave him for several minutes. Paloma should have guessed that Abuela would be thrilled that she was bringing a man home. Her grandmother immediately went to the freezer and started pulling out frozen fruit to make her famous strawberry limeade.

Paloma laid out all the *carne guisada* tacos and pulled some salsa and cheddar cheese out of the refrigerator.

"Mercedes," she called out in a singsong voice that she hoped sounded nonthreatening. It was so hard to tell how a teenager might interpret something. "I brought tacos from Norma's."

Her sister walked into the kitchen wearing a black T-shirt and running shorts and smelled as if she'd just washed her face with astringent. Paloma remembered doing the same thing when she was her sister's age. Warding off zits. God, she was happy not to be that age again. Mercedes must have come home from taking Della Lee to and from the church.

She grabbed a taco without even looking at Paloma and started back to her bedroom. Not a word. Not a thank-you.

"Come join us," she tried again, stepping forward and touching Mercedes's elbow.

Mercedes yanked away her arm. "What are you doing?"

Paloma suppressed the kinds of things she felt like saying and opted for a conciliatory smile. "I want you to meet my friend. And I brought tacos."

"I know. I have mine." She lifted it up to Paloma's face.

An unspoken *Duh* hovered between them. Paloma pretended not to feel the tension in the silence.

"Excellent. Now you can join us at the table."

"Mija," Abuela said to Mercedes. "Your sister's right. We have company. Come join us."

Abuela put her hands on her hips, and Paloma had a sudden vision of the calm before a gunfight in an Old Western town.

Mercedes rolled her eyes and slumped into her chair. At least it was progress. Abuela stirred the limeade, and Paloma brought out glasses of crushed ice. Her grandmother sank into her seat with a bit of a groan.

"So, Abuela," Paloma started. "We think we may have seen Della Lee outside the church this morning and hoped you might have some information that you can share with us."

She caught herself speaking in the plural.

"Oh, the Lees," Abuela said. "So much sadness in that family."

Mick pulled out a yellow legal pad and a blue pen.

"No laptop?" Paloma asked him.

111

"I've got one. They're good for some things. But I don't feel the same way when it's on a screen. There's something about actually writing it, or at least the notes, that feels more real."

"Suit yourself."

Paloma caught Mercedes looking back and forth between her and Mick, as if trying to figure out exactly who they were to each other, despite herself. It would be natural that a teenage girl would read some romance into this, even though the idea was ridiculous. Maybe that would be a good conversation starter for them later. She caught Mercedes's glance and smiled at her, but her sister just rolled her eyes again.

Abuela rubbed her temples. "You understand, of course, that this all happened before I was born," she said. "So everything I know is what was told to me. And I'm an old woman, so the memory isn't what it used to be. But there are things about it that have become almost legendary, so most people my age could tell you the same things."

Mick nodded in understanding, pen hovering.

"The Lee family came to Puerto Pesar from somewhere on the coast, sometime around the turn of the century. Herman Lee's father had the cockamamie idea to bring the fish up from the Gulf and get the cheap labor inland."

"And that really worked?" Mick asked.

"You wouldn't think so, but I suppose it did. I would have thought the cost of the ice and transportation alone would have eaten up any savings. But who am I to question it? Lee and Son's Fine Fish did surprisingly well. It employed most people in town and gave the Lees more than a comfortable living."

Mick started taking some notes.

Abuela continued. "The son, Herman, fell for a local girl, Eva. She was trouble, from what I heard, but a beauty if there ever was one. Long brown hair, big brown eyes. Even after they married, there were rumors, so I'm told, that she wasn't faithful to him, but at first that wasn't really substantiated. I mean, this is a small town, and Herman Lee had more money than almost anyone here, such as it was. So who else would she really go with?"

Paloma noticed that Mercedes had set her iPod on the table and was listening to Abuela. Thank goodness for small blessings.

She took a breath and continued. "They had a daughter, Della, and a few years later, another named Eula. We're talking about the midtwenties at this point. From all accounts, their parents spoiled them. Fancy dresses, shoes, really more than what was necessary in Puerto Pesar. Eva went through Herman's money like water, but he was a slave to keeping her happy."

Abuela cleared her throat and took a sip of the limeade.

Paloma found it hard to read Mick's face. Was this gossip too small-time for him, or did he find it as interesting as she did?

Maybe the latter, as he asked another question. "How does the painter fit into this?"

"Well, a vagabond came through town. He'd come in from El Paso, I think. I'm fuzzy on that part of the story. But he was making his way to Corpus Christi. I don't know why, but they had ports there, and lots of people from South Texas went there for the jobs. So that might have been it. He earned his keep as he went along, painting landscapes, little portraits, and so on. He called himself Teddy Brown, and from what I heard, Eva and Teddy caused quite a scandal. They didn't even try to hide their affair, and poor Herman Lee was so busy at the cannery that he didn't know what was going on right under his nose. They'd even go to the coast together and bring the girls."

Mick stopped writing and looked up at Abuela. "I'm loving this, but please don't take this the wrong way. It seems like this is a lot of hearsay information, especially since you weren't even alive for it. I'm not discrediting it, but I guess it's part of the job description to question what's told to me."

Paloma had been wondering the same thing herself, but she hoped Abuela wasn't offended.

Her grandmother took his hand and patted it. "Oh, you young people. You have no appreciation for oral history. If it's not on the Internet, it can't be believed."

"I just meant—"

"I know what you meant, and don't worry about it. You're right. If this is going to be good, you'll have to check your facts, and generations of retelling might have some holes. But you need to understand something about a small town like Puerto Pesar. Sometimes the stories are all we have. The scandals of the Lee family have been talked about for years and years, and no one has ever told a different version than what I'm telling you. Although I will say that my mother never said too much. She's one of the few who didn't like to gossip about them. But plenty of other people did."

Mick slipped his hand away and raised his limeade glass to her. "Then please continue. I really do appreciate it."

Paloma let go of a breath that she didn't even know she was holding.

"So. After one such trip where Eva and the girls and the painter went out of town, Eva packed up and left while Herman was at work, and the little girls were in the house alone until he returned. I think they were about six and four at the time. Eva never came back, Herman retreated from everything except his office, and the girls had to fend for themselves."

She coughed.

"Do you want to stop, Abuela?" Paloma asked. "I'm worried about you." It was only a couple of days since Abuela had gotten out of the hospital. Maybe this was too taxing for her.

"No, no, *mija*. I'm OK. Just a little water, if you don't mind."

"Of course. Mick?" Paloma looked his way, and he nodded while Abuela talked. "Mercedes?"

"Yes, please."

Well, maybe hell had frozen over because those two words just came out of her sister's mouth.

"Now, this part I did hear from my mother, who was just a little older than the Lee girls. Didn't care for either one of them as far as I could tell. They all went to school in the same room, though, so she knew them well enough, I guess. Eula became very popular after she started singing in church. My mother said that something was off about her, and that she knew Eula had a fearsome temper. Yes. That's what she called it—a fearsome temper. Now, no one I know ever confirmed that. All praise and adoration from everyone else. But Mother seemed certain of it."

Mick was writing furiously now. "Did she ever give any examples?" he said. Even Mercedes seemed riveted. Paloma took that as a good sign.

Abuela sighed. "No, not that I can recall. Years after the fact, when people were still talking about the murder, my mother said she still didn't believe that Della was capable of it. In fact, I remember what she said exactly: 'Della Lee was no angel, but she was no murderer, either.'"

"So your mother thought she was innocent?"

"Well, she said there wasn't any proof, and it was complicated by the fact that Della pled guilty. But my uncle Tomas was apparently convinced of her innocence, too."

"Was that just his opinion?" Mick asked.

"Well, I suppose, but maybe he was biased, since he was married to her."

Wait, what? Paloma and Mick both sat straight up.

Paloma said, "Your uncle Tomas was married to Della Lee? I always thought he'd been a bachelor—that he died before he ever got a chance to get married. I've only seen pictures of him in his military uniform. Nothing about a wedding."

"Well, he might as well have been a bachelor, but, no, he actually married Della Lee just before she killed Eula. Hours before, in fact. My mama said that for that first year, he wrote and wrote and wrote to her in prison, and he even went to see her, but she always refused him. Except once. He went up to tell her that he'd been drafted and was assigned to a stateside unit caring for the army's horses. He didn't expect to see combat. But he came back from that trip to Huntsville a different man."

"Different how?" Mick asked just as she thought it. She was captivated by the intrigue. Maybe Puerto Pesar wasn't quite as sleepy as she'd always thought.

"Withdrawn. Defeated. My mama said he turned down the army position and joined the infantry with the Marines. Got sent to the Pacific, right in the thick of things."

She took a breath and rubbed her temples before continuing. "And he never came back."

Her three listeners gasped.

Paloma spoke first. "Why would he have done that? Volunteered for combat when he had such a safe post with the army here?"

"I don't know, *mija*. He was gone before I was born, so these are bits and pieces I picked up over the years. My mama certainly didn't want to talk about it more than she had to, and she often shushed me when I asked questions. That's as much as I know from her."

Mick's pen had kept up with the narrative. "What else do you know about their childhood? About Eula or about the painter?" he asked.

"Well, I do remember my mother saying that Eula was just like Eva. Carrying on with the boys. Or maybe it was just one. She never elaborated except to say that Eula would get into these rages. But then, that doesn't square with what everyone else says about her. Sweet girl. Angelic voice. *Santa Bonita*."

Even Mercedes jumped in. "Would your mother, as the sister of Tomas, have known things about the Lees that maybe everyone else didn't?"

Mick looked animated for the first time. "Yeah, do you think it's possible that Eula acted one way around family and another way in public? And Tomas's sister, like Paloma said, would have been close enough to the family to see that."

Abuela shook her head. "I don't know. Like I said, just snippets. From what I remember, it was only my mama and my uncle Tomas who ever said a sideways word about Eula Lee. Everyone else was ready to canonize her."

"But, Abuela, you even have one of her holy cards," Paloma said.

"Well, she's the closest thing little old Puerto Pesar has to having a patron saint, so I figure that if she is one, then I'm in her good graces. If she's not, well, then, what do I have to lose?"

Paloma smiled. It was one of many cards scattered around the house. She always felt as if it were a shrine. Saint Cecilia sat atop the old upright piano, patron saint of music. Saint Zita taped to the oven, patron saint of cooking. For her med school graduation, Abuela sent her twenty-five dollars and a holy card of Saint Luke. Patron saint of physicians.

Mick seemed to have more questions, but Abuela stood up, leveraging her arms on the table to pull her weight off the chair. She started to remove the dishes, but Paloma stopped her. "That's enough for today, Abuela."

"I'm afraid so. I'm going to go take my nap. Mercedes, will you clear away the glasses?"

The girl stood, shrugging. "Sure."

Paloma was relieved to see their exchange. Maybe her sister helped Abuela more than she'd thought. Maybe helping Della Lee, even though she was being paid, would be good practice for her. Paloma had to get over the idea that she was spending time with a murderer. Apparently it didn't faze her grandmother or sister.

"And, Abuela," Mercedes added, "I'm staying over at Maria Guevara's house tonight. We're studying for finals."

"I can drive you," said Paloma. She hoped they could grab some Popsicles from the market like they used to when Mercedes was little and spend the afternoon together. She'd love to ask her what it was like to visit with Della Lee.

"No, I can make it on my own." She paused. "Um, but thank you."

At least she got a "thank you." Paloma would consider it progress for today.

Mercedes picked up the glasses and rinsed them in the sink before returning to her room. Mick and Paloma started picking up the taco trash to put it in the bin.

"Wash out that foil, *mija*," said Abuela. "I can reuse it. And put the plastic bag under the sink."

Mick caught Paloma's eye, and they exchanged grins. "I will, Abuela. Now, go take your nap. We've got this covered."

She started walking down the hall but turned back, a hand on her hip.

"I remembered something else. What was it now?" She paused, and then looked up. "That's right. Someone told me that Herman Lee found out something about the painter, Teddy Brown. That's what sent him off looking for Eva. But he never came back. He died in an airplane crash over the Atlantic."

CHAPTER TWELVE

Goree State Farm for Women—1943

By fall, Della was no longer the victim of incessant nausea and had learned to make a guitar fit around her growing belly. It was not yet visible underneath her baggy prison jumpsuit, but it would be before long, and she needed to rewrite the story of how the baby came to be before the other women asked questions that she didn't want to answer.

Only Hazel knew the truth. And Hazel had advised her to stay silent about it. If Eddie the driver got wind of her accusation, who knew what influence he might have in taking the baby from her?

The very thought of it frightened Della past the point where words could even describe. Despite how it had come into existence, she already loved this child. She felt its gentle kicks, and her breasts tingled as they readied for the milk that would nurture it.

More than once since she'd been incarcerated, she'd been tempted to find a way to end her life, even though Fr. Medina called it the

Unforgivable Sin. But this baby had saved her. Now it was her turn to save it.

In the new story she told herself, there had never been an Eddie. There were any number of times when she and Tomas could have stumbled. Could have given in before they were married. And if that had happened, this child could very well belong to Tomas. She liked to imagine that it had happened that way.

She remembered the first time they kissed. If it had not been for Tomas's great self-control, she might have given in that very afternoon.

He'd worked on her family's homestead for four years by that time, and after Herman Lee died on his way to Europe, Tomas checked in on Della frequently.

Despite her best efforts, Della could not afford to keep up the homestead without the income that her father had brought home from the cannery. She had no choice but to start selling off parcels of the land. She started with the most valuable part with its oak tree groves and rich soil. It was not to be the last, and she knew it. Creditors wanted their money. The circumstances were inconsequential to a bottom line.

The first time was the most difficult, and Della's head rested on her arms as she leaned over the kitchen table after returning from the lawyer's office. Her sobs nearly drowned the sound of the screen door squeaking open and the gentle tread of Tomas's boots as he stepped upon the floor.

She jumped up when she heard him, and he ran across the room to her, the well-worn hands of her friend grasping her own. She looked up into his red eyes and saw that he understood the loss this was to her.

"Della," he whispered as he moved his right hand to her neck and pulled her to his shoulder. He was warm and smelled like the sweat of a hard-earned day, manly, and just like she'd imagined it. Ever since the day when they first met out in the pasture, a center of gravity had formed and flourished between them. It pulled them together despite their ardent avoidance of it.

She loved him as if he were a part of herself. And yet Della could see that Eula was in love with Tomas as well. It was the little things. The color of Eula's cheeks at the mention of his name. The thin nightgown she would wear in the mornings when he stopped in for coffee. Della suspected that it was the attachment of a young girl for the only man who was a constant presence in her orphaned life. One she would outgrow in time.

But regardless, it seemed real enough to Eula. And if Della had to choose one or the other, she was going to choose her sister. Tomas understood. He told her they could wait to be together until Eula was on her own. She was already sixteen. It would only be a few more years.

But the sale of the land they all loved signified more than anything else could the desperation she'd fallen into. The realization that her father was dead and was never coming back to rescue them from these circumstances. She had never felt more alone than when the fountain pen drained its thick black ink onto the contract papers, taking all hope with it.

Now she was wrapped in the arms of Tomas Trujillo, and it was better, warmer, sweeter than she had dreamed of. His flannel shirt was softer than a pillow, well worn, and she gripped it, avoiding his skin and where it might take her. He had no such hesitations, though, and lifted her chin to his. She opened her eyes as he closed his own and placed his rough, sun-chapped lips on hers. She gasped, parting her mouth and inviting him without understanding it to press further ahead, until their first kiss became many. The frenetic pace made her step back and him forward, until she heard the shatter of a water glass as it was knocked from the table. When he looked away to reach for it, she put her hands on his face and pulled him to her, erasing the glass, the sale, and Eula from her mind until the thoughts were only the two of them and this delicious, delirious feeling.

His hands reached for the button of her blouse, and she wanted him to undo it, to undo all of them. Her clothes had never felt so cumbersome, not even in the humid months when they clung to her skin and she ached to pull them off at the end of the day. She wanted his hands on her, flesh to flesh, as if there were no other way to be so close to him. But he recoiled as if he'd touched a hot flame and stepped back against the wall. He ran his fingers through his hair and grasped it, pulling his head down.

"Oh, God. Oh, God, Della. I'm so sorry."

She took a breath and moved toward him, but he sidestepped and moved to the other wall.

"Are you all right?" she asked. He looked up and took steps toward her, gently leading her to sit at the table before taking a chair of his own. Her heart raced but started to slow as he took her hands in his and finally looked up.

"I'm sorry, Della. I shouldn't have done that. I saw you there, crying, and I couldn't help myself. I just . . . I don't know. I just had to make it better."

She slid her hand into his slowly and looked into his eyes.

"You did make it better. You always make it better. You're the only good part of today." She added in a whisper, "Of every day." She held his hand tighter and leaned in closer until his breathing slowed. She brushed her lips against his, then pulled back, resting her head against his chest. He slid his hand down her braid, fingering the strands that had broken loose from their plait. They swayed almost imperceptibly to a music of their own creation, a melody of joy and sorrow and comfort and love.

Finally, Tomas sighed and stepped back. "I brought a present for you. It's on the counter." He pointed toward it. Only then did she see that he had brought a small clay pot with him. A little acorn was half-submerged in the dirt, a young, green shoot springing out from its hard shell. "I knew how much you'd hate to lose that oak grove that you and Eula used to play in. So I thought we could start a new one. I've been harvesting this acorn, keeping it in the icebox until now. It's ready to plant. And I think I have just the spot."

Della's heart had just started to return to normal when this sweet gesture quickened her pulse again. She loved this man, and she was certain she had since the first time she saw him.

He took her hand as if they had always done so, and she was happy to follow. The screen door bounced as they raced out of it, and it banged and echoed in decreasing tones until it was silent. Tomas walked about fifteen yards before stopping.

"Here," he said. He placed the pot on the ground and turned, taking both her hands in his own. "I don't know what the future holds or what land will stay and what will go. I do know that I'll do everything I can to help you keep this house. I want to plant the tree here so that whatever happens, this is a permanent boundary. As long as I'm alive, you'll always have that roof over your head, the shade from this tree, a garden to tend, and a yard for your children to play in." He didn't say what she knew he was thinking—that he hoped he would be the one to give her those children and provide her that life. And she wanted the same.

They sat on the ground and pulled away the soil. Together they dropped the little acorn into the hole they'd created. Tomas told her it would be decades before it reached its full maturity, and it would initially need to be protected from pests, drought, storms. Just like the beautiful girl next to him. She kissed him on the cheek.

When they had replaced the dirt and patted it down, they stood, and Della wiped her hands on her apron. Her hair had all but fallen out of its braid by now, and Tomas reached over to pull the ribbon from the end. He brushed his fingers through her hair and smiled before pulling her in to him once again.

This time, the kiss possessed all the warmth and wholeness of an unspoken promise for the future before them.

CHAPTER THIRTEEN

Puerto Pesar—Today

Mick's e-mail was flooded with week-old messages from various colleagues whose poorly disguised words of consolation masked what he really knew to be true: they'd smelled blood, and they wanted to get the scoop.

Not a voice mail, not a text from any of the guys whom he'd gotten drinks with after work in the past. Mick stared at the discolored popcorn ceiling in his motel room and put his former friends into categories. Randy—he'd always liked Stephanie. He was probably swooping in with a muscular shoulder to cry on. Tarek—his wife would have sided with Stephanie. And he would do whatever she wanted. Anthony—he would already be trying to weasel his way into Mick's plum assignments.

Pick a name, pick a reason. Oh, and there was one more type: the ones who saw everyone as a networking opportunity. Mick was out of the picture for the time being, so he wasn't any use to them anymore.

That was the type he used to be.

Between that and all the telemarketers who ignored the "do not call" list, he'd had enough with the interruptions.

He tried to ignore the fact that the *real* distraction was Paloma Vega. He had really enjoyed being with her yesterday. Seeing the painting, getting the tacos, going to her grandmother's house. In fact, all he wanted to do was to find a reason to call her. Right now. To hear her voice, the one that filled him with a kind of peace that he hadn't known in a long time.

Sincere. Paloma seemed sincere.

Then he realized that he'd never gotten her number. Not that it would be too hard to find. But it was just as well. He was here for a reason. And he needed to get on with it.

He needed to go meet Della Lee.

He grabbed his keys and a stale cookie from the registration desk, along with directions to the Lee homestead.

The map ended at the same point that a small dirt road emerged from the main one that he'd been driving on. Not too far out of town, but it still felt isolated. It was hard to believe a ninety-year-old woman lived here by herself.

A rusty white mailbox stood on the corner of the property with red letters that were nearly pink from years of fading: Lee. And above that, in similarly faded gray-black, Trujillo.

He started down the road, no doubt capturing tiny pebbles in the treads of his tires. At least it was a rental.

Before long, a charming stone house appeared, and just beyond its fenced border, an enormous split tree that was unlike any he'd ever seen. The dual trunks separated and then intertwined near the top as their branches reached out, clinging to each other as if one would fall down without the other holding it up.

The metal gate to the small yard was open, and lights were on inside.

Mick walked up to the stoop, tall enough to nearly brush up against its low-hanging cover. He rapped on the screen door.

Inside, he could hear Frank Sinatra crooning "I Get a Kick Out of You" and water pouring from a faucet.

"Miss Lee?" he called out.

The music and the water stopped.

After what seemed like an eternity, the shuffle of steps became audible, until he saw the tiny woman they belonged to. She was slightly hunched at the shoulders but was in otherwise remarkable shape, considering her age. No scars, no markings. He'd half expected to find someone who had wrinkled and faded tattoos. She didn't seem feeble, either. Maybe a lifetime in a prison environment had kept her fit.

In every way, she seemed to be a normal little old lady.

Rather than the murderess she was.

She opened the screened door and looked up at him, adjusting her glasses and peering at his face. "I'm not selling any more land."

"I'm not here to buy land."

"Then I'm not buying anything. I don't have any money, and I don't need any candy or insurance or magazines."

"I'm not a salesman, Miss Lee. My name is Mick Anders, and I just want to talk to you."

"I can't think of why."

She was as tough as any congressman.

"I'm a reporter for the *Daily Talk* in Boston, and I was hoping to visit with you about your return to Puerto Pesar." A deep, musty scent with a dash of mothballs wafted from the house. But he also smelled . . . chocolate. He tried his most charming smile. "Miss Lee, are those brownies I smell?"

She looked him up and down, her opinion of him completely unreadable. But she must have approved of whatever she saw, because finally she opened the door wider and took a small step back.

"Come inside, young man. Wipe your feet."

She led him to the kitchen. "Sit here," she said, pointing to a wooden chair. "Look at this." She plopped a box of Betty Crocker Fudge Brownies mix in front of him. "Have you ever seen such a thing?"

Whatever he'd expected her to say, it hadn't been this.

"A box of brownies? Yes, I have."

"Not brownies. Brownie *mix*. Just add oil, water, and eggs. Oil, water, and eggs. Can you imagine? That and some brown powder, and in forty-five minutes you have a perfectly delicious dessert. I just don't know what to make of it."

"Well, I guess they wanted it to be easier for people to bake?"

"And that's not all of it," she continued. "Cookie mix. Cake mix. Tapioca mix. A whole aisle in the market dedicated to mixes." She waved her arm around the imaginary store.

He couldn't tell if this made her happy or not. How strange it must be, reentering the real world after so many years behind bars. What else might she find surprising? It must be as if she'd traveled through time. Either that, or she was crazy.

"I guess some people see it as progress."

"Progress," she repeated slowly. Then she nodded. "Yes. That's exactly what it is. Next thing you know, they'll be putting a man on the moon."

Mick hoped the shock he felt didn't show on his face. Surely . . .

"Oh, don't look as if you just caught Santa Claus slugging some whiskey. Let an old woman have a little fun."

"Yes, ma'am," seemed the only response for such an exchange.

"Well, I'm sure you're not here to have me prattle on about silly things. You said you're a reporter, so I don't need to ask you what you're here for. You're just another one of dozens who've been writing me. Good thing I don't have a telephone, or it'd be ringing and ringing and keeping me up. Although, I'll say that you're the first one to come by in person. Probably not the last."

Mick felt relieved to be the first one here and bolstered by the attention she seemed to be drawing. His instincts were right about her being a good news story.

He slid his notebook and pen out of his bag and proceeded with the caution that one might in front of a rattlesnake. "Well. I originally came here to see the portrait of your sister. *Santa Bonita.*"

"Oh." She stiffened at the name.

He jumped right back in before losing her. "But I'm not sure that's the story I'm leaving with after all. It doesn't appear to be crying like everyone said for a while. It is remarkable, but not miraculous."

"No, it is not miraculous." She sighed. "It's simply the work of a vagabond artist who passed through this town and painted my sister and me. And at a high price. My mother."

"What do you mean?"

"Not so quick, Mr. Anders. Look." She folded her hands and rested them on the table. "I want to get one thing straight before we continue. There's a reason a bunch of people have been trying to get my story. I may look frail, but I haven't lost my brains, thank God, so I'm not going to tell it to just anyone who comes along."

Mick ran through his résumé in his head. She'd want credentials. He had plenty of those. And more. She might not be aware of everything that was possible on social media. He could dazzle her with all the outlets he could share her story with.

"Are you listening to me?" she said. "Or are you one of those people who spends his time thinking up his response instead?"

"I . . . I'm listening. Please continue." He'd been caught, and she knew it.

"I'll let you in on one little secret. And then I'm going to decide how things go from there."

He leaned in to meet her, and she stared at him as if participating in a contest where neither could look away. At last she spoke, in a whisper. "Things aren't always as they seem. Don't assume that everything you might have read about me is the truth. Only I know the truth. And the only other two who did have long since died."

Including your sister, he thought. Who might be the other? And what truth could she be talking about? He wrote the questions on his legal pad. She watched him as he did so, and he felt her disapproval as if it were made of matter. He set down the pen.

"Look," she said. "There're two reasons I invited you in. The first is that you're the only reporter who has had enough interest to make it all the way down here, so that has got to be worth something."

"And the second?" he asked, feeling daring as he did so.

"The second is that you look a little like Paul Newman, and I liked his movies. We used to get them at Goree. He was a good man. Are you a good man, Mr. Anders?"

The question caught him off guard. This had the distinct feeling of cat-and-mouse. Of the interview being flip-flopped.

"I would like to think so."

She narrowed her eyes and looked him up and down. "I've always been a pretty good judge of character, and I'd hate to think I'd gotten out of practice. So we're going to give this a go, young man. Go ahead. Ask me something."

Mick's stomach fluttered as he flipped back to the pages he'd written after visiting with Paloma's grandmother. He had to get this right. This was the story. Others wanted it. But he *needed* it. Two weeks, his editor had said. Two weeks for a knockout story. And including his travel, one week was almost gone. He stretched out his fingers and picked up his pen again. Time to reclaim control of this interview. Start from the beginning. "You were found guilty of murdering your sister, Eula Lee, in 1943. Is that correct?"

She didn't answer, and he was afraid he'd been too direct. She stood up and filled a teakettle and set it over a mild flame on the ancient gas stove before sitting down again with a sigh.

"Mr. Anders. This isn't going to work."

His heart sank. They hadn't even begun and already she was dismissing him.

"What do you mean?"

"If you're going to ask me questions that any high school sophomore can research for their campus newspaper, then maybe you're not the one to give my story to."

Ouch.

She'd called him out on the very thing he'd been reflecting on yesterday. His "just the facts, ma'am" way of expediting an article. Losing sight of the *people* in the story, what led him to this business in the first place. He'd kick himself in the butt if the board hadn't already done it for him.

"May I try again, Miss Lee? Please?"

She pursed her lips and delayed an answer. He half suspected she enjoyed toying with him. "You have until you finish that brownie to let me decide if we're going to continue. And no dillydallying just to draw it out."

Mick took a breath and slowed down. Took a small bite of the brownie. He rubbed his hand along his chin and considered a new approach.

He tapped his pen on the table, and then placed it behind his ear. No notes. Just conversation. That wasn't how he usually worked. But Della Lee was no usual subject.

"How . . . how did life change for you and your sister when your father left?" He held his breath, and his heart beat in anticipation of whether or not this would save him.

She nodded several times, as if ruminating over it.

"Now, that is a question worth asking. None of this 'You were found guilty' stuff. Because that doesn't give you the whole picture. No one does the things they're driven to without some kind of motivation. It's not the action that's interesting. It's what led up to it. So, yes. I will answer that one."

Whew. He was back on track. He hadn't totally lost his touch. The *Rocky* theme played through his head, although he had to admit that it was probably premature.

The teakettle screamed. She stood up to turn down the flame and poured water into two mismatched cups. He watched how she moved, and he wouldn't have called her "frail," as she herself had said. In fact, she seemed quite the opposite. Miss Lee sliced two lemons in half, letting their juices drip through her hands, her fingers catching the seeds. Then she added fresh mint leaves and drizzled honey into the steaming water.

As she stirred them, one by one, ghostly threads of mist rose. She placed one in front of Mick before setting one at her own seat and sliding gracefully into the chair. The agony of waiting through this ritual made him feel impatient, as he wondered what this *truth* she dangled in front of him could be.

Mick placed the cup at his lips, but it was still too hot to drink. She seemed to have no such problem. Her eyes closed as she began to speak.

"It was 1940. I was sixteen, and my sister was fourteen. Our mother had been gone for ten years. I don't think Eula even remembered her. Maybe bits. We never talked about it. But I marked the date every year. May 23. The day after we'd returned to the coast, and she left with the painter. I would have forgotten her face if it were not for a photograph that my father kept on his desk. Even through the grays and whites of that old picture, you could tell that her lip color was bold and her teeth were bright white. Her face smiled for the camera, but I never saw that face at home. At least, not until the painter had come into town. Or whenever Papa bought something for her."

Mick made a mental note to call his mom when he got back to his room. He might have complained that he never saw her, with as many hours as she had to work, but at least she'd been there. He couldn't imagine what it must have been like to have your mother check out.

"That must have been very difficult," he said.

"It was. My father became absorbed in the running of the can-nery, so I was left with raising Eula. And tending the livestock, cooking dinner."

"What about school? Surely you had some ambitions. Something you wanted to be." Mick remembered that age. Sixteen was tough. Studies. Hormones. Growing pains.

"I was a poor student, Mr. Anders. I was up too early and in bed too late tending to all the chores. It didn't take much persuading to tell my father that I wanted to stay home and do my own schooling. He would buy me all sorts of books when he traveled to Corpus Christi or Houston or Dallas, and I learned everything I needed to know from those. I've been an avid reader ever since."

"And what about Eula? Did she do well in school?" Mick surprised himself with that question. Not because of the content of it but because of how easily it flowed as part of a conversation rather than an interview. He found himself genuinely wanting to know.

"She tried to stay home as well, and for a while I let her. My father didn't even notice. But she wasn't interested in the books, nor would she let me read them to her. She would just take walks and lock herself in her room, singing. I finally told her that she had to go to school, or her new job would be raking manure over the garden and milking the cow. So she went back."

Mick had to hold back a laugh. This woman was a character. Call the *Ellen* show. She'd have a field day with her, and it would probably go viral.

Della Lee drained the last of her cup and continued.

"I know you asked about when my father left. But that's what I wanted to illustrate. He might have left to go find her after the tenth anniversary of her leaving, but he had left us long ago, at least in the sense of being any kind of parent to us. So when he left, it made no difference to our daily lives. At least not right away."

"What prompted his leaving?"

"He was on a business trip in Dallas. He called in to his secretary at the fish cannery and told her that he was flying to Europe. Didn't even mention what country. He had seen an item in a magazine pertaining to our mother, and he had to go find her."

Mick looked for any sign of emotion over these words, but she didn't reveal anything in her body language. Maybe seventy years had been enough to ruminate over them. Was that what prison did? Inoculate you to even the most painful memories? Or did incarceration create new pains that eclipsed the old?

"Miss Lee, I can't figure something out. Why do you think your father didn't go to find her sooner, if he was so in love with her?"

She folded her arms and peered at him. "Young man, what might you do right now if you wanted to learn about the eating habits of koalas in Australia?"

"Easy. I'd look it up on the Internet."

Oh.

She must have seen the acknowledgment in his eyes. A hint of a smile—*smirk?*—appeared on her face. "You see, it wasn't as easy as it would be now. Not that he didn't try. He did hire a few private detectives over the years. But the painter and my mother had slipped out in the night. No trace of them. Where on earth do you start with something like that?"

So whatever was in this magazine was the first trace of his wife that Herman must have found. Mick wondered if he could track it down.

He took the last bite of his brownie and a quick swig of the tea that he hadn't touched. Della continued to let him talk, so he must have passed his audition, at least for the time being.

"After ten years, did your father not think that she was staying away on purpose? I mean, did he really think he was going to be able to bring her back?" He wiped crumbs from his fingers.

"Ah. Yes. It seemed like it might be fruitless. Well, besides the fact that he still loved her, he was a man determined to save her."

133

"From what? I'm assuming she was happy where she was, if she never came back."

Miss Lee softened for the first time and placed her hands on the table as she leaned in. "I don't mean to save her that way. I mean to save her soul."

Mick jerked back.

"Her soul?"

She nodded. "You young people don't pay too much heed to those kinds of things today, but you have to remember that I grew up in a time with stark right and wrong. Heaven and hell stuff. *Sin*. You don't use that word, do you, Mr. Anders?"

He couldn't say that he did. Suddenly he felt guilty about that.

"Exactly," she continued, pressing a finger into the table. "He prayed for her all the time. Not that she would come back and love him, but that she would renounce her adultery and honor her vows so that she could be restored to salvation."

She was right. He didn't know anyone who used language like that. It was something from another century. Literally.

But it was more than that. It gave a new dimension to the meaning of the word *love*. It wasn't just caring about someone's mind and body. Mind, body, and . . . soul? He thought of a tripod. Three legs provided more of a stable foundation than two. Had he ever loved someone that . . . that thoroughly? He couldn't say he had.

Miss Lee continued as she threw up her hands. "We never saw him again, you may know. The plane he was on crashed over the Atlantic in midflight. It was headed to Madrid, but no one knew if that was his ultimate destination."

Again, no particular emotion on her part as she spoke of this, and Mick wondered for the second time what pain she might have suffered later that caused this one to pale. Or was it so remote that it had dulled over time?

To have lost a mother so young and a father so tragically. He began to see why this had been the right question. You couldn't cut to the chase regarding someone's guilt or innocence without knowing what the circumstances were in the first place.

Mick had learned all that in college, of course, but news today was told in sound bites, one hundred forty characters, scrolling headlines on social media. Any anonymous person with a keyboard and Wi-Fi was a self-titled journalist. People were forgotten. Expediency reigned.

Blood pulsed through his hands. They were itching to grab that pen and write down everything she'd said. Everything he was thinking. He felt alive.

Mick shifted in his seat and leaned forward. "That must have been devastating." The words seemed so inadequate, so obvious, but what else could one say?

She waved her hand in the air. "As I told you, it didn't change our day-to-day much. He was home only at night to sleep. At the office during every daylight hour. Life was the same with or without him. For a little while, at least. Then it got worse."

He knew what it was like not to have a dad. His had skipped out when his mom was pregnant. What could be worse? And then he remembered. For a moment he'd forgotten that this enthralling old woman in front of him was a convicted murderer. "What happened?"

"The cannery suffered after he died. There was no board. No right-hand man. My father *was* the cannery. He'd been reviewing proposals for machinery that would speed up automation, but he left before he'd formalized any agreements. The employees tried to salvage what they could, but he'd left a giant hole that no one seemed to be able to fill. They lost their military contract after failing to fill a major purchase order, and one by one, clients dropped off. Desperate, they sold for peanuts to a firm in Houston, but the doors were quickly closed after the new company took off with all the recipes that had made Lee and Son's Fine Fish so popular. Nearly everyone in town was unemployed after that. My father was the cannery, and the cannery was Puerto Pesar. It all died, not just him. And any regard that the town might have had for two abandoned girls left with it. Most everyone essentially shunned us. But I don't hold a grudge. I think people were just searching for someone to blame in their own misery. And we were the natural targets."

Mick's stomach tightened. How horrible to imagine what Della and Eula had gone through.

"And you had no other relatives?"

"No. Well, not any who were close. I know that my mother had family somewhere in California. My father's parents had died before I was even born. Remember, medicine wasn't what it is now, and certainly not in a place like this. People didn't live to be very old."

Then it was nearly miraculous that she had lived so long. But neither broached that. He wanted to know why she didn't search for her family in the west, but she answered him before he could ask.

"And here's the first part of the *truth* that I'm going to tell you."

Mick felt his pulse quicken. She was drawing him in like the Pied Piper, and he danced to the tune she played.

"My sister was very troubled, you should know. It's not something I've talked about before. The voice of a beautiful songbird was the first ray of hope that Puerto Pesar had had since the cannery closed. It was as if an angel inhabited her. And in those times, I felt like I had my sister back. My Eula. The one I adored. But when she was not performing, it was the opposite."

This was definitely not in any accountings that he'd read. He caught himself rocking in his chair, anticipating what she might say next.

"The opposite?" he asked.

"Exactly that. Outside of the church, a terrible darkness would befall her."

A crying portrait. A despondent girl. This was the stuff of a novel, not an article. "Miss Lee—do you think your sister was . . . *possessed?*"

She sat up straight. "Certainly not! If I had meant that word, I would have said it. It won't do to have you embellish my story. Listen to exactly what I said. My sister was *troubled*."

He hoped she would elaborate, caring, genuinely, what might have ailed *Santa Bonita*.

Miss Lee continued. "I was afraid that if we found our other relatives, they might send her away after they lived with her for a while. Staying here was the only way to keep us together, even if it was a difficult life. But there are things you do because they're right, not because they're easy. Sacrifice is sanctifying."

More religious stuff that he didn't understand. It was cryptic. What drove her to murder her sister if so much had gone into protecting her? He wasn't sure how to form the words to ask that question.

As Della started to get up to remove the teacups, Mick placed a hand on her arm and put them in the sink himself. He looked back and saw her rubbing her eyes. This question had led to so many others, but she seemed exhausted. It was the same look he'd seen on his mother's face after back-to-back shifts.

"Miss Lee," he said gently. "It looks as if you might be too tired to continue."

She nodded. "I'm afraid you're right. I spent too much time outside today."

"I'd really like to come back and visit with you again. Would you mind if I stop by soon?"

"That would be nice, Mr. Anders." He felt as if he'd passed a litmus test. At least for today. He wondered if there actually were other reporters contacting her, or if she was really just a lonely old woman who told him what she thought she needed to in order to keep him interested.

Or, another thought. Mick struggled to shake the edginess, the competitiveness of his profession and admit something to himself: he liked her company. He liked this old lady, even if she was a murderer, and he wanted to come back and sit at her table and have tea and a brownie. He suspected that she enjoyed talking to him, too. What else was there to do in a town like Puerto Pesar, especially if you were ninety years old?

Maybe they weren't manipulating each other. Maybe they needed each other.

"Miss Lee," he said with all sincerity. "Can I bring anything for you from town next time? Save you the trip?"

"What a considerate thing to ask. But I do have a girl running some errands for me, so I think I'm all set." She must mean Mercedes.

She led him to the door but called out to him as he was halfway down the steps.

"Mr. Anders!"

He turned.

"Churros. If you can find some churros, I'd love some of those."

"What are churros?"

"You're a smart boy. I'm sure you'll figure it out."

It wasn't until he was pulling into his motel that he remembered something she'd said at the beginning of the conversation.

There were two portraits. One of Eula. And one of *her*.

CHAPTER FOURTEEN

Goree State Farm for Women—1943

The tales of the original Goree Girls All Strings Band reached legendary heights, like Paul Bunyan in a skirt with a guitar. One by one, as they were paroled, the stories would grow, and Della never knew fact from fiction. Georgia's false teeth were made from hippopotamus tusks. Lillie Mae once served President Roosevelt in her restaurant before he was elected. Burma was a heroin addict. Ruby Dell had to sew in order to calm her stage fright before a show, snapping at anyone who distracted her from her stitching. And so on. Of course, they were all gone now, paroled back into life outside the walls, and even Reable Childs was preparing for her own release. Della hoped that would give her a chance to play with them onstage.

"Hold that note longer," Hazel would say. Or, "Just pluck at that top string." She never used terms like *arpeggio, bending, modulation, tuners,* all things Della learned reading books about it. But the older woman knew what sounded good. The string band had been the ticket out for all the original members, and she seemed dead set that Della would have the same opportunity. Prison was no place for such a young girl, even if she had killed her own sister. *And prison won't keep no baby forever,* she'd sworn to Della.

A statement that terrified her. What had begun as a shock had grown into a kind of companion, and Della found herself thinking about the baby all the time. Would it be a boy or girl? Would it be healthy? Would they take it away?

Matron Heath had told her that a child born in prison could stay with his or her mother for up to six years. But that there was also talk of shortening that. She didn't think she could handle it if they planned to take the baby sooner.

At night, Della found it difficult to get comfortable, plagued by backaches and fear about the things that were out of her control. If only she could run away with this child. Run to Tomas, start over.

Hazel could calm her by telling stories. She had an encyclopedic talent for recalling details about even the most obscure inmate.

"Tell me again about the rodeo," Della would say as her lazy speech drawled toward sleep. It was all anyone had talked about lately, from the excitement to its abrupt cancellation.

"The rodeo," she'd start. "Every October we have a prison rodeo, and thousands of people come from all over the state. Except for this year. This year, we have a war. But you'll see next time, my dear. The goat roping. The bull riding. The performances. The crowds. Every Sunday for four weeks, it's a little chance to be normal again. A little chance at freedom."

She spoke it with gentle inflections, up and down, like a spoken lullaby.

"Freedom," Della whispered until sleep took over and she said no more.

Letters from Tomas continued, although not as frequently as at the beginning of her incarceration. They remained unread, unanswered, and still Della waited for the annulment documents that never came.

Uncharacteristically, Matron Heath popped into the dormitory just a few days before Christmas with a wrapped bundle.

"Lee," she said. "There's a package for you."

Hazel looked up. "Why *you* deliverin' it, Matron Heath?"

"I'm not talking to you," she answered. She sat beside Della on her bed. Della wrapped her arms around her belly and shifted her weight so that she could sit up. Her movements were slow and deliberate. The baby had been kicking furiously in the last few days.

Matron Heath placed the package in Della's hands. "Look. Gertie tells me that this boy writes and writes to you, but that you never send out any mail. You know we have to read everything that comes through, and I'm not here to get into all that. But this was important, and I wanted to be sure you got it." She patted it as she stood up. "He's crazy about you, you know. Though I don't know what a fool boy can see in a murderess."

The portly woman hobbled toward the door. "Merry Christmas," she said, and left shaking her head.

Della waited until she was out of sight before pulling the papers out of the package. She'd said that they were important. As much as Della wanted the annulment to happen in order to free up Tomas for a happier life, a trickle of tears escaped at the possibility of that one final link to her home being severed.

It did not contain what she expected. Instead, there were pages and pages of drawings, some on scraps, and even on work orders from the ranch. They were scrawled with pencil, crude in detail, but it was easy to distinguish the subjects. A longhorn calf, born in the spring. Our Lady of Guadalupe church, with a Christmas tree in front. Her beloved homestead, looking the same as always. Tomas had drawn a wreath on the door, and she was certain that he'd placed a real one on there as well.

She looked at each one as if it were its own marvel, tracing her finger along the shaded lines, remembering the things that had been of special importance to them.

The oak tree, grown from the seed that they planted together, looking as if it might be about four feet tall now, judging from the background that he'd drawn behind him. Their wedding cake, never eaten, which must have been committed to his memory, as it had surely decayed along with their future.

They went on and on, twenty-three pages in total, all depicting some element of Puerto Pesar that Tomas saw fit to capture. He hadn't won her over with words, so he'd tried to get her attention with his artwork, drawn from the most intimate places of his heart.

Tears began to fall from her eyes, distorting the pictures as they dropped.

She held them to her chest and rested her head on their jagged edges. The closest thing to holding Tomas himself, knowing how much of him went into them. They were more precious than diamonds.

A note accompanied it, and the familiarity of his handwriting made her stomach tighten in pain. Her hands shook as she lifted it to read.

Della, I don't know why you don't write back to me, but I trust that you have your reasons. Here are some scenes from home. I'll be waiting for you for the day when you can return. I'll be waiting for you even if that day never happens.
Love, your Tomas

"What is it, honey?" Hazel asked. But Della just crumpled the note, clutched it in her hand, and rolled over to face the wall. She cried into her pillow, letting the envelope of drawings fall to the floor.

She felt a terrible, suffocating darkness. She was angry with her mother for leaving, with her father for checking out, with her sister for dying. Eddie for raping her. They'd all failed her, and because of them, she'd failed Tomas.

She withdrew from everything, save for the few chores she was expected to do. She missed the Christmas play put on by some of the inmates, refused to pick up the guitar, and forced down food only for the sake of the baby.

Even Hazel left her alone in her misery as she moped around in the routine sameness of the day. The monotony was broken only once, on New Year's Eve, when Matron Heath summoned her to the front office.

CHAPTER FIFTEEN

Puerto Pesar—Today

Paloma laid strips of bacon on top of the meatloaf and slid it into the oven. Mercedes had always liked bacon, and she thought her sister might enjoy that for dinner. She would set the table with place mats and plan a nice meal for the three of them.

She'd given some thought as to what she might be able to do to help Mercedes. The main question was: What did her sister want? All Paloma knew was that Mercedes wanted to get out of Puerto Pesar. Understandable. That had been her goal at that age, too. But Paloma had known she was meant to be a doctor. Had Mercedes considered what she'd like to do when she grew up? Was California just a dream based on what she'd seen on television, or was there something specific that drew her to it?

If Paloma could find out the answers, she'd know how to help. How to give her guidance once she returned to New York. They could Skype and go over Mercedes's homework together. If she considered college a possibility, Paloma could show her how to apply, how to get scholarships.

Abuela walked in from her bedroom, jingling her car keys. She walked with some effort.

Paloma set down the glass. "Where are you going?"

"Oh, *mija*, I need to pick up my prescription."

"I'll do that for you."

"It's in Harlingen."

"I know."

Paloma sighed. It broke her heart that her grandmother didn't have someone in town to handle all her medical needs. She was happy to do it all for her now, but what would happen when she left in two and a half weeks? What about the other elderly people in town?

Maybe she could enlist Mercedes to start doing some of this. Incentivize her with that allowance she'd send from New York in exchange for stepping up the help around here.

But until then, she would handle whatever her grandmother needed.

"You're not going anywhere, Abuela. I'll drive up there and get it for you. Please just watch the meatloaf."

"You don't have to do that."

"Nonsense. I'll head out now. You go put your feet up."

"I'll go with you."

Paloma jumped at the sound of Mick's voice outside the screen door.

"What are you doing here?" she asked as she let him in.

She could see that he didn't have an immediate answer. Somehow that made her happy.

"Um, I didn't have your phone number. And I wanted to tell you that I went to see Della Lee this morning."

"You did! I can't wait to hear all about it."

"I heard you say you're driving to Harlingen. Want some company?"

145

She looked in his eyes. Cool and blue and earnest. It was tempting. Yesterday had been surprisingly enjoyable, from Mick coming to her rescue to laughing over tacos to listening to Abuela tell the story of *Santa Bonita*. His affable nature made her feel comfortable, safe. She'd been too busy to feel that way about anyone in a long time.

But she was also heading back to New York in a few weeks. She didn't want to start something that would have to stop.

"No, that's OK. I'm going to run some errands while I'm up there anyway. You might be bored."

Paloma avoided eye contact with him, not wanting to reveal anything that would show him that she would, indeed, like his company. She kissed her grandmother on the head and grabbed the keys from her hands. Mick opened the screen door and gestured for her to go through. *Nice touch.*

She looked back. "Doctor's orders. Go sit down and put your feet up. Watch some soaps. Can Mercedes receive calls at school in case you need anything?"

"Yes, *mija*. Don't worry about me."

"Friday is her last day, right?" Paloma asked.

"Wednesday. She just has finals, and then she's through."

That was good. They would have more time to visit then.

Mick laughed as they walked out. "I need a doctor like you. I like that kind of prescription."

He helped her lift the garage door. Abuela's cream-colored Oldsmobile, purchased used sometime before Mercedes was born, filled nearly every inch of the carport. She'd pulled in far to the right side to leave just enough room for the driver to slip in and out. Paloma put her hands on her hips.

"Well, this should be a good trick."

"Would you like any help?" Mick asked.

"Maybe. I'll roll down the window and holler if I have a blind spot."

Paloma's slender frame fit through, but just barely, and she wondered how Abuela possibly managed it. She shut the heavy door behind her and placed her hands on the smooth steering wheel. Ten o'clock and two o'clock. It was strange, now that she thought of it. She'd driven only a few times in the last ten years. There really wasn't a need to in New York, unless she got a rental to drive to the coast on a rare day off. She'd mastered the city's confusing subway system within days, differentiating the express lines and commuter lines and numbered lines and lettered lines.

Paloma leaned in to the headrest and sighed. It was hard to believe how different life was here.

"Everything OK?"

Her eyes shot open at the sound of Mick's voice.

"Yes. Sorry about that. Let me get this going."

She turned the key in the ignition, and it groaned. She tried again, pushing the key to its limit. Nothing.

"Looks like you might have a dead battery there. Or a problem with the alternator."

Paloma stepped out of the car. "I'm going to have to call someone."

Mick stepped forward. "Look, I really don't mind running some errands with you. We can take my car."

Abuela was probably watching from a window and rubbing those rosary beads. Praying for marriage and babies for her granddaughter. Well, given her grandmother's devotion, God probably owed her a couple of favors, and she'd called one in.

Paloma couldn't deny that the turn of events wasn't entirely unwelcome.

"That would be nice. Thank you."

He closed the garage door for her, and Paloma saw him wipe his forehead. Poor thing. He wasn't used to this heat. She'd at least grown up with it. But he didn't complain.

"Do you mind if we make a quick detour before heading out?" he asked as he slid into the driver's seat.

"No. What do you have in mind?"

"I want to go back to the church and take a few pictures of *Santa Bonita* before it's closed up for the day."

"That's fine by me, but do you think that's allowed?"

"Are you always such a rule follower?"

She smiled. "I might have been accused of that once or twice in my life."

"Well, here's Rule Number One of being a journalist. There are no rules."

"Looks like I picked the wrong profession. There's nothing *but* rules when you're a doctor."

"Then let your hair down, hold on tight, and get ready to live a little."

"Right. By taking unsanctioned photos in a prefab metal building outside a small-town church. *Whoa*. You really live on the wild side." She felt the smile that grew as she said it.

"Tell me something crazier to do in Puerto Pesar, and I'm there."

She thought for a moment before responding. "Nope. I think that's it. You've identified the single most daring activity in this town. Congratulations, Mr. Anders."

He tipped an imaginary cap. "Thank you. Thank you very much."

The drive to the church took five minutes, during which Paloma felt very alert to his every movement. It was strange—a good strange—to be together heading to see the portrait, which seemed to have piqued both their interests. They pulled right up to the grave-yard and followed the stone path back to the building that housed *Santa Bonita*. Their steps echoed in the hall, and she didn't see anyone else around.

They walked into the candlelit room, watching the flickers dance across the face of Eula Lee. The second impression was just as powerful as the first. Even as the room dwarfed it, the portrait commanded all attention. The perfection of its execution. The details, so real that it was as if she'd walk right out of it. The eyes. Those enchanting, luminous eyes that seemed to weep as they read your soul.

Mick and Paloma inched toward it, both transfixed, the spell broken only by them bumping into each other as they approached the kneelers.

"Oh, sorry," they said at the same time. They continued looking at each other as they stepped back.

Mick slipped his hand into his pocket and pulled out his phone. "Time for your close-up, Miss Lee," he whispered. He stepped close to the portrait, taking photos within inches of her dress, her eyes, her hair, her lace, the initials of T. B.

Paloma watched his attention to detail, enjoying the tiny glimpse into his professional life. She'd always found it sexy to watch a man work.

"I think I've got everything I need. Ready to hit the road?"

"To Harlingen we go."

They walked toward the door. Paloma turned around and looked into the eyes of little Eula Lee. She genuflected and crossed herself, just in case. She needed all the help she could get. Abuela. Mercedes. Life.

As they walked back to the car, Paloma glanced up. The sky was gray with dark, impenetrable clouds. They hovered, teasing, in a windless air.

It gave her an idea. She grinned just at the thought of it.

"Mick," she said, using his name for the first time. It wasn't unpleasant.

"Yeah?"

"I'm not always a rule follower."

"And what does that mean?" He raised his eyebrows.

"I'll let you in on a secret. The only skeleton rattling around in my closet."

His eyes widened. "I don't know if I should be intrigued or frightened."

"Toss me your keys."

They jingled as he pulled them from his pocket and threw them in a curveball. She caught them left-handed.

"Impressive."

She hit the button on the remote twice, unlocking the door.

The first few minutes were uneventful as they drove out of the town, but she picked up speed as she hit the empty highway.

She could feel Mick looking at her. She pressed harder on the gas pedal. Her pulse started to race. This was what she missed about driving. The thrill she could find on the long stretch of a Texas highway. It was the one thing that was hers. She'd had this in mind ever since returning to Puerto Pesar, this little pastime that once occupied her as a teenager. The part of her that most identified with the restless spirit of Mercedes.

She pressed harder. She could see Mick out of the corner of her eye, gripping the handle of the passenger door as the speedometer sped past seventy. Seventy-five. Eighty. Eighty-five.

With her left hand, Paloma pushed the buttons for all four windows to go down. A fierce wind ripped through the car, swaying it slightly, cooling her face the way an ancient air conditioner could never do. This was where she used to clear her head, to pretend she lived anywhere but this tiny town. And yet it was the one thing that New York could never satisfy. Too many people to ever be truly alone.

The grass was always greener, right?

Mick spoke up, shouting above the air that crossed among the newly opened spaces. "You surprise me, Miss Vega!"

Paloma kept her eyes on the road and felt her lips vibrate as she spoke. "How is that?"

"You fret over taking a few innocent pictures of a thrift-store find hanging in a makeshift metal building, but you have no qualms going— what are we at now?" He leaned in to see the control panel. "Ninety-two miles an hour."

She pressed harder. Ninety-five. She'd made it to a hundred and ten once, when she'd talked Arturo into letting her borrow his then-new truck, promising to make a produce run for him in Harlingen. It had rattled until she thought the screws would fly off. She was tempted to do it now. Ninety-five felt like child's play, even in a small rental car, when there was only a straight road ahead of you. It could go for hours like that.

There was a saying that her dad had taught her. "The sun is ris', the sun is set. And here you is, in Texas yet." He'd learned that during a misspent spring break at South Padre Island, cut short when his father insisted he come home to white-bread Connecticut. But not before he'd fallen for her mother and gotten her pregnant. He'd atoned, though. Paid Paloma's tuition and had created as much of a father/daughter relationship as could be expected for two people who met as adults. She missed out on memories like having him teach her how to ride a bike. But he'd introduced her to baseball, albeit from the luxury of a corporate box. A cynic might say too little too late, but Paloma didn't think that way. She was glad to have him around at all.

A thought hit her like a punch to the stomach. Mercedes *didn't* have that. Paloma's father rescued her just when she needed it, and she hadn't looked back. But not Mercedes. There were no outs for her. Paloma felt more convinced than ever that she needed to use her success to compensate for what her sister's life lacked. It was just a matter of how.

Paloma didn't let the needle go past ninety-five. She supposed that there had to be some accommodation for growing up, even by a fifteen-mile-an-hour reduction of an all-time high. And she had a passenger.

Assured that there were no cars in front of her, she glanced quickly at Mick.

"Can't do this anywhere on the East Coast as far as I know," she said.

"Oh, there are a few places," he answered. "You just have to know where to look. I've been known to clear my head on the roads of upstate New York now and then."

Paloma smiled at the thought that they both found the open road calming. Or maybe it was a side effect of living in a large city. She was just about to ask about his visit with Della Lee—*What was it like to meet a murderer?*—when she heard the faint ring of her phone. She closed the windows, and the air quieted as if it had been vacuumed out.

"Could you get that, please?" she asked, pointing to her brown leather purse by his feet.

Mick picked it up and opened the zipper. The first thing he found was a paperback book. The kind where the hero has nearly lost his billowing white shirt as he embraces the enthralled heroine. He held it up.

"You are full of surprises, Miss Vega," he said, looking amused.

She snatched it from his hands, feeling her cheeks flush, and stuffed it in the pocket of the driver-side door. She might be busy in New York, but she wasn't dead.

The phone went silent. He reached back into the purse to pull it out.

"Looks like a Mason Brown. Boyfriend?" His eyebrows raised just a bit as he said this.

She rolled her eyes. "That's the management office for my apartment. Mason, Brown and Associates. My lease is up next month. I'm sure they want to see if I'm going to renew."

"Are you?"

She hesitated. Why did she hesitate?

"Probably. It's on the Upper West Side, and my new job is across the park, but if you move even a few blocks in New York, it's like a different world. New dry cleaner. New ramen restaurant. New Starbucks. And I like my baristas. They know I like one percent milk and take two sugars in my black coffee. I'd have to start all over again."

Mick nodded in a way that seemed as if he understood. "How are you handling being back in Puerto Pesar? Has it been easy to come back after being away?"

Paloma warmed at the question. Their conversations had been light up until this point, but she had the feeling this was not meant as a casual question. It was as if he really wanted to know about *her*.

"It's been good. Different. Like I don't quite know where I belong. One foot here, and the rest of my body there. I love being around Abuela again. But honestly, I'm having trouble getting through to my sister."

"How is that?"

Paloma sighed. "I don't even know where to start. This might sound crazy, but it's as if the Mercedes I knew—the kid on the bike and then the eighth grader with braces—has been abducted by aliens and this counterfeit version left in her place. I don't know her at all." She tapped her fingers on the steering wheel. "Although it's really my fault. I haven't been back as often as I should have. The poor kid . . . girl . . . young woman probably thinks I quit on her just like our mom did."

"I get it. My dad left before I could ever know him. What have you tried so far?"

"Just silly stuff now that I think about it. I sent her some pajamas from Saks a few months ago. I have yet to see her wear them. I've ordered books that I thought she'd like. I showed her an article about how listening to music as loud as she does can damage her eardrums. I bought her Popsicles from the market, which I know she used to love."

"Could she be feeling as if you're treating her like a little girl instead of the, what, seventeen-year-old she is?"

"Sixteen."

"Still."

"You're right. I've just slipped right back into the role of big sister. But she's not little anymore." Paloma had slowed down to a modest seventy-five miles an hour. "I've been so stupid."

"Not stupid. That isn't a word that suits you. Not by a mile. Maybe . . . maybe you've been growing up at the same time."

Paloma could see him turn and look at her. "What do you mean?" she asked, feeling that he was touching on something that she hadn't fully realized.

"Well, you only just finished your residency, I believe, and you're about to start your first *real* job as a doctor? Don't get me wrong—that's not to say that all your years at school weren't real work. I know how tough college was for me, and I'm not the one who tackled that plus medical school."

He had a point. "You're saying I'm really looking at this through adult eyes for the first time because school is behind me and my perspective is, what, more mature?"

"I didn't mean any offense by that."

"No, no. I didn't take it that way. And I think you might be right. I've been too preoccupied with my own growing up to notice hers."

Just saying it, she felt the release of a tension that had been gnawing at her. Like facing this truth was the first step toward making a *real* connection with Mercedes. Not a cursory one. Not one that sent gifts on holidays and checked that box as if it were enough.

"I don't mean to pile on, but maybe this helps. Like I said, my dad skipped out on us when I was a kid, but he always sent me birthday presents. Do you know what I got on my fourteenth birthday? A package of Hot Wheels. That would have been nice when I was *six*. And do you want to know what I would have really liked? Him. The gifts are useless if you aren't *there*."

Paloma didn't say anything. It hit really close to home. She'd done what her dad did. What her mom did. God, but she hadn't *meant* it that way. She desperately hoped it wasn't too late to make amends.

She slowed down to sixty-five and looked over at him. He'd seen right through her, through her problem, and put it into words that she hadn't been ready to vocalize. Something about him made her comfortable, and he'd drawn out the truth in her with just a few pointed insights. Maybe that was what made him a good reporter.

"Thank you, Mick. You are more right than you can imagine."

~

Mick really liked this girl.

Woman.

As Paloma continued down the highway, moderating her speed after their discussion, he glanced at her and found his breath halted by her beauty. Flawless skin. Hair like molasses. But that was only the outside.

She was smart—a doctor. Compassionate—spending this month taking care of her family. Fearless—well, half an hour on a Texas highway just convinced him of that.

And he couldn't help but like that she read romance novels. That was a side of her he'd like to know more about. Personally.

He turned his head toward the window and squeezed his eyes shut.

No, no, no. In and out of Puerto Pesar. Talk to locals. Take some notes. Try to eke out a story that will get you back to where you were.

A woman was not part of the plan. Not even one like Paloma Vega. But he felt that resolution slipping through his fingers.

Paloma announced that they'd arrived in Harlingen. Mick saw industrial buildings and more taco stands. Pawn shops and motels.

"Jackson Avenue," she said as she took a right. "I can't remember the last time I was here. Maybe when I was eighteen. We used to come up here every six months to go to the dentist."

Palm trees of varying heights lined the street, some towering high above the one- and two-story buildings. The shops were painted all shades of pastel colors, although they may have been faded versions of something originally more robust. They passed a movie theater, and then turned in to a parking lot.

"Where are we going?" asked Mick.

"Someplace special," she said, pointing across the street. "There it is."

Just beyond the main street was a small, redbrick storefront. At the top, the bricks were set in a diagonal pattern, and above the door, a green-and-white awning sagged. A painted sign hanging on the window read LONHILL DRUG.

Paloma led the way. When they got to the door, he reached out to open it, a habit he'd learned from his mother but had abandoned since living with Stephanie. His nerves tingled as he did so, waiting for the reprimand that might come. Paloma didn't need her door opened for her, but he wanted to do it anyway. She didn't say a word.

The smell of old wood and sugar wafted through the air. What was somewhat derelict on the outside could be called vintage on the inside, in the way that people paid big money to replicate. Four rows of shelves carried all basic toiletries and convenience items. Four stools with red leather seats were bolted into the floor in front of a stainless steel counter. Art-deco letters lined the ceiling, spelling out COSMETICS and TOBACCO. And in the corner, behind glass, was an extension to the building that held rows and rows of bottles. A white-haired man in a white coat with pockets stood behind the window, counting dime-size pills into a bottle.

Paloma approached him.

"Mr. Salazar?"

He didn't look up.

She rapped on the window.

"Mr. Salazar?" she said again, louder.

He turned toward her and cupped his hand around his ear.

"You calling me?" he asked.

"Yes, do you remember me, Mr. Salazar? I'm Paloma Vega." She was shouting by this time. "Mrs. Vega's granddaughter. I'm here for her prescription."

He leaned in closer to the glass and lifted a lever.

"Who are you again?"

"Paloma Vega." She drew out the name into long sounds. "My grandmother called ahead from Puerto Pesar."

"Ah!" he said, raising a finger into the air. "Mrs. Vega. Should have just said so in the first place. I have it right here."

His hands shook as he pulled out the blue basket marked *V*.

Mick leaned in toward Paloma. "Should he know you?" he asked quietly, inhaling her vanilla scent.

She shrugged. "Well, maybe not. We came here only after the dentist visits. So I guess not. But I remember him. It's only been eleven years, but he seems to have aged a century. I used to look forward to coming here. He'd play card tricks for anyone sitting at the counter."

Mr. Salazar returned with a receipt, and Paloma slid her credit card through a cubby. He shook his head and pointed to a sign: **Cash Only**.

She looked at Mick. "Who carries around cash anymore?"

He pulled his wallet from his back pocket and counted out enough bills.

"Former Boy Scout," he said.

"Always be prepared." They spoke at the same time, and she laughed.

God, she was beautiful when she laughed.

"Looks like I owe you now."

"Looks like you do." He grinned.

"Well, if I can presume to add to my tab, I have to tell you the milkshakes here are the best I've ever had. Care to try one?"

"And ruin my boyish figure?" he said as he patted his stomach. "How about splitting one?"

"Deal."

Twenty minutes later, Mr. Salazar placed a large scalloped glass in front of them. They'd forgotten to ask for two cups, but Paloma seemed unfazed as she handed him a straw and took one for herself. She offered him the first sip before he could do the same, insisting it was only fair for the guest to try first.

For a moment, he wished he were a food critic, because this might have been the most delicious shake of his life. Rich, thick . . . spicy?

"This is the secret." Paloma leaned in conspiratorially. "Vanilla ice cream—Blue Bell, the best—blended with shaved Mexican chocolate and a dash of red chili pepper."

"What is *Mexican* chocolate?"

"Toasted cocoa beans, sugar, ground almonds, and cinnamon."

"I know what you're doing." Mick smiled.

"What?"

"The sopapillas. The tacos. Now this. It's all part of a plan."

Paloma lowered her head and raised her eyes. "I have no idea what you're talking about."

"Well, a handsome stranger blows into town, and you wine and dine him with the best of South Texas, and a guy can start to believe that there might be an ulterior motive." Mick couldn't believe that he was flirting, like a fourteen-year-old boy. There was something about Paloma that made the last couple of decades disappear.

She rolled her eyes. *"Presumido."*

"Pre what?"

"*Presumido.* Conceited. You've got the big head. That's what my grandmother used to say to Abuelo when he got fresh with her."

And there was that laugh again.

Just a few days ago, Paloma had been wound up. Almost hostile. Now Mick saw those barriers fall away and a woman spring forth who made him feel as if he'd known her all his life.

Boston seemed farther and farther away.

Paloma, however, was closer and closer. Even though they drank from their own straws, they'd ceased taking turns with the glass, sipping at the same time. Mick felt his blood pulse as they leaned in toward each other, foreheads nearly touching, a pretense of sharing a drink that held something more meaningful than he thought possible so soon after meeting someone.

When they were finished, Paloma took her napkin and wiped his upper lip.

"Mustaches don't suit you. Promise me you'll never grow one."

"Yes, ma'am." He rubbed his hand around his chin and cheek. "But what about the scruff?"

"Keep the scruff. I like the scruff."

Score.

He took her hands just long enough to help her slide off the stool. They felt delicate and warm, and he wanted to hold them longer. But he didn't dare.

They walked down an aisle full of feminine products and stopped at an endcap full of egg cartons.

Paloma picked one up and looked at him. "May I add one last thing to the tab?"

"Eggs that should have been refrigerated?"

"*Cascarones.*"

"What are those?"

She grinned. "You'll see."

After paying, they walked to the car. Or rather, Mick walked and Paloma pranced. She held that silly carton behind her back and seemed to skip her way back to the parking lot.

"What mischief are you up to now?" he asked. "You already drove here like a madwoman and nearly had us killed. I'm not sure how much more I'm supposed to take from you?"

Her features sagged, and immediately, he felt bad for hurting her feelings. He stepped in toward her.

"You mean it?" she asked.

"Oh, Paloma, I was kidding. I—"

But he couldn't continue. Out of nowhere she'd cracked a bright-pink egg over his head, and a shower of round confetti fell from his hair, down his face, and landed all over his white shirt.

"What?" He brushed his hands down his chest. "What was that? You played me."

"Oh, I didn't make that clear enough?" She smiled, and he could see all her teeth.

Again, *crack*. Purple. Confetti rain. This was war.

"Apparently not," he said. Mick reached around her back, seeing that there were still ten brightly colored eggs, hollowed and filled, and he intended to grab the majority of them.

Ten . . . nine . . . eight . . . one by one, they pulverized the *cascarones* until the asphalt below them looked like a rainbow had exploded, and Paloma and Mick were covered in confetti until they almost couldn't be seen.

They reached for the last one at the same time, holding it in indefinite suspension. Everything slowed as Mick grabbed her arm to keep her from having this final victory. Or maybe he just wanted a reason to touch her. They froze, even as Mick's heart raced. Their eyes met, laughing eyes that suddenly turned somber. Paloma's lips were flushed, red. Her skin was warm, and he felt her pulse under his hand. The fourteen-year-old boy who had just resurfaced thought about kissing her. She might even let him. She might . . . He leaned in. She followed.

Kissing Paloma sent shocks of electricity throughout his body. He couldn't imagine pulling away from her now that she was in his arms, her lips on his, warm and perfect and earnest and better than he even imagined it; ever since he laid eyes on this woman, he'd wanted to do exactly this.

But he wasn't going to let that get in the way of a little competition.

Crack. He stole the last egg from her grip. This one was good. He shattered it to pieces so tiny that not only confetti, but eggshells decorated her hair, leaving shards of white intermixed with the colors.

"Consider your tab paid."

She shook what she could out of her hair, but it did almost no good.

"Oh, I don't think so, mister. The tab is covered and then some. This means war. You just won't know when it's coming."

"Well, if we don't live past today, then neither of us will have to worry about it. Why don't you give me the keys and I'll drive back?"

"As. You. Wish." She drew out the words like a certain Dread Pirate Roberts.

"And no *Princess Bride* references if there is going to be any chance of a friendship. My mother made me watch it with her at least once a week."

"Your dad must have hated that." Her hands flew to her mouth, and he watched her realize what she'd said.

"I didn't mean that," she said. "I'm sorry."

"Talk about a buzzkill," he said. And then he winked.

"Buzzkill? How old *are* you?" She slapped him across the arm.

Apparently the teenager had returned. She had a way of making that happen.

He slid into the driver's seat and turned up the air-conditioning. Paloma picked up her phone and turned down the vent while she checked her messages. Her eyes grew serious.

"What is it?" he whispered.

"Hold on." She held up one finger, and then pressed it to her ear. She hung her head and ran her fingers through her hair. She played it again, and Mick could faintly hear the shaky voice. It sounded like her grandmother.

"*Mija*? Have you seen Mercedes? Maria Guevara called her wanting to study with her, but I told her that Mercedes was already supposed to be with her. But Maria said they never had plans, and she didn't see her yesterday, and neither of us could reach her on her cell phone. Call me, *mija*. Call me if you know where she is."

Mick looked at Paloma, who seemed to understand exactly what he was going to say.

"Keys?"

"Thank you."

They raced back at a steady eighty-five.

CHAPTER SIXTEEN

Goree State Farm for Women—1943

Della was handed over to the guard named Roy, who gripped her by the elbow and led her through the set of double doors toward the administration offices. But he took a left down the hallway to a door that said VISITING ROOM. She bristled, wanting to tell him that he'd brought her to the wrong place, but she knew better than to be contrary.

Why had Matron Heath called her here?

The visiting room was one place at Goree that Della had never seen. Only Tomas ever tried to see her, but she refused each time. It tore her apart to know that he had been in the building. That he must have driven so many hours to see her. And she wanted to see him. To look again into those brown eyes that had once been her only salvation, that held hope and future and promise. But with the death of Eula, she could no longer return that gaze. She could promise him only loneliness and sorrow. For at least the next twenty years.

Roy opened a heavy door that screeched on its hinges.

"In here," he said.

He looked at her with the lecherous gaze that she'd recognized in that paddy wagon driver nearly nine months ago, and she shivered. She tried to move out of his grasp, but he held on tighter and put his lips against her ear.

"By the way," he whispered. "You just say the word anytime, and I'll come and visit you."

She shoved her shoulder forward, pulling away from him, and walked ahead into the room. One other inmate was there, a Negro woman with her hands buried in her face as she spoke to a younger girl across the bars.

The guard kicked a chair out from its place and told her to sit. She took the seat and scooted up against the table that stretched across from wall to wall as a barrier between freedom and incarceration. It was high, and the seat was low, coming just above her belly.

Della smoothed her hair back through shackled hands just as she saw Tomas walk toward her. She froze, conflicted. Her head spun with elation at seeing him after all this time—handsome, wonderful Tomas. The matron must have decided to play Cupid.

Either that, or she was just cruel.

Her eyes filled with tears, but she bit her lip to hold them back. It might give him hope that didn't exist. Her voice shook as she whispered his name, betraying her. "Tomas," she said softly.

He rushed to his seat and held out his hands to her. She found herself involuntarily reaching back.

"No touching," said the guard on his side, and Tomas pulled away his hands while leaning in.

"Della," he said gently.

And she burst into tears.

"Della," he said more ardently, standing up to hold her arms through metal bars before retracting them under the guard's careful eye. He sat down again.

"Sweet Della, darling, I miss you. I took another chance that you might finally see me and we could talk about this. I can't believe you said yes this time."

She looked into his eyes before glancing away.

He continued. "They gave us only half an hour, so let me jump right in. I know why you've been avoiding me. I *know* you. You think by being stubborn, I'll give up and go meet some other girl and have a happy life."

She breathed deeply as he spoke softly. "I'm right, aren't I? But that's not going to happen. There is nothing you can do to make me seek an annulment. I love you, and you love me, and I will wait just like I told you I would."

Still, she didn't look at him. She wanted to. She wanted to tell him that she loved him back. To accept his offer and know that he would always be hers. But she couldn't. Too much had happened that he didn't know about.

"All right, all right. We won't talk about that. Not yet. I'll change the subject. But please, Della, look at me."

She took a breath and raised her eyes to his. She felt lost in the tenderness that radiated from his face, and she ached to feel his hands on hers.

He smiled and relaxed. "There you go, my girl. My beautiful girl."

She couldn't help but laugh. "I think your eyesight is faulty."

He shook his head. "No, I'll have none of that. You are my beautiful Della no matter what happens."

Tomas always knew the exact right thing to say.

They paused, just looking at each other, until he spoke again. "What is it like here? Are you OK?"

She looked around this room, unfamiliar to her, and yet made of the same gray concrete as the hallways and the cells and the workrooms. How did one say how cold nights were with concrete walls and thin blankets? How hot the sun could burn in an open field? How bland the food, how lonely the heart, how desperate the ache? How did one say that here there could still be joys? The music, the love for a child not yet seen?

Well, he didn't know about the child. Maybe she could spare him that.

"I am well enough," she managed to say. "And you?"

"Lonely, miserable without you, aching for my bride." He smiled at her, and in the rays of his warmth, she couldn't help but do the same.

"But besides that, decent, I guess. The house is in good shape. I patched a roof leak after our last storm, painted all the rooms with a fresh coat, repaired some outlying fencing. But, my love, you should know." He hung his head. "I had to sell off another forty acres. I'm so sorry. But there was just no way to keep them."

Della's heart tightened at the thought of their beautiful land getting smaller and smaller, but she knew that Tomas wouldn't have sold unless it was necessary. Even if she did get paroled, there might not be anything left.

"I understand," she said. "I trust you."

He continued. "And there's one more thing you should know." He sighed. "Good news and bad news, I suppose. I'm going to join the army."

Goose bumps prickled all along her skin. The news should not have shocked her, given the hundreds of thousands of boys being drafted. But in her imagination, Tomas was somehow excluded from danger.

"How is there good news in that?" she asked.

"A buddy of mine at the recruiting office in Corpus has arranged for a stateside assignment for me. The cavalry units at Fort Bliss in El Paso are being replaced with armored divisions, but they need soldiers to care for the horses while their relocation and sale are being managed. With my experience on the ranch, he said I was a natural candidate."

"So you won't see war?" Hope beat in her heart.

"No, darling. I won't see war. And although it's farther away, it's still Texas, and I will be here every chance I can to see you."

"No," she found herself saying.

"No? What do you mean?"

She was ashamed of herself for letting her resolve weaken at the sight of his face and the news of his safe assignment.

"No, Tomas. Don't come see me." She folded her arms. "This was a mistake."

He pushed back his chair and stood up. "What do you mean? How can you say that?"

She raised her voice. "Why do you think I haven't answered your letters? Why do you think I begged for annulment papers? You have to forget about this, Tomas. I will be here for a very, very long time. That's not fair to you."

"Don't *do* that, Della." He shook his head and gripped the table. "Don't do that."

"Do what?"

"That whole martyr thing that you're so good at. I think you've done it long enough. First for your mother, then for your father, then for Eula. I'm not going to let you do that for us. We're in this *together*. We made a decision about Eula—*together*." He pressed his finger into the table. "Your sentence is being here. Mine is having to live without you next to me. It's *our* sentence, Della, twenty years, but they don't have to be difficult if we try to get through it with whatever scraps of time we can."

Her heart beat. He could be right.

No. It wasn't possible. She had a baby now, or was about to. And she could never expect him to accept that.

"This isn't a life, and you know that. This is not what you signed up for."

"I signed up for spending the rest of my life with the girl I love, whatever that looks like, and right now it looks like this."

Della wanted to believe it. She wanted to think that letters and sketches and brief, platonic visits were enough. And they might be for her. This existence was of her own creation, the die she'd cast the day Eula died, but Tomas did not ask for this. She had to do everything she could to break him of his promise.

She sighed and lowered her head. "Tomas, you are more than I deserve. But the time is almost up, and I will leave it at this." She looked back at him. "If you do not initiate the annulment papers, *I will*. And I'll do it soon. It takes a long time to get a decision from Rome."

"You don't have to do this," he said again, desperation in his voice. He leaned in as close as he could and spoke gently. "Didn't you already give up enough for your sister?"

Della finally looked at him. "There is never enough I could do for her. You know that."

Wasn't she already proving that?

He ran his fingers through his hair, and his face reddened. He took a big breath, as if about to yell, but clamped his jaw and continued in a gentle voice.

"Della, there are so many things about you that I love. From the first moment I saw you, the pulse ran from my fingers through the lead of my pencil and I couldn't stop drawing you. Your kindness, your hard work, and everything you've had to do on your own. But above all, your loyalty. To Eula especially. You have been mother and father to her, and I understand there is a bond there, a sense of obligation that is stronger than anything else. I even understand why you did what you did, and I've supported you through that. You have been more loyal to Eula than she deserved, and you've lost so much for it. But *you are not going to lose me.* Do you hear me? You are not going to lose me, and if you think I'm signing the annulment papers, then you don't know me at all. What is twenty years when we are so young? You will be thirty-nine when you are paroled, and I have no doubt of your parole, my angel. It seems like an eternity, but it's not. We can still have many years together. Decades together. I will come and visit you whenever it's allowed, and we will write, and we will make the time go fast."

Della heard his words as she kept her eyes on her hands. Loyalty? That was what he admired in her above all? It would break his heart to know that his fidelity hadn't been returned. Another man had defiled the vow that she and Tomas had made to each other, taken her husband's place in a dingy motel bed, given her a child that should belong to him. Yes. It would break his heart.

There was only one way to convince Tomas that their marriage was over.

Putting her hands on her rounded belly, Della stood up. The buttons on the jumpsuit strained as the baby stretched. She almost lurched forward from the pain but managed to be steady on her feet.

Tomas smiled as he saw her rise, until he took in the length of her. His eyes widened, and then every feature of his face sagged into a portrait of devastation. His hands flew to his face, and he choked out a sob that had his shoulders heaving. He stood up and slammed his chair back against the table.

At last he looked at her, and this time her eyes locked with his. Hers were resolute, hiding the tears that welled inside while his flowed freely.

"What is this?" he said at last. "What does this mean, Della?"

Della pursed her lips because she didn't trust herself to speak.

Tomas balled his hand into a fist and clutched his chest. With the other hand, he steadied himself on the table.

"Della!" he said again, softly. "Tell me. Tell me that this is not of your doing. One word. One word, my love, and I will believe you. You know I'll believe you. You would not do this. The Della I love is mine, and I am hers."

He looked at her, his eyes pleading, and her stomach heaved at the burden of holding his gaze with no expression. She would not lie to him and admit a sin that had not been hers, but she hoped her silence would say it for her instead. She held her breath, which burned every nerve in her body.

She clenched her jaw as it threatened to shake at the effort of holding back all she really wanted to say. *It isn't true, Tomas. I could never lie to you. Believe in me, not in what you see.*

"I'm going to go back now," she said, offering no explanation or apology. But her feet wouldn't move, at war with her head.

Tomas ran his hands through his hair and spoke in measured tones. "What else are you not telling me, Della? What about Eula? How did she *really* die? Can I trust what you told me about *that*?"

No! That had not been her intention. But of course he would have put those together. This breach of loyalty. Eula's death. She wanted to shake her head, to convince him of her honesty, at least on that front.

Instead, she turned to the guard, Roy, who watched the exchange with a sly grin on his face. "I'm ready to go now," she said, and she turned toward the door without a final glance at Tomas. The baby kicked her so hard that she doubled over, but it would not have taken much effort anyway.

She was thoroughly broken.

CHAPTER SEVENTEEN

Puerto Pesar—Today

Where could Mercedes have gone? Paloma's heart raced, an angry brew of fear and guilt.

She'd been in Puerto Pesar for ten days, and she admonished herself for doing such a poor job of relating to her sister. Was this her fault? And more important, was Mercedes safe?

Mick kept quiet as she drove home, something she noted and appreciated. Being with him only added to her guilt, and she didn't want to talk. She'd missed Abuela's call because she'd been kissing him.

That kiss.

In another circumstance, that kiss would have her up all night, reliving it, turning over its meaning in her mind. Wondering when it might happen again.

Shame on her for losing her focus.

She pulled up to Abuela's curb, pausing for only the requisite pleasantries.

"Thank you for going with me. I'm sorry about this."

"I can come with you."

"No, this is family stuff."

"I understand. Here." He ripped a page out of his notebook and wrote down his phone number. "I won't bother you. But please—"

He put his hand on her arm as she slid halfway out of the car. She liked the sincerity in his eyes. But she had too much going on to deal with that.

"Paloma," he said in a tone that was both firm and gentle. "Please call me if you need anything. *Anything.*"

"Thank you, Mick. I will. But you have your work to do. I have to deal with my family. Let's focus on those right now."

He pulled back. "I understand."

She gave him the keys and hurried up to the door.

Abuela was standing in the kitchen, finishing up a conversation on the telephone. Paloma set her purse on the counter and listened.

"Thank you. Yes. Yes. We'll be there. Ah—here is my oldest grand-daughter now. OK. Bye."

"Abuela, who was that? Was it Mercedes?"

"No, *mija*, but she's OK. She's safe."

Paloma felt like a balloon that was deflating. Safe. That much was good.

"Thank God. Where is she?"

Abuela rubbed her hands together. "She's in jail."

"What!"

"That was the sheriff. I don't know exactly what happened, but she and some boy were arrested about twenty-five miles west of here after robbing a convenience store."

If Paloma had stuck her finger in a socket, she could not be any more shocked. That was insane. Her sister might be sullen, but Paloma couldn't believe that she was a criminal.

"Did they say why?"

"No, *mija*. That's all I know."

"I'm going to get her." She grabbed her purse and took a step toward the door.

"I can go with you."

"No, Abuela. I think you should stay here. You've been out of the hospital for only a few days."

"But I don't want Mercedes to think that I didn't want to be there for her."

"I'll tell her, Abuela. Don't worry."

Her grandmother started to cry, and Paloma froze.

Growing up, Paloma might not have had a father or a mother, but Abuela made up for both of those. Her grandmother always had to be the tough one. Paloma learned that from her. Abuela never showed weakness. And Paloma had never seen her cry.

She stepped forward and wrapped her grandmother in her arms. Leaning down, she buried her head in Abuela's shoulder, as much for receiving comfort as for giving it.

Mercedes was the excuse, but in truth, Paloma sensed that they both needed a chance to be vulnerable. Even on phone calls from New York, Paloma never asked how Abuela was feeling. Always how she was *doing*.

What was she doing taking care of strangers in New York when she had family who needed her help here? Not just the physical help Abuela needed, but to *be* there. Emotionally. For her—and for Mercedes.

They pulled away from each other.

"Look at me." She stroked her grandmother's cheek. So wrinkled, so soft. "Abuela, I'm going to take care of this. Not just getting her out of there. I don't know how, but we're going to make everything better, OK? I know it's been hard on you having to raise Mercedes right on the heels of raising me. I'm going to help."

The older woman's eyes were red, but the corners of her mouth turned up slightly. "You're a blessing, my darling. I don't know what I'd do without you."

Paloma felt a pang in her heart.

"Well, you've had to do without me for too long. We're going to be OK. Got it?" She kissed her on the head.

Then she remembered that the car didn't start.

"Abuela, is she at the police station just outside of town?"

"Yes, the one by the highway junction."

About three miles. In brutal heat. She pulled Mick's phone number out of her pocket and thought about dialing it. Her fingers lingered over her keypad. No. She didn't want to bring him deep into her life, nor did she want to use him as a taxi service. She'd have to walk.

She drank a glass of water and headed out.

~

Paloma wished she'd changed into shorts before leaving for the police station. She leaned on the bench outside, wiped her forehead on her sleeve, and breathed in and out until her heartbeat no longer raced.

It wasn't just the heat. She was worried about her sister. Abuela had said Mercedes was safe. That was good. But it wasn't enough. She'd have a record now. That could hurt her future, which was so fragile to begin with. What had driven her to do something like this?

She'd failed her sister. Some part of Paloma was complicit in this.

The police station was really just an outpost of the sheriff's larger offices in Harlingen. With a lack of budget for salaried officers, volunteers ran it. Paloma had only driven past it before now. She'd never had a reason to enter.

The jail was comprised of two eight-by-eight rooms in the back and a small open area in front, where a lone deputy sat behind a desk. Country music came from a radio on a desk in the entrance. Mercedes sat in one of the rooms, head against the wall, looking up, and the boy sat in the other. Paloma could see him through the window to that room. He was the same one she'd seen speeding around the town square a couple of nights ago. A husky guy, probably a few years older than Mercedes.

The deputy opened the door to Mercedes's room and let Paloma in.

"Can you keep that open, please?" Paloma asked as she watched her sister sit so still. "She's not going to go anywhere." Mercedes looked so small in the room, and Paloma felt about the same size. An open door might at least feel less claustrophobic.

"I guess so."

"Do you have any water?"

He pointed to some mugs by the sink at the end of the short hallway.

Paloma picked up two of them, both with coffee stains, one with a dead ant that she rinsed out. She filled them up with warm water that came from the cold faucet and brought them into her sister's room.

Mercedes moved to the opposite end of the bench when Paloma walked in. Her eyeliner had smudged, either from heat or tears. Paloma set a mug close to her and took a seat nearest the door.

She took a breath before she started speaking, keeping her voice gentle. Her sister looked as if she would jump at the slightest noise.

"How are you doing?"

Mercedes turned toward the wall. Paloma scooted in just close enough to reach out and touch the ends of her hair. She remembered when Mercedes liked to play beauty parlor with her. They'd hold each other's strands up to the light and clip split ends with safety scissors, competing to see who had the most complex one.

"I've been worried about you," she began. "I want to help."

"How about start by going away?"

She'd expected something like that. But it still stung. "OK. Let's shelve that discussion for the time being and talk about what happened."

"Like you care."

"I care more than you can imagine."

"You have a nice way of showing it."

Paloma steadied her breath as she continued. She was sure her agitation came across, and she needed to keep that in check if there was going to be any progress. "I'll make you a deal. You tell me what happened so that I can get a lawyer or pay a fine or whatever it will take to get you back home. And *then* you can say whatever it is you want to say to me, and I will listen, and if you still want me to go away after that, I will. Tomorrow, if that makes you happy. But first things first."

Mercedes didn't move at first, and it struck Paloma that this was a real-life version of the Quiet Game that they'd played when her sister was little. *Abuela's taking a nap. Let's see who can be quiet for the longest.* Mercedes had been a champion, sitting on the sofa for as much as an hour while Paloma used the silence to do her homework. She'd even made award ribbons for Mercedes out of construction paper.

But miraculously, her sister turned. Paloma saw not only the smudged makeup but the tears that had caused it. She wanted to wrap Mercedes in her arms, but she held back.

"That's a girl," she said, instantly regretting it. She'd reverted right back to treating her like she was a kid.

"I'm not going to abandon you, Mercedes," she whispered. "I'm not going to leave this room until we get a chance to talk. It's overdue, and it's my fault, but I'm here to make that right."

Mercedes curled up her legs and hugged them. "I hate you."

Paloma felt as if she'd been slapped across her cheek, but she'd promised herself she was going to maintain her composure. She was well practiced. You couldn't panic in the ER. You couldn't lash out at a fragile teenager.

"Well, let's start there." She put her hands in her lap and squeezed them, which strangely gave her the strength to continue. "Look at you. You know what I haven't told you since I've been back? How much you've grown up. Two years, and it's like a whole new person in front of me."

Her sister still didn't say anything.

"I love you, Mercedes. I love you, and I should say that more." Paloma felt a floodgate open inside her. She had a decade of things that should be spoken. "Let's try this. What do you hate about me? I'm ready to hear it."

Paloma would have liked to get back to talking about the more immediate problem of her sister getting *arrested*, and she would have liked to have this conversation at home. But at least in the custody of this jail cell, she finally had her sister's undivided attention.

Mercedes took a breath and unleashed it. "I hate that you left and that you left me behind. I hate that you have a rich dad and I don't. I hate that you got out of here and forgot about us. I hate that you send us gifts from New York but that you don't actually know what we like. You bought me pink pajamas from Saks. I hate the color pink. And I sleep in a T-shirt. You would know that about me if you were here."

Paloma was guilty of all those things.

Mercedes wasn't finished. "I hate that you've come back now and swept in like some kind of savior, like we're helpless, like I can't—or don't—help Abuela."

Paloma felt as if she were on the long end of a shooting range. But these were more words than Mercedes had said in a row in a week and a half.

"You're right."

Her sister looked surprised.

"You're right, Mercedes. Yes, I left. I was nineteen and wanted to get out of here as badly as you do now. I never expected to be able to do so, but yes. I have a rich dad who came back into the picture and rescued me. I felt like, I don't know, Rapunzel? Remember my reading *Rapunzel* to you when you were little?"

Mercedes crossed her arms.

"And you were little when I left, Mercedes. You were six. How could I have taken you with me?" This was agonizing. But like ripping off a Band-Aid, she had to go through the pain if they were ever going to heal.

"Then maybe you shouldn't have gone in the first place."

"Would you leave here if someone suddenly offered to move you to New York and send you to college? Can you really tell me that you wouldn't have done the same thing?" She raised her voice a bit more than she wanted to, became more defensive than she'd planned.

"Then why didn't you come back very often?"

The truth hurt. No matter how much she wanted to defend her choices, she'd made some selfish decisions.

Paloma returned to speaking softly, swallowing the guilt that weighed her down. "I was wrong. So wrong, and I'm so sorry, and I'm not going to even try to say that it was OK. I'm not going to even try to justify it anymore. All I can do is to show you that I'm going to change."

Mercedes lightened her edge momentarily, seeming to let down her guard before putting it up again.

"Well, don't think that you can sweep back in now and make things better. I've grown up without you. I don't need you."

It felt like a slap to the other cheek. Paloma took a breath. She had to tread carefully.

"I know you don't need me. So let's not start from there. How about, I would like for you to be in my life, and I would like to be in yours? I will visit more often, and I'll bring you to New York. You would love New York."

Mercedes glanced up at her. She knew that would get her sister's attention. "I've always wondered what it would be like to visit you there."

"And I would love to have you. Truly." Paloma reached for her sister's hand, slowly, as if trying to touch a caged tiger. Mercedes didn't pull back. This was progress. Maybe they could broach the more pressing issue now.

Paloma continued. "In the meantime, do you want to tell me what happened?"

Mercedes's shoulders slumped. "Not really."

"I'm going to end up hearing your version or someone else's. And if I hear your version, I might be able to help you."

Mercedes sighed and relaxed her arms. "I didn't do anything."

Paloma looked her in the eye. "OK. I believe you. Go on."

"I was running away. I've wanted to for a long time. Justin—the guy in the other room—is someone I know from school. He told me that he was planning to get out of here and that he'd tell me when he was ready so I could go with him."

Oh, God. This was worse than she had expected. What if they had succeeded? The very thought made Paloma shudder.

"And what was the plan?"

"I don't know. All he said was that he had a job lined up somewhere in California."

"So what happened?" Paloma squeezed her hand. She never wanted to let go of her little sister again.

"I spent last night at his mom's house. She was out of town. Then we headed out this morning. But we didn't get very far."

"Yeah. Twenty-five miles or so."

"His truck was low on gas. So we pulled into a gas station, but his credit card was declined. He said he'd be right back. He went into the store, and I could see him through the windows shouting at the cashier. And then . . . And then . . ."

She didn't finish. She started crying.

"Mercedes, what happened?" Paloma scooted closer and took her other hand, relieved that Mercedes didn't pull it away. She would have wrapped her in a hug, but she didn't want to scare her sister away so soon.

"I saw him pull a gun on the cashier, and she opened the register and gave him some money. He ran out and shouted at me to start the car. I slid over behind the wheel. He jumped in, and he was still holding the gun. He never pointed it at me, but I didn't know if he was going to or not, so I just drove off when he told me to."

Paloma pinched her lips tight, terrified at the very thought of her sister being in that situation. She was ready to march over to the next room and wring the life out of that punk. There was a string of expletives ready to burst out, but she didn't want Mercedes to clam up. She was talking. That was good.

"I kept driving, looking for another gas station, but there wasn't one, and I pulled over because the truck stopped. Justin told me we had to keep going, but we didn't walk very long before we heard sirens. He kept running, but I just couldn't anymore. I sat down on the ground, and he kept going. They got to me first, and then they got him."

Mercedes must have been terrified. Paloma couldn't begin to imagine what that had been like.

She patted her sister's hands, and then slowly put her arms around her. Mercedes didn't flinch. "OK. OK. Good girl. We're going to figure this out."

"I didn't mean anything, Paloma." Mercedes sniffed, and Paloma pulled a tissue from her purse. "I didn't know he was going to do that. But they told me that I'm an 'accessory.' I didn't mean to drive off. I was just scared, and he had a gun, and I don't know what I was thinking."

Mercedes curled up and put her head in Paloma's lap, which Paloma thought was equal in magnitude to finding the City of Gold. She stroked Mercedes's hair, all the way to its tips, over and over. They used to do this before going to bed. Paloma would read to her—picture books at first, chapter books later. This was like having the little girl back again, just for a moment, before she had to acknowledge the big girl again.

"I'm scared," her sister whispered.

"I know. That must have been terrible. But it's going to be OK. I'm going to help you. We're going to do this together."

Mercedes wrapped her arms around Paloma's hips, and Paloma felt her shoulders shake beneath her. She was so thoroughly relieved that her sister was here. Safe. They could work out everything else.

"Paloma?" Mercedes sat up.

"Yes?"

She looked right in Paloma's eyes and wiped away her tears with her palm. "I don't hate you."

Paloma closed her eyes for a moment just to revel in that statement. "I know that. I know that, sweetheart."

"I think I've just been jealous of you. Really, really jealous. But I don't hate you."

She laughed. "Well, to tell you the truth, I hate myself a little bit."

"Don't."

She gave Mercedes a tight hug and didn't let go as she talked. The next thing would be difficult to say. "I'm going to go talk to the police officer now and see what our next steps are to bring you home soon. But they may be keeping you overnight."

Mercedes pulled back, looking frightened. "Do you really think they're not going to let me go? The guy who pulled a gun on me is in the next room."

"I don't know, honey. But don't worry. He's locked up, and you won't be alone. I'll go home and get some things that you'll need, and then I'll go sit in that chair all night no matter how uncomfortable it looks and how much that deputy probably snores, and I will do everything I can—*everything* I can to get you through this." It worked. The faintest smile started at the corners of Mercedes's mouth. Paloma kissed her on the forehead and closed the door behind her. She rested her head against it. There had been progress, but there was still a long way to go. Tomorrow she'd go to Brownsville to post bail—words she never thought she'd say.

CHAPTER EIGHTEEN

Puerto Pesar—Today

Paloma had told him to butt out.

Well, not really. But that was how Mick felt. She was right, though. She had a lot going on with her family, and he had no idea where his life was taking him.

Mick unlocked the door to his motel room and threw himself on the bed.

What a roller-coaster day. Visiting with Della Lee. Driving to Harlingen with Paloma. *Kissing* Paloma. That had been amazing. Highlight of the day. The week. The month. It was edged out of his thoughts only by his worry for her. And for her sister. What must Paloma be feeling right now? He wanted to call, and he even reached for his phone to see if he could find a way to get her number, but she'd seemed pretty firm on wanting him to go home. He was going to respect that.

Instead he pulled out his phone and scrolled through the pictures of *Santa Bonita*. Some were too dark, but enough had come out well enough to send to his friend Andy, who worked at the Smithsonian. He did restoration work on paintings, and although this was somewhat parallel to his field of expertise, maybe he could point Mick in the direction he needed to learn more about the painter. He hit Send, along with a brief note of explanation.

He brushed his teeth and went to bed, thinking about that kiss until he fell asleep.

~

The next morning, he checked his phone. A message from Andy. **Looks interesting, buddy. I'll look into it.** A text from Paloma. **Mercedes is OK. Just didn't want you to worry.** His fingers hovered over the numbers. They itched to call her.

He decided to head back toward the Lee homestead. Della Lee was the only story he had right now, and he had lots of questions.

Mick stopped by Norma's food truck, feeling like a local being here for the second time in a week. As he hoped, she had churros, which turned out to be fried dough, cut into long, rippled strips and sprinkled with cinnamon and sugar. He bought four, and he couldn't resist eating one along the way while it was still hot. Amazing. He didn't know how he'd lived before having churros.

He could get used to this. *Lengua. Carne guisada.* Sopapillas. Not that there weren't Mexican restaurants in Boston, but you had to give a border town like Puerto Pesar major props for being the real deal.

The food was still warm as he drove up to the Lee homestead. A snake slithered across the path as he walked up to the house. He stepped back, embarrassed at being enough of a city boy not to know what was poisonous and what wasn't.

He knocked on the front door and heard the radio playing again.

184

"Miss Lee?"

No answer.

"Miss Lee?" he tried again, getting worried.

When no one responded, he walked around the property and peeked in the windows. No sign of her. He tried the back, moving more quickly, and saw the door to a shed left open. Looking out for more snakes but not seeing any, he headed over there and heard a small rustle.

"Miss Lee?"

"Oh!"

And there she was, wearing her sleeves rolled up to her shoulders and a bandanna holding back her wispy white hair.

"You startled me, young man. Is that you, Mr. Anders?" She adjusted her glasses.

"It is. I brought you some churros."

Her eyes lit up as if it were the nicest thing anyone had ever done for her. "Aren't you a dear? Let's bring them up to the house and eat them while they're still warm."

She stepped out to close the door and wiped her hands on her housecoat. He noticed how red her face was.

"Miss Lee, it's too hot for you to be out here." She nodded, so he took her arm to help her as they walked back.

The house wasn't much cooler, but he had her sit down, and he moved a table fan next to her and put it on low.

"How about some water?" he asked.

"Thank you. I should have brought some with me."

He found a glass in the cupboard and turned on the tap. "You shouldn't have been out in the first place. What were you doing?"

"Looking for that other portrait. I thought it might be out there. And maybe it is, but I didn't find it yet."

He handed her the water, which she drank almost all at once.

"That hit the spot."

"Want another one?"

"No, no. That was enough. Maybe after the churros."

Mick pulled them out and handed them to her. In his years in this business, he'd tried to pick up on the things that would help someone be motivated to give him details about the article he was writing. He'd learned to read people and anticipate what they wanted. He realized as he was helping Della Lee that it was different with her.

"Oh my, they taste just like they did when I was younger. Where did you find them?"

"At a little taco stand that someone told me about. Norma's."

Her eyes widened. "I wonder if that's the same one. Well, no, it couldn't be. It must be her granddaughter. Or her great-granddaughter. Gosh, I can't believe how old I am."

It would be polite to interject something about her not being too old, but he hesitated.

She sat up straight. "Well, let's not waste time, as I may not have much left on my lease here on earth. So go ahead and pull out that notebook of yours, and we'll get started on what you're here for."

He found himself almost disappointed with her abrupt readiness to get back to business. He was enjoying his visit. Still, he did as she suggested.

"Did you come with a list of questions, or do you want me to do the talking?"

"Um, let's start with you doing the talking." The good stuff always came out when you let the other person lead the conversation.

"I like that. So, Mr. Anders, would it surprise you to learn that I gave birth to a baby while I was in prison?"

～

Walker County, Texas, prepared a basket annually for the first baby born in the New Year. Large and white, it brimmed with cloth diapers, leather shoes, a rattle, a teddy bear, and handmade blankets crocheted and quilted by old, local women who took any opportunity to work their needles and their gossip.

Cristina Lee took a robust breath and wailed a hearty cry just five hours into the morning. But no such celebrations were to be hers, and Walker County officials eventually presented the gifts to a boy over in New Waverly, born four hours later.

Della's long brown hair was matted against her face, and her breath was faint from exhaustion. The Texas prison system didn't make room in the budget for the kinds of pain-reducing medications that were available, and the baby had made her entrance, all nine pounds of her, unaided. They'd taken her away to be cleaned and examined before Della got to see her.

Gertie was her first and only visitor. She walked into the room with a pen and a folder full of papers and pulled up a chair next to Della's bed.

"Well, well," she said. "I hear you've had quite a time of it. Seventeen hours in here. How are you feeling?"

Della forced words through cracked lips. "Like a bomb went off in my body."

Gertie patted her arm. "I can only imagine. I don't have any of my own, but I've heard the first one is the hardest. Maybe in the future—" She cut herself off.

They both knew there wouldn't be any future babies for Della.

"Well," she continued. "It's not every day we have a baby born here, but we do have our procedures, so I thought I'd go over them with you."

Della's body hurt as if a rock had been hurled at her abdomen. She placed her hands on her swollen belly, now limp and wrinkled. But already she missed her daughter, who was being examined by the doctor. That tiny, slippery, perfect little girl she'd held for one love-at-first-sight moment before they took her from her arms. The world was different in a matter of minutes. She tried hard to concentrate on Gertie's words.

"So. Do you have any family to send the baby to?"

Della shook her head. It shouldn't have been like this. Her mama and Eula should have been at her side, holding her hands as she pushed. Herman and Tomas should have been in the hallway pacing, waiting for word. The child would cry. They would run in. Everyone would marvel at the beauty of this child already loved so deeply by each of them.

No. She did not have any family to send the baby to.

"Well, then. Have you thought of sending her into the foster system, or did you want to keep her here?"

Give her up? It had never crossed her mind. "No. Under no circumstances. She will stay with me."

"Attagirl. As I told you last month, if you want to keep her here, she can be with you for up to six years. We'll move you to a smaller wing. We have two other inmates there, Mouse and Ruth. You may have met them. Ruth is about to be paroled, though, so she and her son will be leaving soon."

Ruth sounded vaguely familiar. Maybe from working in the orchard. Quiet type. She knew Mouse from laundry shifts. Always smelled of cigarettes.

"As soon as little Cristina learns to take a bottle, you'll start rotating shifts with them, one person always staying behind with the children."

Della nodded. She wondered if she'd be allowed to stay in the string band. She was about to ask when Gertie pressed on.

"But you'll have a few weeks to recover, too." She ran her finger down her notebook. "Let's see. That's about it. Do you have any questions?"

"No. Thank you." She wished she could get out more words than that, but she was exhausted after the delivery.

"You rest up. I'll come visit you later. And the nurse will bring in Cristina when she's ready to eat."

Della curled onto her side but couldn't sleep.

Whatever it took, she was going to give this baby the best start possible. She was going to do everything her own mother didn't, even behind these walls. She was going to give her the love that Eula never got from Eva.

The love Della tried to give to Eula.

~

Mick's pen slipped from his fingers onto his lap, and he realized that he hadn't written down one thing after she'd begun speaking. How horrible it must have been. No family around, no family to send her to.

"Miss Lee," he started. "You've just about left me speechless. I—I had no idea that you'd had a child in prison. That didn't come up in any of my research."

"You know, I'd like it much better if you called me Della. You would be doing me such a favor to let me hear myself being called by my own name in my own home again."

It never would have occurred to him that such a small thing could be a luxury. He also marveled at the fact that she steered the conversation better than a race-car driver on a beginner's track. He'd better watch out. Stick her in Boston and she'd give him a run for his money.

"Della," he said, holding back a smile. He wanted to ask, *Who was the father?* but quickly did the math and figured that she must have gotten pregnant right around the time of her wedding. Besides, he knew that Miss Lee didn't like the obvious questions. The ones that could have short answers. She was right. That never told you what needed to be said. "Della," he repeated. "What was it like to raise a child in prison?"

"You're learning, Mick," she said with approval. "And the answer is the same as it would be for any mother anywhere. You do whatever it takes to protect her."

~

Della hadn't expected to be able to love again.

Cristina changed all that. That moment of euphoria when she was born had never ended, only grown. And all she wanted at the end of any day was to run back to the nursery and be with her daughter.

At six months old, Cristina could throw a ball, pull herself up on the bed, and was already cutting her first tooth. She delighted in the company of Ruth's son, Charlie, and Mouse's daughter, Bess. Charlie liked her enough, but Bess seemed to resent, even at the age of three, the newest addition.

But Ruth had just gotten paroled.

Della's daylong shifts in the prison orchard had begun again now that Cristina could eat watered-down oatmeal and applesauce. It was only June, but the heat, even in the shade, felt like a thick cloud that wrung all life out of you. Sweat poured from her skin as she climbed up and down a ladder to pick apples.

On this particular day, the showers were occupied when she came in from working outside, but she couldn't wait a minute longer than necessary to see her daughter. The highlight of her day was the moment when she took the tiny girl in her arms and nuzzled into her neck. Cristina still exuded the intoxicating smell of newness and innocence. Della would close her eyes and inhale it, and everything else was forgotten in that moment except how much she loved her child.

She stepped up to the nursery door and peeked through its long rectangular window. It was Mouse's turn to watch the children, but it wasn't the first time that Della couldn't find her. Cristina sat on the floor, waving her arms up and down and bouncing with excitement over something beyond what Della could see. She pressed her head against the glass and just barely saw Bess pushing a red metal fire engine around the floor in circles. Cristina stretched and stretched until she was nearly on all fours, rocking back and forth, trying to touch the shiny toy. Bess snatched it up and hugged it against herself. Then she headed over to Cristina and whacked the toy against her shoulder.

"No!" Della yelled and pushed her way through the heavy door into the room.

Cristina was wailing as Bess raised her arm to hurl it at the younger child.

Della ran to her daughter and pulled her into her arms.

"There, there," she said, placing the girl's head against her shoulder, while her eyes darted around the room to find Mouse.

She was on the far side of it, in a rocking chair, facing the wall while flipping through the pages of a magazine.

"Mouse!" she yelled. "Bess just hit Cristina and was about to do it again."

Mouse turned another page. "Children will be children. It's not the first time your daughter has tried to take a toy away from mine. Maybe it will teach her a lesson."

"This is the second time it's happened. Last time she bruised badly. I didn't say anything because accidents happen, but this is starting to look like a pattern."

At this, the woman turned to face Della. Her eyes were small and pinched. "You're not going to squeal."

Mouse had a talent for making statements that sounded more like threats. The last thing Ruth had told her was to watch out for Mouse. But she hadn't elaborated.

"Why would you say that? I can't let this go on."

Mouse stood and walked right up to Della, looking down at her.

"You used to have a bed next to that Hazel woman, right?"

"What does that have to do with this?"

"I saw her doing something that would put her in solitary, and I don't think you'd like to see that happen. You being friends and all."

"I don't believe you. Hazel wouldn't do anything that could put her in there. She's not the violent sort."

Della smelled the rancid odor of the woman's long-rotten teeth as she leaned in closer. "I didn't say she was doing anything violent.

Nothing so hateful. In fact, not hateful at all. Quite the opposite. If you call being naked in the laundry closet with Cocaine Maggie love."

An image appeared in Della's mind, forced out just as quickly.

"I always thought you were crazy, Mouse, and now I'm sure of it."

"You're so ignorant. You mean Hazel, that old bulldagger, she never laid a finger on you?"

"No. Not at all. In fact, she's the one who told me to be careful around Cocaine Maggie."

Mouse snorted. "Well, think about it, then. Doesn't that tell you all you need to know? Maybe she warned you so that you'd keep away from her little secret."

"Hazel's not like that. Hazel's always been good to me."

"Maybe there's something in that, too. Maybe she's buttering you up in case Cocaine Maggie ever gets paroled."

Della opened her mouth to protest but didn't know enough about these things to counter her. "If that's even true, I'm sure Hazel has her reasons."

"Sure she does. There's no love in this place. No husbands. Rarely a visitor. People got to take it where they can get it. We're the lucky few, if you can call it that, who have children to come 'home' to after slaving on the farm or in the animal houses. And even that will be gone before any one of us is paroled. Where you gonna find your love, Della, when your baby girl is gone? Only five and a half years. Sounds like a long time. But it will be gone. Like that."

She snapped her fingers in front of Della's face, and Della blinked.

"Gotcha, didn't I? That's right. So here's the deal. You're not going to say anything about my daughter, and you're not going to do anything that robs me of one minute with her. Or the break that I get working in the nursery instead of outside. But you say one word about my Bess, and you can kiss those five and a half years with your precious Cristina good-bye. And you can promise that I'll tell the warden what I saw between Hazel and Cocaine Maggie, and your friend can rot away in solitary for all I care."

She grabbed Bess's hand and led her to their common room.

Della didn't know why Mouse thought she had the power to do any of that, but she was just the sort to have figured out how to gather dirt on someone and how to use it to her advantage.

Della held Cristina tight against her, soothing the little gasps that wound down at the end of a good cry. She picked up the offending toy fire engine and held it up to eye level. She could see a distorted version of her face and could tell that the tears she was holding back were gathering under her eyes.

She had to be careful around Mouse.

Nothing could happen to Cristina. She was all Della had left to live for.

CHAPTER NINETEEN

Puerto Pesar—Today

"You are my hero, Arturo," said Paloma. He'd gotten up early to bring jumper cables to Abuela's house and get her car started. One more walk to and from the police station was enough to have her ready to don feathers and try to fly.

"Oh, you're gonna make me blush with that kind of talk." He slammed the hood shut after Paloma turned on the ignition.

"I can't thank you enough. Three miles to and from the police station yesterday evening just about killed me. I'm not used to this heat."

"You crazy New York girl. You shoulda called me."

"Maybe so. I don't know where my head was."

But she did. On the way there, she'd been so worried about Mercedes that she couldn't focus on anything else. After leaving, she'd walked back to Abuela's house and found herself thinking about Mick. Their drive to Harlingen.

That kiss.

She regretted how she'd left things with him. Engulfed with guilt over Mercedes's arrest, she'd had to compartmentalize things the only way she knew how. And she just couldn't take him into consideration at the moment. It was like triage in the ER. Which crisis was bleeding the worst? Her sister took precedence over any man.

But she needed to call him as soon as she had a chance. She owed him an apology, something she seemed to be getting good at lately.

"You want me to drive to Brownsville with you?" Arturo asked, cutting into her thoughts.

"No. No, thank you. I don't know how long it will take to talk to the court-assigned attorney. And I can't take you away from the restaurant."

"Well, you just let me know how it goes, then. My Corrina and I said our prayers for Mercedes last night." He laid his hand on hers. "She's gonna be OK, you hear me?"

Paloma took a deep breath and nodded. It was so comforting to have a friend who cared like this. "Thank you for that."

Arturo was right. When Paloma arrived in Brownsville, the attorney had already negotiated Mercedes's bond. First time, juvenile offender, just the driver, not the perp, no one hurt, money recovered. And her claim that the guy had scared her into driving away would likely hold up. He had a record that contained breaking and entering, a DWI, and marijuana possession. She had none.

Paloma's blood raced at hearing this, and she shuddered to think of what would have happened to Mercedes if she'd made it any further with this delinquent. It hurt her head just to imagine all the scenarios.

She thanked the attorney for his work, relieved by his extra assurances that he thought there was a good chance of getting her case dismissed before it would even need to come to court. For the time being, she could go home, and she was scheduled for a court appearance in four weeks.

Four weeks. Paloma would be comfortably installed in her new position at Lenox Hill Hospital. But her heart wouldn't be in it. Her heart would be here. In Brownsville, sitting behind Mercedes. That wasn't enough, though, was it? To phone in her support and turn around to stitch up the eyebrow of some drunk who got hit during a brawl.

There was something seriously wrong with that picture.

Armed with a checkbook and money in her account earmarked for rent, she drove back to Puerto Pesar to pay the bond at the police station.

The smile on Mercedes's face was worth every penny.

Paloma had brought her some tacos from Norma's and her iPod. Mercedes turned on the music as soon as they were in the car.

"What are you listening to?" asked Paloma.

Mercedes put her feet on the dashboard and took an impossibly large bite out of the taco. "Polly Tate. Have you heard of her?"

"She sounds vaguely familiar."

"Want to listen?"

Paloma concealed the elation she felt at getting even this far into a conversation with her sister. Mercedes put it on speaker. Paloma braced herself for something loud and heavy, but instead, a rather folky, acoustic song came through, sung by a woman with a most unusual, earthy voice.

"I like it. It's different from what I thought you usually listen to."

"I listen to a lot of things. I like her because she writes her own songs, and they're not always about love."

"Well, you can share your favorites with me anytime."

Mercedes smiled. "I've never told anyone this, but I'd like to work in the music industry. It's why I want to go to California. It seems like everything happens there."

Paloma enjoyed hearing Mercedes open up, but she stayed cool. She didn't want to scare her off.

"But not in a band," she continued. "Everyone wants to be in a band. I want to manage them. Like, find the right venues, help them become famous."

"I didn't know that, Mercedes."

She waited for the snarky "You don't know anything about me" comment, but it never came. She pressed her luck.

"You know, it is possible to work your way up. But if you go to college, you'd probably make some really good connections in that field. Have you considered it?"

Mercedes shrugged. "Not really. It's expensive. And why would any college want me?"

"There're plenty of reasons for them to want you. For one, look at how focused you are in your goal. They like that kind of thing. You're motivated. Look at how you went to work driving Miss Lee. And as for the money, I can help you apply for scholarships. Plus," she added, "I want to contribute, too." She'd done her budget based on her new salary and calculated that she could kick in about $500 a month. It was a start, especially if Mercedes went to school in state.

That got her thinking. "Why don't you look at the website for UT in Austin? It would be much less expensive, and Austin is the live music capital of the country. That's better than going to California."

She heard her sister inhale. She could see the possibilities race through her head.

"Or consider this. You could come live with me in New York and get in-state tuition there. I only have a studio, but if you don't mind my bad habit of leaving wet towels on the bathroom floor, it might work."

Mercedes's face brightened.

"Can you just imagine it, though?" Paloma continued. "You could intern at different venues and work with bands. Maybe you could even own your own agency someday. Either place. Austin. New York. Anywhere you want. I'll help out no matter what you decide."

Mercedes put her head on Paloma's shoulder. Well, here was the miracle for today. Paloma reveled in this and found that she was getting as much out of the conversation as she hoped Mercedes was. She stroked the girl's hair with her free hand.

"Paloma?"

"Yes?"

"I'm glad you're back. I mean, I know you're going to New York again next week. But I'm glad you're back right now."

Paloma felt something she'd never felt before. Homesickness. Anticipating her return to the East Coast at the end of the month, she already missed Puerto Pesar. That in itself was a revelation.

~

Della sent Mick home with some brownies and a promise that he could come back the next morning. She liked that young man. He needed a little smoothing out, of course. He seemed anxious to fall into what were probably long-practiced bad habits. Quick questions, quick answers. But she was pretty sure she'd broken him of that. He was already catching himself. Slowing down. It was nice to have someone to talk to, and she didn't mind drawing it out.

He was the right one to give her story to. But there were two things she wasn't going to tell him. Two things that would be her secrets for as long as she wanted them to be.

First, she would not tell him about Eddie the driver. Her child would have been considered a bastard and Tomas a cuckold, despite the circumstances. Maybe those words were considered old-fashioned to a young person of today, but even if it didn't matter to the world as it was now, it mattered to her. Cristina belonged to Tomas. Tomas to Cristina. Della to both of them.

Second, what happened at the rodeo belonged only to her. It was filled with pain—the memory of what Della's stubbornness drove Tomas to do. And tenderness.

Some things were never meant to be told outside of the people they happened to.

CHAPTER TWENTY

Goree State Farm for Women—1944

The prison rodeo was the highlight of every fall for the inmates of Goree and Huntsville. Between the preparations for it and the actual events on Sundays in October, it brought a sense of energy and excitement that the inmates of Goree didn't know the rest of the year. It was only two weeks away.

Della was assigned two roles: catching greased pigs and playing with the band. This would be the last year that the Goree Girls would be participating, as their spot on the radio had been recently revoked. Interest waned since Reable Childs was paroled, and a territorialism had spread among the women in her absence that leached an irreparable poison into the group.

With all that turmoil, never was Della more thankful to be staying in the nursery. She lived for the few hours of Cristina's company when she wasn't laboring outside or trying to sleep.

Not that it was peaceful. With each day that passed, Bess became more like her mother, picking on Cristina by pulling her hair and taking her toys. Cristina seemed unaffected, but tensions between Della and Mouse were growing.

But today Della's turn in the laundry had been light, and she looked forward to spending a rare afternoon with her daughter. With supervision, they might be able to go out into the yard and enjoy the tentative cool that had begun to descend on the Huntsville area.

The door handle to the nursery shook, and the guard Roy stepped in. He reattached the large ring of keys to his belt.

"You," he said, pointing to Della. "I'm here to escort you to the other wing. The Goree Girls are practicing."

"But that's not until tomorrow." Della looked longingly at Cristina, who had just fallen asleep in her arms after a long session of nursing. Mouse was after her to stop "such foolishness" now that the girl was nine months old, but mother and daughter both loved those tender moments. A drop of milk lingered on Cristina's lip, and a twitchy smile spread across her angelic face. Della hoped that was a sign that she was dreaming happy dreams. She held the child close to her and relished her warmth.

"It's impromptu. The warden wants them to work on their rodeo set. Lots of people are expected, especially on account of there being no rodeo last year."

Della sighed. She didn't want to go, and yet the rehearsals would be over soon enough and music would no longer be a part of her life. She didn't know if she'd even be able to keep a guitar if there wasn't an official purpose for it anymore. And Cristina delighted in her songs as much as she enjoyed playing them.

"Let me put her down first."

"They want you now. Mouse, go take the baby."

Mouse looked put out, but she didn't argue. Della glanced back at Roy as Mouse leaned over the crib. His eyes were glued to her shapely behind in her undersize prison jumper. When Mouse arose, she smiled coyly at him, and Della saw a look pass between them that suggested a familiarity beyond guard and inmate.

She was not going to win here. She rose to her feet and followed Roy out the door.

"Della, my dear!" shouted Hazel as Roy led her into the community room where they were practicing.

For a few weeks after Mouse first offered her salacious rumors about Hazel and Cocaine Maggie, Della kept her distance from her friend. But she decided that whether or not it was true, Hazel had never given her a reason to doubt her intentions.

"Hazel!" she responded as she was swept up into a big hug.

"How is that dear girl of yours? Oooh, every time I see her in the play yard while I'm a-workin', I just want to scoop her up and *pinch* those chubby cheeks. You must love every minute of it."

Hazel had been a mother. She understood the particular ache that a woman felt inside each time she was away from her child. Mouse routinely reminded her of the countdown until Cristina would be forced to leave and be adopted elsewhere. Five years and eleven months. Five years and seven months. Five years and two months now. It seemed like such a long time, but that December day long into the future hovered over Della's heart like an ever-growing weight that would suffocate her the day it arrived.

Altogether, the losses of Eula, her parents, and Tomas wouldn't be able to touch it.

Banjo and guitar strings began to be plucked, and tuning commenced.

Hazel leaned in and whispered to Della. "Rough waters today—watch yourself. I guess everyone wants to go out with a bang."

Della laughed. "That's a specialty of Rose's, isn't it? She's in for dealing in explosives?"

"Funny girl! I always wondered if there was a sense of humor in there somewhere." She tapped a finger against Della's heart. "Look what becoming a mother is bringing out in you. I like it. Keep it up."

Della basked in Hazel's praise. She was right. These past nine months had been different. Brighter. Happier. It didn't matter that her hands were rough from hoeing carrots in hundred-degree weather if she came home to the smooth skin and cool feel of her child. It didn't matter if calluses developed on her fingers as she played the metal strings of her guitar if she came back to play a lullaby for Cristina.

Rose called out to them. "Hazel McKay, you have no business being in rehearsal unless you're going to help wipe down the cases. And, Della, we've put you on lead for 'If I'll Never Have You,' since Bitzie has laryngitis."

"I don't think that's a good idea. I'm not a vocalist." That would have been Eula's domain. Della shuddered.

"You in or out, Della? There're plenty of girls who would like the chance to come inside and practice with us. You may have paid your dues in the last few months, but you're still the newest, and you're easily replaceable."

That struck Della in the gut. She didn't want to give this up. Outside Cristina, it was the only thing she looked forward to.

It took a half hour of tuning before the women were satisfied that they could start a song. Della could now play without looking at her hands, so she glanced up at all the bickering that was going on. No wonder the Goree Girls were coming to an end. The original ones had a goal—early parole. Best behavior, all the way around. And they'd succeeded. No one was left from the old days. Now it had attracted some of the girls who were in for more serious offenses, and even a masterful performance wouldn't buy one day off their sentences.

The intro for "If I'll Never Have You" began as strums of the refrain before launching into a song about a woman lamenting the love her sweetheart had for someone else. This was a new one in their lineup.

Della had already learned the tune, but not the lyrics. She read over the sheet as they began.

It made her veins turn cold.

> Darling, I watch you from afar
> Every kiss you place on her red lips
> Sends a knife right through to my heart
> Knowing, seeing, my love for you eclipsed
> By one whom I adore.

They reminded her of Eula. The envious looks had begun the day her sister found Della and Tomas kissing in the homestead. And every time he came to the house to bring her the wildflowers he'd picked. And when he called on her early on Sunday mornings to walk to the first Mass together.

As Tomas had become hers, Eula had ceased being so. The mother and daughter relationship dimmed with each passing day. Eula threw herself into the music. Adored the adulation that came as word of her anointed talent spread among the county and made the late-morning Mass brim with people coming to hear her. The more her voice and following grew, the more a malaise began to spread in her. As if they stole a piece of her with every performance, draining her of all she'd been.

First she was distraught.

"There, there, now," Della would say, stroking her sister's beautiful hair when she came home exhausted after Mass. The girl was inconsolable, though, and had no words that gave Della even a hint as to what might be the source of the tears. There was no rhyme or reason to her moods.

Then the rages.

A game of cards. "You cheat!" she'd accuse.

Preparing the meal. "Pepper! You know I hate pepper. Are you trying to kill me?"

Finding Della putting the newest bunch of Tomas's wildflowers in a vase. "Go to hell!" she'd shout before throwing it across the room.

Della flinched. Not from the sound of ceramic hitting the wooden walls and shattering. It was the expression of damnation, of the hope for it. The worst curse that could be wished on a person.

But it was easy to believe that her sister meant it. Eula's eyes were full of fire, and the softness that had once been there was almost completely extinguished. Except on Sundays, when Eula would leave for church as Della was arriving home from the earlier service. If Della saw her first, she'd hide behind a tree and let her pass. She never knew which Eula she would get—the beautiful girl whom everyone already hailed as *Santa Bonita* or the volatile one.

Tomas raised his concerns in increasing measure. Eula was unstable. Eula needed help. Della refused to believe it, but in time, she couldn't disagree with him. They learned of a doctor in Houston who was making strides with people as erratic as her sister. And they made plans to bring her to him.

~

The paddy wagon smelled of cheaply bought perfume, the stench of an unseasonable October day, and excitement.

The members of the Goree Girls All Strings Band squeezed into the confined space, with windows barely cracked lest anyone have an idea to attempt an escape.

A hearty voice filled the remaining pockets of air.

"Well, won't this be a mighty fine swan song!"

Della looked up from her seat in the middle to find Hazel muscling her way in and stepping over the girls' uniformly booted feet.

Roy came around to the back door and barked at everyone to hurry up.

"Make way, girls, make way. It's a short drive. You ain't gonna die in here." He looked directly at Della. "Although maybe some of you should."

Roy's visits to Mouse were becoming more brazen, and Della had all but caught them doing the kind of things that would get him fired and send Mouse to solitary. Della figured that he would be better off being nice to her rather than antagonizing the one person who could get them both in trouble. But she never had the impression that smarts were his strong suit.

Hazel grunted as she wiggled her way into a space next to Della, and Della felt her friend's thigh smother her own. Her breath smelled of peppermint covering stale coffee.

"You ready for this, darlin'?" she asked.

Della nodded and tried to breathe through her mouth as she spoke. It was unbearably stifling in there.

"The performance, yes. The rest, I don't know. Catching greased pigs? How am I supposed to do that?"

"Just pretend it's old Mouse, standin' in the way of you and that baby of yours. Ain't nothin' gonna stop a mama from her little one. You'll have that piece of bacon in your hands in no time."

It wasn't difficult to imagine attacking Mouse.

"And another thing," Hazel added. "People ain't comin' to see no professionals here. They can go to any old rodeo for that. The prison rodeo attracts people the way a travelin' carnival might. You know, bearded lady and two-headed calves. To see oddities. Prisoners doin' what cowboys do—that's an oddity."

"How many people will be there?"

"Oh, twenty-five thousand, give or take. Maybe more this year, since this will be the last time the String Band performs."

"Twenty-five thousand? I thought it might be hundreds. Maybe a few thousand. That's so . . . intimidating."

"Well, get used to it. You'll be coming here once a year from now until eternity."

Della swallowed hard. Another reminder that her life wasn't her own.

"Hard to believe that the Goree Girls are over. Almost before it began—for me at least."

The rodeo would be her swan song. Her swan song and her debut. What an odd thought. But she couldn't lament it too much. Even the brief time she had been a Goree Girl introduced her to a love of music that had been dormant in the shadow of Eula's tremendous talent.

"Well, someone will think of some new kind of diversion, I'm sure. I'm hearin' that Beauford Jester is thinkin' of a run for governor, with a platform to improve the state penal system. Not long ago it was considered the worst in the country. That's how the rodeo got started in the first place. It got the community involved. Raisin' funds."

"I wouldn't know what to compare it to. But it can't be the worst thing in the world, I guess. Ask a cotter—they think it's better than being out there looking for work and scrounging for meals."

"Well, maybe it's not so bad at Goree, but I hear some pretty mean rumors about the Walls for the men. Abuse, bad management, malnutrition."

"I'm glad I wasn't born a man."

"Honey, if you was born a man, you wouldn't be here."

Della thought about this. If she had been a boy, would life have turned out differently? Would their mother have left? Most likely. Would their father have retreated into business? She was certain. But maybe an older brother could have dealt a stronger hand to Eula, and maybe her sister wouldn't have gone off so hog wild the way she did. And certainly there would not have been the canyon carved between them over Tomas. So, yes. Maybe it would have been better to be a man.

Except for one thing. A man would never know what it was like to feel a child kick against his belly. A man would never know what it was like to feel the thrill of milk leaving your breasts as it nurtured another human being. The mother and child bond was irreplaceable.

Della decided that she'd do everything exactly the same if it meant being able to have Cristina.

"Oh!" An outcry swept across the paddy wagon as it lurched forward and began to make its way over the bumpy road leading outside the barbed-wire fence that surrounded Goree. Talking was impossible over the noise of the engine, and Della focused on the slivers of light that came from the windows.

In ten minutes they stopped, and Roy came around with two other guards to open the back door and let in the momentary relief of fresh air. It was short-lived, given the blistering humidity that played with the emotions of those who usually found respite in a Texas October.

Della watched as girl after girl descended in her cowboy boots and crinoline-filled gingham skirt. The red and white squares reminded her of a picnic, the one where Tomas gave her a ring hidden in a cake and asked her to be his forever.

It wasn't easy to put Tomas out of her mind, but when she was sweating out in the orchard or holding her baby close, it wasn't as hard as it had been in the beginning. Until little things like the checkerboard pattern recalled some memory, invoking pain in her.

But that was short-lived today as she took her turn to step out of the suffocation and into the vastness of the rodeo arena.

She'd never seen anything like it.

The stands were tall enough to hold maybe fifty rows of people and wide enough to corral hundreds of cattle. It must be magnificent when it was filled. Twenty-five thousand people. Fifty Puerto Pesars could fit in there.

But for now there were only about a hundred people milling around. Most of them were men in black-and-white-striped tops and pants. She wondered if that made it harder for the prisoners to escape—the fact that they would be so visible in their striking getups.

Those who weren't occupied were clustered in the few spots of shade that shadows provided, but the rest were busy. Most were wrangling animals—horses and bulls. She didn't see any pigs yet.

She heard a yelp coming from her left.

A man had just fallen from what appeared to be a large mattress with blue-and-white ticking. It was folded in half and secured with leather straps that looked like a girdle cinching a lady's waist. On either side were two men gripping it. The man on the ground got up and wiped his hands on his pants, creating a small dust storm. He remounted the mattress, straddling it while the men held it still. Once balanced, he wrapped his arm around one of the straps. The ones holding it began to shake it—gently at first, but with increasing rapidity. The man held on, but his legs flew up and down in the air as if they weighed nothing. She heard someone counting.

"Four . . . five . . . six . . ."

And then another hollered as he fell to the ground.

"What's going on over there?" she asked Hazel. She pointed to the man who was once again mounting the mattress.

"He's practicing for the bull ride. Kind of funny when you think about it. It's not as if that contraption is much of a substitute for the real deal."

"Why don't they just practice with the bulls?"

"Too dangerous," she said. "It's a risky sport even for the professionals. For the inmates? Nearly impossible. They don't want any of them injured before the paying crowds are there to see it."

"That's awful! Why do it at all?"

She raised her hand to eye level and rubbed two fingers together.

"The rodeo is big money. And the crowds get a thrill out of seeing the amateurs. Well, except for their families. I'm sure there're more than a few wives and mothers in the audience who will have chewed off their fingernails by the end of the day."

The look on her face must have told Hazel what she was thinking.

"You're right," she said. "It is kind of awful. Not much different from Ancient Rome, where it was sport to watch the kind of violence that happened in the arena."

Hazel swept her hand around their own version of it. "Not exactly the Colosseum. But it goes to show that people never change."

Della wasn't sure she liked the rodeo after all, and it hadn't even started.

"Don't worry, sugar." Hazel placed a hand on her shoulder. "That's the worst of it. I think you're going to have a good time here."

"Lee!" a voice shouted. "Della Lee, get back in line."

She didn't need to face him to know that it was Roy. Not merely because she recognized his voice, but because it was laced with the ever-present sharpness that was unmistakable. She shivered.

Was it possible for a person to be born that way, or did the features of a face and voice form as they became cruel or kind? Even a girl like Mouse could have been pretty once, could have had a sweet countenance, but her temperament left a fixed look of bitterness on her face and a grim sound in her voice. Roy was no different.

Della had known varying degrees of fame in her short life, all unwanted and each widening the circle as time went on. Sister of the songbird Eula, known throughout the county for her mesmerizing voice. Murderer of that songbird, reviled across several counties in South Texas. Latecomer to the Goree Girls All String Band, listened to on airways across the United States.

But nothing like this.

She wiped dust off her boots and fluffed her gingham skirt until it looked as full as those belonging to the other girls. The crowd was restless, shouting out for them to begin. It was one thing for the band to receive letters in the mail from listeners, even marriage proposals among the crazier ones, but to see the living, breathing fans in person was both frightening and exhilarating.

Eula would have loved this, and the irony that it was instead Della standing in front of such adulation was not lost on her. It had just been a way to pass the countless days. Later, a way to make her daughter smile.

And now she was sad that this would be the last time she played.

Horse-riding guards with guns, wearing bow ties for the occasion, escorted the girls. Other musicians gathered on the round stage, preparing their instruments. It was a sea of cellos, violins, banjos, guitars. Della recognized some of the acts, like the Hillbillies, from various studio sessions for "Thirty Minutes Behind the Walls."

G-C-F-A. She plucked the strings of the guitar and adjusted the tuning keys. It was a cheap instrument, always losing its pitch, and she had to tighten them after every song. She gripped the neck and ran her hand along its glossy body. In a short time, it had become an old friend.

Hazel hustled over with a bag in her hands.

"You need lipstick."

She picked out three tubes and opened them. Each was worn to various stages of stubbiness, used by untold numbers of inmates before her. Red. Mauve. Pink.

Della watched as Hazel held up each one to her face and scrutinized them as carefully as she would if she were defusing a bomb.

"Red," she determined, and she slid it across Della's lips. "Open." She pulled a wrinkled tissue from her pocket and blotted the color.

Della watched families and couples and men walking through the bleachers, finding their seats, stepping over one another. Concessioners carried trays of lemonade and Coke and popcorn. Movement everywhere.

Except for one spot.

Della stood on the round stage in the middle of the arena and had a good view of the people. She placed her hand over her eyes to shade the already blazing sun and saw one person standing rigid, looking at her intently.

From where she stood, it seemed as if he could be Tomas. But that was impossible. He was out in West Texas with the army.

But even the idea of it made her heart leap in a way that it never had for anyone else. The love of two people who had endured loss and devastation together. Two people who shared a secret.

She looked right at the man, but he didn't move. Didn't even flicker until the announcer stepped up to the mike and called for everyone to stand and remove their hats for "The Star-Spangled Banner."

Thankfully, that task fell to Rose, and as she warbled on the *rocket's red glare* and missed *the land of the free* by a cracked mile, Della looked again at the man who resembled Tomas, her heart thumping at the possibility. He did not return her smile.

Only when everyone sat did he join them.

"Ladies and gentlemen," the announcer said in a smooth voice. He raised and lowered his hand, quieting the crowd like a magician. "Welcome to the twelfth annual Texas Prison Rodeo here in Huntsville. This is the best crowd we've seen to date. They told me we've got about thirty. Thousand. People. Here. Let's give a round of applause to all of you for making the drive out here to cheer on our contestants and give some cheering up to the residents of the Walls."

He stepped back and clapped his hands before wiping the sweat from his bald head and running his finger under his collar. A line of sweat ran along his spine, saturating his white dress shirt.

"What a change this is from our first days over on the east side of the prison in the baseball field. Your support and enthusiasm have made this possible year after year and helped fund the prison system." He looked back at the Goree Girls and gave a thumbs-up.

Della heard all the laughter and applause distorted through what seemed like a tunnel, as she held her hand over her eyes and searched for the man who looked like her husband.

She snapped back to reality when Rose elbowed her in the side. "You're on," she whispered.

"Ah, here she is. Our own lovely Della Lee to open the last performance of the Goree Girls All Strings Band."

He held out his hand to her, and she stepped forward to take it. He wrapped his arm around her waist and gave her a hard kiss on the cheek before she could pull away. She'd never even met this man, and she winced at the reminder that some men thought they could do anything they wanted to a woman—a prisoner. And that Tomas might be watching.

"I give you our songbird, Miss Della Lee."

She cringed at the word *songbird*. That was her sister's mantle, one that she'd worn a hundred times better than Della. But she recognized that it was just showmanship, and at Goree, you did as you were told. And she had been told to sing if she didn't want to wither in the orchards for more hours than she would have otherwise.

Della stepped up to the mike. She was scheduled to solo for only this one song, a last-minute switch from the one she'd rehearsed. "Save the Last Dance for Me" had been a small crowd-pleaser during the few times they'd played out for prison-sponsored events, and Matron Heath had personally requested it.

The crowd quieted again as the words poured from her red, red lips. She sang with her husband in mind.

"Love," she began, conveying in that one word the years of longing she'd had for him.

"Don't go away. Save the last dance for me."

The man stood up, took off his hat for a moment, and folded his arms. She studied him as the girls in the background played the slow melody before her next line.

It was him. Holy Mother of God, it *was* Tomas.

It had shocked her into blasphemy, but she brushed aside that thought. There was something wrong. It was what he was wearing. It was olive canvas, top to bottom. She noticed the military cap on his head. This wasn't like the army uniforms she'd seen pictures of in magazines. What was it? She couldn't remember.

"*Love,*" she sang again. "*Don't leave it this way. Save the last dance for me.*"

Della finished the song, imploring her unnamed *amour* to forgive her for an unnamed wrong, and to stay by her side until the end.

She had sung it with an emotion that wasn't acting, and the crowd jumped to its feet in thunderous applause and shouts. Tomas left the stands.

Wait! Stay! She implored him in her head. She wanted to talk to him, hold him, regretted every time he'd come to see her and she'd refused him. Maybe it was the lyrics she sang, the uniform he left in, but she felt suffocated by a wave of grief that life had taken the turn that brought her here.

But she couldn't leave. Guards stood everywhere, darting their eyes across the crowds, watching for anyone who might have used the rodeo as a chance to escape.

The emcee walked back across the stage, clapping lightly as he tried to keep the paper program in his hands.

He headed to the mike as she retreated to the back of the Goree Girls, hidden by the much taller Marjorie.

"What did I tell you? Didn't you just love that? But, ladies and gentlemen, we're only getting started. I'd say that was a warm-up, but in this weather, I think we already hit that point. Still, let's get on our feet and move our hands together for the energetic voice of Miss Marjorie Peony. You heard that right. Our own flower. She'll have you stomping your feet in no time."

Marjorie took her spot.

For the rest of the performance, Della plucked, she strummed, she played the notes of every song with precision. If this was the last time she might ever hold a guitar, she was going to do it with every bit of gusto she had. She let her hands say what her words could not. She let them feel everything in her heart. Just in case he could hear her.

When the emcee finally waved them offstage, introducing the Hillbillies as the next act, she looked out into the arena with a storm of emotions. The last performance of something she'd grown to love. Tomas, somewhere here, something wrong.

Eula.

This moment should have been Eula's. And, if she were still alive, her following could have easily expanded into crowds this size. She could have played in Houston. Dallas. Maybe even outside of Texas. New York? She had no doubt. Eula would someday have drawn in throngs of people with her otherworldly voice. Della stopped and closed her eyes before taking that last step off the stage.

She breathed in the energy.

This one was for you, dear sister.

Then she looked down at her hands. The ones that had stroked Eula's hair as she took her last breath.

The dressing room had none of the trappings that one might have for girls who had reached the nationwide fame that the Goree Girls had. The walls were cement, and the floors were matted with dried hay that had been brought in through shoes and mud. A long table with dirty mirrors sat in the corner. It was not crowded, as the show was over and the girls had shed their skirted getups in favor of crisp white dresses and sun hats that would give the impression to the rodeo attendees that the prisoners were well taken care of.

Only Della had not finished changing, as the pig catching came near the end of the program. She favored the relative coolness of this dim, windowless room over the corner stands that were reserved for the prisoners to watch the rest of the events. The lone door was attended by one of the new guards. He stood outside for reasons of privacy, know-ing that there was no other exit for any girl who might have escape on her mind.

She sat in front of the mirror, looking at her drawn face, made up in clownlike colors that were good for the stage but garish in person. It was good that Tomas couldn't see her up close like this. She looked like a harlot. Della found an unused tissue and began to press it hard against her skin until she resembled herself again.

The buttons on her blouse felt tight, so she began to undo them until she was down to her brassiere. The door opened, and she jumped, wrapping her arms around herself.

But it was only Hazel.

Della retrieved her blouse and held it up to her chest. Despite their friendship, Mouse's accusations about Hazel and Cocaine Maggie had never left her mind, and it felt strange to be halfway undressed in front of her. But she shook off these fears as just another way that Mouse tormented her. It wasn't enough to bully her and her daughter; she had to try to darken the one good friendship Della had in this forlorn place.

"What a show, darlin'," Hazel said as she walked over to the corner. But she quieted as she reached Della. "There's someone here to see you. A man."

"What?"

"Shhh . . . I'm going to let him in, but you won't want anyone to hear you."

It was Tomas. It had to be. Her blood raced. What had he come for?

"How is he going to get in here with the guard at the door?"

"That green fellow? He's been at Goree, what, two weeks? All I needed to tell him was that two of the girls were fightin' underneath the stands and that he was supposed to go right away to break them up."

"Who's fighting?"

She smiled. "No one is fightin', you innocent. But you can always guarantee that a man will want to get in the middle of two girls tearing at each other. I told him that they were over at the far end of the arena to give you a little time."

Della nodded, her heart bursting. "Thank you."

Hazel retreated to the door, and in her place stood a familiar silhouette. She took a breath.

It was him. Wonderful, handsome, water-in-the-desert Tomas. Her heart lurched at the very sight of him.

He closed the door and walked over to Della.

Her pulse pounded, not knowing what to expect. It had been nearly a year since he left the visiting room at Goree, upset by her pregnancy. Was he angry with her? Was he bothered that the announcer had kissed her cheek?

Say something, she begged silently.

"Della." His voice was gentle.

She covered her face in her hands and bent over, sobbing.

"Oh, Della." He took long, hurried strides and stood in front of her in no time. He placed his hands on her arms, caressing them as they slid down to her own, where he held them and pulled her to him.

Her arms were stiff. She wanted to return the affection, had thought of the possibility of this moment ever since she last saw him. Her blood raced at his real presence, better, sweeter, warmer than she'd imagined it. And yet she needed to be steadfast. There was nothing to promise him but loneliness. It would be selfish to encourage more.

A moment couldn't replace a lifetime.

"Why—why are you here?"

He pulled back and reached around to his belt, where he pulled out a large envelope, folded in half.

"This is why. But it doesn't matter anymore."

"What is that?"

"The annulment papers you wanted. Straight from Rome."

Her eyes widened. She wanted those papers. And she didn't. It would mean the end of something that never had a chance to begin.

"Why did you bring them here to the rodeo instead of Goree?"

"I drove halfway to Goree a dozen times over the last year, and each time I turned around. Then I thought about mailing them to you. But I'm on my way to Dallas, and when I heard about the rodeo, I thought it might be my best chance to get this done."

"Why are you going to Dallas?"

He smiled at her with soft eyes and cupped her face in his hand. "Why, why, why? You're full of questions, my love, but not the most important one."

Her confusion melted at his touch, and she let her cheek press against him.

He continued, moving his hand down her hair. The blouse she was clutching dropped from her grasp, showing more of her than Tomas had ever seen. Her pulse quickened at his closeness, at her exposure, at the possibility that at any moment someone could walk in.

"Della, I told you that my reason for being here didn't matter anymore. This annulment doesn't matter anymore, because I don't intend to sign it."

Her head jerked up. What was he talking about? Her breathing raced.

He ripped it in half with both hands, and then once more for good measure.

"No—" she started, reaching for the pieces of paper that had fallen to the ground. He drew her in to him again, burying his head in her neck and grasping her waist.

"I'm a fool, Della. A fool. I saw you, pregnant, and I thought that you had cheated on me. It's the only thing that made sense. Why you didn't fight the conviction. Why you didn't write to me. I thought you didn't want me."

"Want you?" she whispered. "I married you."

"I thought that maybe you knew you were with child and used our marriage to legitimize that."

"I wasn't with child. Not then."

"Hush, my love. I know that. I know that now." He pulled her face up to his. "Your friend told me everything. Hazel?"

"What did Hazel tell you?"

"About—about. God, Della, I can't even say the words. I want to *murder* the man who did that to you."

So, he knew now. She was so relieved, and felt a lightness that she hadn't known since—well, since as long as she could remember.

She nodded, acknowledging the truth.

"Della. Why on earth didn't you tell me?"

Didn't he see? He'd heard Fr. Medina's sermons right alongside her. Atonement by sacrifice. The virtue of putting another's needs in front of one's own. Her priest preached it. Her father lived it.

This was how she loved him. This was how she'd loved Eula. Put them first. Put yourself last.

"Because I wanted you to be free of this marriage. Tomas, I'm going to be in here for *the rest of my life.*"

"You could be paroled in twenty years, though."

"You make it sound like nothing."

"It is nothing. I told you that I'd wait for you. And it's only eighteen by now."

She laughed through her tears. "You've always been a romantic. But this is too much. I won't let you do it. Get a lawyer to draft another copy."

"On what grounds?"

"Consummation. Or lack of it."

"I won't do that. I'll tell people that your child is my child. I'll take her home with me. Wait—her? Him?"

"Her. Cristina." She smiled at the mere mention of her daughter, back at Goree, too young to go to the rodeo.

"Cristina. That's beautiful. But how can you have a child in prison?"

"She can be with me for four more years, and then she'll be adopted out." Her chest tightened just saying those words.

"And then—what? Do you receive letters? Do you get to see her?"

"I don't know. I don't want to even think about that day coming."

"What about this? When she's six, I'll take her back to Puerto Pesar and raise her myself. And we will visit, and she will know you."

Della shivered, the impact of the possibility making her feel dizzy. She pictured her daughter running around the farmstead. Climbing up the tree that would someday grow tall. Riding the horses that Tomas would surely purchase again. It was so much better than what it would be to not know her. Still, could she do that to Tomas? Could she foist upon him a child who was not his? A child who would remind him daily of the violation his wife had suffered?

On the other hand, they could be a family. The family they'd always dreamed of. The thought of him raising her daughter as his own, the thought of Cristina being spared from being given to strangers, it was all too wonderful to take in.

She threw her arms around him, forgetting how exposed she was until she felt his hands on her bare back. It sent chills up and down her body. He held her there, swaying her back and forth, placing gentle kisses on her shoulder but not pushing for more. She laid her head on his broad shoulder.

"You are too good to me. I don't even know how to begin to say all that I'm thinking."

"Then it's settled. No one will know she's not ours, together. I will raise her as ours, Della. Just as soon as I'm back from the Pacific."

She pushed away from him as if electricity had just coursed through her body. She picked up her blouse from the floor and held it up to herself.

"The *Pacific*? You told me that you're going to Dallas."

"Only to catch the transport that will take me west. I joined the Marines. That's where they're sending me."

"No, no, no. You didn't. You told me you joined the army. That you'd be stateside and that you'd be safe. The *army*, Tomas! Not the Marines!"

He sighed. "That was my original plan. But it changed."

"What do you mean, it changed?"

"When—when I thought, you know. I was angry, Della. I was angry and hurt, and I just wanted to die. So instead of being safe here fiddling around with army horses, I joined the hardest group of men I could think of."

What had she done? Her silence had propelled him into this. She should have told him the truth when she had the chance. Her mouth felt dry. Parched.

"Then reverse it. Tell them that you made a mistake. That you have a family and you need to be here now."

"That's not how it works, my love. I've already been to boot camp. I'm a Marine. *Semper fi.* Always faithful. Even if I could leave, which I can't, I wouldn't abandon those men. They are brothers to me now."

"But—I'm your wife." *Wife.* Such a beautiful word. It had been years since it crossed her lips. She gripped the edges of his shirt.

He took her hands in his and kissed each one delicately.

"You are. My beloved, darling wife, Della. Who is going to pray for my safe return and raise our daughter until I can come back and take her home. And who will be paroled in eighteen years and live to see our daughter walk down the aisle and give us grandchildren."

How he warmed her heart. Grandchildren. She spent every day just surviving the next breath. There must be billions of breaths between now and grandchildren.

She nodded again. Tomas made it all sound so possible. So perfect.

"You have to promise me two things," he said.

"Anything." She looked in his eyes, ready to give him whatever he asked.

"One. You will actually open my letters when I write, and you'll write me back. I need that, Della. I need to hear from you and know you're OK. It's the only thing that will keep me alive. Living for word from you."

"I promise."

"Two. We put away all talk of annulment. Permanently."

"OK." She smiled. It had just about killed her to fight it these past couple of years.

"I think we need to guarantee that."

"What do you mean?"

He pulled her into him again and kissed the side of her neck, sending shivers through her body more intense than any she'd ever felt before.

Oh.

Tomas moved his hand from her waist to her back, clumsily unhooking her brassiere. She wanted this. She wanted to give him this. It was nearly all that she could think about.

But this wasn't their honeymoon, and this wasn't a hotel. Any minute a guard, a girl could walk in. She opened her mouth to tell him, but he must have seen it as an invitation for more because his lips met hers, and before she knew it, his tongue swept across her mouth in the most exquisite way, and suddenly none of the rest of it mattered.

She would make love to her husband. Here in this concrete cell while the guard went to find the girls who weren't fighting, and the other girls cheered in the stands for frivolities like barrel racing and buck riding.

Here there was no guard, no Roy, no Eddie, no Hazel, no Gertie, not even Cristina. There was only Tomas and his hands and his mouth and his heart, all hers.

They would be married in full at last. And no one could take that away from them.

221

CHAPTER TWENTY-ONE

Puerto Pesar—Today

Mick found a quiet table in a corner of Arturo's. He set his notebook and pen on the table. He jerked when he felt a slap on his back.

"Hey, man. Good to see you in here again."

"Arturo. Thank you. Good to see you."

"You're too early for happy hour, but I'll take two dollars off the margaritas anyway. My Corrina makes a mean mango one. The secret is not to blend the pulp."

"Sounds good. That and a glass of water. And some loaded nachos, please."

"And how about jalapeños? Spice up your life." He nudged Mick with his elbow, and it felt as if a deeper message were trying to be conveyed.

Arturo went back into the kitchen, and Mick started to write down the things he remembered from visiting with Della and what he'd looked up on the Internet.

Della Lee Trujillo. Convicted of killing her sister, Eula, in 1943. Parents were Herman and Eva Lee. Eva ran away with a painter. Herman died on his way to find her. Cannery. Tomas.

The list continued until he'd exhausted everything he could think of. He looked it over and was disappointed with himself. He drew a line through all of it and, for good measure, ripped the page from the notebook.

This was his problem. The very thing that had catapulted his career—hard-nosed reporting—was the very thing that sank it. This was not who he set out to be in the beginning.

Fresh page. His pen hovered as he looked up to the ceiling for answers. An image came to mind. He began writing.

A baby cries its first breath. A woman falls back on her pillow. She is deflated, her stomach a hollow reminder that the child she carried was hers for only a short time. A window lets in light, save for the vertical shadows that fall across the floor. Iron bars mar what little view there was, reflected in the woman's heart. There is no view, no light in a brief life that has known only sadness.

Mick took a deep breath and reread it. His pulse quickened. It was not an article that he was meant to write. It was something more . . . more thorough. More compelling. Della Lee didn't want a rehash of her life. It would be an injustice heaped upon a lifetime of them.

How had he lost his way? No, he knew the answer to that. He didn't need to pound himself for mistakes made, opportunities lost. There was only one way out; it was to look forward and change directions. Getting back to the newspaper would be like crawling into one of the molted cicada skins that were strewn on the ground of Puerto Pesar and trying to fly with it.

More ideas came to mind, largely fed by his own imagination, but it was a starting point, a compass for the things he'd like to explore with Della Lee. His pen flew in an ambitious attempt to keep up.

His phone rang, interrupting him.

Paloma, he thought. But it was only his friend Andy, probably responding to the pictures he'd sent of *Santa Bonita*.

"Andy." He leaned the phone against his shoulder and stretched his fingers, already sore from so much writing.

"Mick—long time no talk."

"Yeah, my friend. Too long. How's the family?"

"Good. Darlene graduated last night. Time flies."

"College?" He wanted to get to the point, but if he'd learned anything from Della Lee, it was to slow down. Talk to the person, not chase the facts.

"High school, Mick. She graduated from high school. Jeez, how old do you think I am?"

Damn. He really had lost touch.

"Sorry, buddy. I don't do math on Tuesdays."

"You never did math on Wednesdays through Mondays, either, as I recall."

"Well, you knew me when." Andy was the studious older brother of Mick's pot-smoking college roommate. Got a summer internship at the Smithsonian and was hired a few weeks later.

"Anyway, I got your texts. Interesting stuff. It's hard to be able to tell much with grainy pictures, but let's just say that you have my curiosity piqued."

A spark of hope grew in Mick's chest. "That's good news. Really good news."

"Slow down, cowboy." Andy laughed on the other end. "Seems appropriate, right? You—out there in Texas. That's the last place I would have imagined you going."

Not long ago, Mick would have agreed.

"Whatever it takes for a lead, you know. Even a hellhole like this."

"Well, I'm not promising anything. But maybe you do have a story. I'll get back to you. I just wanted to let you know that I'm on it."

"That's good news. Keep me posted."

"I will. Stay cool down there, Mick, and hurry home when you can."

"You bet." But the words sounded like a lie as he said them.

What was home?

He turned off his phone and picked up his pen. No more interruptions.

Della Lee steps out of a car, her last connection to all that she left behind. Before her is a wall of cement, dreary and claustrophobic. Behind her is the only life she's known.

Maybe that was too heavy-handed. The narrative style was new to him, but he thought it would be a great format for her story. The best way to tell it.

"Loaded nachos and a mango margarita." Arturo startled him. He leaned over and whispered to Mick. "I threw in an extra splash of tequila. No charge. Looks like you could use it."

It smelled delicious. But once he looked at it, he wondered why he hadn't ordered something he could eat with a fork, so he could write. He would ask Arturo for more napkins next time he came by. And that glass of water.

Mick started again.

> *Della Lee hears a guitar being played down an unseen hallway. The song is played in a minor key, liberties being taken by the one at the strings, a change from the happier way the familiar tune goes when played in a major key. Her sister, Eula, used to sing this melody during childhood days that Della sees through the haze of time and tragedy. This arrangement, however, reflects the soulful cries of her heart.*

Better. Dig into the experience. Not merely the facts.

A chair slid out next to him, and it was all he could do not to pack up and go back to the motel. He couldn't focus here.

Paloma.

Every other thought left his mind as his eyes took her in, glad for this interruption. He jumped to his feet and put his hands on the back of her chair, even though she'd already done it for herself.

"Hey," he said, feeling tongue-tied.

"Hey, yourself." She smiled.

"What are you doing here?"

"I came to talk to Arturo, but it looks like he's busy," she said.

"Can I get you anything? A margarita? Dr Pepper?"

"I think Arturo's already got it covered. Here he comes after all."

He set down two waters, and then handed a margarita to Paloma. Same as Mick's. "An extra splash of tequila for you, my dear," he said as he looked at her. Mick thought he might have even winked.

"I owe you an apology," Paloma started.

"No. Please don't even think that. You've had a lot on your plate."

"That's no excuse," she said, placing her hands on her knees. "I shouldn't have been so dismissive, especially when you'd been such a help."

"How is your sister?" he said. Mick had learned about Mercedes's role in the failed holdup. Big news in a small town.

"Good. She's home now. She'll be in court in about four weeks."

"Four weeks? You'll be—"

"I know. I won't be here. Don't think it doesn't kill me." She put her head in her hands and gripped her hair.

Mick needed to say something to distract her.

He looked at his water glass, etched with a palm tree, and said the first thing he could think of. "We don't have palm trees in Boston."

Well, that was brilliant.

She took a long drink and set it on a coaster. "Tell me about Boston, Mick. Why is it home?" The elephant in the room sat firmly between them, ignored.

"Well, there's the obvious. Fenway Park. I'd have to turn in my man card if I didn't list that first. I try to get to as many games as I can."

"I like baseball," she said. "My dad took me to a few games while I was an undergrad, but I didn't have much time after that."

"Please tell me it was the Mets."

"No, the Yankees."

He folded his arms and glared at her. "We can't be friends anymore," he said in exaggerated seriousness. He hoped she knew enough about the legendary rivalry to know that he was joking.

She shrugged. "Well, it was nice while it lasted."

"Yes, it was."

"But I'm not going to give up my Yankees for anything." She curled her legs around the side of the chair and leaned in toward him, just slightly. He couldn't tell if it was intentional or not. "So, what else?"

She was so close. Kissing distance, he thought, if he leaned in a little more.

He'd say it was like high school all over again, this will-she-or-won't-she debate.

"What else do I like? Hmmm. Watching the tourists snap pictures along the Freedom Trail. The first cold days when the leaves change. Community lectures at Harvard and MIT. The fireworks with the Boston Pops on the Fourth of July. For starters."

What he didn't like: politicians. Prep schools. Ice. But he didn't say that.

"Oh, and the food. Little Italy. There's this hole-in-the-wall bakery on Prince Street that makes the best rum baba. Oh my God. Perfection. And the gnocchi. No one makes gnocchi like they do in Boston." He kissed the tips of his fingers. "You should go sometime." He wanted to tell her that she should go with *him*.

But she didn't take the bait. "Well, New York is not exactly lacking in that department."

"No, I suppose it isn't."

"Do you want to know what my favorite thing is about New York?"

"What's that?"

"The street food. I love that you can get gyros from the same truck that sells hot dogs and tacos. And—" Her smile widened. "This sounds weird, but I love to get falafel with a grape soda."

"That *is* weird."

She looked down at what he'd been writing. He slid the notebook off the table and turned it over.

"I'm sorry. I'm interrupting you." She made a move to get up.

"No. Stay." He stopped just shy of touching her arm. "Please."

She looked down at her hands. "You might have gotten more than you bargained for here in Puerto Pesar. I'm sorry."

He took a chance. He slid his hand over hers, and she didn't move back. "What does that even mean? You don't have to apologize about anything."

"I mean you came here to do a job, and you ended up getting pulled into the little dramas of this town." It was in one ear, out the other. It was a near-impossible task to steady your voice when your whole body raced with electricity. She hadn't moved her hand.

Paloma seemed unfazed. "No, really. I'm sorry for being so dismissive the other day when you were only trying to help. I'm not the best company right now. I have a lot of mixed feelings about being in Puerto Pesar. I can't explain it."

She was too hard on herself.

"Let me guess," he said. "You want to do the right thing. Take care of your grandmother and your sister and save all the people who live here without medical help. But you can't wait to get back to the freedom of a place like New York and all that it has to offer. You're torn."

"Exactly," she whispered, appearing a bit awed. He looked at her eyes and saw them turn red. She pursed her lips, her beautiful lips, and he recognized that she was holding back tears. As he saw it, there were two ways to cheer her up. He could kiss her again. Or he could make her laugh. The fourteen-year-old fought pretty hard for the first one, but this wasn't the place.

"What's that?" he asked her, checking just above her head.

She let go of his hands and touched her hair. "What?"

He peered in, investigating, and touched a finger to the air above her. "Is that—is that a bit of *tarnish* that I see on that halo?"

Her mouth opened, and the smile spread.

Score.

She slapped him on the arm. "Stop that," she said. But she laughed as she said it. "Be serious."

"I *am*. Saint Paloma is doing her duty but wishes she were somewhere else. Congratulations. You're a member of the human race. Stop the presses! Wait, I *am* the press. Or used to be."

"Oh, we are a pair, aren't we?"

He slowed down his words and ran his thumb along her hand. "I'd like to think so."

She looked in his eyes with a sadness that he couldn't pinpoint. It was a make-or-break kind of moment, where he could press in if he wanted to, but the right call was to let her make the next move. And she did. But just not the one he wanted.

She slid back her hand.

"I can't get involved with you right now." Her somber tone returned as she whispered, "I've got too much to figure out."

She stood up, margarita untouched. He felt like downing both of them.

"Mick," she added as she turned to go. "I hope you find the story that you want."

It sounded like a good-bye.

Paloma closed the door to Arturo's behind her. She turned around and gripped the knob, ready to run in and go back, but then she pulled away just as quickly. She'd been right the first time; there was too much to handle right now without bringing another person, other emotions into the mix.

She walked by the church. Weeds were sprouting through the cracks, miraculously green in a town that was plagued by twenty shades of water-starved brown. She wondered how the bad parts of life managed to grow and thrive while the good parts wilted, starved of hope.

She'd never missed New York more. Yet never felt so right about being here.

She slipped into the back of the empty church and sat in a pew next to an icon of Our Lady of Perpetual Help. The Madonna wore a dark-blue veil with an elaborate crown on her head. She held the Child in her arms and was heralded by angels on either side. Paloma remembered that this one was Abuela's favorite. A holy card of this image was attached to the refrigerator, next to *Santa Bonita*.

Paloma lit a candle. She didn't know if she believed it would do any good, but the flicker of the flames was comforting.

She spoke the things in her heart. Get Mercedes's problem sorted out. Build that relationship with everything she had. Prepare for the new job.

And look after Abuela. She was worried that her grandmother had done too much too fast, and it was starting to show in the way she moved. Labored.

But something else had been nagging at her ever since coming back to Puerto Pesar. It was distressing that in the event of an emergency, the town did not have even the smallest amount of medical provisions. It was unacceptable that Abuela and others like her had to drive to Harlingen for doctor's appointments or down to Mexico to buy medicine. What about the children who went unvaccinated and the teens suffering from depression and the young mothers who might not make it to a hospital to deliver their babies?

Something had to be done, and maybe she could be the one to get the ball rolling. It was ambitious, especially from so far away, but she already had some ideas and knew just the right sounding board.

Arturo. Didn't a bartender know a town better than anyone else?

She stayed for another twenty minutes, finding remarkable peace in this spot. No wonder Abuela was so devoted. It was as if you could shut out everything else. A sanctuary by every definition of the word.

Paloma genuflected and crossed herself out of habit. When she reentered the plaza, she saw Mick about a block down, heading in the opposite direction. The sight of him gave her a feeling of comfort akin to what she felt in the church, sparking one bit of hope: Now was not the right time. But that didn't mean it would never happen. Boston and New York weren't all that far away.

"That's not my girl still out here, is it?"

A haze of cigarette smoke preceded Arturo. His bushy, artificially black mustache was dusted with cookie crumbs, evidence of the sweets she knew he couldn't resist.

She smiled. "It is."

"Paloma . . . are you crying?"

She'd seen her red eyes in the mirror this morning, but it was merely due to lack of sleep. Arturo would have certainly imagined a broken heart. The romantic. "No, but I almost wish I were. Might be the only rain we see around here anytime soon."

"You've got that right. I think we're pushing a hundred ninety days. Corrina's started taking wagers at the bar. The pot's up to three hundred dollars. Gonna be a nice windfall for whomever picks the right date."

She reached into her pocket. "Put me down for five. Christmas Day."

Arturo put his hands on his hips. "Sweet Jesus help us if it's going to take *that* long to get any relief."

"Seems like it should be any day now. Look at the clouds. They're so dark. But nothing happens."

Arturo sighed. "I've been here long enough to see these cycles, but this one is longer than others. We either get the flood or the drought. No breaks for Puerto Pesar. Cursed name, I guess."

"Yeah. Port of Regret."

"Speaking from experience?"

"Maybe. But you have a dinner hour starting soon. You don't need to hear my woes."

"Miss Paloma, you should know that a bartender is a psychiatrist second to none. Doesn't hurt that a little of the sauce helps loosen a troubled tongue. I've heard it all. Tell me what's bothering you. Anyone I need to beat up?" He tucked his bag under his arms and curled his fists, eliciting a laugh from her.

"Can we go inside? I think I'll melt if we stay out here."

"Sure thing."

She followed him into the restaurant, enjoying the impressionist rainbows that spread across the vacant saltillo floor, reflections of year-round Christmas lights. A contrast to the dreariness outside.

"Have a seat. I'm going to put you to work. Happy hour starts soon."

She heard the rattle of kitchen noises as he stepped in and out of the swinging door. He came out with a tray full of salt and pepper shakers, plus a Dr Pepper with crushed ice.

"Just like you like it." He set the drink down in front of her.

"Thank you."

He slid the tray of glass shakers over to her. "These need to be filled up and wiped down before we can put them on the tables. You do that, and I'm going to fold the napkins." He picked up a stack of them from the bar top.

The chair groaned as he sat in it, despite his slight frame. "Now. Tell me what's on your mind."

Paloma unscrewed the cap to a pepper shaker and began to fill it.

"I've been here almost two weeks, Arturo, and I'm more conflicted than ever. But I had an idea and wanted to run it by you."

He raised his eyebrows. "Shoot."

"All right. Tell me if I'm crazy, but I'd like to help get a clinic started here. Something simple, enough to handle minor emergencies and regular checkups."

"Well, I think that's a terrific idea."

"Thanks. It would be expensive, though. I don't think the town has the funds. Have you seen the potholes? You could swim in them. Add to that the fact that I don't live here." She rested her elbows on the table and pulled her hair. "Ugh, just as I said the words, I realized what a big undertaking that is. What is wrong with me, Arturo? I should just leave well enough alone, as Abuela would say, and go to New York. Visit more often. Fly them out to the city."

She'd just done the same thing to Mick. Let him in, pushed him back. She felt like she was sitting on a playground seesaw. This was not how she usually operated. Being decisive and unemotional were traits that earned her high honors in med school and recommendations that got her the job at Lenox Hill.

Could those very things be what made her lose touch with her family and her hometown?

"You've made old Arturo here happy just by seeing your pretty face again. And your grandmother and Mercedes. You know they're happy to have you here. And that Mick fellow." He pointed at her. "Well, I don't even need to have my glasses on to see how he lights up when you're around."

She felt herself blush. "You sound just like Abuela. There's nothing to talk about there, Arturo."

"My sources say differently. Sounds as if he's been spending some time with you."

"Do you have a spy team or something?"

"You know it." He crossed his arms and nodded.

She rolled her eyes. "Well, even if there was anything to talk about, I put that to rest. He has work to do and then he'll be off."

"He's talking to Della Lee, right?"

"I think he already did. A couple of times."

"That old lady might not have too many days left. What is she, ninetyish?"

"I think so."

"Did he find what he's looking for? About *Santa Bonita*?" He stopped wiping the counters.

"I don't know. We haven't talked about it."

Paloma stopped and looked at the salt and pepper shakers in her hands. She twirled each of them around on its edges. "You know what I used to do with these when I was a little girl?"

"What's that?"

"Well, once a month, Abuela would meet with her canasta club at that diner that used to be on Route 28."

"I remember that one. Rosa's Cantina."

"Yes. That one. I had to go along because she didn't have anyone to watch me. But I'd get bored, so I played with all the condiments. The salt was the bride in her white dress. The pepper was the groom in a black tuxedo. The ketchup and mustard and salsa were the brides-maids in their colorful gowns. I played out all sorts of weddings. Beach, church, mountains."

"What an imagination you have."

"I used to. I became so serious, Arturo. School. Residency. Work. But I did used to dream about things like love and marriage. I wonder if it's too late for me."

"Aw, you're too young to be talking like that." He patted her arm.

"Maybe not. But look at me. Here I am talking about starting a clinic in Puerto Pesar, as if I don't have enough to do. Maybe I'm too much of a workaholic to have a relationship." She set down the shakers and rested her head on her chin.

"Well, I'm sure we can figure out a way to make it work. And you wouldn't be alone in it. Have you thought about a loan from the bank? That's how I was able to start this restaurant."

"I don't think they'd give me a commercial loan when I haven't even started my new job."

"What about a cosigner?"

"I don't know anyone." This was feeling bleak. Her chest pounded, knowing what she had to do to make this happen. She had to be here. But she wasn't ready to say that.

Arturo wasn't finished with ideas, though. "How about your dad? I heard he's living pretty well up in New York somewhere."

"Connecticut. Darien. Yeah, I know he'd do it in a heartbeat if he could. But he's in the middle of an audit and has to account for every single penny. I'm not going to ask him. And besides, he's done more for me than I could have ever dreamed. After scholarships, he picked up the rest of the tab for college. And medical school. That's why I can even be here in the first place. I must be the only recently graduated doctor who isn't saddled with a mountain of school loans. So he's done more than enough for the cause."

"Well, I always knew you as one of the hardest working kids at the high school. You're going to find a way." She knew his confidence in her was genuine.

Her phone lit up. A text from Mick.

At the risk of sounding like I'm in junior high, I'd like to be friends. I won't kiss you again. I might THINK about kissing you. In fact, I can pretty much guarantee that. But I'm a gentleman, so hands off. I'd just be sorry not to be able to see you again.

She smiled and felt a blush rise in her cheeks.

"I think you got it as bad as he got it. Maybe there's a saltshaker wedding dress in your future," Arturo said.

"What are you talking about?"

"Well, unless you have a boyfriend in New York I don't know about, I'd say that's not the face of a girl who just heard from her dentist."

"And what would make you say that?"

"For starters, you just turned three shades of pink."

She grinned. "It's just the weather, Arturo. And your eyes. Go get your glasses on."

"Don't you think I know you're changin' the subject?"

"You're sounding like Abuela again. I've known the man less than a week."

"As a newly married man who knew two minutes into meeting my Corrina that there was no other woman for me, I highly recommend the institution. Now, you're slackin' off on those shakers. I'll make you a deal. You finish up that job there, and I'll cook up a great batch of chalupas for you and your boyfriend next time you come in. Best you've ever had."

"The chalupas or the boyfriend?"

"Yes."

She slapped his arm and smiled. Then she texted Mick back.

I would like that.

CHAPTER
TWENTY-TWO

Huntsville Prison Rodeo—1944

Della would never know how Hazel held off the guard long enough for Tomas to stay in the dressing room with her. Surely the excuse of two female inmates fighting across the arena would not have kept him away as long as it did. All her friend would say after the fact was, "Sometimes it's best that a woman keeps her secrets to herself."

But whatever Hazel had done, Della was grateful.

Tomas had slipped out after one last, memorable kiss that left her lips raw, and her heart slowly, slowly returned to a new kind of normal. She walked naked over to the mirror and sat in front of its rusted corners. Her cheeks were flushed and brought out a prettiness in her that she had never seen reflected back. What a lovely feeling it was to be so treasured by a man. So different from the last time. Tomas had given her a gift without even realizing it—the memory of that horrific night on the way to Goree was relegated to a part of her mind that made it feel as if it had happened to someone else. Because that had been the Della who was orphaned, sisterless, indicted, despairing.

Tomas resurrected the Della who was youthful and full of hope. When he returned from the Pacific front, he would come and see her whenever he could. And, when Cristina turned six, he would take her home to Puerto Pesar and raise her as theirs.

Della smiled at the thought of what their future could be. She could bear Mouse and Roy and Cocaine Maggie and stale food and suffocating incarceration with the thought that someday, with good behavior, a family awaited her.

One breath at a time. One out of billions.

A rustle sounded outside the door, and Hazel peeked in. "Is he gone?"

"Yes." Della gathered her clothes around her and began to step into the canvas dungarees that she would need for the next event.

"How are you doin', girly?"

"Good. I'm good. I'm *real* good." She grinned.

How did people do this? Share something so glorious with another person and go back to regular life as if the most amazing experience had not just happened? How did people keep their cheeks from reddening, their mouths from widening, their eyes from shining?

Della began to believe that life had just started. And it was beautiful.

"Well, you keep that smile on your face as long as you can, because you's about to catch some pigs. Let's get that blouse buttoned, 'cause they're already startin' to line up, and I still need to go over your technique."

"There's a technique to catching a greased pig?"

"Lordy, girl, of course there is. The easiest way is to drag 'em into the circle by their hind legs. It's a sight to see their little forelegs racin' backward."

"What circle?"

"Really? You never seen this done before? I thought every self-respectin' Texan girl could tell you the ins and outs of a rodeo."

"Puerto Pesar isn't the kind of town that rodeos make a stop in."

Hazel picked up a hairbrush and ran it roughly through Della's hair before starting on a braid.

"We're going to have to go back to basics, then. You'll be one of ten girls. Whites and Negroes both. Two pigs. You got to grab a pig and drag it into a circle that they've painted into the center of the pen. Keep it there for five seconds."

"That doesn't sound too hard."

"It is when you're all greased up, too!"

"What?"

"Yeah, girly. They gonna roll up them sleeves on your skinny arms and grease you all up, too. Now, what do you think of that for some entertainment?"

"I think that when Cristina is older, she'll get a good laugh out of it."

"Well, you just keep that precious little baby in mind, because the girls who catch the pigs gonna have a good meal for their dormitory. I'm countin' on you so as we get some bacon for our breakfast later this week. And your little one's gonna like tastin' that, too. I guarantee it."

It had been years since Della had eaten bacon. Probably since just after Father had left for Europe. After he died, they had to sell off land and much of the livestock, and things like bacon were a luxury she had to do without. How she would love to taste it again, and, more important, let Cristina try it.

She was going to win this.

All thoughts of Tomas left for the moment as she followed Hazel and a different guard to the holding pen where nine other girls waited. Their bare feet were already caked in mud, and they began to fold up the hems of their pants. Della did the same, though it seemed pointless, seeing as they were just going to get filthy anyway.

"I'll hold your shoes for you here, and I'll be a-cheerin' from the sidelines. You go get us a big old hog, Della Lee!"

Della got in line along the fence and pushed up the sleeves of her blouse as rodeo workers came along and basted her arms with thick black grease. Their darkness was a shock after seeing her own pale skin for her whole life, and the first thought she'd ever had of escape crossed her mind. If she could slather this stuff all over herself, she wondered if she could disguise herself as a Negro woman, at least from a distance, and slip out somehow, unrecognized.

It was a nice thought. Escape. What if she could get away with it? Leave with Cristina, find Tomas, run somewhere that they wouldn't be found. They wouldn't have to wait twenty years. They could have each other now.

But there were more holes in that plan than in a cheese grater. First, it would be nearly impossible to leave with a small child. Second, Tomas wouldn't be home until after the war, so where would she go? Third, she'd probably cook herself in this hot sun if she greased herself up like that.

A foghorn blared, and before Della had gotten a chance to size up the competition and come up with a plan, two pigs were released. Beneath the roughly painted grease, she could see their pinkish bodies and curly tails. They were fast little devils.

Della focused on the larger of them. She made eye contact with it before it turned and sprinted off. She couldn't count how many other girls were going after it. She just kept her eyes on that one, chasing him around the large pen until he neared the corner. Taking low and long steps, she reached for his hind legs, as Hazel had instructed, but he zipped off, causing her to fall flat into the mud. She wiped it off her mouth, only to leave a trail of muck in its place. She pursed her lips tight, reminding herself not to open them again until she could get to water.

She looked around the pen and saw the majority of the girls going over to the pig on the left, so she set her sights on the other one, chased now by only two girls. It was the scrawnier of the two, but a scrawny one could still provide a good meal, so she began to race after it.

Bang. Another girl had the same idea, and they collided as they ran after the second pig, sending Della down on her backside this time. She was covered now in mud and grease and the excrement of animals that had been in this pen for various rodeo events. But at least she hadn't gotten any more on her face.

This continued for what felt like ages, but what the clock revealed to be three minutes. Grab, fall, get up, leap, fall, mud, reach, fall, grease, crawl, fall. She was already exhausted.

At last, one of the Negro girls caught the smaller pig and began to drag it into the circle. From the other side of the pen, a line of the rest of the girls chased the remaining one, herding him almost directly toward Della. She spread her legs apart, anchoring them as much as was possible in this mud pit, and remembered what Hazel had said.

Pretend that pig was someone out to get Cristina.

No one would ever hurt Cristina. She drew up all the Mama Bear energy that she could muster, that superhuman strength that only a mother could conjure at a moment's notice.

As the pig raced by her, she leaned toward its right side, causing it to veer left. She turned sharply and leaped on top of it, wrapping her legs around its belly and clamping her hands under its forearms. It shrieked and wiggled and put up a good fight, but she held on and held on and held on, burying her face into its stinking little body, wondering how on earth she would get it into the circle.

Suddenly a cheer erupted, and she opened her eyes. She'd held that pig for a solid ten seconds, not realizing that she was already in the circle.

Cristina would get to try some bacon. And both the white and the Negro dormitories would have a feast as well.

Della stood up and released the pig, which was wrangled by some cowboys into a cage. She felt someone grab her hand. It was the girl who had caught the other one. They raised them up, grinning widely, only their bright white teeth showing through layers of grime.

"I'm Lila," the girl shouted over the crowd.

"Della."

"Good job, Della. Your first time, right?"

She nodded. If she spoke again, the filth would drip into her mouth, so she remembered to purse her lips until she found one corner of her sleeve that seemed miraculously untouched. She wiped it across her face.

"Yes," she finally said.

"Well, good for you. That was quite a jump."

"I did it for my daughter."

Lila smiled, but before she could respond, they were already being pulled apart, shuffled to the side, where buckets of water waited for them.

The girls who had not caught a pig had already rinsed off, and the water was tinged with brown, and on its top floated the oily residue of grease and fragments of twigs and hay. Still, it was an improvement over the state they were already in. They picked up used rags and made the most of what they had.

Lila spoke again, not having to shout quite as loud as before. "I have a daughter, too. Daisy Rose. She's four. I get to see her when I'm released. Should be in time for Christmas."

"How wonderful for you. Who does she live with now?"

"I have a daughter, too. Daisy Rose. She's four. I'll get to see her at Christmas."

Hadn't she just said that?

"Della Lee, my girl, you's a-gone and won us a nice breakfast!"

"Hazel!" She turned from Lila and held out her arms to embrace her friend.

"Oh my, no. If you are thinkin' that I'm a-gonna hug you in that mess that you're in, you're as loony as Lila over there."

She turned around to look at the girl, who had bundled up a bunch of the wet, dirty rags and was cradling them in her arms, cooing and singing over them.

Della whispered, "What's wrong with her?"

"That'll be a story for another time. For now, we gotta be gettin' back to the grandstands. They're corralling us all over there for the last few events before the paddy wagon comes."

"Do you think I'll be able to get a shower as soon as we're back?"

"Girly, I'll make sure you're first in line. I don't want to have to be smelling you for the rest of the evening."

Della trudged over to the covered stands where the other female inmates were sitting in their crisp white dresses. She'd be glad for the chance to truly rinse off once they were back at Goree, before going to see Cristina for the evening. She didn't care if the water was hot or cold, as long as it washed off this mess.

The last spectacle of the day was the most anticipated, and she hoped it went by quickly.

The Hard Money Event put forty red-shirted inmates into the arena with an angry bull. Tied between the animal's horns was a Bull Durham tobacco bag. It was supposed to have fifty dollars in it, but over the years, rodeo attendees had increased its value. The more money at stake, the more risks the inmates might be willing to take to get it. And the danger of it all ignited the crowd.

Today's kitty was said to be $1,200, split in half with the prison. There was a lot a man would do for $600, let alone an incarcerated one. That would more than buy a few packs of cigarettes. A few bribes.

The men poured out onto the arena's dirt floor. A buzzer blared, and the bull kicked up his hind legs as he strutted around. A brave man was the first to start, grabbing at the bag. The bull dodged, only to meet another man trying the same thing.

He stood still, save for kicking up dust with his hoof, looking left and right for whomever might try to attack him next.

Della felt for him. Horns or not, it seemed cruel to surround an innocent creature with a bunch of men who were after it.

Four men lunged forward. The bull lowered his head and rammed one of them, throwing him up into the air before he landed on his back. He rolled over, writhing, but no one came to his aid, as they chased the bull into another area. One by one, the bull tossed them as they came close. Most sprang to their feet and tried again. A few still lay on the field, shielding their faces with their arms, struggling to get up. The bull toyed with a few of them, entangling them under his legs before someone else distracted him.

The crowd went wild as they were knocked off.

Della prayed under her breath that no one would get seriously hurt.

At last, seven men were left. They ran toward the bull, cornering him, and Della thought it would be wise for them to work together and split the winnings. But maybe that wasn't allowed, because there was nothing about their actions that suggested working as a team. Bucking in desperation, the bull kicked and roared and waved his head around, lowering it enough for one man to leap across his neck, holding on tightly with one arm while wrangling the Durham bag off the horns. He ran across the arena to the judging area, waving the bag in the air as rodeo workers whipped the bull back into his pen and helped the men lying on the ground.

Della thought the whole event was sickening.

Lila came over to join her, ignoring the unspoken boundary that hovered between the white women and the Negro women. Della didn't mind. She liked Lila's spunk. It took a resourceful woman to nab a greased pig when she herself was so tiny.

"This your first rodeo, Miss Della?" she said.

"It is."

"They bill it as a break for the inmates. 'Look how much fun you're all going to have!' Oh, it's nice to get out from behind them bars for a few days a year, but if you ask me, this is worse than the prison."

"Why do you say that?" Lila was touching on the discomfort she felt.

"Look around, Miss Della. Everybody still bein' told what to do. Puttin' their lives in danger. People payin' good money to see it all. Ain't nothin' but slavery with a different suit on."

That was it. Despite the new clothes, the chance to be outside, to watch the events, it was the same cage. Della could not walk out and follow Tomas. She could not go buy a popcorn or visit the Ferris wheel. The freedom was an illusion. She knew that, of course, but she'd let the sights lull her into a sense of normalcy.

She rested her elbows on the empty seat in front of her. Lila did the same, but then leaned in and whispered something.

"I can get you things, Miss Lee, if you just ask me."

"What things?"

"Almost anything you can think of. Your favorite whiskey. A photograph of the ocean."

"How much does that cost?" She'd heard that there were inmates who excelled at sneaking contraband items into the prison. She just hadn't met one that she knew of.

"Just the cost of the item itself. I don't charge nothin' on top of that. Keeps things from getting boring. Think of it this way, Miss Della. You'd be doin' me a favor. Think of something hard. Really hard to get. And give me a chance to get it for you."

The only thing Della wanted had walked out of here an hour ago in a US Marine Corps uniform, bound for the Pacific. She was sure Lila had no sway there.

But there was no *stuff* that could replace the hole that was left in his absence.

CHAPTER
TWENTY-THREE

Puerto Pesar—Today

I would like that.

Mick smiled at Paloma's response to his text. He hoped he hadn't pushed it too far telling her that he was thinking about kissing her. It was meant to be funny. To break up the sadness with which they'd left things.

He needed to visit Della Lee again. He stopped at the market before heading over. He didn't want to bring her churros again and thought that flowers might be a better choice.

Daisies. They were a friendly flower. Someone had said that in a movie he watched with his mom. Something with Meg Ryan.

When he arrived, Della looked as if she'd been expecting him, although they hadn't arranged a time or even a day to get together again. He hoped that she was as eager to talk to him as he was to listen.

"Daisies," she said, lighting up at the sight of them. "Let me see if there's a vase somewhere in the closets. You'll have to excuse me. I'm still going through things one room at a time. I don't move as fast as I used to."

"May I help you?"

She shook her head. "You know what? I'm wasting precious visiting time when a sink will do just as well." She walked over to the kitchen sink and filled it with enough water to cover the long stems halfway. She wiped her hands on her apron.

"Can I get you something to drink?"

"No, thank you. I just came from a late lunch." Mick was ready to dive in. He pulled out his notebook and pen this time, hoping that she wouldn't mind if he started jotting things down. He didn't want to miss anything.

She poured herself a glass of water and joined him in her usual spot, a high-backed wood chair next to the fireplace.

"Do you have any particular questions for me, Mick?" She smiled. Was he imagining things or was she goading him?

He took a breath. "Well . . . I keep thinking about the baby. I can't imagine what it would be like to have a child in those circumstances."

She nodded as if he'd asked the right thing, but a dark look came over her face. It was quite unlike her, and it reminded him that she wasn't merely the old lady he enjoyed visiting. She was a murderer. It was easy to forget that. So far, their conversations had steered away from that subject.

She put her hand on her heart and paused, as if considering how—or whether—to continue.

"Mick, not all stories have happy endings. And my story isn't one in which you can romanticize me or anyone else as a heroine. If I'm going to talk about Cristina, I'm going to just give it to you as it is. As it was."

He swallowed. "I want to hear it, Della. Please tell me."

~

Della worked in the fields for the next week, having lost the lottery that would have kept her inside. The unseasonably hot weather had created more work than usual as apples held on to their season, fig trees blossomed with their fall yields, and melons, grapes, and pears were the most robust they had been in a long time. Only the berries had withered, dying at the end of the summer. Their shriveled little remains turned to dust at the slightest touch.

By the last day, she'd been reassigned to picking broccoli, an arduous activity whose only relief was the fact that Hazel was working alongside her. She hadn't been able to visit much with her since the rodeo.

The task was backbreaking. Hours and hours were spent stooping over the broccoli plants, searching for the heads that were just exactly right for picking. The budding ones were too early. The ones that had yellow flowers had passed their peak time and would be too bitter to eat. Della pushed back the enormous, bug-addled leaves to even find the heads, then determined where to cut the main stalk in order to give it the best chance to grow more sprouts later on. This position kept her hunched over for the majority of the day.

Even the euphoria she'd held on to since seeing Tomas and making plans for their future wilted in the debilitating outdoors. She stood up and stretched, twisting her body left and right.

"Let me help you, darling." Hazel set down her undersize knife, watched by a guard.

"Back to work," the guard shouted before continuing his rounds down the orchard rows.

Hazel responded with the kinds of words that would have gotten Della's mouth rinsed out with soap by her mother. She well remembered Eva's insistence on proper language. If Herman wouldn't sell his way out of Puerto Pesar, then maybe daughters with proper manners and a decent education would be her escape when they were older. Except she hadn't waited until they were older. She'd found early salvation in the painter.

Della would forever remember the sudsy taste that would bubble up if she ever said a cross word, and she could taste it even now. Yet Hazel said them so freely.

"Hold still." Hazel spread her hands across Della's lower back and started massaging her spine with her thumbs. The pressure felt so good. A temporary release from a hellish chore.

Della had long since stopped worrying about Hazel and Cocaine Maggie and any shenanigans that Mouse had alluded to. Hazel had only ever been a friend, and at this moment her hands were a welcome thing. What else there might be was immaterial to her, despite her worry for the salvation of Hazel's soul. Fr. Medina had always preached of the damnation of anyone who deviated from doctrine. And Papa lit a candle every Sunday praying that his wife, wherever she and her lover had gone, would confess her transgressions and be restored to the Church. He didn't want to see her go to hell.

Those memories always made her worry for Eula, knowing as she did about her sister's affair with Norma's husband and her suspicions about others. She'd discussed her concerns with Fr. Medina, but he admonished her for gossiping to him, equal in seriousness alongside out-of-wedlock relations, envy, and not giving alms. She dismissed the thought that he didn't want to do anything to jeopardize the Songbird of Puerto Pesar singing in his church and filling his coffers.

But Della couldn't believe that someone like Hazel, despite the horse-thieving or a possible arrangement with Cocaine Maggie, wouldn't be rewarded for being a guardian angel to a girl such as herself in a place such as this.

Hazel pushed one last time on Della's spine, popping something in that good-hurt kind of way that took the pressure off the nerve that had been bothering her. "There we go."

"That is so much better. Thank you."

"Anytime, girly. Hey, how much you got there in your pickin' sack?"

Della peeked in.

"About halfway."

"Yeah, me, too. We'll be due a break any minute."

On cue, the whistle blew. Hazel, Della, and the sixteen other women working in the field lined up to turn in their field tools and collect their lunch and water. A group of white women huddled under the only shade provided by the lone tree, leaving the Negro ones to sit on rocky soil in direct line of the sun. Hazel and Della sat a few feet apart from everyone else, pouring the water over their heads before drinking any.

"You been writin' your man?"

"Four times already."

"That's a good thing. Them boys need all the support from home they can get."

So far she hadn't received any letters in return. She told herself that there might be any number of reasons why that was the case. They had to come all the way from the other side of the Pacific Ocean. They could have fallen out of a mailbag. They could have gotten wet and their ink smeared. It could not be the thing that she feared the most. She refused to consider any possibility that didn't include him bringing Cristina to Puerto Pesar and their becoming a family upon her parole.

"Hey, I've been meaning to ask you something ever since the rodeo," Della started. She swatted a mosquito on her arm and wiped off the trace of blood left behind.

"I told you, I ain't spillin' no secrets about how I kept that guard from you and that husband of yours. Don't need to have no reason to be put in solitary, even for a minute."

"No, that's not it. I was wondering about Lila."

"Loony Lila?"

"Well, yes. Why do you call her that?"

"She gone and got sterilized a few years ago, and she ain't never been the same since."

"You mean like—"

"Yep. They took out her baby-makin' organs. They used to do it to nearly all the female inmates. Thought that criminal behavior was somehow hereditary. Thought they could wipe out crime by never lettin' deviants be born in the first place. It was all against their will, of course. They don't do it so much now, maybe more to the Negro girls. Never to the men, go figure. But that Lila girl, she insisted that she was with child at the time, and she kicked and hollered and fought them, but they got her anyway, and after, they said they hadn't seen no evidence of no baby."

"Oh my God, Hazel, do you think she really could have been expecting?"

"Nah, no one on her block thought that was true. They would-a seen somethin' if she'd-a been carryin' on with anyone. That girl *wanted* a baby, though. Lordy, I didn't have much of nothin' to do with her, but when I did, even before the procedure, she was always countin' on gettin' out and havin' a big family. I think after it happened, she went and got herself a little bit crazy. Been talkin' about a daughter that no one believes exists, and how she'll get out and see her at Christmas. But even that ain't happening. She's a lifer, like you."

"What did she do?"

"Killed her mother."

"What? She doesn't seem like the type."

"Well, you don't seem like the type to kill your sister, and yet here you are, darlin'."

Hazel held her gaze for a moment, making Della feel, not for the first time, as if she were trying to root out the story.

"Here I am," she responded, revealing nothing. Eula's death was not something she felt ready to talk about, even with her friend.

Hazel continued. "Lila had a defense, at least, but it wasn't enough to get her off here in the South. You see, Lila's mama was a white woman. Married to a wealthy farmer much older than herself, but she kept company on the side with one of the slaves."

"There aren't any more slaves. That's illegal."

"There's that innocent mouth of yours spoutin' off 'bout things you don't know. It might not have been slavery as history books talk about, but it is what it is, and there still be people who take advantage, and Lila's mama's husband was-a one of those. Her lover got her in the family way with Lila; she had to tell her husband the baby died, lest he see that it was a Negro child. Took the girl in as a servant years later but was wicked to her. Licked her somethin' good. Maybe takin' out her own guilt on the girl. Lila took enough beatings till she beat back and gone and killed her."

"Bless her heart." Della crossed herself, Father, Son, and Holy Ghost. What would Fr. Medina say to something like that? Would he believe that killing was forgivable if it was to save your life? How long a tether did mercy have? More or less than the one for judgment?

"Then she gone and got herself locked up here and sterilized, and that dream of havin' babies ain't never goin' come true for her."

Della's arms ached for the child she would see in only a few hours. She couldn't believe the joy that had come from an atrocity. A joy that girls like Lila would never know.

"Mouse, too, you know. After that baby of hers been born, she got the sterilization, but if I recall, she asked for it. No more babies for her."

"Why is that?"

"You think she carries on with guards like Roy because she likes to? Well, maybe Roy is the exception. She's been with him for longer than the others. But before, she'd get all sorts of favors. Easy jobs. Cigarettes. Real shampoo. Nail polish. And didn't want to have to worry about no more babies."

"So it's true about her and Roy."

"'Course it is. You nearly caught them a few times, haven't you? It'd be great, though, wouldn't it, to catch 'em for real and somehow have evidence. Might get him fired. Get Mouse sent to solitary for a while. Might shut up that big, braggin' mouth of hers."

"I'm not looking to get them in trouble, Hazel. Mouse scares me."

"Lordy, girl, you gots that baby to think about. How many times have you told me that you've walked into the nursery and there ain't no one there but Cristina all by herself when Mouse is supposed to be watchin' her? She's gettin' bigger. She's goin' start climbin' up things and fallin' and hurtin' herself if someone's not there to watch her. And Mouse just don't care. Not sure she cares about her little brat, but certainly not your precious girl. You make a plan to catch Roy and Mouse, and you might even have a shot of spendin' more time in the nursery with her out of the way."

"And how would I even do that? It's not as if I can predict when Roy's going to be in the nursery."

"Beats me. I think this sun is a-fryin' my old brain. I'll try to come up with somethin', though. We got to catch 'em with their pants down. Literally!" She cackled in harmony to the whistle that blew, announcing the end of the break.

"Damn. Never enough time to eat, let alone go take a piss somewhere before it's back to the fields. You go on, girly. Get back in line. I'm gonna try to find me a tree before they notice."

Della popped the last crust of the sandwich in her mouth and followed the other women over to the guards who were ready to hand out
the tools for cutting the broccoli once again.

Hazel was right. Mouse's actions had gotten downright negligent,
and it was only a matter of time before Cristina got hurt.

As she waited her turn, she looked at the Negro women behind her.
Lila had told her that she could get her things.

Della knew exactly what she needed. And Lila might be the one
who could get it.

CHAPTER
TWENTY-FOUR

Goree State Farm for Women—1945

It took three agonizing months, but Lila came through. After a false
start with a defective one, Della now had a camera in her hands. The
film in it was used with only three photos left. But it was all she had.
And none too soon. Mouse had become more brazen in her neglect.
Most recently, Della found Cristina sitting in a soiled diaper that had
already begun to leave a rash down her legs.

What if something even worse was to happen?

Della sat down on the mattress, her tired legs feeling every squeaky
coil beneath her. Their sharp ends had begun poking through in the
most well-used spots, exposing rusty tips. Requests for a new one had
gone unanswered.

She turned the box over in her hand. It had a hard-shell case, black
with raised gold lines. She found the clasp that released it, and it popped

open, revealing a lens on a leather accordion base. She touched the dials and buttons, trying to learn what they did without pressing them and wasting the precious film. Three pictures wasn't much, but all she needed was one. Should she practice now to make sure she knew how to use it? Or take all three when the moment was right in the hopes of getting one that achieved her purpose?

A sticky hand rested on her arm.

"Dat?"

Cristina had toddled over and pointed to the camera.

"A camera, baby girl. Mama is going to save us with this."

Her daughter's big brown eyes looked at her without comprehension but with the mutual adoration that they shared in every moment they were together. She never wanted to forget this, the shape of Cristina's eyes, the light that shined when you looked at her straight on. Her beautiful curls that bounced just like Eula's. It should be easy to pass her off as Tomas's daughter.

If she were at the homestead at Puerto Pesar and she was a normal mother and they were a normal family, she would take as many photographs as she could afford to develop so as to never forget the changes that happened on an almost daily basis as children grew.

Three pictures. Surely one could be spared to immortalize her daughter.

"Let's sit over by the window."

She took Cristina's hand, not minding the honey that seemed to have laced her fingers. Bess was sleeping, and she didn't want to do this while that little terror was awake.

"Sit here, baby." She spit on her hand and wiped it on her pants so that the honey didn't get on the camera. She looked through the lens, past the dust that had settled in the crevices, and saw a hazy version of Cristina through it.

"Turn for Mama. Turn, honey?" Her daughter didn't understand the word, so Della shifted her slightly to the right and tilted her chin up to catch the sun.

"Stay right there, Cristina. Don't move."

Click.

It worked. She didn't know how or when she might be able to get it developed, but if the next picture turned out the way she hoped it would, she'd be able to give it to Matron Heath and hope that she might be able to talk her into letting her have just this one.

"Good girl. Give Mama a hug. Play some blocks?"

Cristina wobbled over to the corner that held a sparse amount of toys, none that contained a complete set of anything. The blocks were missing a *C* and an *A* despite being made up of several mismatched sets, each incomplete in its own way. It made it impossible for her to ever spell out words like *C-R-I-S-T-I-N-A* or *M-A-M-A* or *D-E-L-L-A* or *D-A-D-D-Y*. She hoped, as Cristina got older, to show her how to spell and read with the help of stubby crayons and scraps of paper. Until then, she used the blocks to spell out *L-O-V-E*. Surely the state would have some kind of plan for her daughter's education, but she wanted that one word to be theirs.

Bess stirred, and Della prepared herself for the inevitable disruption of the peace. She tiptoed over to her own bed and slipped the camera into her pillowcase.

"Da," said Cristina, pointing to the toys.

"Doll? You want to play with the doll?"

"Da."

Bess was possessive of Doll, the only one in the pitiful nursery, not enough for two little girls. Doll had long hair on one side and short hair on the other, the unfortunate result of some past child pulling at it. Her cloth stomach was stained with a rainbow of colors from years of food and drool, and her batting spilled out past roughly sewn seams. Still, Bess and Cristina, whenever they had a turn with Doll, would wrap her in a blanket. Della was sad for Bess. There were moments when a real tenderness came through, but on the other hand, she had Mouse's blood in her veins, and that spelled *T-R-O-U-B-L-E*. There were certainly enough blocks for that one.

Click.

Della's head whipped around at the tiny sound, and she saw with horror that Bess was holding the camera.

The girl giggled. "Button!" she shouted, looking down at it and starting to press it again.

"Bess, NO! Put that down!"

Della had never run so fast, leaping across the room. Her heart raced. *Please, no,* she thought. *Don't take the last picture. It's all I have.*

Bess yelped as Della pulled her arm away and grabbed the camera out of her hands.

She looked at the register and stilled. She took a deep breath, relieved at what she saw. There was one picture.

Only one. She was going to have to make it count.

~

By the end of the week, Della was ready.

Cristina looked like an angel when she was asleep, and Della kissed her red cheeks, lingering a moment longer than usual. They were warm. Almost hot. She was immediately alarmed, but the sleep was good for her daughter. She'd make sure she had plenty of water when she woke and would take her to the infirmary if needed. But there was a bigger picture to consider. Literally.

"This is it, baby," she whispered. "I'm going to get Mouse out of here for good so that you'll be safe and I'll get to spend more time with you."

Her words were steady, but her hands shook. Fifty things could go wrong. But one needed to go right. Everything depended on this.

She slid under the bed, having prepared a wall of blocks and toys at the side, and pulled down the bedsheet in the hopes that it looked like a makeshift child's fort—not the hiding place of a desperate woman. She hoped that Roy would not realize that Bess and Cristina were not old enough to construct it, even roughly. Or that his attention was diverted toward Mouse. In fact, everything hinged on that.

It was Mouse's shift in the nursery, a post she'd been getting more and more often, leaving Della to the outdoors. The weather had cooled, so there was less to do in the fields, but cows still needed milking and chickens still laid eggs. A guard had come for her moments ago, but she'd hunched over in the back of the line of women, watching, watching, waiting for him to be distracted, slipping away as soon as he turned his head.

She snuck back into the nursery just in time to kiss her daughter and secure her hiding place.

She heard voices in the hallway. Roy and Mouse, likely. The door rattled, and its steel frame echoed as it shut behind them.

Her heart pounded, and she feared that they would hear it.

Della saw their feet. Mouse took off her shoes and curled and flexed her toes.

"Where's Bess?" Roy asked.

"Out in the play yard with Gertie. I begged her to take her out."

"But what about this one?"

"Cristina? She's got a fever. So Gertie agreed that she needed to stay in. I didn't want Bess near her anyway. That's why I sent you the note. Cristina won't wake up for a while and Bess is out. Gertie even said she'd take her into the office to draw."

"And what about the bitch?"

Mouse laughed. "Cleaning up cow dung as far as I know. Serves her right."

"So it's just you and me."

"Just you and me. Did you bring me the stuff?"

"You know it. I like to keep my girl happy."

Della heard the rattling of a bag and a deep inhalation by Mouse, followed by Roy.

She saw their legs through the crack between the toys under the bed. The mattress springs squealed one bed over as one and then both lay down on it. A clear packet fell to the floor, full of a sugary-looking white powder. Della flinched but recovered just shy of knocking over the blocks.

She heard things she wished she hadn't. Words she knew and words she didn't know. It was rough, an ugly ordeal, not like what she'd had with Tomas just that once.

The springs began a rhythmic beat, squeaking. Della could see the four feet of the bed, shaking and sliding. The bed was meant, at best, for a child. Not for two adults.

It was now or never. She had to get this right.

Della moved quietly but quickly, reaching for the camera that she'd set near the toys. The box was already open, the lens already extended, every precaution taken to do this soundlessly.

Roy and Mouse provided just the right amount of noise to cover up any sound the camera might make.

The bed shook violently, and Della feared that it would break. But it also signaled that this moment would be over quickly. She scooted closer to the wall of blocks, carefully moving the one that obstructed her lens.

She wanted to close her eyes, to avoid seeing the mass of skin and arms and legs and hands. But that didn't give her what she needed. She needed faces. She had one shot, one chance, to capture an image of Roy and Mouse, to prove to Matron Heath what had been going on while Mouse should have been watching their daughters. She wished she could get the white powder into the frame, but maybe she could just add that to her tale, and they'd set up a search to find it. Roy might be fired. Mouse might be moved, if they could find another place for her to be with Bess. Cristina would be safe, kept under the eye of her watchful mother.

Della had never prayed so hard.

The bed slowed, and Della still didn't have her shot. But they remained undressed, and that was enough, if only she could see their faces. Then it seemed as if Roy was turning. She saw his chest, hairless, shift in her direction. *Now, Mouse, now,* she thought. *Turn toward me.*

Della inched forward, thinking that if she angled the camera just a bit, she'd be able to see enough of Mouse to make it count. She shifted the camera.

Mouse looked her way.

Click.

In her enthusiasm, she backed away, but the lens grazed a block, and the small tower she'd built came tumbling down.

Her stomach lurched at the noise, and she clasped her hand over her mouth.

"What the hell was that?"

Roy looked straight at Della while Mouse pulled the sheets across her body.

"What the hell do you think you're doing, you bitch?"

Della shoved the camera across the floor to the head of the bed, hoping that in seeing her, he missed the fact that she'd had it. Roy lunged for her hair, pulling her out from under Cristina's bed, dragging her across the cold tile floor. It hurt. It hurt so much, like her head was on fire at its roots. He let go at last, taking a wad of her brown hair with him. But then he stood above her, naked, pinning her hair with his foot so she couldn't move. Cristina woke, flushed and screaming.

"Ma! Mama! No!"

Cristina. There was nothing she could do. No way she could get to her.

Roy ignored her.

"What did you think you were going to do? Tattle on us? You really want to go up against me, Della Lee?" He pushed her aside and stooped down to the ground, grabbing her by the collar and pulling her up until she was face-to-face with him.

Mouse kept the sheet around herself but stepped over to the bed to pull Cristina to her, clasping her hand over her mouth to keep her from yelling.

Roy continued to rant. "Maybe I've got this all wrong." He laughed. "How about this, Mouse? Maybe she wanted to watch? Think that's it?"

Della was disgusted at the very thought.

"Stay there," he ordered.

He grabbed Mouse's clothes. "Get dressed and keep that baby quiet."

Roy then scooped his uniform off the floor and stepped into his pants. Della saw her chance to move, and she lunged to grab Cristina, but he stood between them in a flash.

"If you know what's good for you, you'll stay exactly where I put you."

Della nodded. He was entirely capable of killing her. Of killing Cristina.

And she was powerless to do anything.

"Don't," she choked. "Don't hurt her."

"You think I'm going to hurt her? How stupid do you think I am? Oh, no. She's not going to be the one who gets hurt."

He finished buttoning his shirt and ran his fingers through his hair.

"You stay with her," he said to Mouse. He pulled the keys from his pocket and yelled out the door for two guards to join him.

"You're getting what's coming to you," Mouse snarled at Della under her breath.

Della was on the verge of hyperventilating but remained quiet, knowing that she was outnumbered. She couldn't do anything to put Cristina at risk.

"That's her," he said, pointing at Della. "Take her to solitary. Two weeks. Bread and water."

"No!" Della screamed, flailing her arms and kicking her legs as they grabbed her.

"Straitjacket for this one," the older guard said. The younger one ran out of the room and returned with it. They held her down while Roy stepped up and forced her arms into the jacket. He crossed them over her torso, pulling them tightly around her back, tugging the ropes much tighter than necessary. Her arms throbbed in pain, her shoulders burned, but it was nothing like the pain of seeing her daughter watch this happen. What would she do without her mother for these weeks?

And, worse, *what might Mouse do to Cristina?*

As soon as she arrived in the cell, she fell to the concrete floor and screamed.

~

Della sat in near darkness for an untold number of days, the cell lit only by the half-inch distance between the damp concrete floor and the door. The light came from a hallway bulb, nowhere near a window that might give her some reference of day and night.

She felt herself slipping into insanity every time she thought of Cristina, and her blood raced so hard that she thought she might die from its pain. She imagined the worst possible things.

She was sick. She was neglected. She was scared. She'd forgotten her mother.

The very thoughts made her feel like a caged tiger, and had she been able to claw her way through the thick walls by fingernails or teeth or anything else, she would have gladly sacrificed it to find her daughter.

When the small food door opened once a day, she would cling to it, shouting at and begging the guard to give her *any* information about her daughter, but her pleas went ignored.

The not knowing was, in the most literal sense of the word, maddening.

But when she got out of this, she needed to be strong and sharp. She would not ever let Cristina be vulnerable again.

So she tried to find some way to mark the two weeks, but there was no pattern that she could attach to that could give her a sense of the passing time. Even the meals, bread and water as promised, were sporadic. No breakfast, lunch, and dinner with which to mark time.

The bread was stale, and she chipped a tooth the first night trying to take a bite. After that, she learned to soak it in her mouth, letting the saliva soften it before chewing and swallowing.

She'd heard horror stories of women who came out of solitary. They were never the same. Had she been alone in the world, she might have found respite in losing her mind, in creating an imaginary world that didn't hurt as much as this one. But she did have something to live for. She needed to live for Cristina and Tomas and the future they were going to have.

So she made a plan to combat that. She would count to a hundred, forward and backward, and do the same with the alphabet. Then in Spanish, what little she knew. Then in French, of which she knew even less. Her mother had begun to teach them before she ran off with the painter, saying that it was what all elegant people spoke. *Un, deux, trois, quatre, cinq, six. Six. Cinq, quatre, trois, deux, un.* That was as much as she knew. Up to the age she was when Mama left.

She recalled everything she learned from catechism classes with Fr. Medina, although she hadn't been since childhood. The seven sacraments. The Ten Commandments. The nine gifts of the Holy Ghost. The books of the Bible, Old and New Testament.

When those became monotonous enough that they did more harm than good, she ran through her multiplication tables and scraps of literature that she remembered reading.

Lethargy overtook her just days in, and she feared the weakness that would spread if she let that continue. She jumped up and down in the small cell, stretched her limbs, and pretended to punch the wall as a boxer might. That was the best part of her days.

When she'd exhausted everything she could to keep her mind and body active, she lapsed into memories.

Mama's beautiful hair falling over her impossibly thin waist. Father stepping into the kitchen to wrap his arms around her, leaning in for a kiss and receiving her cheek. The painter visiting at the bungalow on the water, the sounds she heard from her mother's bedroom when Della thought the painter had left.

Tomas, and the time she came upon him in the barn. When she told him her concerns about Eula's rages and the men she suspected she was sneaking out with. When he took her in his arms and kissed her to console her and it became more and more intense. They had pushed boundaries before, but nothing like this. Then an admonishment from Fr. Medina came to her head, and the description of the spirals and fires of the afterlife, and the moment ended.

Her cheeks warmed and her lips ached just remembering him. And the time just months ago when they'd made all thoughts of an annulment an impossibility.

She imagined him out in the Pacific, but she discovered that those thoughts made her feel nearly as caged as when she thought of Cristina. A memory was a foothold to something solid. But trying to visualize that of which she knew nothing made her feel lost. Was he on a battlefield? Sitting under a palm tree? Did he drink out of rusty canteens, or were treats like pineapple juice available to troops? Were his bedmates other soldiers, weary and dirty, or did bare-breasted native girls in grass skirts comfort the men far from home?

That kind of thought was enough to make her stop. She trusted Tomas and their love and their plans, but she also knew grave loneliness, especially in this dark and empty space. It was supposedly why the Cocaine Maggies and the Hazels and the countless other women at Goree did what they did—desperation for human touch. And she almost wouldn't have denied Tomas any kind of company if it kept him alive and ultimately brought him home.

Anything. Just bring him home.

Stay strong. Tomas and Cristina. Their family. Tomas had promised her their future. She had to trust in that.

The only thing that seemed safe was reflecting on Eula. The memories were fixed points in history. Things she could hold on to. All the years of worrying about Eula, Della's substitutions as a mother—caregiver, consoler, protector—from mosquito bites to creating forests out of sheets and branches, from Eula's mood swings to her ethereal voice.

The good and the bad buried in the churchyard.

A kind of salvation. For everyone.

Della's best memory of Eula was the day that Father left. He'd read something in a newspaper or a magazine, something that made him believe that Eva was alive and he was going to go find her and bring her home. When he found whatever he'd found, he'd immediately contacted a buyer in Dallas and said that he was ready to sell the cannery as long as the terms included guaranteed employment for all the workers for at least five years, and a carrying-out of the plans for automation that would make it more profitable for everyone. He told the girls that he planned to present the contract to Eva to prove that he was ready to sell everything because he wanted to put this family back together. They would fly back to Dallas on their way home from Europe, finalize the details in front of a lawyer, and he'd be taking her shopping to the best places before returning home to the girls.

He left that day as the father they remembered instead of the father he'd become. He was full of hope and love and optimism.

Della had little expectation that he would be successful. If Eva Lee wanted to return home, she'd had a decade to figure out how to do it.

But Della would not be the one to dampen her father's or Eula's enthusiasm.

Eula had remembered that Mama's favorite dessert was chocolate cake, so the girls, now teenagers, planned to spend the weeks perfecting recipes. With Tomas helping on the homestead, they were free to spend hours after school trying variations. Tasting their results. Slicing it and sharing the pieces with friends. They would turn on the radio and dance while they mixed and sifted. Eula would sing to some of the songs under her breath, but Della heard and thought that she was a million times better than anyone else. When Mama and Papa returned from Europe, Eula had said she hoped they would leave Puerto Pesar and move to a city—Houston, Dallas, maybe even New York—and she would have a career on the stage and they would be a family again.

They talked about the adventures they would have in a city. Bookstores. Concerts. Baseball games. No more cleaning up after horses, no more chafing their hands digging up parsnips and carrots.

For a couple of blissful weeks, life was as good as it had ever been—until word came of the plane that crashed into the Atlantic and, with it, every hope that those dreams would come through.

They lost the friends they had. Few supported the girls in their grief, instead blaming the entire Lee family for the devastating unemployment that ensued. *Why hadn't Herman Lee gone to Dallas first?* they wondered.

Della knew. The minute Papa knew where his wife might be, there could be no wasted minute getting to her and winning her back. But without a will and without a plan, and her father having never delegated responsibilities to a secondary manager, the business was in flux, tied up in probate court and languishing without its leader.

Della didn't mind being shut out. She had kept to the homestead during school hours anyway and preferred the company of Tomas. He came out to help even though there was no longer any money in it.

It was Eula who suffered. She was born for greatness, and now she was a penniless orphan with no one but her sister to look after her. Something snapped. The homestead only brought her aggravation. She came home with marks on her neck that alarmed Della, calling them "love bites" and saying no more about it, and Della prayed that it was the worst of what was happening.

Her deceptions were imperceptible to anyone but her sister and the man—men?—she carried on with.

But on Sundays, she was triumphant. Her audience was ever growing, and the collection baskets were overflowing, and the county named her the "Songbird of Puerto Pesar," and she was loved once again.

Her death was a blow to the town, the second tragedy at the hands of the Lee family.

And all eyes turned to Della.

Della remembered that morning. Every word Eula said. Her prewedding accusations of Della cheating on Tomas. Every movement was a ghastly choreography as the girls circled around each other.

And the knife.

Della shut her eyes and shook her head. She did not want to remember that day. It had broken her heart.

The memories played like a movie reel. Hour after hour, day after day, marked by a time unknown to Della.

It was brutal. She couldn't take any more of this nightmarish solitude. She skipped a few rounds of bread and water, testing herself to see whether starvation might be a better option to end all this once and for all. Her only salvation from that fate was the thought of leaving Cristina without a mother.

But finally the door opened, squeaking along its hinges, and an unfamiliar female guard stood silhouetted in the hallway.

"Della Lee?" she asked. "I'm bringing you back to the dormitory."

With what scant strength she could muster, she replied, "You mean the nursery."

"I mean the women's dormitory."

A shot of panic raced through her body, and her pulse quickened as they walked back to her old bed.

She learned three things as she fell into the arms of Hazel.

Gertie had left to take care of her ailing mother.

Della had been in solitary for five weeks.

And Cristina was dead.

CHAPTER TWENTY-FIVE

Puerto Pesar—Today

Mick felt as if an emotional anvil had fallen from the ceiling. He stared at what he'd written, jottings that seemed meaningless in light of what Della had just told him.

He looked up at her, and she seemed to have become frail almost before his eyes. She put her hands over her face and rubbed her temples. He didn't know if he should say something. He hated being helpless.

She shook her head and spoke first. "I'm sorry, Mick. I don't think I can talk about that anymore. In fact, I'm going to go lie down now."

"Of course. I understand." He got up and helped her to her feet, holding her elbow, but she stopped him at her bedroom door.

"I can take it from here."

"Della," he said. "I'm worried about you. Please let me check on you tonight. You don't have to talk to me. I just want to make sure you're OK."

She turned to look at him. Her skin had sagged, and her eyes were understandably sad. "You don't have to do that."

"Please. I want to. I won't sleep if I don't know you're OK."

"If you want," she said flatly.

She closed the door, and he rested his head against it. There was nothing more he could do here.

~

Mick started the air conditioner as soon as he got in the car, but he didn't leave right away. His hands rested on the wheel, and he stared ahead, still stunned by the horror of what Della had said.

To survive solitary confinement for five weeks only to find out that your child had died was unimaginable.

He looked at his phone to check the time. Four o'clock. He had a message waiting for him. Andy. He almost didn't care about the portrait at this point. He was concerned about the old woman in the house behind him.

"Mick, you might be on to something with that Teddy Brown. I don't want to get any hopes up, but a couple of my colleagues think it looks like the work of a European artist. I would love to get down there and see it myself, but I can't do that for a few weeks. If you're free in a couple of hours, though, and can get over to the portrait, maybe we can Skype while you're in front of it. Call me."

That would be the perfect excuse to visit Paloma. See if she wanted to go to the church with him. But the truth was that he felt spent after his visit with Della. She'd just told him the most horrible thing imaginable, and he found himself caring more than he might have in the past.

But thinking of Paloma brought him peace. He felt like the best version of himself when he was around her, and he needed to feel something good right now.

He pulled up to her grandmother's house and found her sitting on the porch with her sister. Paloma ran inside when she saw him.

Gut punch. Maybe this was too soon.

But she came out a moment later with something in her hands. Popsicles. He smiled.

The screen slammed behind her, bouncing in and out until it settled. Her bare feet seemed oblivious to the splintered flooring, whose painted light-blue slats looked crackled in the heat.

He walked up the steps and took a seat next to Mercedes in a frayed fabric lawn chair whose patches had patches.

"Hi, there," he said. Mercedes smiled, but it was Paloma who spoke.

"Hello, Mick." She looked different from how she'd appeared just a few days ago. Happier.

"Cherry or grape?" Paloma asked.

"What's your favorite?" asked Mick.

"Grape, but—"

"Then I'll take cherry," said Mick. Mercedes took the other one and said she was going to eat it inside. He saw her wink at Paloma as she walked by. He wondered what that meant.

Paloma sat next to him in an only slightly less tattered chair. Already the Popsicles were melting, their drips pooling in the crinkled package. Mick licked the side of his, making an embarrassing slurping sound.

"You probably didn't expect to see me this soon," he started. Might as well be up front about it.

"Well, you *did* give it a whole three hours."

"I know. And I meant what I said. I know you have a lot going on, and I don't even know what's going on with me, so let's not start anything. But I would like to still know you."

She nodded. "Me, too."

"Well, then. Just so you don't think I'm some kind of stalker, I do actually come bearing news."

"Wait. You're dripping," she said. Paloma pulled a napkin out of her pocket and handed it to him. He wiped his chin clean of the red juice that was just about to slide down to his shirt collar.

"Thanks."

"You're welcome. Side effect of living here. So, what news do you have?"

He brought her up-to-date on his conversations with Andy.

"But, Mick. That doesn't make any sense. It wasn't a European artist. It was an American artist, wasn't it?"

"That would seem to be the case. I texted him back and said I could Skype him in about an hour from the church. I thought you might like to join me. You know, since you were there with me from the start."

Her face lit up. "Thank you. I'd love to hear what he says."

They each finished off their Popsicles, and Paloma stood up to take his trash. When she returned, an awkward silence sat between them.

"There's something else, Paloma," he finally said, relishing the opportunity to have her here, to say her name. It would all be over too soon.

"What's that?" She sat up and really looked at him.

"I realized that I've been approaching journalism all wrong. Maybe everything. Life." He crossed his legs. "I got into this business to change the world. Tell the stories of the downtrodden. You know, the naive things we envision for ourselves when we're younger. But I lost it along the way. I got sucked into trying to get a bigger byline. Felt heady when I met famous people. Just wrote down the facts of people's lives without ever considering *who they really were*. It was a slippery slope, and I didn't even know I was on the slide. But talking to Della Lee . . . I just don't know how to describe it. It was like going back to the naïveté, but having experience now. Having the hindsight to do it right. I toss around the word *story* like it means something, but it's really just a misguided synonym for *article*, or even *fluff piece* in some extreme cases."

He took a breath to make sure that he hadn't lost her, but she seemed to look at him with anticipation.

"She has *stories*, Paloma. With a capital *S*."

"I'm sure she does, seeing as she killed her own sister."

"Believe it or not, we haven't even touched on that." He saw the look on her face. "I know, that's the whole *reason* I started interviewing. And don't think that it's not in the back of my mind most of the time. But you've got to get to know her. This isn't just an article. This could be a book, and I'm going to need to spend more time with her to flesh that out. And what about other prisoners' stories? I've reported on the policy side of things, but I see now that it's so incomplete. I could start a website where people could share their experiences. I could call it People Over Policy. P.O.P."

She laughed, and he pulled away, but she leaned forward and patted his arm.

"I'm not laughing *at* you, Mick. I love it. It's like you've been plugged into the socket of humanity or something. Those are all great ideas. I'm laughing because I had the same kind of revelation."

"Please don't tell me you came up with something even more brilliant than P.O.P. I'm so embarrassed that that even came out of my mouth."

"No, Mick, I don't think I can top that genius." She smiled. "What I mean is that I realized that my initial interest in medicine got overshadowed by pursuing my grades, and then the magna cum laude that my dad wanted for me, and then applications to grad school, then competing for internships. It's just been the *business* of becoming a doctor. But not the *substance*. Taking care of Abuela lately and being back in Puerto Pesar and just starting to reconnect with my sister, I've been asking myself what I'm doing practicing medicine for strangers in New York when my family needs me here."

She looked down at her hands and spoke more softly. "Would you think I was crazy if I told you that I'm thinking about staying? Oh my gosh, I can't believe I'm even saying that out loud."

He wanted to take her hand in his, but he didn't dare risk it. "I don't think it's crazy. I think it's brave."

She smiled as she looked up at him.

The alarm went off on his phone. "Nearly five. Did you want to go to the church with me for this call?"

"You bet. Let me just tell my sister where I'm going, since Abuela is sleeping. Mercedes is studying for finals. Can you believe it? Small victories."

"You never told me what happened with her, but I've been wanting to ask you."

"I'll bring you up-to-date on the way. But we're going to be fine."

As she followed him to his car, he felt like he could bounce. Stopping by her house was the best thing he'd ever done. He felt attracted to her in a way that went far beyond how beautiful she was. That their paths had not merely crossed but merged somehow. Maybe might actually be going in the same direction.

He wondered if she glowed inside the way he did.

~

"Mick!" Andy's booming voice came over a mediocre video signal as they stood in front of *Santa Bonita*.

"Andy. Good to see you." Mick noticed that Andy had a sunburn everywhere except his eyes, and he remembered vacation photos on Facebook of a recent cruise in the Caribbean. Saint Thomas, if memory served.

"This is my friend Paloma. I thought she'd like to join us today."

"Hey, there. What are you doing with this clown?" Andy said. "I have some dirt on him if you ever want it. I went to college with him, you know."

"Thank you," she said, louder than they might usually speak in a chapel. It was difficult to hear, and Mick suspected that the metal building blocked Wi-Fi.

"Hey, Andy. I'm going to cut to the chase while we're here, since I don't know how long I'll have a signal. I can always call you later from the motel."

"That's what I love about you, Mick. You're always straight to the point. No small talk."

Ouch. That's not who he wanted to be anymore.

"So," Andy continued. "Remember, I restore American art, but a few of my European colleagues took a look at the pictures you sent, and they think it's reminiscent of a famous Spanish artist from the thirties. Teodoro Marron. He was especially known for eyes. Glassy and almost miraculous in their realism. Like Vermeer with light. That didn't sound like our man, but my assistant did some extra digging and found out that an artist, a drifter, came through that part of Texas in the late twenties. He did landscapes. She found some of them on eBay of all places. He called himself Teddy Brown."

Paloma spoke up. "Abuela used to drill me in numbers and colors. That's about as much as I remember of Spanish. But *marron* means 'brown,' doesn't it?"

"Right. That was my assistant's theory, too. So she did a bit more research on Marron. She was familiar with his work, but she needed to see if he had any connection with Texas. What she found is that although Marron claimed to be Spanish, there is no actual record of a birth certificate. He seems to have just appeared on the scene along with his wife, the beautiful Evalyn Marron. Adrienne couldn't find anything about Evalyn's history, either."

Paloma tugged at Mick's shirt. "Didn't Abuela tell us that Della Lee's mother was named Eva? And that she ran off with the painter?"

"She did."

"Oh my God, Mick, could it be the same woman?"

Andy spoke up. "What is this you're saying?"

Mick and Paloma told Andy about their conversation with Abuela, stumbling over each other's words, remembering what the other forgot, until, at the end, they all agreed on one thing.

Teddy and Eva were very likely Teodoro and Evalyn Marron.

Mick saw beads of sweat trickle down Andy's forehead, and he wasn't even the one in Puerto Pesar. "Wait until I tell everyone here! I think that's the piece we were missing."

Paloma grew serious. "If what you're saying is true, then *Santa Bonita* was painted by a famous Spanish artist, or so-called Spanish artist. You say his work is well known?"

"In Europe, certainly, and among art historians, definitely. He's not a Monet or a van Gogh or anyone like that, but his portraits have been known to fetch six and seven figures at auction. So, yeah. Famous enough."

Mick looked at Paloma, whose expression matched the thrill he felt. He didn't know what it could all mean yet, but it was certainly exciting.

Mick stepped in. "Andy, I know someone would have to come out here and look at it in person, but what can we do from here right now?"

"Glad you asked. Run your phone over the portrait—I'd like to take a look as best as I can. Especially around the eyes."

"Yes," Paloma added. "What would make them appear to be crying?"

Mick slid the phone across the upper part of the portrait. Andy directed him left and right until he saw just what he was looking for.

"Unless it's just the phone, it looks to me as if there might be a little scratch on it. My guess is that when it got moved from point A to point

B, wherever those were, it got scraped across the face and may have been a little deeper where the eyes are. In what was surely a well-intentioned gesture, someone painted over it, matching quite well what was already there. Except for in one regard."

"And what is that?"

"At the time this was painted, our Mr. Brown would have used linseed oil, which was a popular medium. However, in the last couple of decades, some paints have been made with sunflower oil. They're cheaper and easy to get. At first, it can look just like any other paint. But it doesn't dry like linseed. And when exposed to heat, it starts to run, causing streaks."

Paloma put her hands on her hips. "So, if I'm understanding this correctly, the portrait was moved here, the heat began to melt the sunflower oil paint, but the way it dripped could have made it look as if it were leaking—crying."

"Right. And I'm guessing that no one ever called in an expert to verify it."

Mick enjoyed watching her get so involved.

"Not that I know of," she said. "These really aren't people of science, they're people of faith. In their euphoric, uh, devotion, I guess the word would be, they just might not have thought to have it examined."

"Again, right. And in my experience with these kinds of things, you draw in two kinds of people. The ones who want to believe in the miracle and the ones who want to profit from it."

Mick and Paloma could hear another phone ringing on Andy's side. "I gotta get this, man. I've seen what I need for now. Call me later—and be nice to that girl."

So, there *was* a story. That cigar-smoking editor of Mick's had a hunch, and here it was. Totally different from what they expected it to be. Not a miracle of tears but a miracle of . . . something. It was most certainly newsworthy. Not just the finding of it but of filling in a piece of missing history for a well-known artist.

Mick said to Paloma, "So it wouldn't have been in anyone's best interest to believe anything otherwise. And it probably wasn't a big deal beyond the local area, so it wouldn't have attracted the attention of skeptical outlets."

They stared at it for a moment. Poor Eula Lee wasn't trying to communicate from the grave. She'd just been melting in the heat like everyone else. Except quite literally.

"Who does it belong to, anyway?" Mick asked.

"The church, I guess," she said.

"But what about Della Lee?"

"Oh, you're right. It would have to belong to her."

Mick saw the disappointment in her eyes—a find like this belonging to an old lady rather than the church, which might have done some good with it. He was more than a little pleased that he knew her well enough to guess what she was thinking.

"We need to bring it to her, Paloma."

"I know. But we should ask Father Reyna first. Want to come with me?"

Father Reyna wasn't in the rectory, so after a little debate, they left a note telling him that it was in their possession.

"On to Della's, then?" Mick asked.

"On to Della's."

CHAPTER TWENTY-SIX

Puerto Pesar—Today

Thick gray clouds cast shadows onto the dirt road leading just out of Puerto Pesar. The windshield was hit with sporadic droplets, none of which was enough to collect in a thimble. But it was more than anyone had seen in months, and it was glorious.

Paloma leaned her head against the passenger window as they headed out to see Della Lee. She felt as if a reset button had been pressed somewhere in the universe. That somehow the miracle of Eula Lee, while not what they expected, had given her a sense of hope. How strangely parallel her life was to Mick's. They'd pursued big things in big cities, and yet each claimed an affinity for what they'd found in this smallest of places. She was back in Puerto Pesar, where she began, and it had been a long road to get here.

Mick pulled over just before they entered the Lee homestead.

"You're quiet," Mick said, breaking her from her musings.

"Lots on my mind, I guess."

"Good stuff, I hope."

"Good stuff." She smiled. And he was part of the good stuff. She just had to let go of overthinking everything and enjoy this moment, come what may.

"Care to share?"

Paloma felt playful, and she turned toward him in her seat. "Is this the Mick Anders who trudged into town a couple of weeks ago with a chip on his shoulder and tassels on his shoes?" She leaned over and pointed to the raffia flip-flops he was wearing.

"That Mick Anders? I don't know the man."

"Oh, you should have seen him. Good-looking guy. But arrogant. Really arrogant. Went on and on about some weird food in Asia."

"Sounds like an ass. Glad I didn't run into him. There was a girl in town around that same time, though. Her name was Paloma Vega. Pretty. But she was kind of wound up. Didn't smile at first. Haven't seen her in a while, though."

Paloma scooted over to the gearshift, enjoying the look of surprise on his face. She slid one arm behind his neck and whispered in his ear.

"I like this Mick Anders. The one who wants to write books and build websites with names like P.O.P."

He turned to look at her, their faces so close that she could see the stubble that had grown by the end of today.

"I like this Paloma Vega," he said. "The one who smiles and apparently changed her mind about just being friends."

She laughed and kissed him lightly on the lips. It sent a shiver through her as she remembered their kiss in Harlingen. She thought about all she'd been missing by working so hard all the time.

The droplets on the windshield grew stronger, though still just a tease of the actual rain that was so craved, but it made loud pinging sounds that echoed through the car.

"We should go in," he whispered, pressed up against her mouth.

"We should," she agreed. But neither moved.

"Wait." Mick pulled away first. "I haven't had a chance to tell you about my visit with her earlier, but she told me some pretty rough stuff. I don't know how she's going to be feeling when we go in."

"What kind of stuff?"

"Solitary confinement. Having a baby in prison. Losing a baby in prison."

"What?" Paloma sat back in her seat.

"I'll fill you in later. Just know that she was feeling pretty fragile when I left her."

"Well, then hopefully the news about the portrait will brighten her spirits."

Mick parked in front of the porch and threw his jacket over the painting. He followed Paloma up the stairs and knocked.

Della Lee answered the door looking tired. She opened the screen for them and headed back in without a word.

Paloma marveled at the house. It was old, as old as anything else she'd seen in Puerto Pesar, but it looked as if it had once been elegant. Like Miss Havisham might have been if she were a sprawling ranch house. It had stone floors with decades of dirt settled in its grooves. A faded mural of bluebonnets stood proudly on a wall in the kitchen.

She wondered where the murder had taken place. Was it the kitchen? The living room? A bedroom? She'd heard it was in the house but not where. And it wasn't the sort of question you blurted out.

"I wanted to check on you, Della," Mick said. "And to introduce you to my friend Paloma Vega."

She was glad he'd left off the "doctor" part. No need to unsettle an old woman and confuse the situation. Della Lee nodded wearily and patted Paloma's hand.

"What a pretty girl you are. And Mick, thank you for stopping by. I'm good. Just feeling a bit worn out in this heat."

Mick said, "We brought something amazing for you to see."

"Let's go into the parlor."

Della Lee led them into the sitting area, where they sank onto an aged couch that engulfed them both. She sat across in another high-backed chair. Paloma was filled with a sense of fascination that she was in the home of a convicted murderer.

"So what is it you wanted to show me?"

Mick jolted up, excited to present the portrait to the older woman.

"Miss Lee—Della—I know you've already seen this since you've been—well, since you've returned. But we spoke to an expert from the Smithsonian in Washington, DC, who told us some interesting things about it. So we wanted to bring it to you."

He whisked his jacket off the portrait.

She remained stone-faced. "Yes, I've seen it. Don't need to see it again."

Paloma looked at Mick. "Miss Lee," she said. "I don't think you understand. It's not just that it's a portrait of your sister. It's about the artist. The man from Washington thinks this may be very valuable."

She nodded. "I'm sure it is. It was painted by Teodoro Marron. But my sister and I just knew him as 'the painter.' Our mother called him Teddy."

Paloma was just about to jump up to her feet, elated by this confirmation, but Mick grabbed her hand and squeezed it. She settled back onto the cavernous cushions, wondering why he was holding her back.

"Look. You don't get to be my age without figuring out a thing or two. Now, Goree wasn't much for education beyond the beauty salon and the sewing, but when the women got moved to Mountain View in the eighties, things were a little different. Mountain View had a much better library and an honest interest in rehabilitating its inmates. Since

I was a lifer, there wasn't much need for that. But I had the time and the resources to answer a few questions about my own life. Starting with Mr. Brown."

Paloma could feel Mick's rapid pulse in his hand and understood that he was just as eager as she was to hear this. But he stayed silent, and she took his lead.

Della said that she had been curious as to the whereabouts of her mother and what her father might possibly have seen that sent him racing off to Europe. Through help from the librarian and a few notes to well-connected people, a printout from microfilm was sent to her about fifteen years ago. It was from a society page in London, where the celebrated new artist Teodoro Marron and his wife, Evalyn, were unveiling a new portrait of a British duchess. Her father must have run across this while on a business meeting in Houston. He liked to stay in the kinds of hotels that carried periodicals from all over the world. She could only imagine his surprise when the face of his lovely wife looked back at him from the pages.

When Della received a copy, she recognized Marron as the painter.

Mick asked, "So you knew, even when we saw you at the church a few weeks ago, how valuable the portrait must be?"

"Well, I couldn't give an exact figure, and it's not as if I care much. I've seen my sister's face in my dreams for the past seven decades, and I'm not overly excited about seeing it for much longer. I did my time, quite literally. If *Santa Bonita* gives some joy to others, then I don't need it collecting dust over here."

Paloma couldn't help but jump in. "So you want us to bring it back to the church? But it will get ruined there." It made sense that a murderer might not want such a reminder of her victim, but Paloma was having trouble reconciling that image to that of the old lady in front of her.

"It's no matter to me. Do with it what you want."

A timer in the kitchen dinged. Della began to stand up. "Where are my manners? Would you both like something to drink? And a slice of pecan pie?"

"Let me get it, Miss Lee," Paloma said, rising to her feet.

"No, you stay there. It's good exercise for my old bones."

When she was out of earshot, Paloma grabbed Mick's hand. "What do you think of all this?"

He sighed and looked up at the ceiling. "Well, I know that Andy will be ecstatic. I can tell you that."

"But what do we *do*, Mick? She doesn't want it, and it's not safe at the church."

"Maybe she'll sell it. Look around here. She could spruce up this place. Maybe get back some of the land that her family lost. Find a relative to give it to."

"Does she have any relatives?"

"She must have a cousin or something. Private investigators are good at searching out long-lost relatives."

"Perfect!" Della shouted from the kitchen. "Come and get a hot slice."

Mick and Paloma joined her, following the intoxicating smell. Mick whispered, "She's in somewhat better spirits than when I left her earlier. Enough to make pie."

"I may be ninety, Mick," Della said, "but I am not as deaf as you'd think." Paloma saw his face go ashen. "I had a good cry followed by a good nap, and it's not as if I hadn't had many decades to remember all those sad things."

She scraped her finger over the bottom of the pan and tasted it. "Oh, I wish I had thought to get ice cream from the store. There's nothing like ice cream with hot pie. Tell me, is Blue Bell still around?"

"Yes," Paloma answered. "It's every Texan's favorite." She found she liked Della Lee and could see why she interested Mick. There must be a treasure trove of history to mine when visiting with her.

"My father used to bring Blue Bell home from his trips to Corpus Christi," Della continued. "He'd pack them into the ice with the fish, and Eula and I would tug at him, begging to find out what flavor he'd brought. I always liked the vanilla."

"That's my favorite, too," Paloma said. "I'll come pick you up sometime, Miss Lee, and we can go get some." It surprised her that she thought of the old woman so warmly. She was not at all what she had expected a murderer to be like.

"That would be nice." Della dug into her pecan pie, blowing on it before taking a bite.

"Miss Lee, do you have any other family around?" How would a woman of her age take care of herself? Having considered Abuela's needs so recently, it was another confirmation that she could be so useful here. But working at Lenox Hill was a once-in-a-lifetime job. The debate in her heart continued.

"No, none at all. There was just Mama and Papa and Eula and me. And Tomas, of course. But he didn't have much family, either, and they didn't have anything to do with me."

"He had a sister, right? Teresa?" Paloma remembered Abuela mentioning that.

"Yes. That was her."

"I think she was my great-grandmother."

She might have expected a glimmer of something in Della's eyes, but even that did not seem to rouse much emotion. How very broken the woman must feel to talk about her relatives with such detachment.

"That may be. I wrote her a few times from Goree, but she only responded once. And it was clear that she didn't want me to write again. So Teresa Trujillo was not really family to me."

Mick spoke up. "If you don't mind my asking, Della, what happened between the two of you?"

Della sighed and slumped into a nearby chair.

"Nothing," she said. "And that has always been a mystery to me."

~

Loony Lila disregarded the segregation of the dining hall to walk over to Della, who stared listlessly at a bowl of vegetable stew and the scant carrots and zucchini floating in the oily broth.

"I made this for you," she whispered. And she slipped a stuffed heart into Della's hands. Its borders were jagged, and the stitches were made in two colors, as if done with scraps. "Turn it over."

Della didn't want to turn it over. She didn't want to breathe. She didn't want to eat. She didn't want to live. But if there was anyone whom she felt pity for, it was Lila, who had her own sad tale. She flipped it over and had to hold her breath to keep from crying.

CHRISTINA

It was misspelled. It was sloppy. But it was the greatest present that Della could remember receiving.

"Merry Christmas," Lila said. "I'm sorry about your little girl." She left as quickly as she'd come, and Della remembered that this day was a hard one for Lila, too—the one in which she always thought she'd get paroled and return to a daughter who didn't exist.

Grief was the most terrible feeling possible. Suffocating under the heaviness of regret. A body filled with rocks, each one placed there by a pain that grew until it hurt to move. Lila wasn't loony for feeling such profound loss. Everyone else was crazy if they thought that despair was something that could be bottled and masked and set aside. Lila *felt* her grief. Felt it enough to let it consume her.

It was more honest than hiding it.

Della admired her for it. There were times when she screamed into her pillow, muffling it so that no one could hear her anguish. But maybe she just needed to scream out loud. To stand in the prison yard and yell until her vocal cords became raw and until the guards dragged her away, maybe to solitary again because then she'd let herself go crazy for real, and she could live in that new reality where Cristina was alive and real and still with her.

Maybe she was already on her way there.

She'd asked around. No one could say which grave was Cristina's, so she didn't even have the exact place to grieve. She'd stand at the end of the cemetery, looking across the final resting places of so many unfortunate ones, wondering which might belong to her daughter.

At last she mustered up the strength to write Tomas and tell him. Tears dripped onto the page, blurring the ink. She left the envelope open, always to be screened by Matron Heath before being sealed and mailed out.

But like those first few weeks after the rodeo, she received nothing in return. Only back. No forth. Every letter sent since getting out of solitary went unanswered. She watched the newsreels before the prison movies, hungry for snippets of activities in the Pacific—Saipan, Leyte Gulf, the Philippines. Nothing. She was desperate for word of his safety.

She wrote his sister, Teresa. Once a week, she begged Teresa for any information that she might have.

It was not until March that she received a response.

Tomas was killed in action at Iwo Jima. Please do not write to me again.
Teresa

CHAPTER TWENTY-SEVEN

Puerto Pesar—Today

They heard the rumble before they saw the lightning.

Paloma raced outside to Della's front porch to see storm clouds that grew black in the distance. The sky lit up as if there were paparazzi in the heavens, flashing their cameras almost in a pattern. She put her hands together and prayed that a breeze would blow them over Puerto Pesar and that, at last, rain would fall on the parched ground.

They'd stayed for dinner, all pitching in to make a casserole out of whatever they could find, which ended up being ground beef, potato chips, and barbecue sauce. Della said that it was better than any prison food she'd ever gotten, though, answering the first of many things that Paloma hoped to learn over time.

She went back inside, where Mick was wearing a ruffled pink apron and helping Della with the dishes. It made her smile. And kind of love him.

To even think that word, especially in so short a time, surprised her. She didn't have any good examples of successful love in her life, as her abuelo died when she was just a little girl. So, yes—her grandparents. But she hadn't had long to see it in person. Certainly not her mom, who dropped boyfriends almost on a four-week schedule. And not even her father and stepmother, who'd divorced just a year after Paloma came to New York.

But Mick made her believe that it could be possible, even though the word had never been spoken between them. What was there not to fall for in a man who would wear an old lady's apron as he helped out in the kitchen?

Mick placed the last dish in the cabinet and dried his hands on a towel. He gave his arm to Della, who took it as he walked her back into the sitting area. She smoothed the strands of her silky white hair.

"You young people are such a spot of sunshine. I can't tell you the joy it brings to an old lady to have you here. My, I haven't made a proper dinner since I was younger than you. I might impose on you to come over again sometime."

It warmed Paloma to hear that.

"Of course, Miss Lee. And you'll have to come over to my grand-mother's house. She makes lasagna that's so authentic it would make you think that she's Italian, and she promised to teach me. And I'll be sure to have some Blue Bell, too. Vanilla."

"You be careful what you promise. With an offer like that, I may just get a ride over there tomorrow evening and knock on your door."

"Well, let's plan on that, then. Abuela is back on her feet again, and I know that she's itching to get my sister and me to cook with her." Some new company might be good all the way around. "In fact, I think you already know my sister. Mercedes."

Della lit up. "Yes, of course. Dear girl. How wonderful that you are sisters."

Paloma looked at her watch. "Oh, dang. I forgot to check on Abuela's prescription. I have five minutes before the pharmacy in Harlingen closes. I'm sorry, Miss Lee. I hate to be rude, but I need to make this call."

Mick excused himself to the restroom, saying that they should be getting back to Puerto Pesar.

She dialed the number and was grateful that it didn't go to an automated message. That was something to like about South Texas versus New York. The girl on the other end of the line sounded as if it was the end of a long and tiring shift.

"Lonhill Drug."

"Oh, I'm glad I caught you. This is Dr. Paloma Vega. I'm calling in to see if the refill for my grandmother's heart medication is ready. Cardioletrovex. Her name is Cristina Trujillo Vega. Cristina without an *H*."

Crack. Thunder rolled right over the house, and the power went off. The daylight that came in through the windows was dim as the sun was shut out, even as it set. Mick rushed into the room to see if the women were all right.

Paloma answered for herself, but Della Lee was silent.

"Miss Lee?" she heard Mick ask. "Are you OK? Miss Lee?"

She turned on the flashlight on her phone and directed it across the room. Della Lee was sitting on her chair, pale as the whipped topping she'd put on the pie. Mick stood over her, fanning her with a book.

Della looked up. "That name. What was that name?"

"What name?"

"The one on the phone. The one you just said."

"Abuela's name? Cristina. Cristina Trujillo Vega."

Della started shaking, and Mick took a crocheted blanket off the back of the couch and wrapped it around her shoulders.

"But she's dead."

"Who's dead, Miss Lee?"

"Cristina. Roy told me she was dead."

"Who told you that? She's just fine. A little worse for wear after a heart attack recently, but she's alive and well."

Della looked at Paloma with desperate eyes. "You said your great-grandmother was Teresa Trujillo. She's Cristina's mother?"

"Yes."

"And who was her father?"

"She never knew. She was adopted."

Della's shoulders quivered, and a guttural cry seemed to come from nowhere.

"Of course. Of course. Of *course* she was adopted. Tell me—what is her birthday?"

"January first. I can't remember the year. 1942, 1943. Around that time. Miss Lee, is everything all right? Why don't you lie down so that I can examine you?"

Paloma stepped forward to cross the room, but Della had sprung up.

"It all makes sense. It all makes sense now. Roy and Mouse. Of course he would have done things by the book. He wasn't stupid. But he *was* cruel. It would have been just like him to lie to me just for the sport of it. Or revenge. And he probably paid off a couple of people to keep up the ruse. Or intimidated them. Oh, what a son of a bitch that man was." She had gone from spectral to boiling in a matter of seconds. "And now that I think of it, he'd had the perfect opportunity, too. While I was in solitary, Matron Heath was on vacation, and Gertie left to take care of her mother."

Mick and Paloma looked at each other, bewildered. This time Mick spoke. "Miss Lee, I don't understand what you're talking about."

"Roy Hildebrand. He was a guard at Goree. He told me that my daughter had died. I don't know how he did it or how he didn't get caught. He's just the sort who could have made up a believable story and had everyone buying into it. But he must have gone through the proper channels. Since I didn't have any family and my husband was overseas, they would have talked to *his* next of kin. That was Teresa. No wonder she didn't want me to contact her. She had my daughter. And she would have had no problem never telling me."

"Are you saying what I think you're saying? Miss Lee, is my grandmother your daughter?" Paloma's heart began to race at what this meant. "Is that even possible?"

Paloma began to understand the fullness of what this meant. For her. For Mercedes. Della. Abuela.

"Yes, my dear. She has to be. The dates match up. Teresa never married but always wanted children." She pranced around the room, clapping her hands. "We must go now. I have to see her. Where are your keys? Is she awake? Will she remember me? Of course she won't; she was too little. What am I thinking?"

At last Della stopped, walked toward Paloma, and took her hand. Her cheeks were rosy, and she looked as if she could power the city of New York with her enthusiasm. "My dear, this is a miracle. I thought I was alone. I made decisions; I stayed in the prison because I thought I had no one. But all along, my daughter was alive."

Paloma could not conceive of a more horrible realization—the knowledge of a hideous lie that robbed you of a lifetime of love. She thought it was remarkable that the woman seemed filled only with joy.

"And you—my great-granddaughter. I have a great-granddaughter!"

"Two, Miss Lee. I have a sister. Mercedes. I think you already know her."

Della clapped her hands and squealed. "Mercedes! Of *course* I know her. She's been quite a darling to me, helping me run errands. Goodness, I have *two* great-granddaughters! If you tell me that you have a baby and that I've got a great-great grandchild, I'm not sure my heart is going to be able to take it."

Paloma laughed. "You sound just like Abuela. No, Miss Lee, I'm not married. I don't have any children."

"Well, not yet." She took one of Paloma's hands and one of Mick's and put them together. "You're a fine young man, and I've enjoyed visiting with you. And my vision may be going, but I see how you look at my great-granddaughter here. You help her out with those things, promise me!"

"Miss Lee!" Paloma said, but she really didn't mind the thought. Even if she felt her cheeks redden.

"No more of this 'Miss Lee' stuff. I don't have many days on this earth, but in the ones I do, we're going to have to come up with something else."

Della had taken to this news so quickly, and Paloma wondered if it was the desolation of years in prison or if older people, faced with an impending eternity, lived at a different pace, filling the remaining time they had.

She walked over to a coat rack and exchanged the blanket for a shawl. "So when do we get going?"

Mick spoke up. "No worries, Della. The way your great-granddaughter drives, you'll be there in two minutes." He slid his arm around Paloma's waist and pulled her to him, kissing her on the cheek.

She loved the comfort with which he did that.

Paloma pulled away first. "Miss Lee, there is nothing I want more than to bring you right over to Abuela's. But as a doctor, I think I need to intervene. Her heart is weak, and I think a shock like this, even a good shock, will be too much for her. She did not care much for her mother—Teresa—but she'd been the only mother she knew."

She did not add the fact that it might come as an additional shock to learn that her birth mother killed her aunt for reasons that they still didn't know. "I think it would be best if I sit down with her tonight and break this to her gently. Why don't you come by in the morning when she can expect you? Maybe Mick will pick you up?"

He nodded. "Of course I will."

Della's shoulders slumped, her disappointment so palpable that Paloma nearly recanted.

"You know best, my dear." She sighed. "I think tonight will seem longer than all seventy years in prison, but I survived that, so I'll survive this."

Della put her hands on her hips. "Well, if we're not going anywhere tonight, then please stay a bit longer. There is something else I want to tell you." She returned to her seat and gestured for them to do the same.

"Now that we're family, I can't have you thinking—I can't have Cristina thinking—that you are related to someone who would do something so vile as to kill her own sister."

Paloma grabbed Mick's hand and squeezed it. He squeezed it right back. What had she just said?

Della turned to Mick. "I told you not to believe everything you read. And that the only two people other than myself who knew what really happened that day were both gone. If you'll indulge me for just a few minutes longer, I'd like to answer the first question you asked me. About my conviction. The answer is, I didn't do it."

CHAPTER
TWENTY-EIGHT

Goree State Farm for Women

Weeks in prison turned to years, and Della learned to live with heart-ache as if it were a benign tumor. There would be no way to remove it without her slowly bleeding out, so she filled the hole made by the pain of loss through lesser things. Mostly in books, especially after the move to Mountain View. She read history and science fiction and the classics and even browsed encyclopedias as new editions came out.

She avoided romantic stories.

Friendships came and went as women came in, as they got paroled.

Hazel left about three years after Cristina was gone. She visited monthly until she got remarried and moved to a couple of acres in Napa Valley, where they grew grapes and attempted to make wine. She wrote a few times a year, all the way up until her death in 1976.

Gertie left the office after her mother became ill, and she returned to Alabama to care for her.

There were new friends, increasingly younger as the years passed by for Della. When the wrinkles set in and the joints ached and the hair turned gray then white, they ceased calling Della "The Murderess" and started calling her variations of "Grandma." The most recent one was "Granny D," circulated by a group of young upstarts in for gang activity. She cherished the title. It dulled the pain that never really went away.

Della's first parole hearing was in the early 1960s, and it was generally thought that she would make it. She was a model prisoner. But it was also the first time she understood the "cotters"—the girls who figured that three square meals and a roof over their heads was a better bet than making it out there in an increasingly unfamiliar world. She'd seen the pictures in the magazines—the shorts were too short, the music was too loud, the economy was too bad.

What was there to go home to?

She'd seen others sabotage their parole, and there were several ways to do it. Most of them were violent.

She enlisted her friends, and even Cocaine Maggie, with whom Hazel had encouraged a friendship before she left. It was clear that Cocaine Maggie was in love with Hazel, something that never did turn physical, as Mouse had rumored. Hazel turned out to be as straight as could be, but she was also just as kind, and she never defended herself against the gossip. She just went on being friends with Cocaine Maggie and letting people think what they wanted to.

So when Hazel asked Maggie to take care of Della in her absence, the older woman took that seriously.

The plan was this.

The young librarian, who told Della that she might not have a job if Della didn't come in to get books so often, agreed to let Della hold her hostage at knifepoint. She'd been a stagehand for a few plays in high school and was excited at the chance to act in a dramatic performance for once.

Cocaine Maggie was the backup, planning to stage a physical scene, one in which both she and Della would strip down to their underclothes, covered by sheets in carefully arranged places, pretending an intimacy that was all for show. The free-love revolution hadn't quite made its way to the guards and wardens of the prison system, and such an offense, widely practiced as it was, was punishable enough to lose eligibility for parole if caught.

So they planned to get caught.

And if all else failed, Della was to scream out threats and profanities during the breakfast hour, convincing everyone that she was out of her mind and unfit for release.

Turned out that all of it was unnecessary. While rehearsing how they'd set up their bedroom scene, Cocaine Maggie accidentally left a bag of her treasured white powder on the pillow. Della's red nose—she'd worked a barn shift on a particularly cold day—and the discovery of the drugs convinced the parole board that she was not, in fact, rehabilitated and would remain at Goree for another decade before it would be reconsidered.

Every ten years, the players changed—Cocaine Maggie died of an overdose, new inmates took their places in the beds that belonged to ghosts of Della's memories—and every time she came up for parole, she found willing participants to put on the charade.

It was in 1983 that Della first reconsidered. She'd reached her sixtieth birthday, marked by a bout of pneumonia that had her in the infirmary for weeks. With all that time on her hands, Della was brought books and magazines by the librarian. Della had been through all of the regularly stocked items—some several times over. So she looked forward to newspapers and the donated items that gave her a chance to read new material.

It was a headline buried in the religion section of the *Dallas Morning News* that made her reflect on everything that had happened since the day of her wedding.

Catholic Church Reverses Position on Burial for Suicide

A scan of the article said that the Vatican had for centuries banned funerals for those who took their own life, believing it to be a sin from which the committer could not repent. While no absolute judgment of damnation would ever be decreed, they hoped the restriction would dissuade people from considering such a terrible thing. To be separated from family plots and to endanger their eternal salvation were punishments that struck terror in even the least devout believers. To be denied the graces that came with a church burial was a sentence that devastated families.

Many suicides were covered up as grieving families made them look like accidents, hoping to keep their loved ones safe from separation and hellfire. But a new understanding of psychology led them to see that all the conditions for the kind of serious sin that could merit such a consequence might not be fulfilled. It needed to be a grievous matter, seriously reflected upon, and acted on with full consent of the will.

It was that last bit that changed everything. Someone with a mental illness might not act with such methodical consideration.

And so the churchyards were opened once again and families found at least a touch of peace at the thought of the mercy that might await their loved one on the other side.

But when they were girls, Fr. Medina's weekly sermons had revolved around the hot flames that burned somewhere after death. So when Della walked in on Eula with the ivory knife in her hands, blade pressed against her heart, she knew she had to do something.

≈

It had been just a couple of hours after the ceremony. Tomas stood across the tent talking to his sister, Teresa, who had not yet come over to greet Della as her new sister-in-law. One of Della's first plans for this marriage was to win Teresa over. Their onetime friendship ended when the cannery closed and Teresa's family was left as destitute as everyone else in the town. Tomas dropped out of school to work, and Teresa's dreams of going to college scattered like fall leaves in a strong wind.

The sparse guests began to leave, and Della realized that she hadn't seen Eula since leaving the church. So she was surprised when she stopped into the house to freshen up her hair and saw her sitting on the sofa.

She had the sharp end of a knife pointed toward herself.

"Eula!" she shouted. "What are you doing?" She raced toward her sister, panicked, but Eula shot to her feet and turned the knife toward Della.

"Get out of here!" she yelled. "Get out of here before I use this on you instead of me. I don't ever want to see you again!"

Della took a deep breath, laid her bouquet on a table, and took slow steps forward. This was not the first time that Eula's erratic behavior had brought them to this point. But she should have known that her wedding day might intensify her sister's feelings. She'd learned from past episodes the importance of remaining calm. "Let's talk, Eula," she said softly, belying the terror she felt inside. For Eula. For herself. "Why are you doing this?"

"Don't act like you don't know. I heard you talking with Tomas. You're married now. He chose you, and you plan to get rid of me like some old rag."

"How could you possibly think that? We love you."

"You said it yourself. You're going to figure out a way to bring me to Houston, and you're going to leave me there."

"Oh, Eula." She must have heard them talking. Of course she wouldn't understand. "Oh, Eula . . . not like you think. Come sit with me." She stepped to her left, never letting her eyes leave her sister, and felt her way to the sofa. She patted it, but Eula didn't budge. Della took very steady breaths.

"We were not going to leave you in Houston. Not permanently. Eula, I'm worried about you. You have to know that. The mood swings. The lack of appetite."

There was so much more than that.

"That's none of your business! Just because things have worked out so well for you doesn't mean you can tell me what to do." She clenched the hand that didn't hold the knife and screamed.

"I'm not telling you what to do, Eula. Do you see the dark circles under my eyes? That's because I don't sleep when I don't know where you are at night, and I think you might be hurt, and I wouldn't know how to get to you. And when you do come home, you're so angry. And then you're not. I don't know which Eula is going to walk through the door or when. And so I've been writing to doctors. Eula, there is hope. There is hope, my darling. There is a doctor in Houston who has many patients with similar characteristics, and he has been trying some treatments that seem to be working. I just want you to see him."

Eula had no idea about the letters, the expensive phone calls. The research she and Tomas had done to try to find help. Della was exhausted. This had to work. They had no other alternatives, and she feared what Eula might do if they didn't intervene.

"You'd like to be able to tell people that I'm crazy. Then I wouldn't be your problem anymore, and you could get your precious sleep and have your precious husband and build your perfect life away from me."

"Of course not! You have to know that's not true. Eula, all I've ever wanted, more than anything else in the world, was to be the mother that you never had. The friend you needed. The sister you deserved. And it was so good. We were so close. And then Papa left, and I lost not just him but you. I have failed you. I don't know how, but somehow I have, and I need to make this right." She ached with desperation.

303

"I'm going to save you the trouble. You don't want me around, and I don't want to live to see you married to *the only man I have ever actually loved*. Oh, don't tell me that you didn't know it. You're the smart one, remember? I'm only the pretty one. But stupid Tomas somehow loves you. And I'm not going to stick around to watch this." Eula's eyes looked wild with anger.

Della reached out a hand. "Eula, he loves you and wants what's best for you, too."

"Well, obviously not, because he married you today. So, hello to your new life and good-bye to your old one."

Eula turned the knife to herself again, and Della saw that she was serious. She lunged toward her, trying to grab it, but Eula was quick and turned, causing Della to slam into the wall. Eula sank into the corner of the couch, curling her knees up to her chest and facing the knife to her belly.

"You're not going to win, Della. I dare you to come over here and get it. And who am I going to use it on? You or me?"

Della seized up in terror. She had usually been able to calm Eula down. For the first time, she truly feared for Eula's life. Where was Tomas? Hadn't he noticed that she wasn't outside?

"Eula, I am hoping so desperately that you are doing this just to scare me, but if not, please, please know that I love you so much. I love you so much, Eula, and I would be devastated if you weren't here. Please don't do this. Please go to Houston with me and let me help you. I'd do anything to make things right for you again." She was sobbing now, and she barely understood her own words through the tears.

"It will be right when I'm gone, because I won't feel the pain that I feel." She laughed.

"You don't mean that. Say you don't mean that."

"Watch me!" she screamed.

Della had countless nightmares over the years wondering what might have happened if she'd done something differently in that moment. If she hadn't leaped onto the sofa to grab the knife. If she'd waited a second longer, might there have been a chance that Eula was bluffing, just one more manic episode that eventually passed?

But she didn't wait; she raced over to her sister—just as Eula plunged the knife into herself.

Since then, Della lived a torment that was worse than any prison sentence, wondering forever what she could have done differently to save her sister. Not just in that moment, but through all their young lives.

She grabbed the knife out of her sister's hands, tossing it to the floor and pressing her fists against her, hoping to stop the bleeding. But with each second, her sister's skin whitened.

"Stay with me, Eula! I'm trying to save you," she cried. Tears fell from her face; her hair fell from its ribbon as she gathered the ruffles of her homemade wedding dress and tried again to stop the life from leaving her. "I love you."

Eula nestled into Della's chest, looked at her briefly before her eyes closed, reminding her of the small girl who used to ask her to read to her before bed. "Too," she whispered through pale-pink lips.

It was the only peace Della would have about that moment.

She laid her body across Eula's, which was curled up tightly. She rocked her sister, kissing her forehead and moving the hair from her face. A sob roared from her throat, released after years of keeping it in check.

It was then that Tomas walked through the screen door, with Teresa behind him.

He later told Della that he'd seen her walk into the house and had convinced his sister to welcome his new wife into their tiny family. But the sight of Della, the knife on the floor, the blood on her dress, sent her running for the sheriff and Tomas running after to stop her.

And it was in those minutes between that Della decided that several things were true.

One. She'd killed her sister. Not physically, but if she hadn't married Tomas, maybe Eula wouldn't have had a reason to get upset. And if she'd figured out long before how to better take care of the troubled girl, if she'd found the psychologist sooner, maybe she could have gotten the help she needed before it was too late.

Two. She knew that Eula may well have been speaking the truth and was intent on taking her life no matter what Della did and how little she understood why. But Fr. Medina would never bury her in the churchyard. The faith of the people would be shaken over this betrayal by their beloved songbird. And worse, Eula might lose the salvation that Della so desperately wanted for her.

Three. There was something she could do about it.

She'd exchange her freedom, her life, for Eula's, and hope that a merciful God might accept the trade.

When the sheriff's car pulled up to the house, Della was waiting.

CHAPTER
TWENTY-NINE

Puerto Pesar—Today

The Truth Days. Della had only ever told Tomas what really happened, and he gave her all his support. But she'd had so many years to think on the regrets, the choices, the consequences. Now it was all redeemed in the light of last night's discoveries. She was going to see her daughter again.

She had two great-granddaughters.

It had been an unimaginable relief to tell those two young people what really happened. They'd stared at her, dumbfounded. Paloma had blinked several times afterward, as if waking from a dream. Della knew that feeling. Today was going to be a dream.

She'd asked Paloma one favor. "Tell your mother, please, my dear. Tell her the truth so that when she learns that I am coming to see her, she knows that what she's surely been told of me is not true and that she can welcome me without reservation. I would not want her to have that burden."

Paloma agreed. Nothing could mar the reunion of mother and daughter.

They deserved to hear the truth. They needed to know that she wasn't a murderer. That she'd loved her sister deeply enough to try to save her, both physically and eternally. It might seem bizarre to a modern world, but they didn't know what it was to hold a belief so deeply that it drove you to do things that seemed inexplicable.

Mick planned to pick her up at ten o'clock. It was six thirty, and the sun was just beginning to rise. She was already dressed, shoes on, rouge applied. She was going to see Cristina today. And eventually she would tell her the story of Herman, Eva, Eula, Tomas, Hazel, Gertie, Lila, Cocaine Maggie, Roy, Mouse. The story of how she came to be. That something beautiful could come out of something hideous. Not today, not all at once, but she might yet have a few years left to share each other's histories and create a new one together.

It was a miraculous feeling.

Three and a half hours. It felt longer than all her years at Goree and Mountain View combined.

Della had told her story in court, a narrative in which what transpired had been an unfortunate and heated argument between the sisters, resulting in Della killing her in an emotional moment, something that she regretted more than anything she could imagine. By pleading guilty and being cooperative, her best hope was to get a minor sentence, a few years, perhaps. But her baby-faced attorney, who had barely passed puberty let alone law school, chewed his fingernails while the indignant county prosecutor acted out his vendetta through a prodigious twisting of the facts.

The judge looked like he just wanted to go home and get dinner.

The prosecutor was allowed to have great creative leeway with the details, cheered on by a standing-room-only mob that was intent on seeing Della pay dearly for the death of their songbird. Eula had been the only light Puerto Pesar had seen in years, and the darkness left in her absence turned to vitriol.

He tarred and feathered Della as the jealous older sister who couldn't stand Eula being in the spotlight. All attempts to answer more than "yes" or "no" and to explain anything were shut down by the judge and a raucous crowd.

So she gave in. Accepted the role of the premeditated murderess rather than someone caught up in a rare moment of anger. Stayed silent about the suicide. It seemed inevitable anyway, and it clearly satisfied the courtroom. Maybe a few strategic tears, an admission of regret would soften the sentence, minimizing the time that she would have to be apart from Tomas.

At least he understood. He'd been there to see her devotion. Her anguish. Eula's determination to separate them. And she'd won. But Della didn't resent her. This was the product of a troubled mind, a girl abandoned first by a mother, then by a father. God would sort it out.

Tomas told her that the grave in the churchyard was hidden under a pile of flowers. Even three weeks later, people gathered with candles and rosaries and prayers for the girl who they were already calling *Santa Bonita*. Or maybe praying *to* her. The mutual devotion had united the town in a way that he hadn't seen since before Herman Lee left.

This was the only legacy Della could leave to a town originally torn apart by the closing of the cannery. A martyr for whom they could rally.

Everyone from that time was long gone, and anything said since then would have been told through the distorted lens of time, the tale changing shape with each telling.

She was glad that Cristina would have the chance to know the truth.

～

Paloma fidgeted as she made the morning's coffee, spilling it over Abuela's white linen tablecloth. She wished that they'd picked an earlier time. Or that she'd ridden out with Mick to pick up Della Lee.

Abuela walked in. Her eyes were sagging, and it didn't look as if she'd gotten any more sleep than Paloma.

"Sit here, Abuela. I'll make you a cup."

"No thank you, *mija*. I'm nervous enough. I don't want to be shaking when I meet her."

Paloma reached out her hand to her grandmother. "Are you OK with this?"

She nodded, a smile coming to her face.

"Oh my, yes. I don't feel guilty anymore."

"What do you have to feel guilty about?"

"I always regretted that I didn't have a better relationship with my mother. I always felt as if she didn't like me. Now I know why. This is a happy day. A happy day."

"You knew Teresa adopted you, though, didn't you?"

"Yes. She told me that she knew a couple who was going to South America for missionary work and that they couldn't take me with them and that I'd probably never see them again. That's about all there was to it. She always said, 'Never mind that,' whenever I asked more questions, so I stopped asking."

Paloma scooted her chair over and wrapped her arms around her grandmother. "I'm so sorry you had to go through all that."

She saw the holy card of Eula Lee on the refrigerator. "Abuela, I just realized that *Santa Bonita* is your aunt."

"Oh, let me see that."

Paloma walked over and brought it to her. Abuela closed her eyes and kissed it. She traced a finger along the edge and held it against her chest. "What a poor, poor thing," she said. "How I wish I could have known you. You'll be in my prayers."

The root of Eula's troubles had started when her mother left. Paloma realized the similarity to her own life. She could have gone off the rails herself without Abuela being there. She hugged her grandmother extra tight. "Thank you."

"For what, my darling?"

"For being there. You picked up the pieces for Mercedes and me. If you hadn't taken us on, either one of us could have ended up like Eula. I owe you everything."

As she held Abuela, she knew she didn't want to let go. She couldn't return to New York. Not when her family needed her. Not when she needed them.

Mercedes eventually ambled in, wearing the pink pajama set that Paloma had bought her from Saks in New York. In hindsight, it was too juvenile to buy for a teenager, but that was just one of the reasons she wanted more time to get to know her sister and what she liked. Last night Mercedes had introduced her to an indie band called Green Ocean. They were good. Mercedes had a talent for seeking out little-known musicians.

Paloma jotted down the names of a few groups later, and she wanted to go online to see when any of them were coming through Austin. She hoped to surprise Mercedes with a trip there soon to see the campus and visit a few music venues.

"Are they here yet?" Mercedes asked.

"Any minute. Want some coffee?"

She shook her head and rubbed her eyes, taking a seat at the old upright piano and playing a one-fingered song.

A car rolled into the driveway, and Paloma saw Mick hop out and open the passenger door. She wondered if Abuela and Mercedes felt as nervous as she did at this moment.

He moved to the trunk, where he pulled out a large manila envelope and a cardboard tube.

He kicked the door shut, as his hands were full, and put the envelope in his mouth while he opened the screen door for Della.

Abuela stood, and Della stared at her for what seemed like minutes. Then she put her hands to her face and said, "Cristina."

The old woman doubled over, sobbing, until Abuela walked over to her and took her in her arms. They stood there, swaying, hugging, consoling. Each crying and holding the other's face in their hands, mother and daughter exploring decades of creases in their skin, looking at each other in awe. Paloma ached to join them, but it was too beautiful a moment to encroach on. There would be time. She wasn't going anywhere. She needed to draft an e-mail to Lenox Hill and to her landlord. For the time being, she was going to stay at home. Puerto Pesar was home.

Paloma glanced at Mick, and he nodded, escorting Della and Abuela, one on each arm, to the living room, where he helped them take their seats.

They sat next to each other, holding hands, even when they spoke to everyone else.

Della shared with Abuela all that she had told Mick and Paloma. And every detail beyond that. She said that she'd planned to tell this story over time, but suddenly time seemed like something that could be snatched away before you knew it. And she didn't want to waste a second.

Paloma watched her grandmother's face, looking for some flicker of alarm as she heard about the rape by Eddie, the deception of a guard named Roy and an inmate named Mouse. But there was nothing other than rapt awe between the two older women.

"Oh my, I'm sorry. I have been going on and on," Della said. "And if you can spare me just a bit more of your time, I have a few things to show you."

"Take all the time you need, Miss Lee," said Paloma.

"You know, you can't call me 'Miss Lee' forever. I had a nickname from some of the inmates, and I rather liked it. They called me 'Granny D.'"

"Granny D? That sounds a little hip-hop."

"Well, I don't know what that means, but I grew rather used to it."

"I like it," said Mercedes. She had curled up on the floor with a glass of orange juice.

"Well, Granny D it is, then." The name felt weird as Paloma said it, but she was prepared to call her great-grandmother whatever she liked. And it seemed to make Mercedes happy.

Della turned to Mick. "Be a dear, please, and get me the things I brought from the house."

"As you wish," he said, winking at Paloma. He brought them over from the counter.

Della shook the contents of the envelope onto her lap. There were seven photographs. She laid them out one by one.

"My friend Lila got me a camera once. The film had only three pictures left. I hid it under my bed, and another friend, Hazel, found it. She kept it hidden until she was paroled. She had the film developed and sent these to me. She said that there were more, but some were damaged or wouldn't have made it past Matron Heath, save for these. Here. These two show the prison rodeo. I don't know who took them."

"A prison rodeo?" Mercedes asked.

"Oh my, yes. We had a prison rodeo. Every Sunday in October. I'll have to tell you about it sometime. You see here, this is one of the Huntsville inmates, dressed as a rodeo clown. And another in a cowboy hat."

She set those aside. "Here are a couple of pictures of what I assume is the Huntsville prison. I think that's where Lila got the camera. These pictures were already on the film. It was different from the Goree prison but looks more like the one that I got transferred to in Mountain View. Bars and cells and all."

And she set the last one on the table, facedown. She took a deep breath and turned it over. It was the picture of a little girl, about a year old, and a young woman, sitting on the floor playing with blocks.

"Who is that?" Mercedes asked. Paloma was happy to see her engaged in what the family was doing.

"That, my dear, is me. And the baby is your grandmother."

Everyone gasped at once, in a way that would have been comical if it weren't so serious.

Abuela reached out to pick it up, releasing her mother's hand for the first time. She took off her glasses and held the picture up to her face.

"That is me? I've never seen what I looked like as a small child." Her eyes grew huge as she took it in. At last she handed it to Paloma, who passed it on to Mick and Mercedes. They all handled it as one would a relic, marveling at the strange existence of such a thing.

"I was so angry at little Bess for taking this, for wasting the film, but it's been my treasure ever since Hazel sent it years ago. I'd taken one of you myself, but it faded over time, since I kept it on me always."

She handed the photograph to Abuela. "Cristina, I want you to have it. In looking at this, I looked at my dead child and pined for the memory of her. But I have you back, and I don't need it anymore."

Abuela took it from her and looked at it once again before placing it in her apron pocket.

"And now," said Della. "My last surprise. This is a gift for Paloma."

"For me?" Paloma already had everything she wanted. The day could not get any better.

She took the cardboard tube from Della and pulled off its plastic lid. Her fingers felt for what was inside, a thick canvas roll. Carefully, she tugged at it until it was all the way out. Mercedes jumped up to clear the coffee table, wiping a condensation mark with her pajama shirt. Paloma unrolled it.

It was a portrait, even more stunning than the one of Eula Lee. The girl in it was older, maybe by two years, in a taffeta dress that defied its medium. The eyes were exquisite, shining with an otherworldly light, yet realistic enough that it seemed to be a photograph. The room was silent as they all stared at it.

Then Mick noticed the initials in the corner.

"It says *T. B.*"

"Yes, Mick. This is the other portrait painted by Teddy Brown. This is the one of me."

A collective "Oh!" was heard in the room. Mercedes got up and stood next to Paloma to look at it. Paloma's hands flew to her mouth, and she traced the outline of her great-grandmother's young face. Time and temperature had damaged parts of it, but for the most part, it was unscathed.

"It's the most beautiful thing I've ever seen. Where on earth did you find it?"

"Oh, I've been spending these days going through the shed in the early morning before the heat swelled, living through some memories. And I found this. I don't know what happened to the frame or who might have put it in this roll, but there it is nonetheless. And how it got separated from Eula's, I'll never know. Maybe a tenant moved it. But they're together again. And I want you to have them both."

Paloma felt as if the world had stopped.

"I—I love them. I do, but why me?"

Della walked over to her, and Paloma wrapped her arms around her great-grandmother. This was all so overwhelming.

"Look, dear. I'll testify to whomever wants to listen that these are the early works of Teodoro Marron, the first portraits by him that are known to exist, if that's of any use. I can't say exactly what the numbers would be, but I can imagine that they would fetch a pretty price at an auction. Enough to pay for a college education for your sister, and maybe, oh, maybe a medical clinic for a town like Puerto Pesar."

Paloma felt a rush of blood to her face and squeezed Mercedes's hand. Her sister glanced at her with an astonished expression. Abuela looked as if Christmas snow had just fallen on the house.

"Mija?" she asked. "What does that mean?"

"You're stuck with me for a while, Abuela. I've been thinking about staying in Puerto Pesar and starting a clinic so that people don't have to drive all the way to Harlingen."

She turned abruptly to Della. "How did you know?"

Della pulled her down to ear level but spoke loudly enough for everyone to still hear. "That young man of yours told me quite a bit about why you're here in Puerto Pesar. And it occurred to me that this was the best use for the money."

Paloma looked at Mick and knew that love didn't know the boundaries of time. Love could be found in a week or in seventy years. It was someone's heart that mattered. She blew him a kiss and smiled. He caught it and placed it against his cheek.

She looked at Della again. "But these are yours. They are of you and your sister. They should be in your home. Not in some museum."

"Of course they should be in a museum, dear. Art never belongs to one person. And think of what you could do with the money. Besides, how much are they going to help an old lady when she needs a doctor and she has to drive into Mexico to find one?"

"Well, when you put it that way . . ." Paloma laughed.

"Exactly."

She hugged her great-grandmother and then Mercedes and then Abuela, stopping in front of Mick and looking at him before wrapping her arms around him.

"Thank you," she whispered.

"You're welcome," he whispered back. Then he placed a kiss on her nose.

Abuela invited everyone into the kitchen as she made the best batch of *huevos rancheros* that Paloma ever remembered eating.

Mick and Paloma sent everyone back into the living room while they did the dishes. He wrapped a wet hand around her waist and turned off the water with the other one. "Do you hear that?" he said.

"No, what?"

"Listen."

Paloma heard thunder crack in the distance. "Oh, that. It's just teasing us again."

"No, I don't think so. It sounds different. Let's go out onto the porch."

She started to take off her apron, but he told her that he liked it on her, and that he'd like it even more if it was all she was wearing. She slapped his arm and laughed but took the hand he held out and joined him on the old lawn chairs on the porch.

The sky was black, the clouds ready to burst.

"Thank you for what you did," she said. "Telling Della about the clinic."

"Don't thank me. She asked me questions about you and I answered. She came up with that entirely on her own. But isn't it wonderful? Think of all the people you're going to be able to help."

"It is. I was a little too stunned in there to say more than 'thank you' and give her a hug, but I need to think of something more to do to show her what this means to me."

"I think all she's going to want is to see you succeed. You've already given her everything she wants. You've just given her a family."

Paloma felt as if she'd just received a family herself. She'd found her way back home, back to Abuela and Mercedes, and gained a great-grandmother in the process.

"What are you going to do now, Mick?" She hoped that the answer would keep him close to her, but she wanted him to be happy wherever it was. "You have what you came for. Your pick of headlines. 'Exclusive Interview with Old Lady Incarcerated for Seven Decades.' Or 'The Art Discovery of the Century: Early Portraits by Teodoro Marron.'"

"Yes, I do have those stories. And I've already started to write the art piece."

Paloma bit her lip to hide her apprehension. "I think it might upgrade you from being that termite burrowing back up that ladder in the journalism world. It might send you back to Boston. Or even New York."

"I have no doubt. It's a big piece. It's going to ignite my career. But that's not the only story I'm going to tell."

"What else?"

He took her other hand in his. "Paloma, I want you to write a story with me. One in which two people from the East Coast visit a small border town and fall in love. I don't know the rest of it. But I want to find out."

Her face welled with tears. He'd said exactly the thing she wanted to hear. She nodded. "I do, too."

She looked in his eyes, which were telling her something more than what his words were. She was ready for this. Ready to make room in her life for someone.

He pulled her in to him and kissed her lightly. "I need to be here, Paloma. With you."

She felt as if she could drown with joy.

He kissed her harder, and she wrapped her arms around his neck. It was even better than the last time. This was two people who had found the beauty in simplicity. Two people transformed by a place that didn't even show up on most maps.

She felt *whole*.

When they pulled back, they stood side by side, watching as the clouds broke and the rain began to fall. It trickled at first, then came down in sheets that cascaded off the porch. As it hit the hot asphalt, which had been hoarding its heat for too many months, it sizzled like steam, creating a ghostly fog that floated in the wind. The sidewalks became a river, and Paloma knew that with a rain like this, it might be days before they could leave the house, as it would surely flood the streets.

But she didn't mind. Everyone she loved most was in that house or, in Mick's case, next to her.

As far as she was concerned, it could rain forever.

ACKNOWLEDGMENTS

First and foremost, I am grateful to my agent, Jill Marsal, for her support and guidance, and superpowers. She keeps me on track, too. The very day I turned in the draft for this book, she told me she was ready to see the next one.

Thank you to my editor, Danielle Marshall, and the whole Amazon Publishing/Lake Union team. I am astounded by the professionalism, scope, creativity, and overall awesomeness of all of them. They are just terrific people, too. Danielle—it is an honor to work with you.

Big, gigantic thanks go to my developmental editor, Tiffany Yates Martin. This woman worked *hard*, y'all. I turned in a first draft that admittedly needed a lot of revisions. She saw the potential, though, asked all the questions that made me dig deeper and deeper and deeper until I wrote what you have in your hands now. I compared it to a literal root canal. I think I made her laugh with that comment. Thank you for the education. I hope to carry it over into future books. With less commas.

This would not have been possible without my family. With a deadline looming, I spent more time in coffee shops than I did at home, and Rob and the kiddos—Claire, Gina, Mary Teresa, and Vincent—did the Herculean task of running the household without me. Never complaining, always supportive. They are my life and the reason I do everything I do.

In the theme of family, and in addition to the sisters mentioned in the dedication, I am grateful for the following: my mom, Chris Remmert, for encouraging me from a young age to write and believing I could do it before anyone else did. She should have a career as a copy editor. My dad, Pete Remmert, for thinking everything I write is wonderful and ready to print. My brother, Paul Remmert, for your memorable quotes of "My Band" and "Dear Journal," which prompted me to actually make something come of them. Well, the band thing turned out to be a pipe dream. But the writing gig is real. Truly, though, I appreciate all your support.

My very favorite thing about writing has been entering the world of readers, authors, and promoters in ways that I never imagined.

To the people who promote books just for the love of it: Andrea Peskind Katz—you have built a reader community like no other. Thank you for the home that I've found in Great Thoughts Great Readers. You keep it classy. Liz Fenton and Lisa Steinke—I am totally fangirling at being your friend. You are not only amazing writers, but you support other authors in exciting and creative ways. Melissa Amster, Kayleigh Wilkes, Barbara Khan, Suzanne Kelman, KJ Waters, Suanne Schafer, Jolene Navarro, and the many others who build writing communities—thank you.

To my new author friends—I have loved your books but loved getting to know you as people more. There are so many, but these are a few: Thelma Adams, Emily Carpenter, Kerry Lonsdale, Lynda Cohen Loigman, Teri Wilson, Nicole Waggoner, Steena Holmes, Patricia Walters-Fischer, Anjali Banerjee, Caroline Gnagy, Loretta Nyhan, and Leila Meacham.

To the readers who deserved gold medals for the love and support that they show to me and to so many authors. Particularly: Susan Peterson, Nita Joy Haddad, Andrea Bates, Kathleen Basi, Carol Boyer, Jenny Belk, Athena Kaye, Rebecca Chaffin Hill, Brigid Cooley (really, the whole Cooley family), and Casi Solis.

To Marcella Turner, for writing the little book about Tuff, Texas, that rounded out details for much of the setting of this book.

To Razmik Boghozian, my inspiration for the character of Arturo. You were such a welcoming host, and you are missed.

The Ladies of the Lake—you know who you are—are a constant source of wisdom and encouragement. I thank you for leading me through these authorly waters.

No writer can exist without the support of some pretty fantastic organizations and the people in them. I am grateful to SARA, WFWA, and RWA.

Finally, thanks and praise to a loving God who has given me this path.

ABOUT THE AUTHOR

Photo © 2015 Gina Di Maio

Camille Di Maio always dreamed of being a writer, and those dreams came true with her bestselling debut novel, *The Memory of Us*. In addition to writing women's fiction, she buys too many baked goods at farmers' markets, unashamedly belts out Broadway show tunes, and regularly faces her fear of flying to indulge in her passion for travel.

She and her husband homeschool their four children and run an award-winning real estate team in San Antonio, Texas. Connect with her at www.camilledimaio.com.